DEATH AND THE NAKED LADY

Mac McLean, successful international singer, boards the Dauphiné on his way to New York, unaware that his patron, Georges Fournier, has just been murdered in Paris. But death is also on the passenger list of the luxury liner as it makes its way across the Atlantic. It starts innocently enough when McLean finds a case under his bed filled with Fournier's precious jade figurines.

Everyone seems interested in these statuettes. Lady Harcourt, playing around on her husband Albert, is intrigued when she finds them under McLean's bed. The unsavory Gonzales makes it clear that he wants them. So does Joseph Pasquela. But why does a man so rich ask McLean to spy on his wife Elisabeth, formerly the Naked Lady of the Folie Bergère? And why does movie star, Lili Fenwick, keep showing up in his stateroom? When death makes an appearance, it is not entirely unexpected.

FACES TURNED AGAINST HIM

Bert Mason's wife Myra has disappeared. Was she cheating with Milt, as everyone says? Bert laughs them off. Milt wouldn't cheat on his wife. Not Lillian. Then they find Myra's body...

THE LADY AND THE CHEETAH

After a bogus interview is published, everyone thinks that Rafferty Valois is an international man of adventure when, in fact, he is simply an out-of-work newspaper man. But that doesn't stop him from accepting a job from the Countess Becellini to retrieve a packet of stolen letters for her. The Countess is trying to make sure nothing comes between the marriage of her daughter Bianca and the deposed King of Movania, soon to be reinstated to the throne. But there are others who want the letters, and are prepared to offer Valois large sums for their deliverance—Bianca's grandmother for one, "the bitch of Rome;" and Carlo Cattoriere, a deported gangster who has other plans for the former king that involves his niece, Maria. They all think Valois such a clever man that surely he can find them for him. Because if he doesn't, his life won't be worth a damn.

JOHN FLAGG BIBLIOGRAPHY
(1885-1970)

The Persian Cat (1950)
Death and the Naked Lady (1951)
The Lady and the Cheetah (1951)

Hart Muldoon series:
Woman of Cairo (1953)
Dear, Deadly Beloved (1954)
Murder in Monaco (1957)
Death's Lovely Mask (1958)
The Paradise Gun (1961)

As John Gearon
The Velvet Well (1946)
Faces Turned Against Him (1951)

Death and the Naked Lady

- - - - -

Faces Turned Against Him

- - - - -

The Lady and the Cheetah

JOHN FLAGG

Introduction by James Reasoner

STARK HOUSE

Stark House Press • Eureka California

DEATH AND THE NAKED LADY / THE LADY AND THE CHEETAH

Published by Stark House Press
1315 H Street
Eureka, CA 95501
griffinskye3@sbcglobal.net
www.starkhousepress.com

ISBN-13: 978-1-944520-16-8

Book design by Mark Shepard, SHEPGRAPHICS.COM
Cover art from "Reclining Nude" by George Hendrik Breitner

First Black Gat Edition: January 2017

FIRST EDITION

A Pair of Ladies
from John Flagg

By James Reasoner

John Gearon (1885-1970), former journalist, radio script writer, literary agent, and playwright, holds the distinction of writing the first novel ever published by the iconic Gold Medal Books, *The Persian Cat*, published in 1950 under the pseudonym John Flagg and reprinted in 2015 by Black Gat Books. It must have been successful, because the next year, 1951, Gearon/Flagg was back with two novels, the provocatively titled *Death and the Naked Lady* and *The Lady and the Cheetah*.

Like *The Persian Cat, Death and the Naked Lady* is a novel of international intrigue, with the plot touching on events in England, Germany, and South America in the tense days following World War II. But in an unusual twist, Gearon places the novel's action in a very confined setting, the French ocean liner *Dauphiné*, which is sailing across the Atlantic toward New York. On board is the American narrator Mac McLean, who has made a name for himself in France as a nightclub singer, following his service as a bomber pilot during the war. Mac is on his way to the United States for a breakthrough booking at a swank New York club. (I can't help but see Eddie Constantine, who shares some background with Mac, in this part.)

Mac is a bit of a womanizer, and his current mistress, the wife of an English lord, is also traveling on the *Dauphiné* with her husband. Then there's the sleek and somewhat shady South American businessman and his wife, a fantastically beautiful German girl who's the Naked Lady of the title, a nickname bestowed on her because she worked at the Folies Bergiere before marrying the sinister Joseph Pasquela.

Before leaving Paris, Mac was warned by a friend of his that some sort of intrigue was going on, that the powerful men who have been supporting his career may actually be plotting against him. Once aboard the ship, Mac discovers that someone had planted a bag full of jade owls in his cabin. His friend back in France turns up dead, and Mac is the most likely suspect in the murder. A man with a gun keeps popping in and out of Mac's life. Mac has to juggle the affections not only of the notorious Naked Lady and the English lady, but also those of a lovely blond American actress with troubles of her own. Throw in another murder, a dogged French cop who boards the *Dauphiné* in mid-ocean from a seaplane, poison, microfilm, a masquerade ball, and a plot that threatens the world's new-found peace, and it's enough to wear a guy out. Mac's going to be doing good to survive until the ship reaches New York, let alone do boffo biz at the Persian Room on Broadway.

To ratchet up the tension in this tale full of twists, turns, and double-crosses, Gearon uses the technique of opening each chapter with the date and time it begins. Most of the action takes place over a couple of days, and the suspense is great enough to have the reader flipping pages rapidly when the final showdowns and revelations arrive. Gearon also does a fine job of capturing the luxurious but slightly claustrophobic atmosphere of a cruise ship at sea. As the web of intrigue and dangers tightens around Mac McLean, there's literally no place for him to go. He has to sort everything out or die trying.

Gearon's next novel, *The Lady and the Cheetah*, is also set against a background of international intrigue. Down on his luck French-Irish newspaperman Rafferty Valois is in Paris when he's approached by a man with a mysterious proposition. The man's employer, an Italian countess (who's actually American, and the heiress to a fortune made in plumbing supplies), has a job for Rafferty, but he'll have to travel to her magnificent villa on an island in an Italian lake to find out what it is. Intrigued, between jobs, and wanting to get away from a daffy British blonde who's attached herself to him, Rafferty agrees to visit the countess's island.

He finds a lot more trouble waiting for him there than he bargained for.

For one thing, the countess has a pet cheetah she leads around on a leash made of thin gold chain, and Rafferty is afraid of cats. For another, the countess has a beautiful daughter with an apparent abundance of suitors, some of whom are definitely on the shady side. When the countess hires Rafferty to recover a bundle of incriminating letters with which she's being blackmailed, *The Lady and the Cheetah* begins to read much like a hardboiled private eye novel with the benefit of vividly rendered settings, one of which is a medieval torture chamber under an ancient castle, and a cast of interesting characters including American gangsters, deposed European nobility scheming to get back on the throne, and

Rafferty himself, described in a newspaper article as an "international man of mystery" (yep, just like Austin Powers). Then one of the characters winds up with a knife in the back, a beautiful young woman may be framed for the killing, and the novel becomes a slam-bang thriller written in a breezy, very appealing style.

Also like *Death and the Naked Lady, The Lady and the Cheetah* comes to a rousing climax involving a big party. In the first book, it's a masquerade ball; in this one, it's a ball at the countess's castle being held to announce the engagement of the young king of Movania to the countess's daughter. At one point in the story, Rafferty makes a wisecrack about Graustark, and Movania is that sort of country, all right.

Also included in this volume is the novelette "Faces Turned Against Him", which originally appeared in the Spring 1951 issue of the digest magazine *Suspense*. It's more of a traditional mystery than the novels, as the chief of police in a ritzy New England town investigates the disappearance of a young socialite, and it's told in third person rather than first, but it shares Gearon's sharp dissection of the upper crust and the cop in charge of the case is an outsider/observer in the mold of Mac McLean and Rafferty Valois. The story also generates a considerable amount of suspense.

John Gearon went on to write six more books for Gold Medal under the pseudonym John Flagg, all of them featuring international troubleshooter Hart Muldoon. Although I haven't read any of them yet, I suspect that Muldoon is cut from the cloth as Mac McLean and Rafferty Valois: smart, funny, and inclined to land in trouble up to his neck, often involving beautiful women, and set against exotic backgrounds. Gearon's career as a novelist seems to have ended with the final Muldoon novel in 1961. But he left us with these well-written, quirkily plotted thrillers that paint an unforgettable picture of Europe with all its beauties and dangers. You can see for yourself by turning the page and traveling to the distinctive landscape of John Flagg's novels.

It's a pretty place to visit, but you wouldn't want to die there.

—September 2016
Azle, TX

Death and the Naked Lady

By John Flagg

Excerpt from the theatrical trade paper Variety, *September 8, 1950:*

Among legit and Hollywood celebs sailing Statewise from Le Havre today on the French Line's crack *Dauphiné* is Mac McLean, Yankee performer who skyrocketed to top money in class French cafés. McLean, who is the current pet of the international glitter set in the French capital, has created loud talk along the main stem because of his coming engagement at the swank Persian Room (opening Oct. 2) at a tag reputed to be in the Hildegarde, Piaf brackets. The wiseacres are saying that what constitutes a boff in Paris, which is noted for its easy attitude toward American acts, doesn't rate this top New York booking against the competition of tried and proved Yankee turns. Opening promises to be plenty tough for the singer, who will have to face a "show me" Broadway mob. Before his success in France, McLean was a complete unknown to show business.

Chapter One

SEPTEMBER 8, 5:00 P.M.

The *Dauphiné* moved away from the pier in a wide arc, and through the porthole I watched the last of France swing about in a manner unknown to land masses. My head continued beyond the arc, made a circle, and then came around again; I was coming out of a two-day drunk with Georges Fournier in my mind and I didn't like it.

The luxurious stateroom was quiet as a tomb. Out there, the new buildings, sprung out of war ruins like too neat, too bright geraniums (fertile soil, I thought goulishly), seemed painted on billowing canvas, sliding away from me with the past four years of my life. In a few minutes the great liner would be headed into the Channel and the night, headed toward the States and home.

Home? Outside in the corridor someone laughed.

Home was where my luggage was; London, Paris, Rome, Cortina, Biarritz, Cannes, St. Moritz— all the plush and glittering places with Mainbocher women and hundred-an-ounce odors. The time before that, the time of dreary rooming houses and pensions where the roses peeled from the walls and the only odor was the odor of poverty, was a dream in the past. No one was scaring me back to that.

Home? There was no gray cottage covered with vines waiting for me back in the States, no little lady to simper sweetly over the gas range, no family, no friends waiting at the station to meet the five-fifteen, thank God! Only a fifty-a-day suite at the Plaza or the Pierre, and that was plenty all right by me.

And yet ...

The song Jacques Renoir had written for me to introduce in New York began running through my head, *"J'ai tout— ce n'est rien."* I have everything— it is nothing. Hell, I thought. Snap out of it or you'll be as bad as Fournier.

I went to the mirror and adjusted my tie. My hand was shaking the way it used to shake in those days so long ago when I would come back from a mission over Cologne or Hamburg or Berlin. Too many Paris farewells.

Goddamn Fournier, anyway! He must have thought it was Halloween or April Fool's Day with a banshee in the background. Or maybe he just wanted to scare a smart American out of a good job. Or maybe he was just nuts. Fournier had too many years, too many women, too much wine, too many ancestors behind him. He was beginning to jump with terror at the sight of his own distinguished shadow, to see death in crystal balls. He had another dream coming if he thought I was buying his mystic mumbo-jumbo or his oblique little Grand Guignol tales of grim faces watching silently from the gloom of an ancient palace on the Avenida Espagnol, moving their chessmen toward destruction.

The light in the stateroom was beginning to fade. But I stood there by the mirror unable to get Fournier out of my mind. At three in the morning, when my head was still full of music and champagne bubbles from Laura Richards' party at the Ritz, he had stood with his back to the windows of his suite at the Crillon and quietly said, "A man might regain his soul."

I had given him a "So what?" grin, wondering why he had insisted on my coming there to hear this rot. And he had turned and looked out onto the Place de la Concorde, deserted in the early dawn. "You are like Cinderella, McLean. It is almost the witching hour. Time to run away from the party. But there is a difference. You see, they do not let you leave this party of your own free will."

The antiseptic silence of the stateroom was becoming unbearable. It was time for laughter and people. Time to get back to the party. Time for over-the-falls-in-a-gilded-barrel. From far away came the muffled shriek of a tugboat.

And then, with my hand on the doorknob, I remembered that other thing he had said: "Like many Americans, you do not really understand the legend of Faust. You don't believe in the Devil. You have been handed the world, but you do not believe in— how do you say?— the pay-off.

The day of reckoning has come for me. I can no longer turn back. With you, we shall see."

I had laughed.

Now, as I stepped out into the corridor, I laughed again. To hell with Fournier and his neurotic riddles. I'd bought a merry-go-round and I intended to grab all the brass rings I could. And the merry-go-round was tinkling away up on the main deck. Time to jump back on. Time for another drink.

I left the black mood down on C deck and decided to try the charming veranda café overlooking the bow and the white wake that ran across its gentle roller coaster back into the approaching night. But I should have gone to another bar, because the first person I saw was Irene Harcourt. It had been off and on in a kind of mechanical manner between Irene and me for some time. At the moment it was definitely off, as far as I was concerned. Irene was sitting at a corner table with, of all people, her husband. It was a novelty seeing them together. Sir Albert Harcourt was something red-faced in tweeds, inclined to such phrases as "hip-hip" and "dear boy" and to sonorous pronouncements on steel. He was very British in that Tory manner which most Americans believe exists only on the musical-comedy stage and completely indifferent to Irene's not-so-innocent sources of amusement.

Irene, sleek and smart in the style of *Vogue* (Paris edition), waved gaily, and with an inner groan I joined them. I had seen her only three nights before when a party of us had gone to show some visiting firemen the less sedate entertainments of the Rue Blondel. And then again on the following night, before I had left Laura Richards' party at the Ritz to go to Fournier's suite at the Crillon, I had danced with her beneath the crystal chandeliers. She had mentioned nothing about a projected trip to the United States.

"Darling!" she cried. "What fun! I had no idea you were aboard!"

She was well along on her usual chain of champagne cocktails, but it was difficult to tell how far along.

"That's the fourth time she's said that," Albert announced indifferently. "To four different men."

"You remember Mac McLean, darling," she said to Albert, who didn't remember or care. And then to me, before he could reply: "Going back to New York for a holiday, Mac?"

"Not exactly. I've been engaged to appear in the Persian Room. It will be the first time back to the States for me in four years."

"I never think of you as an American," Irene said kindly.

"Thanks," I said dryly. I ordered a drink. And then, suddenly, I thought, She's right, of course. I'll be an alien in my own country. I don't know what they think any more, or care.

Albert harumphed and said, "Appear in the Persian Room? What does that mean?"

"My dearest," Irene said impatiently, "Mac is a nightclub entertainer. One of the best. Ladies swoon when he sings."

"I *thought* he was too good-looking to be a businessman or—"

"Gentleman," I finished for him.

"Not at all," Albert said, flustered. "Thought never entered my mind. Must be damned fascinating work, I suppose. Bad hours, though. Devil on the liver."

"Haven't done it long enough to find out."

"Sort of hobby, eh?" Albert said hopefully.

"Sort of a way of eating well," I said. "It was a lucky accident."

"Georges Fournier was his lucky accident," Irene said. "Mac was playing in some dump on the Riviera when Fournier heard him. Have you ever met Georges, darling?" She paused for breath, not for an answer. "Always interested in singers and dancers and the arts. He practically kept a whole ballet company at one time, I'm told. That is," she said innocently, "he paid their *professional* expenses. Simply devoted to the Theatre, Georges is." I could practically see that capital T. "Even when he was a diplomat, he played at it as a sort of dilettante's game. The last of one of the most ancient families of the *ancient régime*. Charming. Has the world to his villa near Cannes, and his parties at his chateau near Versailles are famous."

"I know who he is, of course," Albert said.

"Anyway," Irene continued, "he liked Mac's style of singing. He hired him to entertain at one of his most important parties. Mac was a sensation. He got an offer to appear at the Casino in Cannes, and since then he's simply been rolling in francs and duchesses."

"Irene is so well informed," Albert said without irony. "Amazing fund of odd information."

"I like to know how my friends got there," she said. "And sometimes I'm amazed." Then quickly: "Fournier collects artists the way he collects jade."

"I'm very grateful to him," I said. But I wanted to forget Fournier. I wanted to forget that interview in his suite at the Crillon.

"Aside from Laura's party at the Ritz, the last time I saw Mac was when a few of us went to an exhibition in the Rue Blondel at four in the morning. One of those houses, you know."

"Funny time to go to an art gallery," Albert said. "Don't go in much for that sort of thing myself."

"No, darling," Irene said. "You don't."

Albert yawned and got to his feet. "You'll forgive me, I'm sure, if I snatch a little shut-eye before dinner, eh?"

We forgave him and he went off through the crowded room like a coal barge in midstream.

Irene changed her tune. She put on the old record: "Why didn't you show up after Laura's party, as you promised?"

"Friday's my bad day. Superstitious."

"Where did you go? I saw you leave the ballroom, but when I called your hotel you weren't there."

"Georges Fournier wanted to discuss something with me. I went to his suite at the Crillon and didn't get away until almost dawn."

"If I didn't know you better, I'd say you were queer for him."

"Don't worry. Georges is still old-fashioned enough to prefer women. So am I."

"I suppose you think I'm following you to the States."

When I shrugged, she said, "Well, I am!"

"Now, Irene, let's not ..."

"What number is your stateroom?" she asked in a no-nonsense tone of voice.

"Never notice those things. I'll find out."

"Don't be absurd!"

"Anyway, I'm sharing it."

"Oh?" She put her glass down very carefully.

"With a priest," I said. "Delightful old fellow."

"You're lying!"

"Yes."

"Why?"

I sighed into my Martini. "I'm coy. I like to be persuaded. Your feminine subtlety has undone me. I'm putty in the hands of an old-fashioned girl like you. The number is three-thirty-four on C deck."

"Shall we say eleven?"

"Shall we? Why not?"

Why not, indeed? I thought. I was remembering certain pleasant accomplishments of Irene's.

She looked me in the eyes defiantly, and then suddenly her expression changed to one of doubt.

"There's something about you, Mac, that puzzles me."

"What's that?"

"Well, I thought at first that you had the quality I most admire in men.

Hardness. A sort of amoral, adventurous quality. The man who belongs to no one and gets what he wants from the highest bidder. But recently I've begun to wonder. Perhaps it's because you're American."

I laughed. "Don't worry. I haven't developed a conscience, if that's what you mean. I lost that about the time you lost that old-fashioned attribute of womankind."

She grinned. "Darling! So *young!*"

I ordered more of the same and looked around at the crowded café, nodding and waving when I saw a familiar face. As a well-known night-club entertainer, I had to nod and wave at every faintly familiar face, even if I had no idea of the name that went with it. It was a well-dressed crowd, still very much on its Continental manners. Housewives from New Rochelle, grass widows from Texas, whores from the East Sixties, movie directors, a few Hollywood stars, V.I.P.'s from General Motors and the U.N., a couple of Midwestern Senators returning from some committee investigation at the Ritz in Paris, full of French wine and memories and vocal observations on the "decadence of Europe," international riffraff, hardworking members of the theatrical profession, café society, titles on the run from Attlee, and some of the men who might be called on to make the decisions that influence history. The Americans in the room were behaving as though they were still in the Casino at Cannes, while the few French were trying their best to pretend the Americans weren't there. This, in microcosm, was the world through which I had been riding a gawdy roller coaster for two years.

The drinks didn't seem to be helping as much as usual.

I happened to look toward the main entrance of the café. Something quite interesting began to happen to my blood pressure. Standing there beside a stocky, overdressed man with glittering black hair was a startlingly beautiful woman, in fact the most beautiful woman I had ever seen. During the past two years I had known many beautiful women— God knows it's easy enough for a night-club entertainer who has his own hair and teeth— but this was something off nobody's assembly line. She was tall without the Empire State effect of a mannequin, with a figure exactly right for her height— or for anything else, for that matter; a figure, incidentally, that was pleasantly available to the public gaze through something lacy by an expensive couturier. Her hair was jet black and drawn in a tight roll at the back of her neck in a manner that, I suppose, was out of fashion, but was just right for her particular beauty. And her face was more youthful and fresh than any other face in that room, yet it had about it a kind of brooding seriousness that may or may not have been an act.

I guess I must have been giving a frozen-statue performance, because I suddenly became aware of Irene's not too pleasant laughter. Quick to such responses in her men, she said cynically, "You can look, but you mustn't touch."

"What does that mean?"

"The beautiful bit of bric-a-brac belongs to Daddy— the gentleman on her right."

"Belongs?"

"Oh, yes. And legally, at that. Though God knows how she did it."

"Who is he?"

"Joseph Pasquela. One of those international mystery men. Very romantic. Appeared from nowhere and is reputed to have a fabulous fortune. He could have married almost anything he had wanted instead of— "

"Who the hell is she?"

"Really, Mac! You mean to tell me that you haven't heard? It's one of the most delicious stories in Paris. Surely you know!"

I watched the girl as she moved like a princess through the crowd with the slow-moving man behind her and joined a large party at a table by the great window overlooking the ship's bow. The others in the party were all jabbering and laughing like the animated monkeys they were, but the girl who belonged to Pasquela sat silently, smiling occasionally, looking far off into the distance. At what? I wondered.

"I haven't the faintest idea who she is."

"But, darling," Irene said, "that is the Naked Lady."

Chapter Two

SEPTEMBER 9, 2:30 A.M.

Irene put on her brassiere and slipped back into her Schiaparelli dinner gown. She was extremely professional about it. Speed was sometimes essential to her way of life.

"Well," she said with a contented yawn, "don't think it hasn't been delightful."

"I won't," I said.

"I'm very fond of you, Mac."

"Leave the ten bucks on the mantel," I said.

"What a rotten thing to say!" She made an angry little gesture and then said sharply, "What do you *do*, Mac?"

I kept the bored look on my face and drew the sheet up around my chin. I didn't allow her to see that she had startled me.

"It's no secret," I said. "My French press agent calls me 'heir to Crosby,' and my American press agent describes me as the 'American Jean Sablon.'"

"Oh, that," she said. "That's the sort of thing I tell Albert. I know better. You sing all right, and you're better-looking than most of them, but it might have been any one of a thousand American boys who could croon a tune. Why did Georges Fournier put you up there?"

There was so much truth in her words that they stung.

"Some people like my singing."

"It's all right," she admitted. "But what else do you do, Mac?"

"Sleep around with inquisitive women."

"You're a disgusting oaf!"

"I'm sick of you, Irene," I said.

She started to retort, checked herself, and then said calmly, "Where will I find a cigarette?"

"You heard me, Irene."

"I never hear what I might find unpleasant."

"I'm sick of myself, too."

"Oh, God," she said. "Don't dramatize yourself. It's not in character."

I'd said it involuntarily, without thought, and now, suddenly, very clearly, I knew it was true. I was sick to death of the person I had become. Mechanically I watched her as she rummaged about for cigarettes among my keys and watch and wallet on the glass-covered bureau. At her feet, discreetly tucked into the alcove beneath the long modern chest of drawers, was my luggage. For some reason, the sight of that luggage made me uneasy.

Irene found the cigarettes and turned. She fished out one and lit it and handed it to me and then lit one for herself. I kept watching my luggage, trying to figure out what was wrong.

"You Americans should stay at home," she finally said. "You never grow up. You get bitter as soon as a bit of the world rubs off on you. You blame other people for making the playroom a brothel."

And then I saw it. A small leather case matching the rest of my luggage with my initials stamped on it. A leather case I had never before seen.

"What's wrong?" Irene asked sharply.

"Wrong?" I looked up almost guiltily. She cast a birdlike glance at the luggage. I had to divert her attention quickly.

"Why did you follow me, Irene? I have nothing to offer that you couldn't get without the expense of a trip to the States. You haven't anything to offer me I haven't already had."

"Why, you conceited son-of-a-bitch!"

"Right on all counts."

I was trying to remember. I was almost positive that the leather case had not been in my stateroom before I left for dinner.

"You're utterly impossible, Mac!"

She perched on the little stool before the low chest of drawers. Her foot tapped against the little leather case. I tried to keep my eyes off her tapping foot. The annoyance left her face and she gave me one of those looks that I suppose she would have described as "melting."

"You've been slapped, Mac," she said. "I suppose it was the war. I'd like to keep you from being slapped harder."

"Mother Machree!"

She tilted her head back, her eyes half closed. "You know, darling, I've led the life of a slut. I was born in Liverpool and my mother was an incorrigible climber. She got rid of my father when I was about ten years old and carried off a good part of his fortune to London. I was brought up to be nothing more or less than a de luxe prostitute. Only she held out for a marriage license and a title. In a way, I was lucky to get anyone as tolerant and as stupid as Albert. But there's never been anyone who mattered. Not really. Until you. Mac, darling, I think I could stop being a slut if— if— if— darling, *if*."

She stopped, leaving the romantic "if" a breathless possibility.

I grinned. "Don't spoil a beautiful thing with talk, Irene. Leave me with the ecstatic memories of those nights we—"

She smashed out her cigarette to the accompaniment of a phrase involving a four-letter word and an impossible feat of acrobatics. Her tapping foot kicked out angrily. The little leather case toppled over, unfolding like a letter in the wind. Some tiny objects, bright and sparkling, came spattering out on the red rug.

Irene looked impatiently and, in the act of rising, sank back on the stool, her face a picture of stupefaction.

I thought, This is a dream. For a moment neither of us said a word. Then Irene swooped down, picked up one of the objects, and held it toward me, her eyes glittering with excitement. It was a tiny owl carved from green jade. And all around her on the rug were more owls of green, red, and white jade.

"What are you doing with these?" she whispered.

I got my mind working. I had to think of something quick. What the owls were doing in my stateroom in a leather case stamped with my initials was something for me to figure out. Irene must be thrown off the scent at all costs. There was no good denying the ownership of the collection. There was only one in the world like it, and it belonged to Georges Fournier. Hundreds of people had admired them lined up on their glass table in his chateau at Versailles.

"I'm sorry you saw them," I said.

"Yes!" she cried triumphantly. "I *knew* there was something about you, Mac. I knew it!"

"Don't be so goddamned romantic," I said as casually as possible. "I'm doing a favor for Georges. He asked me to bring them to the States. They're going to be in an exhibition at a Fifty-Seventh Street gallery."

"Georges trusted you with a collection worth easily a hundred thousand dollars? Come, now!"

"Why not? They're unique. Robbery would be impossible. No one could ever get rid of them."

"I don't believe you!"

I got up from the bed and took the green owl from her fingers. Calmly I collected the ones scattered about the rug, returned them to the case, and snapped it shut.

"All right," I said. "I'll tell you the truth. But you're not to breathe a word of this. It's between us."

"Yes!" she said. "Between us!"

"Well, it's nothing lurid or melodramatic. Georges happens to be in financial trouble. He wants me to act as his agent in America, because he thought I might be discreet about it. He didn't count on a lady kicking over a leather case in my stateroom."

"It wasn't even locked."

I let that go. "He wants me to contact certain rich collectors in the States and make a good sale. It's as simple as that."

I looked her straight in the eyes. For a moment she returned my gaze. Then I saw the disappointment in her eyes. I thought I had convinced her. She shrugged her shoulders and got to her feet.

"A naked man is ridiculous," she said.

I shoved the case back under the chest and returned to bed. "Good night, Irene."

"I don't believe a word of it," she said calmly. "What do you intend to do about it?"

"Don't worry. I shan't talk. But I intend ..."

"Yes?"

"Never mind what I intend!"

At the door she turned. "Don't forget. You're lunching with Albert and me tomorrow."

"I can't wait!"

"Good night."

"Give my love to Albert. Hip-hip!"

"Heel!"

In the half-opened door she turned back again. "You may come crawling on your knees for help yet!"

Then she was gone with a slammed door behind her.

I leaped out of the bed, locked the door, and fished out the leather case. It was of cowhide and matched the rest of my luggage exactly. The little owls fitted into niches and stood above one another in three layers. Obviously the case had been designed to hold the owls. It didn't make sense. Unless Georges Fournier was in reality a mental case. Certainly it was easy enough to believe after what he had said during that interview in his suite at the Crillon. I looked at my watch. It was nearly three A.M. I turned to the phone on the commode beside my bed. I could put in a ship-to-shore call to Paris and talk to Fournier. But something warned me against that move. Better wait. Perhaps I would hear from him in the morning. Mechanically I reached for the cigarettes Irene had thrown on the glass-covered chest. And then I saw that my wallet was gone.

I grabbed for my clothes and was half dressed when I decided I was behaving like a fool. I undressed again, got back into bed, and lay there in the darkness smoking one cigarette after another. What was Irene really up to? What was the leather case with the damned owls doing in my stateroom? Was it possible that there was some element of truth in Fournier's nightmare? Was it nearly the witching hour and no way out?

Chapter Three

SEPTEMBER 9, 2:00 P.M.

Irene was waiting near the entrance to the main dining salon.

"Albert said to go ahead. He had to make a business call to his office in Paris."

"All right with me."

She handed me my wallet. "I can't imagine how it got into my bag," she said blandly.

"Was it worth it?"

"No."

"I'm an old hand," I said. "I never keep anything incriminating in my wallet."

"Darling! How wise!"

The maître d'hôtel bowed low, and we made our entrance— or rather Irene made an entrance with me as an appropriate background— down the grand staircase into the lovely dining salon. ("My dear, don't look now, but there goes that Lady Harcourt with her current lover. Yes, darling, Mac McLean, that divine singer everyone is talking about.") The room, probably the most beautiful room afloat, was filled with color and laughter. Wine gurgled into graceful stemmed glasses, the crepes suzette sputtered blue beside the tables, guinea hen and pigeon stuffed with grapes were born triumphantly aloft, and salmon stared surprised from the midst of secret sauces. We were seated with a flourish and I began the ritual of selection, only recently acquired. It was a far cry from the echo of "One corned-beef hash coming up!"

Over the edge of the menu I suddenly became aware of Irene's hand, tense on the blade of her knife. For the first time I realized she was seething with some secret excitement. I looked into her eyes. They were bright and evasive.

She looked away and her voice was casual enough, but her fingers on the knife's edge remained stiff.

"The night of Laura's party," she said. "The night you didn't show up. You say you went to Fournier's suite at the Crillon."

"I told you I did. Why?"

"And you talked about— jade?"

"What are you driving at?"

"Did he give you the jade then?"

I couldn't make out what she was up to. But some inner voice warned me not to answer that one. "What difference does it make?"

"You were wearing tails," she said. "And you had a blue cornflower in your lapel. I remember, I thought it in such bad taste."

"So?"

Instead of answering, she laughed. It was unnatural, shrill laughter, and very much unlike Irene. I began to feel uneasy. But before I could pursue the subject, I saw Albert majestically making his way through the dining salon to our table. And behind him, descending the grand staircase, was Pasquela and his wife.

As Albert took his seat, Irene put her hand on my arm and said, "Your naked lady, Mac."

"Naked lady?" Albert said. "I realize this is a French boat, but ..."

"They call her the Naked Lady, darling. She came out of nowhere— little American girl, I believe— to become the leading nude at the Folies Bergère. Reputed to have the most beautiful body in Europe."

"Well, well!" Albert said, looking toward the lady with renewed interest. "I must say she doesn't look like the sort who would go about naked in public."

"She doesn't any more," Irene said. "Now the exhibit is solely for the gentleman beside her. Her husband, Joseph Pasquela."

"Pasquela! That rotter aboard? Wonder why he's going to the States this time."

"Probably to take over American Tel and Tel. From what I hear, he has practically everything else."

"Nonsense!" Albert said. "His power is highly exaggerated. Probably has a clever public-relations chap."

"What's his nationality?" I asked.

"One of those impossible little Central American countries, I believe. The sort of place where you put on gold braid and grab a shotgun and seize the government, while all the time a band plays. He got his start smuggling munitions in some revolution down there, unless I'm very much mistaken."

"It wouldn't be the first time you've been mistaken, darling," Irene said sweetly.

Albert said, "Quite," with so much feeling that even Irene seemed slightly taken aback. Then, to my surprise, she let the conversation drop. She seemed to be waiting. And now, for the first time, I realized that Albert had the haggard, worried look of a St. Bernard.

"I suppose Irene told you the news," he said.

"News? What news?"

"About poor Fournier."

Irene's fingers drew back from the knife. "I was waiting to tell him, darling. I was afraid I'd bungle it, knowing how fond of Georges Mac was."

"What's happened?" I tried to keep my voice calm, aware all the time of Irene's malevolent eyes.

"He's been murdered."

For a moment I was unable to speak. The laughter and chatter around me receded to a meaningless whisper. Then it came back, louder, more shrill, more insistent.

"Murdered? Georges?" I heard myself say stupidly.

"It's in the ship's paper. Irene insisted I call a chap we know with the Paris police. He gave me some more details— the little they know."

So Fournier had not been dreaming up a nightmare, after all. He had predicted his own violent death and I had laughed. But even now I couldn't bring myself to encompass the full meaning of the event.

"When? Where?"

"That's the odd part of it," Albert said. "The news was released to the press only last night. Yet the murder took place three nights ago. Rather, three mornings ago."

"The night of Laura's party at the Ritz," Irene said quietly.

"He was found in the morning when his valet went in to awaken him. He had been throttled to death. Part of his jade collection is missing."

"Have they apprehended... the murderer?"

"No. A young man in evening dress left his suite at about three-thirty A.M. So far, the police have not been able to trace or identify him. They seem fairly certain he must be the murderer."

The coldness seemed to be spreading from my head down my back. I didn't look at Irene. She said nothing. I knew, of course, that she had been attempting to trap me. And the jade owls; Irene knew they were in my stateroom. I turned to her, challenging her to speak.

"Poor Mac," she said calmly. "You can see it's a terrible shock to him."

"Only a fool would steal Fournier's jade collection," I said hotly. "He couldn't hope to dispose of it."

Albert sighed. "I'm afraid, my boy, I'm a bit more cynical than that. Collectors of jade are an odd lot. With some of them it's a passion— or a vice. There might easily be buyers, with no questions asked."

"Well!" Irene said. "Whoever has the collection would be delighted to hear that!" Her foot touched mine ever so lightly. I drew back.

"But surely the police have some idea who this man was. The man seen leaving his suite at three-thirty."

"Apparently not," Albert said. "Although, of course, Brilton, my source of information, may not have been told everything. The puzzling part of the whole business is why it was withheld from the press. And even now the press does not know about the missing jade collection. Most of the stories in the Paris papers seem to assume it was the work of a jealous husband."

"Just think," Irene said. "I danced with Georges earlier that evening at Laura's party. You must remember seeing him, Mac, before we all went off to Countess Verona Rozelli's for breakfast."

She said it so casually that for a moment it didn't register. Then I said quickly, "I do remember catching a glimpse of him. That was quite a session at Verona's."

"I should say!" Irene said. "I didn't get home until eight in the morning. You dropped me at my house in a taxi."

I looked at Albert to see how he was taking it. He still had the hang-dog look of the St. Bernard. There was no suspicion in his eyes.

"It doesn't seem real," I said.

"Yesterday I was bored!" Irene suddenly cried. "Today I'm not bored any more."

"Shut up, Irene," I said.

Albert looked up sharply. "What's this?" he blustered. "What are you two talking about?"

"But, darling," Irene said. "There's no good going into a decline over Georges Fournier's death. It's too bad and all that, of course, but he was hardly a man anyone really loved. And it *does* make sort of an exciting mystery."

In the silence that followed her words, there was a sudden crash behind me. I half rose from my chair and turned defensively. A waiter, two tables away, had dropped a tray. For a moment the conversation in the dining salon ceased, as though a little chill of fear had run through the crowd. A captain was descending on the poor waiter, his face black as thunder. Irene's laughter broke the silence like a knife through feathers.

"Too many Paris farewells," I said, sheepishly sinking back into my chair. "I've got the good-by jitters."

With the subtlety of a bulldozer, Irene switched the conversation. She began talking about a cocktail party to which we were all invited later in the day in the suite of Lili Fenwick, a new and highly publicized Hollywood star. The subject offered rich material for Irene's special brand of vitriol. I heard myself laughing mechanically, and giving point for point, while all the time a kind of panic was beginning to take hold of me.

Fournier had predicted his own murder and I had laughed. Now I was in it up to my neck and apparently someone intended that I should be. But why? Even if these were the rough boys Fournier had described, and they never "let you leave the party of your own free will," I had never given them any reason to distrust me.

Surely, if it were only a fall guy they wanted, there was no need for such elaborate preparations. The leather case that had held the jade must have been ordered days before they had actually murdered Fournier.

And now Irene, through inquisitiveness or motives of personal blackmail or maybe worse, was making things damned awkward. Could I trust her to keep her mouth shut until I discovered what their game was or figured a way out?

The dream noises in the dining room against the machine-gun staccato of Irene's onslaught on the human race added to my sensation of unreality. I looked toward Pasquela's wife. There she sat, cool and detached, like an iceberg glittering in the sun beside a sinking liner.

And then, suddenly, I was certain that someone was watching me, had been watching me for a long time. I turned to meet the eyes of a stocky man in a badly cut wool suit. He stared back at me without the slightest trace of embarrassment, and all the time he kept dishing soup into his mouth while it dripped onto the napkin tucked into his vest.

I pushed back by chair and got to my feet.

"Anything wrong?" Irene asked.

"I'm not a good sailor."

"But that's absurd! The sea is like glass!"

"Water never agreed with me in any form. But I'll be all right for the cocktail party. I always am. See you then."

I walked toward the staircase designed for the entrances of such persons as Irene, and passed Pasquela and his wife, who sat not speaking, and again I got the impression that she was staring off into some memory or hope or fear that existed for her beyond the confines of the room. Even then, in the midst of my own anger and concern, I was acutely aware of her, and she was there in my mind mixed up with Fournier and the jade owls and Irene as I made my way through the lounge to the elevator.

Down on C deck the corridors were empty and still. My footsteps made no sound on the thick carpet. At the door of my stateroom I turned to look back. There was no one in sight. The distant throb of the ship's engines was a lonely sound. Luxury and laughter seemed very far away in this narrow corridor. For a moment I felt as though I had been kicked out of a gay and tinseled excursion, and never again would I get back.

I opened the door and stepped into my stateroom.

"What are you doing here?" I shouted.

The steward turned in mild surprise. "I just finish with the bed, monsieur. I am sorry, I startle you."

The jade owls were lined up in a neat row across the top of the dressing table.

"Who told you to take those things out of the case?"

The man looked genuinely puzzled. "I do not touch them, monsieur. They are there on the table when I come in. I do not touch anything on the table."

He gestured toward the jade figures and I saw the little slip of folded paper. Quietly I snatched it up and read, "Your cabin. Ten o'clock tonight."

I rolled the note up into a tight ball and stuffed it into my pocket. The steward's face was a study in innocent indifference. I had the sudden conviction that he had read the note. I wondered if the jade owls meant anything to him. It was too late to do anything about that now. He would make an excellent witness for the opposition.

"Get out!" I said rudely. "I don't need you now."

The steward shrugged. His face showed nothing. He left the room quietly, with a backward glance toward the jade owls. I locked the door, got the jade owls back into their case, shoved it beneath my bed, and slumped into a chair. Fear and confusion were giving way to anger. Anger at my own stupidity in not believing Fournier's story, anger with the people who were drawing me into the center of a tight web.

Apparently there was a stopping point with Fournier, a point when his conscience had won out over his material needs; a point beyond which he refused to go. Knowing the possible consequences of his act, he had called me into his suite to warn me. Deep down, he must have known he had signed his own death warrant.

I lit a cigarette and puffed at it nervously. One thing was certain. I was not the free agent I had imagined myself to be. I was no lone rover with the world in the palm of my hand. I had sold myself down the same river as Fournier, and sometime before ten o'clock tonight I must make a decision. I didn't intend to let them lick me if I could help it, but I was equally certain my decision would not be Fournier's. I wasn't going to die for some moral abstraction. I wanted survival, and at a high level, at that! And yet ...

Through the porthole I saw some distant land, probably the south of Ireland, a lonely bit of rock flung out of a slate-gray sea. The sea blurred, and for a moment I saw the man in evening clothes fallen across the bed with his head hanging crazily to one side, like a rag doll's. I thought, Not you, baby. Not while there's any fun to be had.

And then suddenly I thought, What fun?

I went to the bathroom and was sick with an illness that had nothing to do with the sea.

Chapter Four

SEPTEMBER 9, 6:00 P.M.

Lili Fenwick, the Hollywood star who just three years before had been a hash-slinger in a coal-town lunch wagon, was a promotion man's creation of an American dream: blonde, perfectly groomed, starry-eyed, and utterly unreal. Clad in purple silk cut so low that her navel might have been the pendant to the diamond necklace she wore, she was now playing the role of gracious hostess at a cocktail party, spouting all of Irene's clichés without Irene's sometimes trenchant wit. Somehow or other she gave the impression of being a sort of outboard motor for the astounding breasts she propelled so proudly through the crowd. And from time to time she looked down nervously as though terrified that these carefully tended sources of her income might disappear. These breasts, with the rather frightened child at their helm, turned this way and that, bestowing favor in a royal manner, sailing majestically up to the more illustrious and sometimes flabbergasted guests, swerving and retreating gracefully from the nobodies. The bewildered navigator, the blonde child, had taken on all the attributes of a de luxe attraction at a circus side show. At times the great starry eyes seemed to be saying, I'm sorry, it's really not my fault at all.

Someone had drummed a series of dreadful bromides into the poor girl's blonde head, and she was being frightfully "international set" after her first visit to the Riviera, calling a maharajah "darling," a tennis star "my pet," and a polo player by a name used only by columnists, while she chattered on and on about Paris in the spring, the beauties of the Sistine Chapel, Lord Somebody's yacht, Wimbledon, and the Ritz. I felt vaguely sorry for her. Something deep down whispered, We small-town hicks should stick together.

This was the most de luxe of the de luxe suites, and it was packed to the walls with the more celebrated passengers, guzzling champagne and popping French Line delicacies into their mouths between shrieks of merriment. It was all *toujours gai*; too, too *toujours* and too damned *gai* to be convincing. But it was my world, the world I had wanted, the world that had been handed to me, the world I intended to retain, hard and gold-plated, cynical and in the know; the wise people who sold but never bought the Brooklyn Bridge.

A great many of Lili Fenwick's guests had known Fournier; none of them well, of course (he had turned a suave and urbane mask to the world, but I suspected blood was thicker than American Martinis, and his heart had belonged to the inner world of the Faubourg St. Germain), but well enough to say, "Poor, dear Georges." Fournier's well-advertised success with women added spice to the general atmosphere of scandal surrounding his death. None of them here knew about the missing jade, so it was assumed the young man seen leaving his suite at three-thirty A.M. had been a jealous husband. The fact that the suspected murderer had been immaculately clad in evening clothes created a certain chic, although the manner of death, it was said, was a bit on the crude side.

For some reason, Irene avoided me. I suspected it was because she was saving it all up for a Big Scene. This was something novel in her life— a lover who might be a jewel thief and a murderer. I felt that she intended to make the most of it. Albert, drooping even more than usual, was hip-hipping and harumphing to some properly reverent relatives of a Kansas City department-store owner. As I wandered about from group to group and glass to glass, I became aware that I was searching for someone. And, after a while, I realized that it was Pasquela's wife. I knew that the Pasquelas must have been on the invitation list, but I searched in vain.

Finally the inevitable happened. I was dragged to the white piano in the corner of the sitting room. Lili Fenwick turned her breasts on the room like two commanding headlights and without a gesture brought the room to silence.

"And now, darlings," she cooed with frightened eyes, "Mac McLean has kindly consented to honor us with— kind enough to play the piano— for— those divine songs, and he's going to sing them."

After which the headlights made a beeline for the champagne buffet like the Twentieth Century coming into Chicago.

I gave them my teeth in my best boyish manner. This was business. A great many of these people might be present at my New York debut; it was the better part of wisdom to soften them up first. I sang a couple of naughty things and then switched to *"J'ai tout— ce n'est rien."* Under the spell of Renoir's haunting words and music, the chatter died down. This song said something to everyone in the room, no matter who sang it; something they never spoke of, something of which they were barely conscious, but something deeply felt. Up ahead, through the champagne bubbles, they were seeing the end of the line, and it ended in darkness.

I had never really liked this song. For some reason it disturbed me. But today I forgot my surroundings and the words seemed to take on a new meaning. Faces receded into the haze of cigarette smoke and there was a kind of foggy space with the poignant words floating out across an abyss of half-articulated yearning, regret, and dimly realized needs. As the last notes died off in the odd and unexpected dissonance, I looked up from the keyboard and saw across the room, by the door, Joseph Pasquela's wife. She looked directly into my eyes.

There was polite applause and the voices raised again in laughter. Lili Fenwick shrieked:

"Divine, darling! Divine!"

I sat at the piano, aware only of one woman in the room.

Pasquela's wife moved away from the group surrounding her and came toward me. I waited with the curious feeling that this moment was important, as important as any moment in my life. I had thought I would never again experience this special sense of breathless waiting, of suspended excitement.

"What is this song?" she asked.

Irene had been wrong; she was not American. Her accent was the meticulous British of the well-educated European.

I told her. "It's extraordinarily good," she said. "And you sing it with great understanding."

"It's my job to seem to understand," I said. "Whether I sing about pots at the end of the rainbow or mother love or how it feels to be in Europe in the spring."

"You made me feel sorry for myself. It's the purpose of such a song. So you see— you succeeded."

"Should I feel sorry for you?"

She looked into my eyes and again I was aware of the remoteness of her manner, a preoccupation with other worlds, other thoughts. She said nothing in reply.

"May I get you some champagne?"

Her eyes flickered in surprise. She hesitated, looking over her shoulder toward her husband, who stood talking to a group on the far side of the room. His back was to us. She said:

"Yes. That would be nice. Thank you."

I brought the champagne to the corner behind the white piano. She looked at me gravely over the rim of her glass as she took her first sip.

"The human race is noisy this afternoon," I said.

"Perhaps there's too much of it in too small a space."

Behind that soft voice and the manner in which she moved was a tradition that included British governesses and exclusive schools. Of that I felt certain. It was difficult to believe that she had been a nude at the Folies Bergère. Almost as though she read the question in my mind, her eyes mocked me.

"I am Mrs.—" she began.

"I know. Of course. And I—"

"I know," she said, and she smiled for the first time.

But the smile died quickly. The air of detachment returned, and there was a nervous contraction of her mouth when she looked toward her husband.

"Why is everyone so hysterical?" she asked.

"That's the way they always are."

"Really? It will take time for me to become accustomed to it."

"I can see you're not enjoying it. Would you like to take a turn around the deck— with your husband's permission?"

To my utter astonishment, she laughed. "That, my dear Mr. McLean, is not at all necessary. I would be grateful if you took me out of this room."

After that I moved fast. I steered her through the crowd, past Irene's narrowed, speculative eyes and Pasquela's masklike indifference, muttered something to the by now inebriated Lili Fenwick, and got the door of the suite closed behind us.

"Should we go to the veranda café?"

"I think I would prefer sitting out on deck for a bit, if you don't mind."

I led her to a deserted section of the promenade and we settled back, side by side, on the deck chairs.

She leaned back and closed her eyes for a moment, then opened them quickly, almost guiltily, as though for a second she had forgotten my presence. She said nothing, waiting for me to direct the conversation. For once I found myself as tied up in knots as any eighteen-year-old boy fresh from an Iowa farm.

"You don't seem to belong to that crowd," I said ineptly.

She smiled. "I don't, really. I bought my way in, you know."

"Was it worth it?"

She looked thoughtful. "You're very American, Mr. McLean. I think it's a quality I like. Directness. In exchange, I shall be direct with you. Perhaps then you will not wish to sit here beside me."

"Why not?"

"I'm told you were a pilot in the U.S. Air Force. I was your enemy, Mr. McLean. I am German. I worked against you."

"That's all over," I said harshly.

"I have my own special guilt," she said.

When I said nothing, she said, "You are not leaving me?"

"No," I said.

The mockery left her face. She looked me in the eyes and the depth of the feeling she caused in me almost shocked me.

"That is the wonderful thing about you Americans," she said quietly. "You give other people a chance."

"Never mind other Americans. I'm only speaking for myself."

"And you deserve an explanation— weak and odious as it may be."

She leaned back and closed her eyes. When she spoke, she seemed at the same time to speak deliberately and yet to allow her words to flow without thought.

"My father was German. I was never allowed to forget that he came of one of the very oldest and most distinguished families of Hannover. My mother was from Central America. Her father had been ambassador to Germany from his country. When she married my father, they settled in Hannover, and my mother never left Germany again as long as she lived. I was brought up in the atmosphere of an enclosed garden. Although my father was a doctor, his main interests and those of his friends were music and literature. The world of the poor and suffering was very far away. When Hitler came into power— I was a child then, of course— the walls of the beautiful little garden seemed to grow even higher. They disapproved of Hitler as a vulgar upstart. But, like many others, they did nothing to oppose him. I was sent to school in Switzerland, but when the war broke out I was home in Hannover. My father was ordered by the government to a Hamburg hospital. We had a very comfortable house near the zoo, and I remember my father speaking softly of the blessed day the British would come in and end it all. But no one spoke those thoughts above a whisper. I went to the university in Hamburg. The air raids began. And then one night, after an evening lecture, there was a particularly bad air raid. When it was over and I got to my street ..." She stopped a moment, and though her face showed no deep emotion, she sighed. "It was gone. Everything. My mother was killed outright, and my father was so badly wounded that he died next morning. It was the end of the enclosed garden. I had nothing left in the world, not even a toothbrush. Except my body! I knew I had to begin again, learn everything from the beginning— that all I had known had been wrong. And I knew I had to survive. I was nineteen."

I remembered the raids over Hamburg and the bombs— innocent little pin pricks in the night, dropping silently the relief map below. You had tried to think of it as only a relief map without people. Had I piloted the plane that dropped the bombs that killed her parents?

"I went back to Hannover, and I was there when the English came in. It was difficult, but my English stood me in good stead. And I was determined to live, to survive. I won't go into all the grimy details. Anyway, with the help of an English officer, I got to Paris. He wanted to send me to London, but I knew that England was not the place for me, so he finally agreed to help me get to Paris. After that— well, I got out of something unpleasant. Then I got a job at the Folies Bergère. It seemed rather idiotic, posing in the nude, but it didn't matter much to me. I had one dream— that was to get to America. Now I'm married to a rich man and I don't have to worry about food and heat and clothing and— and men, and I'm going to America."

"Why is it you want to go there?"

"To find life," she said.

"Life?"

"Belief. I lost it."

"You don't have to believe in a merry-go-round," I said. "You just enjoy it."

"You talk the way a great many people I've known feel," she said. "The difference is that you are acting. You are even fooling yourself. I knew, as you were singing, you are a person who has not given up— a person who still believes."

My heart sank. She was talking about some other guy. What I still believed in wouldn't fit into an open pore. I couldn't even act the part of the kind of person she was talking about.

"I don't have to know much about you," she went on, "to know that— well, if one were in trouble, you would help. There is something of the knight about you, Mr. McLean."

"The name is Mac. And it doesn't go with knight, Mrs. Pasquela."

"My name is Elisabeth," she said. "And I like Mac."

Suddenly, as I looked at her, my former enemy, all the emotion the first sight of her had induced returned. And it came over me that despite her hard shell, her apparent ability to give and to take it, there was something lonely and frightened about her.

Without thought, I said, "Being a knight for you might make sense. The first time I saw you, I thought—"

She moved her head impatiently and looked down the deck as though she regretted having left the party.

"This isn't a line," I said quickly. "At least, I don't think so. I'm usually pretty good with a line. It's part of my stock in trade. You can see I'm bungling too much to be throwing a line."

She thought about that for a moment, and decided to smile. "You mustn't get serious. I came out here on an impulse."

"What impulse?"

"The impulse for fresh air," she said coolly.

"You're laughing at me."

"I'm in no position to laugh at anyone."

"What impulse?" I insisted.

"I wanted to learn. I know few Americans. I want to know how you feel. To share it. You see, I think I've made a terrible mistake. I didn't know, I ..." She stopped.

"Go on."

"Your words haven't helped. It's what I sensed so strongly in you while you were singing that song. You don't like the— how do you say— the top dogs. You belong with others."

I'd forgotten how to blush long ago, so it didn't show. And then some desperate note behind her words caught my attention. I stopped feeling guilty in the urgency of the new thought.

"You need help!"

She didn't answer.

"That's why you came out here! You're so desperate, you turned to a complete stranger on the hunch he would turn out to be O.K. You took the chance. You're in some kind of trouble."

She made a move to rise. I felt she was near panic. I put a restraining hand on her arm.

"Elisabeth, it may seem fantastic to you, since I've only spoken to you a few minutes, but goddamn it, if there's anything I can do, I'd be willing to ..."

"To what?" Her voice was almost harsh.

"Ask it."

She hesitated a moment, then said, "I might ask you to kill a man." And then she laughed.

It was a joke, of course, but I felt my blood running cold. Underneath the mockery, the laughter, the casual gesture of her hand as she drew shut her handbag was an emotion so intense that it left her trembling. And I knew the emotion was hatred.

"Pasquela," I said.

She gave me a startled look. "What's that?"

"It's Pasquela you hate. It's Pasquela you would like to kill."

She looked at me without expression. I withdrew my hand.

She smiled. "You're rather sweet to take me seriously. I was merely experimenting. I proved my point about the knight. However, if you have any doubts, my husband is the last person in the world... After all, look what he has done for me."

I took a deep breath and said, "You can't stand going to bed with him!"

She relaxed, put her head back, closed her eyes, and laughed. But this laughter was too loud and too long. It was hysterical laughter in which I felt she was laughing at Pasquela and me and the whole damned show.

"Cut it out!" I said savagely.

After a bit she stopped. There were tears in her eyes.

"The sophisticated man of the world! The famous heartbreaker, McLean! You don't know."

"Know what?"

"The joke. The terrible joke. Oh, Mac!"

She spoke as though she had known me all my life and underneath was a plea for understanding, and desperation.

"You've been through a lot," I said.

She said, "There's something I should like to tell ..." and stopped. She was looking beyond me. I turned. The stocky man in the badly cut suit who had stared at me in the dining room was standing at the rail, his back to the sea, watching us.

The color left her face. "I must go," she said.

"Who is he?"

And now, for the first time, it occurred to me that Elisabeth Pasquela might be more entwined in my own fate than I had imagined.

"I haven't the faintest idea. But I must go." She looked out toward the sea, bathed in a late-afternoon color of rose. "I shouldn't have come out here with you. You can't help me. No one can."

She stood and I jumped up, disregarding the man at the rail, and grabbed her arm and held her.

"Please ..." she said.

"Listen to me. I may be nuts, but there's something about you— something ..."

"You can't very well hold me by force on the promenade deck," she said wearily. "People are watching."

"When can I see you again?"

"It's no use."

"Don't give me that. You came out here with me of your own free will. You need help. I may not be a shining knight, but—"

"All right," she said without enthusiasm. "I'll call you in your stateroom later this evening. Perhaps I'll be able to meet you about midnight."

"Good."

"As a well-behaved young bride!"

On that note of self-mockery, she went off down the promenade. A shadow fell on the deck chair beside me. I turned to face my admirer in the ill-fitting suit. He gave me a stiff smile, full of badly made false teeth.

"Pardon, monsieur. This is my deck chair."

"Is that all you want?" I asked rudely.

He arched his eyebrows. "Allow me to introduce myself. Armando Gonzales. I do not believe that it is good to get mixed up with strangers on a ship. It could lead to trouble. Especially women."

"What does that mean?"

"Perhaps we will leave it by naming it— generalization. And now, if you please ..."

I moved away to let him have his deck chair. Far down the deck, Elisabeth Pasquela gave a backward glance as she turned into the entrance to the main lounge.

Chapter Five

SEPTEMBER 9, 9: 15 P.M.

There were plenty of reasons why I had dinner alone in my stateroom. I wanted to avoid Irene and her questions until after the ten-o'clock meeting. I wanted to straighten out my rather high-pressured reactions to Elisabeth Pasquela. I wanted to prepare myself for whatever contingency might arise when my unknown visitor arrived. Among my preparations was making sure that all was well with my German Luger.

In the meantime, I carefully examined the meager reports of the murder in the ship's paper.

> Georges Fournier, internationally known art collector and the last surviving member of one of France's most distinguished families, was found dead by throttling in his suite at the Crillon at nine A.M. on the morning of September fifth. The brutal murder has created a mystery inasmuch as the facts of his death were reported to the press only this morning, two days after the crime. The police refuse to divulge their reasons for withholding the news. Beyond the fact that a young man in evening clothes was known to have left M. Fournier's suite at three-thirty A.M., about the time established for the murder, no facts or motives have been disclosed. The press associations have filed a vigorous complaint on the grounds that no valid reasons for the peculiar actions of the authorities in keeping secret the murder has been given.

Peculiar was hardly the word for it. For one thing, I was fairly certain that at least two employees of the Crillon knew me by sight— the night concierge and the elevator boy. Surely they must have identified the "young man in evening clothes" by this time. And why had the police not disclosed the fact that the jade was missing? I intended to get rid of those damned owls, but not until after the ten-o'clock meeting with the writer of the note. I wanted his story first.

About nine-thirty the phone rang and I picked it up to hear Irene's voice at the other end.

"Hiding, darling?"

"From whom would I be hiding?" I asked, annoyed.

"Jealous husband."

"Albert?" I asked ironically.

"Don't be a fool. You've succeeded in getting yourself well talked about. Everyone at the cocktail party noticed you leaving with her. But perhaps you don't realize that Pasquela doesn't let anyone near his precious little piece of— well, let it go at that. It wasn't discreet to kidnap her in front of the whole world."

"If that's the whole world, I'm moving to Mars."

"Pasquela might help you to get there!"

I said nothing. There was one of those silences that are correctly described as pregnant— and this one was pregnant with feminine fury.

"I'm curious about some things," she finally said. "As you can well imagine. What time?"

"Tomorrow," I said.

"So!" she cried in sharp suspicion. "You're occupied tonight, are you? I didn't think she worked that fast."

"Nothing to do with that."

"You could have had her in the old days for five American dollars if you'd waited around the stage door of the Folies Bergère. What are her rates now, darling?"

"I wouldn't know," I said evenly. "The other women I know don't even put five bucks' premium on their— shall we say, gifts."

"Now, Mac, I'm warning you!"

"Warning me? Of what?"

For a moment there was silence. Then she said in a rather tired voice, "Please. Don't let's quarrel. Forgive me for behaving like a jealous bitch."

"We'll talk about it tomorrow."

"Yes," she said. "All right." Then, after a short pause, "Mac, I've been lying here alone in my room, thinking. Maybe I'm wrong to treat everything as a game. I don't know what it's all about, but suddenly I'm frightened."

"Nothing can happen to you."

"Frightened for you, darling. It's so queer— the reports in the paper, and ..."

"Not on the phone!" I said sharply.

"Here comes Albert," she whispered and hung up.

I lit a cigarette. It tasted acrid. I had the vague feeling that I should take a shower. Wash it away. Wash what away? I walked to the window and looked out on the dark sea.

At ten sharp there was a knock on the door. I put my hand into my dressing-robe pocket and kept it there on the Luger. I took a deep breath and opened the door.

Joseph Pasquela stepped over the threshold.

For a moment I was so astonished I just stood there gaping. He closed the door behind him and smiled.

"You were expecting maybe Mrs. Nussbaum?" he said pleasantly.

"You had that note left here?"

"Yes. Please, if you don't mind." He locked the door, crossed to the couch, settled back, and lit a cigarette.

"There's no need to be so tense," he said. "I expect you have your hand on a gun. Guns make me nervous— except when I sell them, of course. Please."

I took my hand from my pocket.

"It was very good of you to take my wife away from that party," he said, without the slightest trace of irony. "I myself only stayed for business reasons. A vulgar brawl. My wife appreciates your kindness."

"She wanted fresh air," I said, still in a daze.

Pasquela was looking at the leather case tucked under the bed. "I am glad to see you have not panicked, Mr. McLean. A hysterical type would have got rid of the jade long ago."

"You had it put in my room?"

"Certainly not! I discovered quite by accident. Though, of course, we knew there must have been some motive."

"Motive?"

"Behind the rather premature death of our friend Georges."

"Don't give me that!" I said angrily. "I had nothing to do with Fournier's death, and I'm beginning to suspect that you have good reasons for knowing it. As for the jade, it was planted on me!"

"That would be difficult to prove," he said calmly.

"You've seen to that?"

He smiled. "I'm afraid you have a rather lurid conception of my activities, Mr. McLean. I don't go in for murder. Unless, of course, it's absolutely necessary."

He said it so blandly that he might have been talking of some new book or play or sport event.

"I don't give a good goddamn what you go in for or what you don't, as long as I'm out of it. What the hell's behind all this hocus-pocus, Mr. Pasquela?"

He looked pained. "Your tone of voice might annoy the average employer."

"Employer! Since when have I been working for you? I was working for Fournier and no one else."

"Fournier was only a sort of public-relations man. He was working for me, and therefore you also are working for me. Georges hired you at his own discretion. Perhaps it was one of the few really constructive acts of his rather confused and unfortunate career."

"Listen," I said. "Fournier gave me a break by arranging an engagement at the Casino in Cannes. In return for that, I was merely to extoll the virtues of Beldenez Frères and Company of Lyon and Madrid. A sound business investment, I was told. As a successful night-club entertainer, I was thrown in contact with many American businessmen and their wives. I arranged meetings with Fournier. That's about all I know."

Pasquela sighed. "Except, of course, what Fournier told you in his suite at the Crillon."

I thought quickly. The murderer of Fournier might have been hiding in the suite all the time I was there. In that case, he would have overheard what Fournier told me. It was safer to admit the truth; that Fournier had told me certain things; that I had not believed him.

"Fournier warned me against Beldenez Frères."

"Warned? How?" Pasquela's voice was suddenly sharp. I was certain that he was surprised I was telling the truth. Obviously, he had been prepared for evasion.

"He told me that I had been tricked. That Beldenez Frères were merely a front for a powerful Spanish syndicate engaged in promoting uprisings in Central and South America. He told me that, in fact, I had been acting as an agent for an unscrupulous political group. He told me that he was disgusted with himself for having lent his name and prestige to their machinations, and had told his superiors so. He said he expected to be— to be ..."

"Well?"

"Liquidated."

Pasquela leaned back and blew a cloud of cigarette smoke out into the room. "What did you say to this, Mc Lean?"

"I laughed at him. I thought he was drunk and a little nuts."

"That was very wise of you. Have you repeated this wild tale of Fournier's to anyone?"

"No," I said. "It's none of my business. I'm out for Mac McLean, Esquire, and no one else."

"Yes," he said. "Besides, it's such a wild tale no one would believe you. They would know, of course, that you were covering up your own motives in killing Fournier."

Cat and mouse, I thought. Don't be the mouse.

"I have no interest in who murdered Fournier," I said. "But, in the end, I may have to resort to 'wild tales' in order to clear myself."

"I doubt that," he said. "I believe you will never be implicated. That is, if ..."

"If what?"

"If you stay on our side of the fence, Mr. McLean."

"How can you guarantee it?"

"Never mind that."

"The Paris police are looking for a man in evening dress seen leaving Fournier's suite at three-thirty A.M. You know damn well who that man is. I know for certain that two employees at the Crillon could identify me. I don't understand the silence of the police."

"The employees you speak of are safe. At least, for the moment."

"The steward for this stateroom has seen the jade you planted on me."

"I repeat, Mr. McLean, I did not plant the jade on you. And if the steward has seen it, so much the better. It will remind you to be careful. You would not want any loose tongues wagging, eh? If you do as you are told, you will not have to fear anything. We will see to that."

"Am I worth all this trouble?"

Pasquela smashed out his cigarette. For the first time, he dropped the easy casual manner. His voice, when he spoke, was like steel. "That remains to be seen!"

He looked up at me, and there was something veiled and intense in his gaze. "You see, McLean, I myself am only an employee. I too act under orders. It has been well worth it. I believe you are like me in this respect. We have left our illusions in the past. We wish to have a little wealth and a little power. We wish to have the good things of life. After all, why should we concern ourselves with a few miserable people like Fournier or the natives of some country in which we have no interest?"

The last was said with such bitter cynicism that I was surprised. There were hidden places in the man, contradictions, doubts. Almost immediately he got control of himself and said in a hard voice:

"These are your orders, McLean. In return for them you will be well paid. Also, everything will be done to assure you of a success in your chosen profession."

Again I remembered Fournier's allusion to Faust and the Devil. Like Faust, I was being offered the world. In exchange for what?

"I'm waiting," I said.

"There is a dangerous agent at work among us. A traitor. A spy. We have narrowed our suspicions down to one person, but as yet we have no proof. It is your job to obtain that proof. The methods we leave entirely up to you— although we rely somewhat on your well-known success in obtaining the confidence of women."

"A woman!"

"Yes." He turned away from me, his face stony and expressionless.

I began to feel sick to my stomach again.

"If I should refuse?"

He shrugged. "You are too intelligent for that. You would be turned over to the French police. Your wild tales of Beldenez Frères would be laughed at. The employees at the Crillon would come forward to identify you. The steward would talk about the jade. You wouldn't have a chance."

"I'm not that stupid," I heard myself saying. "I'll play ball on one condition."

"What's that?"

"That after this job, I'm through."

He hesitated a moment, then said, "I myself cannot guarantee it, but I will confer with my superiors. I believe that they will consent."

Shakily I reached for a cigarette. I needed time. If I could get out of this mess on top, it might be worth it. I might even outwit them. In the act of lighting the cigarette, I thought suddenly of Irene. Did they suspect that she knew about the jade? Could I keep her quiet if for no other reason than her own safety depended on it?

I got the cigarette lighted and was about to speak when the phone rang. I looked at it as though it were a rattlesnake. Pasquela's eyebrows arched ironically. He sat there waiting. After a moment, I crossed and picked it up. I said, "Hello," looking into Pasquela's blank face.

"I can meet you in the library at midnight," the voice at the other end said.

"Good," I said, and hung up.

Pasquela's face had not changed expression.

"A lady," I said with a nervous laugh.

"Yes," he said. "Already you are making headway."

For a moment I didn't get it. "I don't understand," I said uncertainly.

He stood. For a moment the mask was dropped, and I got a momentary glimpse of a man plunged in pain and despair.

"Your assignment," he said in a dead voice. "The lady we suspect is my wife."

Chapter Six

SEPTEMBER 9, 11:50 P.M.

Now at midnight the four women carved from stone that stood beneath the glass dome in the ship's library resembled the last survivors in an atomized world. This room, with its cherrywood shelves lined with the fantasies, insights, and obsessions of literary men, was deserted. Up on the boat deck most of the passengers who had not retired for the night were dancing to the latest hits from Paris and New York, but down in this enormous room, two decks high, with its deep chairs and sofas, there was a granite-like silence.

There were still a few minutes left before the time appointed for my rendezvous with Elisabeth Pasquela. Despite a turn around the promenade deck, the adrenalin let loose during Pasquela's brazen visit to my cabin was still coursing through my veins. I went to the far corner of the room and stared rather blankly at some blue leather volumes of Voltaire. I saw the gold letters of *Candide*, and I thought, At least I'm not fool enough to believe that this is the best of all possible worlds. But Pasquela's words hung to me like slime. Beneath his cool exterior, contempt had been as obvious as his insulting assurance that I would find nothing objectionable in my "assignment." There was no doubt about his opinion of me. The "For Sale" sign that Fournier had pinned on me was being altered for the fire sale. They had apparently decided to add a line reading, "Secondhand Goods; Marked Down." I knew I had it coming, but apparently my glands did not. I was shaking with anger.

I lit a cigarette and tried to calm down. This was no time to lose my head. I certainly couldn't afford the luxury of righteousness. Fournier had been more right than he could have known when he spoke about the day of reckoning. Pasquela, or the gang he worked for, had framed me as tight as a Cezanne apple in the Modern Museum. The murder of Fournier had been carefully planned to coincide with my visit to his suite at the Crillon. A leather case had been ordered with my initials stamped into it, and had been sent with Fournier's fabulous jade collection to my cabin on the *Dauphiné*. If they chose to turn me over to the authorities, I would have one hell of a time talking my way out. Certainly no one would believe my wild tales about Pasquela and a frame-up. He had power and immunity, and besides, I hadn't the faintest idea what his real motives were.

It seemed incredible that they should have spent all the time and effort to frame me simply to use me for what Pasquela had termed an "assignment." My success with women had been fairly well publicized, but surely they had other methods of discovering whether or not Elisabeth Pasquela was dangerous to them. It was more than likely that they were keeping me in reserve as the lamb to be sent to slaughter in case the French authorities got too hot on the trail of Fournier's murderer.

After Pasquela had left my stateroom, my first impulse had been to get rid of the jade as quickly as possible. Aside from Irene, the steward was the only one— at least to my knowledge— who had seen the stuff in my cabin. But some unaccountable impulse had vetoed the idea. I had the curious feeling that, dangerous to me though they were, the sinister little owls were the key to saving myself.

Myself. Myself and Elisabeth Pasquela.

Since I had first seen her at cocktails in the ship's café she had never been long out of my mind. Yet everything was against the girl: her childhood in Nazi Germany, the fact that she had been a nude dancer at the Folies Bergère and had obviously married Pasquela for loot, and the way she had allowed herself to be picked up at Lili Fenwick's cocktail party. But by this time hard-boiled logic wasn't working. She did something novel and highly disturbing to my blood pressure. And of course Pasquela's cold-blooded announcement of his intentions regarding her future had awakened in me a protective instinct that only fanned the flame. A few days before I would have laughed at anyone who might have accused me of latent gallantry; it didn't fit into my plans of being the lone rider on the brightest horse of the merry-go-round. But now I was trying to figure a way out, not only for myself, but for her.

There was a soft whirring sound, a kind of warning whisper. I turned from the books and looked at the empty room. The deep chairs and sofas were huddled together in small groups like old ladies dozing in the late afternoon, forsaken and without thought, waiting for the end of the whirring in some distant home for the aged. I had the sensation of life among the inanimate objects of the room; life that listened. The whirring ceased. A small gilt clock above my head began to chime shrilly, swiftly, racing through twelve metallic strokes as though taking a petulant satisfaction in the death of another day. The stone women stared off into space, oblivious of the chirping clock, deaf to its warning of approaching death.

As the last note died out, Elisabeth Pasquela came into the library from the main lounge and stood just inside the archway looking uncertainly about the room. For a moment she did not see me, and for that moment I remained still, astounded once more by the impact of her presence. She wore a simple black dinner dress, conservative almost to the point of prudishness, a gown that would have made a wallflower out of most women. On her it was perfect. There was nothing here to distract from the lovely figure, the pale floating beauty of her face, the brooding softness of the large brown eyes, the sheen of the dark hair. Against the black gown she carried a large pink chiffon handkerchief and a tiny gold mesh evening bag.

She saw me and smiled nervously. I rose and she came quickly across the room to me. She looked directly into my eyes. There was nothing veiled in that look. It expressed, quite candidly, interest.

"I feel terribly wicked." She sat on the sofa and looked up at me with a frank smile. "And I rather like it."

For the first time I sensed something childlike behind the facade of poised beauty. Something lost and reaching out for warmth. Something supremely feminine that cried out for male attributes, too often atrophied in a world where the sexes smoked the same cigarettes, used the same curses, and approached one another in a twilight zone where passivity and aggression merged into indifference. But there was nothing servile in all of this, nothing that suggested the harem woman, nothing of the slave calling for a master. On the contrary, behind that glance I sensed the one supreme quality she undoubtedly possessed: the proud assurance of her sex, with all that that assurance implied— a woman who had waited.

In the moment that we looked into each other's eyes, the smile died on her lips. She turned quickly away.

"I didn't really believe I would meet you here. Even when I had the phone in my hand to call you I didn't believe it. But, as you see, apparently I have a great deal to learn about what my own intentions really are."

"Luckily for me!"

"You must not misunderstand," she said quickly. "This is not— how would you say— an assignation. I want you to realize that."

"'Assignation' sounds so trivial!"

There was a flicker of annoyance in her eyes. "No. Please. It is not necessary to flirt with me. You asked me to meet you here. This afternoon on the promenade deck, I felt ..."

"Yes?"

The blush was faint but apparent. I was surprised. I hadn't seen a woman blush in many years. She turned away and busied herself with inserting a cigarette into an amber holder.

"It's really fantastic what I felt," she said quickly. "I'm acting on sheer impulse. It is probably unwise."

"I hope not, Elisabeth."

She gave me a searching, questioning look, then smiled.

"One's feelings are often dangerously deceptive."

"Suppose you tell me what you feel first. Then I'll interpret."

I leaned over and held a light for her cigarette. We sat very close on the sofa. If she was uncomfortably aware of the proximity, she did not show it. Certainly she did not seem to be as disturbed as I.

"While you were singing at that cocktail party— that wry, sad little song— I watched you. It suddenly came over me that without ever having spoken to you, I knew you. Knew you better than ..." She stopped and then said simply, "You see, I have been fighting alone for a long while. There have been a few kind persons, but most of them... I have had no friends. No one I could trust."

"You trust me?"

After a moment's hesitation she said, "I have never acted on pure instinct before. But I am desperate." She glanced nervously around the deserted room.

"It's all right. We're alone."

She gestured toward the books. "Alone with the past."

"And the future."

"Yes," she said, "the future! I made a vow you know, after the nightmare in Germany. After it was over, I made a vow to let the future take care of itself. All my life I had been surrounded by humorless persons who were forever planning the future— every hour of the day and night— and most of those plans were evil."

"The master plan for the master race!"

"Exactly." She leaned back and shut her eyes as though suddenly tired. "I hadn't considered one thing. The planners weren't finished. They were— they are— working as coldly, as ruthlessly as ever. They haven't given up. I tried to shut my eyes to it. But there it was, the past rising again to become a hideous future."

"There's not much your planners can do now."

She gave a short dry laugh. "I wish that were true. I wish I didn't know as much as I do. I wish I could shut my eyes and dream. But I know them too well."

She turned and put her hand on my arm and spoke with sudden intensity. "That's what I saw in you, Mac McLean. I saw you at that cocktail party with your eyes shut and dreaming away the past. Trying to forget the nightmare. Trying to live in a gay present you couldn't really feel. I saw the fear in you. Suddenly I felt I could talk to you— that maybe you would help."

"Look, Elisabeth," I said gently. "The Nazis are finished. They're not the real danger today. There's nothing much they can do."

"Oh, Mac! That's what they're counting on— that sort of naïveté. I know how they work. I know only too well. I saw your men come into Germany, the army of occupation, young raw troops who had not been in the fighting. They talked glibly of denazification, but it began to work in reverse. It was the Nazis who began to win over the soldiers, the officials, the officers. Oh, it was all soft and well concealed, but ..."

I patted her hand. "It's not your problem, Elisabeth. It's not mine. We have X number of years and X number of possibilities for enjoying them. The bombs are coming from another direction this time. As the song says, enjoy yourself while you can. It's all chop suey anyway."

She snatched her hand away. "It's easy to say. It's what I said for a time. But I found something out. You can't stay out of it, Mac, there's no place to hide. There's no good dreaming. After a while you can't sleep nights, and when you can't sleep, you can't dream."

"It's not like it was," I said patiently. "It's harder than that now, honey. No one believes any more. There's no good fighting a one-woman battle for humanity. Joan of Arc is something for the museums."

"You don't imagine that I see myself in the role of the savior of humanity! Me? It's not that at all. Only it's caught up with me. I must do something or I can't go living with myself."

"I'll take over when you give up," I said.

"Please," she said. "Don't joke."

The feeling of impatience was growing. I didn't want to hear any more. The thought of politics evoked the stench of a rotting barrel of apples. I was wasting time.

"What kind of help do you want?"

"There's something I suspect. Something I must find out. I don't know quite how to go about it. I need help."

"Your husband?" I said.

"Yes."

Once again she looked nervously about. The silence was deep and complete. She took the cigarette from her holder and smashed it out. She began to crumple what was left of it; shredded tobacco fell through her fingers to the onyx ash tray.

"Do you know him?"

I hesitated a moment. Some instinct warned me against telling her that Pasquela had been in my stateroom. I rationalized that instinct into a feeling of protection. The girl was wrought up enough without this new horror.

"I've never met him," I said. "Tell me about him."

She clasped her hands together. "After my success— or notoriety, if you will— at the Folies Bergère, I began to go to parties. About three months ago at a supper party at Versailles I was introduced to Joseph Pasquela. I knew nothing about him except that he was from some small Central American country, had traveled a great deal, and had been living for the past few years in Europe, mostly in Madrid and Paris."

At the mention of Madrid I suddenly remembered Fournier's warning. I would have given a great deal not to hear more from Elisabeth Pasquela. I didn't want to hear. I didn't want to know.

"He became interested in me immediately. And after a bit I realized that his interest was more serious than the others'. Even then I never dreamed he was considering marriage. I was quite cynical about my position. Most of the offers I had received were generous— town houses and cars, and in one case even a chateau in the Loire. But no one had offered a marriage license. To my amazement, he asked me to be his wife. He had charm and tact and he offered security. I would have been a fool to refuse. At least, that's what I thought."

"And ..."

"We were married in a civil ceremony. We went to Biarritz on our honeymoon." She looked away. "Never mind that. Anyway, for a time I was too dazed by my new position to think of anything else. Joseph went occasionally to Madrid on business. I had no idea where his money came from, except some vague references to investments in his own country. It didn't matter. In fact, for a time I even thought the atmosphere of mystery surrounding him was vaguely romantic. And then the letters begin to arrive."

"Letters? From whom?"

"Anonymous letters. At first they were vague, filled with bitter denunciations of Joseph and myself. Accusing me of working for the Nazis. I was disturbed, of course, but thought they were the work of— how do you say— crackpots. But then one day there came to me a letter from his country. It was signed. It was written by a man who claimed he had been a senator in the government that had fallen from power. In cold, carefully chosen words, he described this former government as democratic. He claimed my husband had worked for the overthrow of this duly elected government by helping to arm a military *coup d'état*."

I smiled. "Look, honey. Maybe you don't understand about Central America. Revolutions are a dime a dozen there. No one takes them too seriously."

"No. Wait. This was not a hysterical letter. It mentioned names. When I read them I began to feel ill."

"Names? Who?"

"The writer claimed the revolution had been financed by my husband and his friends but had been carefully planned and executed under the leadership of former Nazis. Many of them were S.S. men who had escaped to Central and South America before the war ended, and some time later."

I felt a coldness in my stomach. Was this the answer? Was this the evil behind Fournier's warning? Were these the people for whom I had been working?

I lashed out against the idea. "People are always writing vicious letters to well-known people. You can't believe …"

"One moment, please." She put a detaining hand on my arm and spoke quickly. "My first impulse was to go to Joseph with the letter and ask him if there was any truth in it. Then I decided to wait. To watch. Sometimes when he had been drinking he spoke of his country with a strange sort of bitterness. Once I found him weeping late at night. He wouldn't give me any reasons for his odd behavior. There were other things— things I can't speak of. I began to pity him, and then I began to despise him. One night he caught me going through his desk."

"Did you find anything incriminating?"

"No. But his reaction was frightening. It was the first time I had ever seen him enraged. He struck me. The next morning he apologized, but there was something there between us that grew into suspicion and animosity. I was torn between two emotions— gratitude for his having given me material security and position such as I had not dreamed possible, and the growing feeling that if there was any truth in that letter, it was my duty to do something about it."

"And how do you think I can help?"

"I need someone to advise me— to help me." She clasped the empty cigarette holder so tightly that her knuckles turned white. "Mac! Don't you see? I know what they are, what they're capable of. If there is any truth in that letter, they must be stopped, wherever they are."

After a moment I said harshly, "Stay out of it."

She recoiled as though I had struck her. "You don't understand! My life— what it was in Germany— I couldn't go on living if I thought ..."

"It's funny how you do go on living anyway. I know. It's too big for you, Elisabeth. It's all very well to go on believing in the best of all possible worlds, but don't advertise it. It's dangerous. The good people are the foolish people today. They're bitched coming and going— the Russians on one side, the greedy on the other, and the good in the middle. There's a phrase we have in my country that expresses it all: Get hep!"

She drew away from me to the far side of the sofa. Her face was pale. "You don't believe that," she said quietly.

"You're goddamned right I do."

She regarded me soberly for a moment, and then, with a smile I was unable to interpret, she relaxed against the sofa and said, "Mac McLean, you've been badly hurt."

When I said nothing, she went on, "Am I right?"

"Once I was a sap," I said wearily.

"Do you want to tell me?"

"No. It's past and done with."

She smiled. "Then don't go taking it out on the rest of us."

She was very near, and I felt that some of the tension had left her. Without thought I took her in my arms. She didn't resist, but neither did she respond. After a moment I let her go.

"It was an idea," I said.

"I don't blame you." Her voice was suddenly tired. "I'm sorry."

"Why? You have no respect for Pasquela."

"It's not even that. Please forget what I've told you."

"Listen to me," I said with sudden urgency. "I'll help you. I don't quite know how, but I'll find a way. But only on one condition."

"What's that?"

"That you give Pasquela no more reason to think you object to, or even suspect, whatever you believe he's up to."

"But Mac ..."

"I'm serious! You're in real danger, Elisabeth. These babies play for keeps. If they thought that you had got hold of something, and planned to spill the beans, you might not live to see the Statue of Liberty."

"Then you do believe me!"

"Never mind that. Do I have your promise?"

She looked puzzled. "You're hiding something, Mac. You know something I don't. What is it?"

"Stop asking questions."

"But what can you do?"

"I don't know, but goddamn it, I'm going to do something!"

The words were said almost without thought. It was true that I wanted to please her, but there was something more than that, an inner sense of relief that came with the words, as though some pent-up guilt had been released.

"Listen," I said. "That guy who came up to us as we were talking on the promenade. Why were you so startled? Why did you suddenly leave?"

She turned away, so I couldn't see her expression, and her voice told me nothing. "He looked at us so strangely. It occurred to me he might be one of Joseph's men."

A small feather of doubt brushed the edge of my mind. For the first time there was a false note. But before I had a chance to pursue the subject, she arose. "I must go."

"At least he's tolerant," I said.

Puzzled, she turned. "What does that mean?"

"How did you manage to leave your stateroom without his knowing?"

"What are you getting at, Mac?"

"For a husband, he seems oddly indifferent to where you go at night."

"We have separate bedrooms. He said good night about ten. He was going to play bridge in the lounge. He said good night chastely. You see, that's the way it's been."

When I didn't reply she said in sudden concern, "Why do you look at me like that?"

"I was just wondering," I said, "whether I may not be the world's prime sucker."

"Don't be enigmatic!" Her voice was sharp now.

Instead of replying I stood and looked into her eyes. Her gaze didn't flinch.

"How well did you know Georges Fournier?"

"Fournier?" She backed away from me. "Mac, what is in your mind? Why do you ask me this?"

"Answer me."

"I knew him only slightly. Joseph and I went to a party he gave in Versailles. He came once to dinner in our suite at the Crillon."

"The Crillon! You and Pasquela lived there?"

"Certainly. Is there anything wrong in ..." She stopped.

"What floor were you on?"

"The second floor."

Fournier's suite was on the third floor of the Crillon.

It had not occurred to me that Pasquela might have killed Fournier himself. Up until now I had thought it the work of a hired hood. I felt a surge of excitement.

"Elisabeth! Fournier was killed sometime between two and eight on Friday morning. Can you remember ..."

"Friday." She spoke carefully now. She looked at me a moment with the expression of a child trying to please its parents. She frowned. "Why, of course. We dined at the Argentine Embassy. We got back to the suite a little after midnight. We had separate bedrooms, of course, and I went to bed almost immediately. I didn't awaken until the maid came in with breakfast and to finish the packing."

When she saw my disappointment she said, "But what in the world did you imagine? Surely Georges Fournier was murdered during a robbery. Joseph said the police were certain that when they tracked down a young man who was known to have left his apartment ..." Her hands dropped to her sides. "Besides, why would Joseph want to kill Fournier? Surely a man of Fournier's reputation— his position, his intellect— could not have been mixed up in this."

The little wisp of suspicion vanished. Looking down into her tense face, I was aware of a strong desire to take her out of this lousy business, to get her away from Pasquela, to protect her.

I placed my hands on her shoulders and said in a low, serious voice, "No more questions tonight. You must do exactly as I say!"

A tiny smile flickered at the corners of her mouth. "My! How forceful!"

"Seriously, don't give Pasquela any cause for further suspicion. If he should ask you any questions about me, act bored."

"You have given me courage," she said simply. "How hopeless things can seem when one is alone! But two people together... Good night, Mac."

She turned and went quickly across the room and through the archway into the lounge. After a moment I started to follow.

Behind me there was a burst of laughter.

I wheeled about to see a woman rising from the depths of a high-backed chair placed not three yards from where Elisabeth and I had sat.

"It's better than any book in this room!"

"Irene!"

She calmly lit a cigarette and said through a cloud of smoke, "Why did you kill Fournier, darling?"

"I didn't kill Fournier. I didn't steal his jade. I don't know who did, but I intend to find out."

"Why don't you go to the authorities? Why don't you tell them the truth?"

"Because, as you know, I was in Fournier's suite that night. There are things you don't understand. Things that won't sound good. Someone is trying to frame me, and until I can prove who really did it I haven't a chance."

She looked at me thoughtfully for a moment. Then she said, "I might be able to save you."

"What are you driving at?"

"Suppose I should testify that you spent that night in my apartment. Suppose I swore that you came to me— as you jolly well should have— after Laura Richards' party at the Ritz."

"What's the price?"

The smile left her face. "Simply that you steer clear of the Naked Lady."

"This is a new kind of blackmail."

"Call it whatever you like."

"What are you really up to, Irene? What's behind all this?"

"I'm too tired to discuss it now. I've had enough shocks for one night."

"Shocks?"

"Yes. I went to a gentleman's stateroom. Very unladylike and all that, but considering I had been there last night … Anyway, I was beaten to the barrier. There was another— shall we say lady— there already. A very drunken lady, and to my sorrow very much at home."

"What are you talking about?"

"Don't act so dumb, darling. She's waiting for you now."

"My stateroom?"

"Where else would I have gone?"

"Irene," I said wearily, "I don't know what the hell you're talking about."

She wasn't convinced. "I can deal with that kind of competition. I'm not giving up, Mac."

"I swear I didn't ask anyone to my stateroom."

"Irrelevant. Listen, darling, I'm your kind of woman, and the sooner you wake up to it, the better. I think you will before we dock in New York. You need a silent woman, you know. Very silent. In the meantime, you'd better get back to your goddamned rabbit warren!"

At the door she turned and said coolly, "You may need help yet. Call me when you're— ah— rested up."

She laughed and left the library.

The statuary stared off into space, lost in a dream of stone. Lucky statues, I thought, and headed for whatever awaited me in my cabin.

Chapter Seven

SEPTEMBER 10, 1:05 A.M.

The scene presented when I opened my stateroom door had all the appearance of a brothel episode in a French film— a scene deleted by the censors for American distribution. A woman was sprawled on my bed, one shoe off, hair askew, lipstick smeared, gown more off than on. On the bedside table were a half-empty bottle of champagne and two glasses. The lady pushed herself up on one elbow, grabbed one of the glasses, raised it to me, and grinned.

"Welcome home! All is forgiven!"

"How did you get in here, Miss Fenwick?"

The shining star of the silver screen thought about it for a moment, then said, "Jet propulsion. Door open, open door, walk in."

"I locked that door when I left."

"Wise baby. Always lock doors after horse has been burned down, I say. Never can tell what drunken slob might walk in. Door open, though. Never break down doors. That's me. Ask anyone."

"What are you doing here?"

"Jus' resting, honey. Don't scold me. Don't be like the rest of those lousy crumbs."

Instinctively I looked toward the spot where I had left the leather case under the bed. It was still there.

The lady sat up in bed, swung her legs over the edge, and noticed her exposed position. "Oops! Didn't come here to do a strip tease. Sorry."

"Don't apologize."

With exaggerated modesty she tugged her dress up over her breasts.

"Can't talk to any of those snooty bums," she said. "But you're my class, honey. That's why I came."

"Bums?"

"Sure, sure. They put us up there and now they're going to knock us off, the lousy sons-of-bitches!"

"Knock us off?"

"That's where we get to the story line, Mac, old boy. That's where we get to the gimmick. Have a drink, honey. It's on me. I ordered it."

My head was beginning to throb. I'd had enough of the distaff side that evening to last me the rest of my life.

"Look, Lili," I said, "I don't know what you're doing here, but it's damned late. You need some shut-eye. I'll take you to your cabin."

"Giving me the brush, eh?"

"Now listen ..."

"No!" she said with explosive finality. "See?"

She got hold of the bottle and managed to pour some champagne into the glasses. With a vacuous smile she thrust one of the glasses in my direction. I managed to get hold of it before most of the wine spilled on the carpet.

"That's better. Sorry about the lady, Mac." She giggled. "My God, you should have seen her face when she walked in. Don't you worry, though. Explain everything to her in the morning."

"I'll order some coffee."

"Don't be a stuffed shirtie!" She straightened up with drunken dignity. "I happen to be cold sober, if that's what you're 'sinuating. Cold sober. I came here to do you a favor, you bum!"

"All right," I said, exasperated. "Take it easy."

I couldn't figure this one out. I'd met Lili at a couple of parties in Paris, but had known her no better than how-do-you-do and good-by.

"Take it easy. That's right." She spoke solemnly, as though I had made a profound philosophical observation. "Might as well take it easy. So what the hell, the little men are going to get us anyway."

"The little men?"

She looked around suspiciously and lowered her voice. "From Mars," she whispered.

"Oh. I see."

"I read it in a book. They're keeping it secret from the public. The big brass. But they know, all right. They found these here little characters in a flying saucer. Two feet high. Jesus, I can't sleep nights since I read it."

"We'll talk about it in the morning."

"No, we'll talk about it now. Not the little characters. But anyway, I say to myself so what if they're giving me the bum's rush, so what if they're pushing me over the falls? It won't matter none. I mean, it won't matter anyway. They'll get it too from the little guys."

"Who's giving you the bum's rush, Lili?"

"We got the news right in the middle of the cocktail party. The studio's not renewing my contract. You should have seen the rats beat it to hell out of there!"

"There are other studios."

"Nope. I'm washed up, honey. Some bitch has been writing a lotta lies about me in a column. I forgot to give her a Christmas present last year.

This is her Christmas present to me. I'm 'morally unfit,' it seems."

"Is it true?"

"Hah! You want a sock in the jaw?" She teetered belligerently on the edge of the bed. "I was supposed to be sleeping around the Riviera with a prince."

"Were you?"

She laughed. "If it was true, the Medical Society or whatever it is should pin a medal on me for achievement."

"Then it wasn't true."

"No. So I deny it. No one believes it. Not a fit representative of American womanhood." She laughed. "Honest to God! It's funny. One minute I got the world kissing my you-know-what and the next minute they're giving me the boot in the same place. You gotta admit— you gotta ..."

She put her hands to her face and began to weep.

My reactions, which had been flitting from suspicion to amusement and back, now veered in the direction of pity. I went to the bed and put my hand on her shoulder.

"You'll lick it yet, Lili. You've got too much guts not to lick it."

"It's a scream," she sobbed. "You know, for a time I even believed my own publicity. American girl as pure as Ivory soap and all that. I thought I had something to live up to for all the kids who were like I was— going to the movies and seeing someone up there on the screen and thinking, I want to be like that! But after my first picture came out, I knew. They weren't selling me, they were selling these!" She indicated her breasts. "I never had anything else. No talent. Nothing but these! And they were selling them to every drooling schoolboy and frustrated businessman in the country, and all the time calling me America's Dream Girl and then give me the ax when they think I really put them to some use!"

"Stop talking like a tramp."

"I learned quick! Ever been in Hollywood?" She didn't wait for my answer. "Oh, it's not that I think I deserve something more. I been lucky, I guess. It's just that people can be such rats!"

"I'm on your side, Lili."

She looked up at me and the childish candor was almost shocking emanating from this Hollywood mask. I wondered what she had looked like before the studio beauty experts had gone to work on her.

"You know why I came to you?"

"No."

"I listened to you sing today. That sad song about having everything and yet having nothing. It said something to me. And I watched you and suddenly I thought— especially later— it's the same with him."

"The same?"

"They're all kissing your feet now, baby, but you got enemies."

"Enemies? What do you mean?"

"There's something... I forget... Honey, the plumbing— quick, I think—"

I got her across the room and into the bathroom. I heard her being violently ill inside. I thought, This is all I need! I went to the phone and ordered coffee, giving thanks to the French Line's all-night service.

She was in there quite a few minutes. When she came out she had rearranged her hair and straightened out her lipstick. She seemed somewhat more sober— as well she might be.

"I'm sorry, Mac," she said.

"Forget it. Sit down. I've ordered some coffee."

"All right, Mac. Anything you say."

Like a dutiful child she sat on the armchair near the porthole, sat very primly as though posing for a Madison Avenue photographer.

"How am I going to face them, Mac?"

"Who?"

"The whole damned ship. By tomorrow everyone will know that I'm finished in pictures."

"Look 'em in the eye and laugh. Being in pictures isn't the whole of life."

"I never wanted to be in pictures. Not really. I liked the loot, of course— who wouldn't?— but I was scared all the time and I kept thinking, It isn't me."

"Where is your home, Lili? I mean, before Hollywood?"

"Highstone, West Virginia. Some dump! My old man was a miner. He was killed in a cave-in when I was only six, so I don't remember much about him. I remember the waiting that night and the expression on my ma's face. I was the youngest of three kids. All girls, so help me. My ma had one hell of a time. We were all working by the time we were thirteen. My oldest sister, Pearl— well, I won't say how she worked. I was sixteen when this guy came into the lunchroom where I slung the hash. I thought he was kidding about a screen test, but— well, look what happened! I managed to buy a little house for Ma. It's up in Connecticut, back of Stamford. All paid for, too! I got Pearl off the streets and my other sister, May, married to a nice guy, a technician with Metro. I got all of that done, thank God, and I even have a little put away."

"Wise girl!"

"I'm not a lush, Mac— not really. It's only tonight, and when I had to face all those rich people in Europe. I never had much grammar. They told me what to say like a parrot." She laughed. "Champagne! Lili Wielenski drinking champagne! What a laugh! Underneath I'm nothing but a dumb hunkie."

"A nice hunkie."

"You mean that?"

"I mean, come to me whenever you want to blow off steam and call them by their right names."

"That sounds awful platonic."

"It is."

"Oh," she said. "You got a girl."

The simplicity of her reasoning was irresistible. "I don't know," I said with a laugh.

"O.K., Mac. O.K. by me. Matter of fact, I always wanted a brother, but I never could find a man who would play it that way."

"I don't wonder!"

"For some reason they always get ideas."

"Don't put any in my head, honey." I lit a cigarette and looked at her thoughtfully, trying to see her the way she had looked as Lili Wielenski in the West Virginia lunch wagon. "Look, kid," I said after a moment, "Why don't you sit at my table in the dining room for the rest of the crossing? We can face them together."

"Oh, Mac, I knew you were an all-right guy. I knew it."

"Now I want to ask you some questions."

She began to twist a ring on her finger. Although her expression didn't change, I sensed a shrinking back, the lowering of a veil.

"Questions?"

"You're sure this door was unlocked when you came here?"

"Oh, yes. In fact, it was partly open. That's why I walked in. I figured you'd just stepped out for a few minutes and would be right back."

"You didn't see anyone else?"

"No one except the steward when I ordered the champagne. And of course your girl friend Lady Harcourt."

"You're positive that's all?"

"Positive."

"No one sent you here?"

She looked at me in wide-eyed surprise. "Sent me here? What the hell do you think I am? A set of books or something?"

There was a knock on the door. "Here's the coffee."

I opened the door. Armando Gonzales stepped briskly across the threshold, gave me a shove back into the room, and shut the door behind him. There was an Army revolver in his hand, and he held it as though he knew how to use it. His eyes, no longer heavy and indolent, were bright with excitement. He gave Lili a startled look.

"Sorry if I interrupted ..."

Lili giggled. "So what B picture is this?"

"Shut up, Lili!" I didn't take my eyes off Gonzales.

Although he spoke calmly enough, I could see that his whole body was at trigger tension.

"But the guy's strictly out of a Monogram quickie!"

"It's no gag, Lili."

"I am glad you realize that," Gonzales said evenly. "Now then, if you please, I have come for certain objects of art. Part of a well-known collection." When Lili made a move as though to rise, he said harshly, "Stay where you are!"

Lily sank back into the chair. The blood began to leave her face. It was obviously just dawning on her that this was not a practical joke. If it had not been for her presence, I might have tried to stall, but I didn't like the look in his eyes.

"I'll be glad to get rid of it," I said, trying to act as detached as Bill Powell in a *Thin Man* scene. I stooped down and dragged the leather case from under the bed.

"It was stupid of you to steal it in the first place, Mr. McLean. I will have better use for it."

"Someone planted it on me," I said. "And I think I know who it was." I threw the case on the bed and faced him. "You can tell your friends for me that all this wasn't necessary. I would have handed it over without a whimper."

He regarded me without expression for a moment. Then he laughed dryly. "Perhaps you are more clever than I imagined. You do not fool me. Open the case." Out of the corner of my eye I saw Lili's hand creeping toward the phone. Looking directly into Gonzales' eyes I said sharply, "No!"

Lili snatched her hand back. Gonzales gave her an amused glance. "Obviously the lady does not realize the danger of calling for assistance. Perhaps you will explain to her after I go."

I shrugged, leaned down, and flipped back the lid of the case. Something cold seemed to touch my spine. I straightened up, waiting for the explosion. It came almost immediately.

"One of the pieces of jade— it is gone!"

"How do I know?" I said with studied indifference. "I never counted them."

"You're lying!"

The empty niche was all too obvious. I turned to face him as he came slowly across the room.

"Mac! Watch out!" Lili whispered.

"All right," I said. "I'm lying. It's just as much of a shock to me as it is to you, Gonzales. All the pieces were in place early this evening. I can swear to that."

He stood just out of arm's reach. His mouth was set in a rigid line. The hand that held the gun was entirely too still.

"I'm telling the truth," I said quietly.

After a moment he said harshly, "Who has been in this stateroom besides the lady?"

"Do you know who I mean when I say Mr. P.?"

"Ah!" The hatred in his eyes was unmistakable.

"I was here with him all the time," I said. "He couldn't have taken it."

"Who else?"

Suddenly I remembered Irene. But she had come to my cabin only after Lili was already ensconced on my bed. She could not very well have taken the jade owl from under Lili's nose. While I hesitated, Gonzales' eyes shifted suddenly to Lili.

"The lady? Was she here alone at any time?"

"No," I said without hesitation. "I brought her here."

He eyed the champagne uncertainly. "Someone brought this. A servant?"

"The steward. We were both here when he came, naturally. He couldn't very well have crawled under the bed before our eyes."

Lili, tense and pale, looking suddenly very sober, sat stiffly in the chair, her hands clutching the arms. "In that case, someone must have come into your room while you were out. But why should they take only one owl?"

I shrugged. "Damned if I know. As a matter of fact, why should anyone take any of them? They're too hot to handle."

"Get into the corner, both of you!"

Lili pushed herself to her feet with an effort and came to me. We backed into the corner. I put my arm tightly about Lili's shoulder. She was trembling, and I knew she was very near to passing out.

With extraordinary dexterity Gonzales began to go through my things. He was almost catlike in the manner in which he managed to do a thorough job while never giving me an opportunity to leap. He emptied drawers and suitcases in a matter of seconds. When it was quite obvious that the owl was not in the room, he frisked both Lili and myself.

Then he snapped shut the leather case, held it tightly in one hand, and backed up to the door. His eyes were dark with anger and frustration.

"You are a meddler, McLean. And you are a fool. The price for being either is high. As you will discover."

"Thanks for the advice," I said.

"And you can tell your friends for me, no matter what happens, in the end they will lose!"

He backed out into the hall and slammed the door. When I got the door open and stepped out into the hall he was already out of sight. The long corridor looked like an empty plush tunnel. I stood there for a moment listening. There was no sound but the throb of the ship's engines. I tried to figure the next move. I was aware of Lili in the cabin behind me, waiting for an explanation. After a moment I re-entered the cabin, shut the door, and went to the phone. I called Pasquela's suite. I heard the phone ringing insistently for a full two minutes.

Behind me Lili said, "Aren't you going to call for help? The purser? The captain? Whoever you call? The man took your jade."

"It wasn't mine, honey." I turned and looked down into her white face.

"Not yours?" she repeated blankly.

"I was taking it to the States for a friend."

"But he— he had a gun. He took it. Aren't you going to report— Mac! What is it all about?"

I watched her, closely fighting off the little germ of suspicion that had lodged in my mind. It was impossible to believe that her anxiety was not genuine, and yet there was something that didn't quite ring true. Someone had lifted that missing jade piece; she had been alone in my room for almost an hour before I had returned. It would have been simple for her to slip the jade owl to a confederate in the hall.

"Look," I said quietly. "It's important. You haven't seen or heard anything. Do you understand, Lili? You've got to trust me."

"Oh," she said after a moment. "I see." She seemed suddenly tired. She avoided my eyes.

"You don't see anything!" I said angrily. "I can't explain all this, but you've got to promise me you won't say a word to anyone."

"O.K.," she said dully. "I promise."

I didn't like the way she turned her back on me and busied herself with lighting a cigarette.

"You don't sound as though you mean it," I said.

She wheeled about. Her eyes were blazing angrily. "Listen," she said. "So you're going to turn out to be a crumb like the others. So what? It's none of my goddamned business! I'll make like I've never heard of you if that's what you want, and boy, it won't be difficult!"

"Now look, Lili ..."

"No!" she shouted. "You look! I came here because I thought you were a decent guy. I came here because there was something about you I thought was good and kind and— well, what do I find? A trigger man and some jade that sounds as though it's awful hot. I suppose you're smuggling stuff into the States or something. It's none of my business, but Jesus, how wrong can a girl be?"

"Lili," I said, "I swear ..." And I stopped.

"Swear what?"

"Nothing."

We stood looking at one another from across the room. The anger died in her eyes. After a moment she said,

"Who the hell am I to pass judgment? I don't know anything. If you say it's all right, I'll go along with you."

I started to answer but stopped at the sound of a knock on the door.

"Yes?" I called.

"The steward, monsieur."

"Good."

He came in carrying the tray with coffee. It was the same man who had been in the cabin with the jade pieces on the table the afternoon before. With hardly a glance at Lili he began to place the cups and coffeepot on the table.

"Are you on twenty-four-hour duty?" I asked sharply.

"I do not comprehend, monsieur," he said politely.

"You understand, all right. Since when is a steward on duty morning, afternoon, and all night too?"

"Oh. Now I am comprehending," he said impassively. "The night steward, he is ill, monsieur. *Mal de mer*. His first trip, monsieur. I take his place."

"You've been in this room earlier this evening?"

"Yes, monsieur," he said with an insolent smile. "I have brought to the lady champagne, no?"

I snatched the check from him and signed. He took it back with the mere suggestion of a shrug. I had the distinct impression that he was laughing at me. "Get out!"

A shadow of anger passed across his eyes. He bowed slightly, gave a quick raised-eyebrow look at Lili, and left the room, closing the door softly behind him.

"Lili," I said as soon as he had left the room, "try to remember what happened when he brought the champagne. Did he fuss around the room, or ..."

"I don't know."

"What do you mean, you don't know? You were here, weren't you?"

"Well, when he came in with the champagne he looked at me so queer, and I knew I was pretty soused. I signed the check quick and told him to put the bottle and glasses on the little table. Then ..."

"Go on, for God's sake!"

"It's just I'm such a goddamned fool for not having told you right away. I don't know why I didn't think of it. After I signed the check I went into the can until he was gone."

"*What?*"

"I know I should have told you. I know I— Mac! Where are you going?"

I turned at the door.

"Drink your coffee. Then get back to your own cabin and lock the door. Forget what you've seen here and try to get a good night's sleep. Maybe I can explain to you over lunch tomorrow."

"All right. Good luck, Mac. And ..."

"And what?"

"And love."

"Oh, that!" I said, and went out into the corridor.

Chapter Eight

SEPTEMBER 10, 2:30 A.M.

Despite the late hour there were still two tables of bridge in play on the far side of the lounge. Pasquela was not at either table. I was turning to leave when I noticed Albert Harcourt among the players. He frowned as I approached and signaled for me to wait until he finished playing a hand. Impatiently I watched him make the wrong finesse to go down two tricks doubled and redoubled. His partner, a hawk-faced elderly lady with much tulle around her scrawny neck, glared at him as though she were about to swoop over the table for the kill.

"Brilliantly played, partner!" she said with shrill sarcasm.

Albert blinked modestly. "Dunno. Think I might have done better, eh?"

"Impossible! My deal, I'm afraid."

"I'm sorry to bother you," I said.

"Not at all. What is it, old boy?"

"Have you seen Joseph Pasquela?"

Albert arched his eyebrows (an almost athletic feat, considering the John L. Lewis growth he had to lift). "What you looking for that Pasquela chap for?"

"Business," I said shortly.

"I bid two spades," Albert's partner announced in icy tones.

"Business? Take my advice, old boy. Stay away from that rotter."

"Pass," said the opponent to Albert's right.

"What do you know about him?"

"What is your bid, partner?" the female vulture shouted.

"Bid? Oh." Albert examined his hand. "I pass."

There was an electric silence. I decided to leave before the storm broke. Even I knew enough about bridge to realize it was a major crime to pass your partner's opening bid of two spades. As I left the lounge I heard the hawklike lady making choking sounds. I made a mental note to question Albert more closely next day about Pasquela. It was possible he might have some interesting information. One thing was certain: I must find Pasquela immediately. My failure to report what had happened in my stateroom would be, in his eyes, highly suspicious. I had no intention of offering myself up for slaughter as Fournier had done. Once I was off this boat I might have time to indulge in the luxury of moral values; in the meantime I intended to keep breathing.

I stamped out my cigarette and went up to the Café Atlantique on the boat deck. There were still a few people sitting around the bar. Beyond, in the main room, four or five couples moved slowly about the glass dance floor to the beat of a tango. Sitting at the far end of the bar was Pasquela, engaged in animated conversation with a woman whose back was to me. As I approached them the woman turned. It was Irene.

For just the fraction of a second before the sardonic mask slid into place I caught a flicker of consternation in her eyes. But she recovered quickly. "Well!" she you "Your appearance here doesn't speak very well for your gallantry, darling."

"No gallantry involved," I said. "The young lady wanted fatherly advice."

"It sounds vaguely like incest. Do you know Mr. Pasquela?"

I caught the warning in Pasquela's eyes. "We've never met," I said.

"How do you do, Mr. McLean? I heard you sing at Miss Fenwick's party. Delightful."

In the strained silence that followed, while Irene turned to her drink, I tried to telegraph a message to Pasquela. There were tight lines of annoyance about his mouth. Irene turned from her drink, darted a quick glance at Pasquela, then, with all the casualness of a cobra about to strike, said to me, "I was about to call it an evening when I ran into Mr. Pasquela in the lounge. We decided to join forces for a nightcap— inasmuch as we were both deserted by our lawful spouses."

I decided to spike her guns. "I can understand how Mr. Pasquela must feel about such a desertion. I have had the pleasure, sir, of a delightful chat with your wife. In the library. About an hour ago. You're to be congratulated. A charming woman!"

For once Irene was stopped. The last thing she had expected was a brash admission from me about my rendezvous with Elisabeth. Not knowing, of course, that Pasquela was fully aware of that meeting, she was astounded at what she must have thought of as my daring.

"Thank you," Pasquela said shortly. He was still simmering at what he obviously considered my indiscretion in approaching him. I wondered whether Elisabeth had given him a report, whether in fact he had seen her since my talk with her in the library.

The tango had come to a conclusion. The musicians were packing their instruments and were leaving the stand. The place had taken on that lethargic atmosphere of night spots just before closing. At a table in the corner of the bar a woman was complaining in nasal drunken tones. The man with her kept up a patient resigned monotone: "Now, Wilma, 'nough's 'nough. Huh, baby? Nough's 'nough. Time to be tucked in, baby."

"I'll tuck *you* in!" the woman announced belligerently. "I wanna another drink."

"Now, Wilma ..."

"It's time for *this* child of fortune to be tucked in," Irene said. She finished her drink and turned to Pasquela with a smile. "Thank you, Joseph. Perhaps you can persuade your lovely wife to join us at luncheon tomorrow."

"I'm sure she will be delighted."

"I just left Albert at the mercy of some bridge friends in the lounge," I said.

"Albert in the lounge!" She seemed startled.

"What's so surprising about that?"

She reached for her bag. "The old darling needs a truant officer. He should have been in bed hours ago. Doctor's orders."

Irene still waited, though, as if she expected one of us to make a move. But Pasquela had finally caught my urgency.

"Perhaps, Mr. McLean, you will join me in a final drink before the bar is closed," he said.

"Good idea."

Irene raised her eyebrows first at Pasquela, then at me. Nothing happened. Slowly she got off the stool. "I guess I can find my way to my stateroom alone. I'm used to it. Good night, darling Mac. Give my best to— ah— Hollywood."

She made an important exit. I could see her standing waiting for an elevator in the foyer. She caught my eye and smiled sardonically. Pasquela ordered two more drinks from the bartender. The doors of the elevator slid open and Irene stepped in. She turned and smiled once more. The doors slid shut.

Pasquela waited until the bartender had set the drinks before us and retreated to the other end of the bar. "You should know better than to approach me publicly."

"It's important."

"As long as you're here, I might as well tell you what I planned to tell you later in your stateroom. I have decided it will be safer to turn the jade over to me."

I felt as though someone had knocked the wind out of me. With the jade on the tip of my tongue, this bland announcement changed my plans.

"When?"

"Bring it to my stateroom tomorrow. After lunch would be a good time. And be sure you do not advertise your arrival. It is important."

I watched him closely. If this was a trick— if he already knew that the man who called himself Gonzales had lifted the jade— he was a damn good actor.

"All right," I said. A lot could happen in twelve hours.

"Now then, what is it you have to tell me that is so important?"

"I saw your wife."

"Well?" His voice was soft but I saw his fingers tighten about his glass.

A group was moving from the main room through the bar toward the elevators. They were jabbering gaily in French. Pasquela said in an undertone, "We cannot talk here. Go out to the boat deck. I will meet you by the last boat on the port side in a few minutes."

As I left the bar a man and woman detached themselves from the party and approached Pasquela, but I could not see who they were. I went through the foyer, past the elevators, and out to the boat deck. The wind was rising and the ship was beginning a slow sickening pitch. The stars were completely obliterated now, and as I walked toward the stern I was aware of liquid mountains, their great black sides glittering in reflected light from the ship's portholes. The gale, whistling through the radio antenna, was like the vengeful scream of a night-born Lorelei. It was lonely out there, exposed to the wildness of the night. I stood in the lee of the last lifeboat and waited for Pasquela.

He appeared suddenly from the darkness and moved in close to me.

"I have only a moment," he said. "What is it you have to say?"

"I didn't get to first base."

"What does that mean?"

"It means that I think you're crazy to suspect her. The only reason she met me in the library was that on the promenade this afternoon I told her I must talk to her about something that involved your safety. When I couldn't come up with a plausible story she walked out on me in the library. She's not remotely interested in whether I live or die."

"Maybe that is just as well."

I didn't like the calm manner in which he spoke. A gust of wind whipped round our legs. Pasquela put his hand over my shoulder to steady himself against the lifeboat. His face, very close to mine, was impassive. I waited.

"Is this all you have to report?"

"I'll try again, of course, but I think you're barking up the wrong tree. She spent most of the time telling me what a wonderful guy you were."

He smiled. "This is very interesting," he said quietly.

There was nothing overtly threatening in his manner, but suddenly I didn't like the position I was in, my back against the lifeboat, Pasquela practically pinning me to the spot.

"You will have to do better," he said. "Much better."

"I tell you I think you're wasting your time."

"Yes. Yes."

He didn't move away. I knew now that despite his masklike composure, his body was as tense as a taut steel wire.

"That's all I have to say."

Still he didn't move away. After a moment he said, "Perhaps now is as good a time as any to explain something to you, Mr. McLean."

"Let's move out of this wind first."

"This will do." He didn't move. I looked over his shoulder down the dark deserted deck. I didn't like it. "Shoot."

"The work I am engaged in," he said quietly, "is more important than the life of any of us involved in it. More important than your life, than my life." He hesitated a moment. "Than the life of my wife."

"But I tell you, you can trust her. You can—"

He interrupted me in a voice like steel. "I will judge that. In the meantime I wish to explain to you fully your own position."

"I would appreciate that," I said, not without irony.

"Yes. Quite." The cold contempt was breaking through his apparent calm. "I have had to sublimate my own personal emotions to a bigger cause. These are things a person like yourself could not understand."

"What are you driving at?"

"Mr. McLean, no doubt you have in your time found it necessary, when more legitimate sources were not available, to visit a house of prostitution."

"What the hell has that got to do with—"

"One moment, please." He went on evenly in the same measured tone of contempt, "The creature involved— the woman— meant nothing to you. She fulfilled her purpose. That is all. She was only one of a thousand and one whores."

His arm touched my shoulder. He was as tense as a wound-up elastic band. "I use this allegorical method, Mr. McLean, so that you may see clearly your own position."

"My position? I don't get it."

"We have found it necessary to employ your particular talents, Mr. McLean, much as a gentleman might find it necessary at certain times to employ the talents of any whore."

I stood there with my back against the lifeboat feeling as though someone had dumped a bucket of slops over my head. I was so stunned that words and movement were completely atrophied.

He smiled. "It would be most unfortunate for you if you overstepped your proper functions, Mr. McLean. We will pay you well and expect certain services. As long as you continue to function on your particular level, we will go on paying you. But if the whore were to imagine, let us say, that she was a lady— and an inquisitive lady at that— well ..." His shrug was eloquent.

I controlled the impulse to strike out at him. "Is that all you have to say?"

"I do not think more words are necessary. Orders are more appropriate. You will bring the jade to my stateroom after lunch tomorrow. After that we will make a decision as to your future."

I spoke then completely without thought, intending to lash as deeply into him as he had lashed into me.

"I suppose it gives you some feeling of self-assurance to play the big boss with me, Pasquela. But you're not fooling me. You're just as much a tool as I am. You'd rather cut off your right arm than lose your wife, but you're acting under orders. Who do you take orders from,

Pasquela?"

I had backed away into the darkness and I couldn't see his face. But his very silence expressed the murderous hatred I knew he must be feeling. In the momentary elation I lost all caution.

"I'm going to take her away from you, Pasquela."

I moved quickly to avert the expected lunge. But nothing happened.

"Do you hear me?"

I moved forward. There was no one there. I strained my eyes into the darkness, and far down the deck I saw Pasquela's shadow glide across the oblong patterns of light thrown by the windows of the Café Atlantique. He was headed for the foyer.

I cursed myself for having given way to emotion. I knew that Pasquela was a deadly enemy. If I expected to save Elisabeth and to get off this ship alive, I had to work fast. Time was running out on me.

I walked to the rail and looked the out the dark sea. Here and there white crests reflected light from the portholes, and across the stars fled sinister, fast moving shadows. Standing here, away from the perfumed interior of the great liner, smelling the salt tang of the sea and hearing the rising scream of the North Atlantic gale, I thought of a brightly colored Easter egg tossing about in the endless blackness of the night. I thought of Irene and Albert and Pasquela and the steward and Gonzales and above all Elisabeth Pasquela, whose safety I had risked for the sake of venting my spleen on her husband. Above, stealthy shadows were obliterating the stars. None of us could survive any more out here in the elements. We had forgotten how to shout defiance into the teeth of the wind; we were left to piddling self-annihilation, chirping with venom inside our scented Easter egg.

There was no use going to the captain or anyone else in authority with my wild tale. I didn't have a shred of evidence. I would be only sticking my neck into a noose. Somehow I must obtain proof of who had murdered Fournier.

But how?

Who was Gonzales and where did he fit into the picture? Was he one of Pasquela's men? I suspected he wasn't. And why were the jade owls so important both to him and to Pasquela? I was certain now that they were significant far beyond their place in the attempt to frame me for Fournier's murder.

In a few hours Pasquela would know the jade was missing. In the meantime I must get hold of Gonzales and attempt to extort the truth from him. I was convinced that once they discovered that the jade was gone, I would be quickly liquidated.

I went to one of the outside stairways and down to the promenade deck. Deck chairs were piled up and seamen were swabbing down the decks. I entered the lounge and went down to the offices on B deck. On the pillar by the purser's desk was the passenger list. I found Gonzales' name and stateroom number. It was on D deck, and from the number I knew it was not far from my own. I turned away from the desk, went to the stairwell, and descended to D deck. I found Gonzales' stateroom, and after a quick look up and down the deserted corridor I knocked. When there was no answer I tried again. Nothing happened. I put my hand on the doorknob and turned it. To my surprise the door swung inward. Warily I stepped inside the darkened stateroom, felt along the wall for the light switch, and snapped it on. I found myself in a small room, one of the least expensive ones. It was deserted. The bed was neatly turned down for the night, but had obviously not been slept in. Toilet articles were lined up with military precision on the bureau. A large, battered suitcase covered with hotel labels from Europe and South America rested on the luggage stand. I opened the closet door and found two suits and a dinner jacket. Below them on the shoe rack were a pair of worn patent-leather shoes and some heavy English brogues. Swiftly I went through the pockets but found nothing more damaging than a half-filled package of stale Egyptian cigarettes, a ticket stub from the Opéra Comique in Paris, and a folded menu from the Lido Café on the Champs Elysées. I went to work on the suitcase and the bureau drawers. The suitcase contained nothing but soiled laundry. In the drawers I found shirts made in Milan and Paris, underwear, socks, pajamas, and handkerchiefs. Nothing to give me a clue to Gonzales' identity or profession. Methodically I lifted the mattress and searched every possible hiding place in the room, but there was no sign of the jade owls. The very fact that there was no symbol of personality— not even a letter— was suspicious. This was the room of a man who wished to remain anonymous.

As I stood there trying to decide whether or not to wait for Gonzales' return, I noticed the slip of white paper on the floor near the door. I picked it up and unfolded a sheet of ship's stationery. On it, in large printed letters, were the words "Swimming pool. Immediately. Urgent." There was no signature.

As I stared at the words, a faint prickle of uneasiness touched my spine. Gonzales had left my cabin no later than one-thirty. It was now almost three in the morning. How long ago had he received this note? And, unless he had secreted them somewhere outside the cabin, he had with him the leather case and the jade owls. Here in the small inside cabin there was no sound except air hissing through the ventilation tube.

The list of public rooms was posted by the cabin door. The swimming pool was two decks below. I knew that the pool must have been closed to the public hours ago. The note and the peculiar place of rendezvous pointed to the fact that the writer was known to Gonzales, but for some reason felt it inadvisable to be seen entering Gonzales' cabin or meeting him anywhere else on the ship where he might be recognized.

How long ago had Gonzales left to keep his strange appointment?

The uneasiness grew more insistent. Perhaps at this very minute they were meeting. The identity of the writer of the note might be a key to the whole enigmatic puzzle of the jade owls. I took a final look about the cabin, switched off the light, and stepped out into the hall. I stopped long enough in my own cabin to pocket the German Luger. I reached the tiny foyer by the entrance to the swimming pool. The elevators were frozen in their shafts for the remainder of the night. I'd passed no one from the time I'd left Gonzales' cabin; the great ship might have been devoid of human life, the passengers sprawled in death in their staterooms, victims of some terrible plague while the ship plowed on untended through the Atlantic gale. But now as I hesitated in the foyer I heard a faint sound from behind me, apparently emanating from the corridor through which I had just passed. I wheeled about. The light bulbs hung dim and evenly spaced down the long passageway, but there was no one in sight. The corridor tilted gently up with the pitch of the ship; it looked like the narrow entry into some mechanical hell. I turned back to the doorway on the opposite side of the foyer. On the other side of it, according to the sign, was the swimming pool and gymnasium. Down here in the bowels of the ship the air seemed metallic and cool.

I pushed open the swinging doors and found myself on a sort of railed-in dais overlooking the main room and the pool. On the dais were several metal tables and foam-rubber chairs for the comfort of those who mixed their Scotch with salt water. The place was bathed in a greenish night light and had the cold stillness of tile and stone and metal. On either side of the pool was a line of dressing rooms. At the far end was the archway leading into the darkened gymnasium. The sides of the pool rose and fell with the motion of the ship while the water remained level. There was something eerie about the steady movement, one side rising from the uprippled depths, the other sinking silently into the smooth green sheet of water. There was no sign of Gonzales or of anyone else. For some reason the place made me think of a mausoleum. It was difficult to believe that only a few hours before, the cavelike chamber had reverberated with laughter and the hiss of bodies cutting through the clear water.

The very silence of the place was unnatural. There was something listening about the stillness; something waiting.

I stood motionless by the rail.

The sound was so slight that at first I thought I had imagined it. A faint, very faint squeaking, as though somewhere a door had been opened stealthily. It seemed to come from beyond the darkened entrance to the gymnasium.

My hand went into my pocket and closed around the Luger. Quickly I stole down the steps to the main room and along the row of dressing-room doors toward the gymnasium. I stayed in close to the walls out of range of that gaping dark portal. If there was anyone in the gymnasium with a gun, I had about as much chance as a duck in a shooting gallery. I reached the far wall and flattened up beside the entrance, listening. I was probably there no longer than a minute, but it seemed an eternity. I heard no further sound. I took a deep breath and ducked around the edge of the door into the gymnasium, throwing myself quickly to the right out of the patch of light, back against the inner wall of the gymnasium. Nothing happened.

The green light from the pool threw only a faint oblong patch on the floor of the gym. Beyond that I could see nothing. I figured the light switch must be near the door, and I felt along the wall behind me. I was in luck. My fingers found the switch and snapped it on. The small gymnasium with its electric horses and iron bars was suffused in a garish light. Grouching in the far corner of the room, her hand pressed to her mouth in terror, was Elisabeth Pasquela.

I was too stunned for words or movement. I stood tense against the wall, looking at her as though she had been projected there by a lantern slide.

Neither of us moved or said a word. Finally her hand dropped from her mouth. She leaned back against the wall, and for a moment I thought she was passing out. Instead she stumbled across the room. I caught her. She slumped down for a moment, then straightened up.

"Thank God," she said.

"Elisabeth ..."

"I heard someone coming. I was out there by the pool. I thought it was a trick. I thought maybe it wasn't you at all. I rushed in here. I ..."

"What are you doing here?"

"I couldn't see who it was. And I thought it was a trap— that you hadn't written the note after all."

"Note? What note?"

She looked up at me and the terror came back to her face. "Mac! You did send the note to my room?"

When I looked blank her arms tightened on my arms.

"Quick!" she whispered. "It's a trap. We must get out of here."

For some reason I couldn't move. It was a dream in which something had registered on my unconscious mind. Something noticed in the first flood of light. Something that held me in this room.

"Mac!" She was tugging at my arm, trying to pull me to the door.

"Wait," I said.

"You fool!" she whispered furiously. "Don't you see? They got us both here under a pretext. You don't know them."

I tried to push her away. I felt like a sleepwalker.

"There's nothing here! Nothing!"

It must have been the oddness of her words that brought back that first impression. Over her shoulder I saw now what had registered on my unconscious mind when I had first switched on the lights.

She was pressed close to me, and even in the urgency of the moment I was aware of her breasts and the whiteness of her arms. She looked up at me and said in a dead voice, "What is it?"

I pushed her aside. "Stay here by the wall."

"Mac! Be careful!"

I walked across the gymnasium to where the trickle of brownish red oozed out beneath one of the dressing-room doors.

I threw open the door. After a moment I shut it and turned back to her.

"What was in there?" she whispered. Her face was chalk white.

"Nothing," I said.

I was back in the dream. I walked toward her. I didn't see it, I thought.

I took her arm and heard my own voice say quite calmly, "There's nothing to be afraid of. Come on."

Chapter Nine

SEPTEMBER 10, 3:30 A.M.

We had fled through endless silent corridors, through the midst of sleeping passengers, out and away from the stone quiet of the gymnasium and the swimming pool, and now in my darkened stateroom I stood intently by the locked door hearing behind me Elisabeth's agitated breathing. For this moment there was an illusion of safety.

"No one saw us," I said after a moment.

"What did you see in that dressing room?" Her voice trembled with anxiety.

"Nothing."

"But your face when you turned!"

"I thought I heard a sound there. I was wrong." I was couldn't bring myself to tell her. Not yet.

"I was certain that note I got was from you," she said. "I was so certain!"

"It was a pretty clumsy bit of business."

"I don't understand. If you didn't write it, who did?"

I couldn't very well tell her what I really thought. Even I found it difficult to believe that Pasquela had planned what looked like a frame-up. Yet I was certain that if I had not gone to Gonzales' cabin and from there to the pool, another few minutes would have found Elisabeth Pasquela in a position that at best could be described as compromising. Probably by this time ship personnel would have been summoned by an anonymous phone call to the swimming pool. If I had not arrived when I had, she might have had a difficult time explaining her presence there with the body of a murdered man.

She was waiting for an explanation.

"Pasquela probably saw us in the library," I said glibly. "He looks like a hot-blooded, jealous sort of character. Maybe he jumped to the conclusion that you and I were carrying on an affair. To make sure, he forged that note to see how you would react. Naturally, if you sallied forth at three in the morning to meet me in a secluded part of the ship ..."

"I don't believe that!" she said. "God knows Joseph is capable of almost anything, but it is not like him to use methods so crude."

I turned from the door. She was only a few feet from me in the darkened room, but I couldn't see her. Quite suddenly I made a decision. I moved away from the door and touched her. I found her hand.

"Why don't you turn on the light?" she asked nervously.

"I've got to say something. It will be easier in the dark." I stood with my back to the room and lit a cigarette. The first glimmer of dawn was a soiled streak of light on the horizon.

"About five hours ago a man came to this room and gave me orders."

"Orders?"

"I was to gain the confidence of a lovely lady. The man who gave the orders suspected this lady of spying on him. For some reason he thought she might be susceptible to my reputed charms. The man was Pasquela. The lady in question is his wife."

She said nothing. I pictured her standing there near the door frozen with shock.

"I'm just the kind of guy they would hire for such a pretty little job!"

"You're trying to frighten me!"

"I've unknowingly been part of their organization for several months. Now I know, and I'm still playing along. I'm rather attached to my neck, you see. I didn't— and don't— know what their game is, but I never was naïve enough to think it had anything to do with the Boy Scouts."

I expected fear or fury, denunciation, even tears. But when she spoke it was with infinite weariness. "Wherever one turns ..." she said. "Wherever one turns ..."

I talked quickly now before I lost my nerve. I stood there by the porthole and in a calm voice told her everything, from my first meeting with Fournier in Cannes to Pasquela's visit to my stateroom. I took an almost masochistic delight in destroying any last remnants that might have survived in her mind of a bright and shining Galahad.

When I had finished, I said, "Now I'll turn on the light."

"No," she said.

I turned. I could not see her in the darkness.

"I'm glad," she finally said. "I'm glad you told me."

"Now you know what kind of a joe I am."

"Yes," she said. "Now I can trust you."

"What!"

The elation in her voice astonished me.

"You see, Mac, I suspected you were involved with Joseph in some manner. I know now, by what you have said, that you are not really one of them. You didn't know what they were really about. None of us are angels— God knows I haven't been one— but I know now that I can trust you."

"You suspected I was mixed up with Pasquela? You suspected that even when you were telling me all that stuff in the library? I don't get it."

To my astonishment, she laughed. "I suppose there's a joke in everything. Even in death!"

"What do you mean?"

"I have a confession to make also, Mac— a confession to be spoken in darkness."

I started toward her, but she must have sensed it or heard the slight movement. "No. Please stay where you are until I finish."

I stayed there, puzzled and apprehensive. I couldn't make any sense out of the way she had received my admission.

After a moment she said, "You see, I too was acting under orders."

Apprehension changed to panic. "Pasquela!" I managed to say. "It was a trick!"

"Certainly not. I am breaking an oath of secrecy in telling you this, Mac, but I see now that you and I will be in this business until the end—whatever it may be. We cannot be dishonest with one another. I must tell you—"

"Tell me what?"

"You remember in the library I told you I had received a letter from a man who had been a senator in the former government of Joseph's country?"

"Yes."

"That was true enough, but I lied about something else. At least, I lied by implication. I did not tell you the man who wrote that letter was in Paris at the time, or that I met him by appointment two days later in a café on the Left Bank. What he told me convinced me that my suspicions about Joseph were more than justified. I agreed to help him obtain proof of Joseph's guilt. After the ship sailed I discovered that this man was aboard. We met secretly on the boat deck. He told me that he suspected you were unwittingly helping Joseph and his crowd. I agreed to attempt to gain your confidence. I took a chance in telling you all that I did in the library, but I was working on sheer instinct. When you didn't confess then that you were involved with Joseph in some manner, I was terribly disappointed. I called this man immediately afterward to report. But I persuaded him not to— how shall I say— go to work on you himself until I had another chance. At least I believe I persuaded him. When I got that note. I thought you had changed your mind, and I decided it was worth the chance of going to the swimming pool. You can understand how relieved and happy I am that you have finally told the truth."

With a sense of foreboding I asked, "What did this man hope you might get from me?"

"It all sounds fantastic, but then, we are living in fantastic times. It seems that he had been in touch with Georges Fournier on the afternoon of his death. Fournier told him he was entrusting you with something of great value. Something that might be instrumental in proving Joseph's collaboration with the criminals who have come into power in his country. Something that would prove who he worked for."

"Something of great value," I repeated dully.

"Yes, Mac. Surely you know what it is?"

"I know what it is, all right. I never suspected that it was Fournier who sent them to my stateroom."

"But now that you know ..."

"They are no longer in my possession."

"Mac!"

"Elisabeth," I said quietly, "this man from whom you took orders—his name was Armando Gonzales, wasn't it?"

"How did you know?"

"You weren't successful in persuading him to lay off me. He came to my stateroom after I had seen you in the library. He had a gun. He took the jade owls."

"That was stupid of him!" But her voice rose with hope. "It doesn't matter, though, Mac. He is a good man. He'll understand when I explain. And now that he has the jade owls, he will know the meaning of Fournier's message. Everything will be all right."

When I didn't answer she said, "Mac! You know something! What is it?"

"I couldn't tell you before, Elisabeth. Now you had better know. There *was* something in that dressing room."

"Something?"

"A man. He had been stabbed to death. It was Armando Gonzales."

I heard the gasp of horror.

"Someone wrote him a note telling him to go to the pool. He probably thought it was from you. He was murdered for the jade owls."

"Armando dead!" she whispered. "Always the good people. Always the good. It's too much to bear."

"It means that Pasquela has got hold of what he wanted. It means now that he has …"

I left the sentence unfinished. Neither of us moved. We stood silently in the darkness.

After a moment she whispered, "We're just the two of us now. Just you and I."

The despair in her voice drew me to her across the room. In the darkness I took her in my arms. For a moment she resisted; then her lips responded passionately. She reacted as dry kindling to a match. I lost my head completely. I had not really expected her to respond. In a sudden frenzy of desire, I loosened her shoulder strap. She pressed close with undisguised passion, a kind of desperate urgency.

But when I got her to the bed she began to fight me off with an intensity that matched her former passion. The sound of her sobbing finally forced me to let her go and move away from her.

"Sorry!" I said harshly.

Gradually the sobbing subsided. Shakily I groped for a cigarette and lit it. In the flare of the match I saw her adjusting her dress.

"You'd better go," I said coldly.

"Mac, forgive me. I hate a woman who leads a man on and then… I'm so dreadfully sorry."

"Forget it. We've got other things to worry about. Like getting off this boat, for instance."

"I must explain. I want you to understand."

"No explanation necessary. My mistake. Won't happen again."

"Darling, you sound like a petulant boy."

The "darling" registered, but I was still boiling.

"The boy singer!" I said.

"There's a reason ..."

"There always is. I suppose this one is being faithful to the Nazi bastard."

"But Mac, I thought you understood. I've never slept with him."

I was astonished enough to forget my anger. "You can't be serious!"

"But I am. It's not the sort of thing one discusses, but with you... There's something not right about him that way. He's not been right with women for a long time. He'd die if anyone knew."

"Well, that disposes of one good reason. The other, I suppose, is that I make you sick to your stomach!"

"The other," she said quietly, "is a selfish reason. You see, Mac, I love you."

I had the sensation that the stateroom was drifting off into the half-light of the dawn trickling in at the porthole, away from danger and intrigue, hate and death. My resentment was completely obliterated by wonder.

"If this is your idea of a joke ..." I began.

"I love you," she repeated calmly. "I knew it for certain a few minutes ago. And I know also what that could do to me. I've never loved a man before, Mac. Maybe because I couldn't love the men I grew up with— maybe because I never thought much about it."

"Elisabeth ..."

"No, please— stay where you are. It's difficult to explain this. It's because I love you that I didn't allow— well, what would have happened. I sensed that if it did happen I might never get over it. I might go on being hurt for the rest of my life. This way it won't hurt quite so much when it comes time to say good-by."

"But why—"

"If I hadn't loved you I might have submitted. But I have too much ahead of me, Mac. Too much to face. I must not be dependent on a man like you."

"A man like me?"

"A man for whom the good-by is never far off."

"What kind of heel do you take me for?"

Ruefully she said, "Oh, darling, I don't blame you. You simply would be bored with one woman for any length of time. You can't help it. I'm afraid that deep down I'm a one-man woman. The kind who would drive you to distraction. Why is it that women like me always find themselves in love with men like you?"

"You make me sound like Alphonse the boulevard gigolo."

"I don't mean to. It's just your nature. Today it's me. Tomorrow it would be Lady Harcourt, or—"

"Irene! Listen to me, Elisabeth. You're wrong about me. When we were talking in the library you said that you thought I had been hurt. Remember? Well, that's true. I'm not like you, Elisabeth. I've been in love before, and I married the girl. She— well, it didn't work out. That's the usual cliché, I believe. I suppose all the details are just clichés too, but it never seems that way when it happens to you. Anyway, we were divorced. I admit I've played around a lot since then. There was no reason not to. But all the time I've really been looking for someone like you. If I thought you'd have me, I'd tuck my slippers by one fire and never look at another woman again. I mean that, Elisabeth."

When she didn't reply I took advantage of what I thought was indecision and approached her again. This time there were no fireworks. I was careful. Very gently I kissed her. Right in the middle of the kiss the damned bedside clock chimed four.

She broke away. "Darling, I must go."

"Yes. I suppose you must. But for God's sake, Elisabeth, give me a chance. Give me a fair trial. Watch me. From now on I don't even look at anyone but you."

I switched on the light.

She was smiling. It was good to see the tension and the fear gone from her eyes for that one moment, at least. It was good to see her smile into my eyes.

"Mac McLean. Dear Mac McLean. If you can convince me of that, I shall come to you of my own free will. You will not have to ask."

But even as I looked at her, the smile vanished. The world around us began to close in once more.

"It's fantastic," she said. "Fantastic that after what happened to poor Armando, we... Is it that we are heartless, darling?"

"There is nothing we could have done to prevent it. Right now we've got to worry about the two survivors. You in particular. Pasquela knows you went to that gym. In a moment of jealousy or worse, I think he planned to frame you. From now on you've got to watch every step."

"The jade," she said. "If we could only get hold of the jade... If Joseph has it in the cabin, I'll find it. It's our one chance to prove—" And then, struck by a sudden thought, she said, "Mac! You're certain it was Joseph who lured poor Armando to the pool? You're certain that it is he who must have the jade now?"

"Who else?"

"Does anyone else know it was in your cabin?"

"Yes," I said uncomfortably.

"Who?"

To my knowledge, three persons knew: the room steward, Irene Harcourt, and Lili Fenwick. After what had just transpired between us, I couldn't very well tell her that two women had been in my cabin earlier in the evening.

"The room steward," I said lamely.

"You're certain he is the only one? Think, Mac. It's important. Even someone you might imagine to be not even remotely connected with Joseph. I know how they work. People you would never dream ..."

There was no point in telling her about Lili and Irene. Aside from the embarrassing explanations involved, I was positive she was barking up the wrong tree. Pasquela was our man. The idea that Lili or Irene could be connected with him was idiotic.

At least it seemed idiotic. But even as I said, "No one else, as far as I know," a little wisp of doubt crossed my mind. Just why had Irene come to my cabin? And for that matter, Lili's sudden interest in me was— in the light of what had happened— a trifle precipitous.

Elisabeth started to say something, changed her mind, and shrugged rather sadly. "Ah, well," she said. "You know best. Now I must return to my husband."

I put my hands on her shoulders. She looked up into my eyes with an expression of trust and courage.

I said, "If you can discover anything about the jade, let me know immediately. In the meantime, for God's sake— and mine— be careful!"

"Don't worry. And you, darling— don't try to be a one-man F.B.I. I know these people. Be very cautious."

She managed a laugh. I saw suddenly the resiliency that had seen her through the terrible years of the war. I saw in that laugh the weapon of the oppressed. She wore that laugh like shining armor.

I tried to match her bravado, fighting the impulse to keep her here within my sight, by my side, to face whatever we had to face together. "We'll lick them yet!"

"Of course we will!" she said, just as though we did not both know that without the jade— whatever it might signify— or some tangible proof, our chances were as bright as a butterfly caught in the intake ventilator of a blast furnace.

Cautiously I unlocked the door and opened it a few inches. There was no one in sight. I gave her the signal. As she brushed past me our hands touched and held for just an instant. Then she went quickly down the long corridor. At the corner, where it branched off toward the foyer and the stairs, she turned and smiled. Then she was gone.

I locked the door once more and began to pace back and forth, trying not to think of what she might have to face. I tried to reassure myself with the thought that, now that Pasquela had the jade, he would have no reason to turn to violence. But I remembered the hatred in his eyes on the boat deck. His pride and his twisted emotions were involved in this, too. If he suspected that Elisabeth had not only been spying on him for some time but was also interested in me, there was no telling what steps he might take. From now on every minute would count.

For one mad moment I considered going to the captain with the whole story. I got over the moment quickly. Without a shred of proof, I could accomplish nothing except to arouse suspicion. What had I been doing in the gymnasium? What was Fournier's jade doing in my stateroom? Why had I not confessed having been in Fournier's suite shortly before his murder? And even if the authorities took enough credence in my tale to question Pasquela, the result of that would be putting my head in a noose. Pasquela would see to it that the frame-up came into play.

Time, I thought. Time and sleep. Maybe tomorrow. Tomorrow! Today. Today, with its ominous gray dawn.

But beneath the sinister theme of my thoughts there was a counterpoint, an incongruous tune that sparkled with life and loveliness. Elisabeth! The way she had smiled into my eyes, the sound of her voice when she said, "I love you," the touch of her hand on my cheek, the explosive moment when her body had pressed close to mine. Elisabeth, went the strange and lovely tune, Elisabeth... It went on singing while I prepared for bed and continued singing as I dozed. But somewhere it got lost again in the foreboding crescendos of the main theme. I began tossing about in a nightmare in which Gonzales struggled in the darkened gymnasium with a shadowy figure. I tried desperately to reach him in time, but I was rooted just outside the gymnasium by the swimming pool. Only the pool was now a cold tomb. I couldn't move. I was dead there on an icy slab. Elisabeth called from outside, but I couldn't answer. I saw the gleam of the knife's blade slashing across Gonzales' face, and the final sickening thrust to the chest. I saw the murderer turn toward the sickly light of the tomb. Where there should have been a face there was a gaping hole, and from the hole came a shrill, pulsating scream.

Chapter Ten

SEPTEMBER 10, NOON

I woke from the nightmare to the sound of screaming. It was a full minute before I realized the sound was actually the shrill ring of the telephone. Sun was pouring through the porthole, and the ship was no longer pitching. We must have left the storm behind. I lay there listening to the telephone's ringing, trying to shake off the labyrinthian darkness of my sleep. I looked at my watch. It was a few minutes after noon. The sound of the phone took on a new and urgent meaning. I pushed myself up on one elbow and grabbed the instrument.

"Hello?"

"Mac! Thank God. When you didn't answer I was afraid—"

"Elisabeth!" She was there, able to speak at the other end of the phone! My panic began to subside.

"I'm at the hairdresser's," she said in a low voice. "The attendant has left me alone under the dryer. But she'll be right back."

"What did he say?"

"Not a word. He— But never mind. Something has happened. The thing we talked about— the art collection— you know. I believe I know where he has hidden it."

"For God's sake, be careful. When can I see you?"

"That's why I called. There's a gala performance tonight in the theatre. The ship concert or some such thing. Afterward there is a masquerade ball in the Café Atlantique. You'll be there, won't you? I'll manage to get away for a few minutes. Say, one-forty-five on the promenade above the boat deck."

"Can't wait that long."

"Please, Mac! Don't try to speak to me before then. I've spent a good half hour at breakfast denouncing you for an outrageous mountebank and gigolo."

"That wouldn't be difficult!"

"Quite brazenly— considering he knew already— I told him that I met you at the swimming pool. I made sound like a malicious adventure on my part. He may not be entirely convinced, but it made some impression."

"Good! Make me out a baby-snatcher or a sex maniac, if it throws him off. But about the jade ...”

"She's coming!” Her voice rose to an affected social tone. “Why, yes, my dear Lady Harcourt. Delightful.”

The phone clicked. I grinned to myself. There had been just a touch of malice when she had used Irene's name.

I got out of bed and fought off the cobwebs. The sunlight and the sound of Elisabeth's voice gave me a momentary illusion of well-being. It was almost impossible to believe that a web was closing about both of us. Things like that didn't happen to people like Elisabeth and me. Things like that didn't happen in the gay and luxurious atmosphere of a de luxe liner. Things like Fournier's murder and Gonzales' mutilated face were part of some nightmare. There must be a way out.

But as I shaved and dressed the feeling of sunlight began to dim. There wasn't much I could do until I met Elisabeth that night. Over twelve hours to go. A lot could happen in twelve hours, a lot of very unpleasant things. I began to feel like a squirrel in a cage, feeling desperately the need for some decisive action. When I left my stateroom I turned, against my better judgment, toward the stern and the rear stairway. I knew that my actions were foolish, even dangerous, but some deep-rooted impulse drew me down to F deck and the pool. I was fairly certain that there would be no signs of the night's tragedy; even normal deaths are kept very quiet in expensive hotels and on luxury liners. I sympathized with the ship's officers, who were probably scratching fruitlessly at the stone wall the murder must present to them. I knew how little Gonzales' cabin would reveal; it was going to be difficult for them even to begin an investigation.

I reached the swimming pool. A couple of stout gentlemen were drifting about in the still green water like two tired walruses. I went on into the gymnasium. A bony gentleman in shorts dangled listlessly from the flying rings. He looked at me mournfully over the top of an untidy beard. In the far corner another walrus type, closely related to the species in the pool, was being pounded by a masseur. Instinctively I looked toward the floor in front of the dressing room where I had found Gonzales' body. There was, of course, no sign of a stain; the floor glistened obscenely beneath fresh wax. It was almost impossible not to believe I had dreamed the sinister scene of the night before.

The masseur, who had looked up casually from his walrus, now said rather sharply, “Yes, monsieur?”

"I'm looking for someone,” I said hurriedly. Too hurriedly. The bag of bones hanging from the rings regarded me balefully. The walrus exposed an eye, barely discernible behind rings of fat. The masseur no longer seemed casual. I didn't like the bright interest in his eyes.

Without another word I turned and hurried out past the pool to the foyer. An elevator was ascending to the next deck. Through the open steel frame of the shaft the operator gazed at me in stony silence. Then his face was gone and the car slid upward out of sight. I wanted suddenly to get away from the pool, as far away as possible. I started up the stairs. Halfway up to D deck I stopped, rigid with listening. Something was wrong. It took me almost a minute to realize that the curious sensation of sudden deafness was due to an unheard-of occurrence. The distant throb of the ship's engines had ceased. In the unexpected stillness came the sudden clatter of the elevator gates opening somewhere above. Puzzled and uneasy— it was inconceivable that the *Dauphiné* would come to a dead stop in mid-Atlantic— I hurried up the stairs to the promenade deck.

Passengers were crowding out of the public rooms chattering excitedly. The chairs down the long deck, usually completely occupied at this hour, were empty. For a moment it seemed that the entire passenger list was at the rail. Something not on the schedule of shipboard entertainment was obviously happening. Unceremoniously I elbowed my way through the crowd to the rail. The storm of the night and early morning had been left far behind. The sea was an undulating carpet of glass, gently glistening beneath a clear sky. Several hundred yards off, floating like a giant duck on the glittering sea, was an enormous plane, one of the Air France flying boats familiar to travelers on the African and Far Eastern routes. A motor launch had been lowered from the *Dauphiné* and was cutting its way toward the plane.

Beside me someone said, "Someone on the ship must be ill. Probably bringing in a crack surgeon."

I could have told him who was feeling ill at the moment, and he wouldn't have had far to look. I had a pretty good idea of the plane's mission. Fervently I prayed its object had nothing to do with me.

The launch made a wide arc, slid up to the plane, and cut its motors. Down the railed ladder hurried a man. From this distance he was a man and that was all, a man in a rather badly fitting overcoat who clutched a brief case in one hand. Two sailors reached up and snatched him into the launch as it drew smartly away. The plane's engines roared to life as the ladder was drawn up and the door slammed shut in its belly. She swung about and began to plow laboriously away from the ship. She gained momentum, sliding down the long slope of one glassy wave, climbing heavily into the next. It seemed impossible that she could lift her bulky weight from the sea. The roar of the engines filled the noon air. Now she began to skip clumsily over the crests of the waves, and then suddenly, just as it seemed she would never make it, she was free, a duck with its legs drawn up, heading slowly east.

The *Dauphiné* had come to life once more even before the launch reached its side; beneath my feet I felt the familiar throb. The launch drew in close to the mother ship. The cables were attached in a matter of seconds. I could no longer see the small boat, but I knew that she was scraping up the ship's side.

The crowd dispersed, back to the bridge games or preparations for the first luncheon service or the latest novel left open on a deck chair. I knew that within an hour all sorts of weird rumors would be spreading like prairie fire, and I was equally certain none of them could match the lurid truth.

I went into the lounge, planning to take the elevator down to the dining salon and some overdue food. As I waited a voice said softly in my ear, "You look lonely, darling. Remember, if you ever need a friend, you can count on me."

"I wonder," I said, turning. "I wonder, Irene."

Irene Harcourt, looking extremely smart in something tweedy, grinned. "Could it be that our hero is being pursued by the Mounties— this time by plane?"

Beneath the mechanical smile and the careful make-up I noticed that she didn't look too good. There was something very unfamiliar to Irene in her eyes. Worry.

"You've been reading too many bad novels," I said.

"Maybe the information I get in them will prove helpful."

She shut up as the elevator door slid open and we stepped in. Several others followed us into the car. All the way down to D deck she hummed the Cole Porter tune "Friendship." As we stepped out into the foyer before the entrance to the dining salon, Albert got up from a sofa where he had been waiting and came up to us. For the first time I detected something chilly in his manner. On the surface he was polite enough, but as we made social conversation for a moment I sensed that in some way he blamed me for Irene's rather washed-out appearance. After a moment he said, "Well, old boy, we shall see you again before the end of the voyage, no doubt."

It was a definite snub, a pointed indication that I was not invited to sit with them at lunch, and coming from the affable Albert, it was equal to another man's direct insult.

Quickly Irene said, "Albert is in a vile temper. He's furious with me. Last night I invited Joseph Pasquela to join us at lunch— never dreaming he would remember. His wife called to say they would be delighted. I'm sorry, Mac, that you have other plans."

"I do wish you had consulted me before issuing indiscriminate invitations, my dear," Albert said. "It's going to be quite an ordeal being polite to that bounder."

"Concentrate on the Naked Lady. It shouldn't be difficult. Her charm is quite obvious. Extremely obvious." Irene dripped acid.

"Seems to me I have spent a great portion of our married life being polite to cads and bounders," Albert said. His gaze rested glassily on me for only a moment.

He turned to make conversation with a horse-faced couple who had just marched out of the elevators, very county, very arrogant, very bored. In an undertone Irene said, "Mac, I meant what I said about helping. Just like the song. If you need an alibi— I'm serious."

Albert turned back and harumphed an impatient order and she left me to enter the dining salon. I took a moment to finish a cigarette. I tried to shake off the growing uneasiness that had been with me since the first sight of the seaplane. It probably had come because of Gonzales' murder. No one could connect me with that. I was certain that neither Elisabeth nor I had been seen near the pool. There was no reason for anyone to connect Gonzales' death with Fournier's murder. The arrival of the plane had nothing to do with the Fournier case. And yet ...

I stubbed out the cigarette, went down the grand staircase to the main floor of the dining salon, and gave the maître d'hôtel my name. So far on the voyage I had not sat at the table officially assigned to me in the dining room. Now I was led across the great room to a table for two in one of the least desirable spots near the pantry doors. A girl was sitting there. She looked up and smiled. Her blonde hair was brushed back into a demure knot above a well-scrubbed face almost devoid of make-up. She looked like someone's daughter down for the holidays. It was a couple of seconds before I recognized Lili Fenwick.

"I took you at your word," she said uncertainly. "I'm on your hands— at least at mealtime— for the rest of the voyage."

I did my best to hide my annoyance. Why the hell had I asked the girl to sit at my table? I had enough to cope with without playing father-confessor to a Hollywood queen on the skids. She looked at me doubtfully and I forced a smile. Instantly her face lit up. But as I watched her it suddenly occurred to me that perhaps I had been engineered into this. Did Lili Fenwick have some other motive than the professed need of a friend during a difficult period in her career?

I sat opposite her, remembering the scene in my cabin on the previous night. Come to think of it, her reaction to Gonzales' melodramatic visit had been extraordinarily casual. Surely it would have been more normal on her part to express suspicion, to ask questions, and when she got unsatisfactory answers to report the incident to the ship's officers.

But when I looked into her eager face it was impossible to believe there was a touch of Machiavelli in the girl. I pushed the ugly thought out of my mind, but I was left with annoyance.

"What role are you made up for?"

"The real me!" she said gaily.

"Almost convincing. Kind of nice. But look, Lili—"

"Yes?" The grin faded. She looked like a kid about to be spanked. I didn't have the heart.

"Nothing. It's just that you look as if the wardrobe mistress and prop man of *Rebecca of Sunny brook Farm* have been at work on you."

The grin returned. She began to rattle on about how certain people had avoided her like the plague on the promenade deck. I didn't bother to listen much at first, and suddenly as I looked over the top of my menu I wasn't listening at all.

Elisabeth was coming down the main staircase with Pasquela at her side. Although my eyes were all for her, I had to admit they made a handsome couple. As she reached the bottom step and paused for a casual glance around the room, her eyes met mine and then shifted expressively to Lili. Uncomfortably I remembered her words about my promiscuity. She crossed the room, cool and remote, preparing for the ordeal of lunch with the sweet-tongued Irene.

"Gee, Mac," Lili said, "I never thought of that angle. I'm sorry."

Startled, I turned back to her. Was she referring to Elisabeth? How could she have known?

Her next words reassured me somewhat. "Your friend Lady Harcourt finds me drunk in your cabin and now here I am with you at lunch. She probably thinks we've been together ever since last night. I am sorry, baby." Her tone expressed no remorse.

The waiter stood over us. "Cocktail, Lili?"

"Not for me. I've had my last drink for a long while. How revolting can a female souse get? I guess I answered that last night."

For a girl with a hangover, she looked surprisingly fresh. I ordered a dry Martini and an omelet for myself.

Lili had ordered her own lunch before my arrival and was half through it now.

When the waiter had gone she lowered her voice and said, "About last night ..."

"Not now."

"O.K. I won't ask questions. I thought maybe you might volunteer an explanation."

"I'm sorry you were involved in that show of firearms. I can't explain it now, but I will before we dock in New York. In the meantime I'm counting on you to keep mum."

"Don't worry. I have your initials carved on my right arm. But I'm nervous for you, honey. You haven't been dumb enough to fall in with Luciano's boys? You're not trying to smuggle in dope or something?"

I laughed. "This isn't the Republic lot, kid."

"I thought maybe you had cocaine hidden in those owls."

I stopped laughing. "What do you mean, hidden in the owls?"

"Well, I got a pretty good look at them when you opened the leather case for Gonzales."

"How did you know his name?"

Her eyes flickered but she said quickly, "That's an easy one. You mentioned it yourself while he was in the room. Anyway, having a Hollywood education, it was the first thing I thought of after I was tucked in bed. Those owls were mounted on polished wood bases. The wood could have been hollow."

At the expression on my face she said, "What's wrong, baby? You look as though you'd struck oil or something."

"I just had an idea. Or rather, you did. Maybe it was dumb of me not to have thought of it before."

I signaled for her to shut up as the waiter approached with my cocktail. During the silence I had a moment to watch Lili carefully. Her face showed no more than a childish sort of curiosity. She acted as though we were discussing a scenario in which everything was bound to turn out right in the end.

My nerves were beginning to do tricks again. I took a swig of the cocktail but it didn't help much. Here in this beautiful room in the midst of laughter, once again I had the sensation that time was running out on me. The Easter egg. The bright-colored Easter egg. Elisabeth and I were right in the heart of the gawdy egg now, but I sensed the closing in, the death that hid just outside the thin shell. Somewhere in this room were the merchants of death; the buyers and the bought.

"Drink up," Lili said. "You look as though you needed it."

Obediently I lifted my glass.

"You better get a few days of sun before you open at the Plaza," Lili said. "You could use it. I have a hunch, though, your whole system will operate better back where it belongs."

"Back where it belongs?"

"The States. You're like me that way, Mac. We're out of our depth in Europe. Our blood circulates better back on Main Street. You're the kind of apple a smart Old World character could squeeze dry in no time. Despite your smart talk. We play better on our own playground. Outside, the rules are different; we play wrong and lose our shirts."

"Could be." Was there something concrete behind her abstract observation? Nonsense, I thought. Yet the girl was, to say the least, surprising. Just when you thought you had her typed, she started a new role.

A middle-aged guy in Bond Street's best, silver at the temples, carrying himself as though he had just bought out General Motors, got up from a table not far away and descended on us with the sincerest of all sincere smiles.

"Watch this," Lili said under her breath.

"Lili, baby! No time long see. What's new, honey?"

"Mac," Lili said with a dead pan, "this is Bert Stetson, the great director."

"In our town, everything is 'great,'" Stetson said. Especially himself, his tone implied.

"I saw your last picture," I said. "Very significant."

"It was a gamble," he said modestly. "But I tell the boys the public will go for adult entertainment these days."

"When are you going to start giving it to them?" I asked blandly.

He gave me a murderous look, then decided to treat it as a joke. "Got a comic here, huh, Lili? Sorry I couldn't get to your cocktail party. How about joining us at the masquerade tonight?"

"You haven't heard the news, have you, Bert?"

"News? Look, baby, this is the first I've been out of my cabin. Seasick from the time I climbed the gangplank. Anything I should know?"

"For your own good, yes," Lili said with a wink at me. "A guy like you shouldn't waste his time. You see, the studio isn't taking up my option."

The sincere smile stayed in place, but the rest of his face looked suddenly green. He had been standing bent over Lili with his hand on the back of her chair. Now he straightened up like a ramrod.

"Sorry to hear it," he said politely. He darted a nervous look around the room.

Lili didn't help. She didn't say a word. Stetson fidgeted in his own silence for a moment. He shifted from one foot to the other, looking off into the distance as though he expected the U.S. Marines to come to his rescue.

"Too damned bad," he said mechanically. Apparently he realized the Marines were going to fail him this time. "I'm sitting with L.B. Got to get back. Don't understand why they should drop a talent like you, Lili."

"I was sleeping around too much," she said sweetly.

"Oh, come now!" There was a thin streak of viciousness in his voice. "If you mean that item in Amanda's column— after all, the Industry comes first, you know. She has the interests of the studios at heart. A great girl."

"It was awfully sweet of you to ask me to the masquerade," Lili said distinctly. "It sounds like fun."

Stetson stopped smiling. "Oh, that," he said. "I'll call you on that, Lili."

"No," she said mockingly. "I'll call you."

Stetson muttered something that must have been a farewell, because he left us abruptly. Lili watched him walking away as though from the scene of a disaster. The smile never left her face.

"Good girl!" I said.

"I couldn't have done that yesterday. I would have boiled over. It's being here with you that made me see it the way it really is." She put down her fork and leaned forward. "You know, Mac, I woke up this morning, and even with the hangover I felt right away as though I had got out from under a terrific weight."

"Anyone I know?"

"No, I'm serious!" Disregarding my restlessness, she continued, "I don't give a damn now what they think in Hollywood. I've made a little money. I have some loot cashed away in a good bank. My name is still fresh enough to rate TV guest shots and club dates. I might even get a musical show on Broadway. But if it don't, though, I'm not going to worry about it any more. Jesus, considering the talent I had to begin with, I was pretty lucky. Let the other dames get old trying to stay up on top of the heap. I think I'd rather be one of those things the radio people call homemakers."

While she had been talking I glanced toward the Harcourts' table. Irene was rattling away in her usual machine-gun fashion. Elisabeth looked like a Marie Laurencin borrowed for the occasion. Albert, though he probably thought his manners impeccable, had the appearance of a British colonel in the Malay jungle forced to break bread with the local chieftain.

"Did you hear what I said, Mac?"

I turned back politely. "Sure, Lili."

"I mean about homemaking."

"So what?"

"Look, honey, the kind of homemaker I mean is making with the home for some guy."

"Well?"

"That's my only trouble. Persuading the right guy to play house with me."

"You won't have any trouble persuading him."

She grinned. "That sounds real encouraging."

I didn't like the way the conversation was going. "Now, look here, Lili ..."

"Oh, eat your your omelet and shut up!"

"We agreed ..."

"Who said anything? I didn't say who the right guy was, did I?"

"No, but ..."

"For instance, it might be that Valentino type at your girl friend's table."

"Girl friend?"

"Lady Harcourt."

"You mean Pasquela?"

"Whatever his name is. He was giving me quite a play this morning on the promenade. The guy tucks an awfully mean steamer rug. And I don't usually tingle before noon."

"Pasquela made a pass at you?" I exclaimed incredulously.

"Don't be crude. A Continental type like that doesn't make passes. But whatever he was doing was pretty damned charming."

Before I could speculate on this unexpected development, I saw a page making his way across the crowded room. I watched him, thinking, Not here, not this way, kid. But he kept coming. Apprehension turned to certainty as he stopped at our table.

"Monsieur McLean?"

"Yes."

He handed me an envelope. My throat began to feel dry. I smiled idiotically and said, "Thanks," as though he had handed me the crown jewels. He turned on his heel and marched off. So there won't be an answer to this one, I thought. As casually as possible I tore open the envelope. The note read: "Will you please come immediately to the purser's office on Deck B." It was signed by the captain.

I looked up from the note. Pasquela was looking directly at me. His eyebrows were raised ironically. I began to feel sick.

"What's wrong?" Lili asked anxiously.

Carefully I folded the note and stuffed it into my pocket. I gulped down the rest of my cocktail. "Business," I said. "I'll see you in your stateroom later. I hope."

"Yes," she said. "Good." And then as I started to rise, "Oh, I forgot. I'm going to the movies with—" She stopped.

"With whom?"

"The Valentino type."

"Pasquela! You certainly work fast."

"I'll try to ditch him, Mac. But look." She fished into her bag and brought forth a key. "If I'm not back by the time you get to my suite, go in and wait."

Mechanically I took the key.

"Mac!" she said in sudden concern. "Something's wrong."

"Smile," I said in a low voice. "People are watching."

She obeyed. I looked into her eyes, trying to find the answer to a couple of questions that were bothering me. She met my gaze for a moment, then looked down at her plate. She gave a nervous laugh. "A hell of a homemaker I am!"

"I wonder."

And I kept on wondering as I started across the room toward the stairs.

There was no good kidding myself. The note was not a request; it was a command. Fournier or Gonzales, I thought, and with a silent prayer crossed my fingers. At the top of the stairs I gave a look back, the look of a gallows-bound criminal. My world, the world handed to me by my particular Mephistopheles, was a glittering carpet strewn with jewels. I turned away. My credit has run out, I thought. The sound of the crowded dining room was throttled by the closing door. The foyer was empty. The elevator, like a *deus ex machina*, slid silently down through the open grillework to fetch me.

Chapter Eleven

SEPTEMBER 10, 2:30 P.M.

A man in uniform turned the handle, swung the door inward, and said, "You are expected, Mr. McLean."

I entered the office. The door closed behind me. The captain sat behind a large desk. Standing to his right was a stockily built man with an olive complexion, stiff black hair plastered close to his head with some sort of oil or vaseline, dark eyes that were reassuringly mild at the moment, and one of those indefinite mouths that seem never to be quite in position. He looked like a shopkeeper in a provincial French town, and his rather shiny dark suit heightened that impression. But almost immediately I noticed the hands. Small hands, incongruously small for a man of his build, very white hands, delicately formed, tiny hands, the hands of a child. My first mistake was not to look away from those hands quickly enough. They disappeared behind his back, and when I looked up there was no mildness any more in his eyes.

There was a smothered cough off to my right. I turned to find a blank-faced woman sitting in the far corner of the room, pad and pencil poised in a businesslike manner.

The captain, who was renowned for his charm and tact, rose from behind the desk with an apologetic smile. Almost immediately I sensed that he resented the presence of the man beside the desk and the necessity for the interview. Murder was out of place on his beautiful ship.

"Forgive me, Monsieur McLean, for bringing you away from the dining salon. It appears to be a matter of some importance."

"I don't understand."

"Perhaps I understand even less than you. Allow me to introduce Monsieur Louis Devois of the Deuxième Bureau."

The Deuxième Bureau! This might be even more serious than I had feared, if the French F.B.I. was taking a hand in it.

"I was most reluctant... An artist of your fine reputation... But even on my own ship there are limits to my authority. I am certain there has been a mistake that will be corrected."

Devois cleared his throat impatiently. The captain bowed stiffly in his direction.

"You will pardon me now. I have duties."

"Yes. Thank you."

Devois snapped out the words. His manner was not reassuring. Here, apparently, was one Frenchman who dispensed with polish and frills.

The polite smile left the captain's face. He hesitated a moment, shrugged, and came across the room toward the door.

"I know you to be an intimate friend of Lord and Lady Harcourt. They will be my guests at dinner on the last night out. I should be honored if you also will be my guest."

"*Enchanté*," I said. I was wondering whether I would be anyone's guest after this interview, except possibly an unwilling guest of the French government.

The door closed behind the captain.

"Sit down."

I looked from Devois to the chair, placed at an angle in front of the desk, and then back to Devois. I didn't move.

"Did you hear me, Monsieur?"

"Your English is plain enough, Monsieur Devois. And I might add that so is your manner. Would you be kind enough to explain what this is all about?"

"No need to be alarmed, McLean," he said dryly. "That is, of course, if you will answer a few simple questions to my satisfaction. I would prefer that you sit."

I controlled my annoyance and obeyed. I tried to act detached and casual, crossing my legs and lighting a cigarette. I managed to keep my hand quite steady.

"Police always make me nervous," I said lightly.

"You have experience of them, no doubt."

"Oh, many times! In my wild youth I used to get tickets— summonses, you know— for speeding on the average of one a month."

"You are fortunate if that is your only contact with the law."

"I will have to disappoint you, I'm afraid, by admitting to my good fortune. Until now."

"Ah. Yes."

His small hands made me restless. They didn't move or fidget, but hung at his side in a curiously lifeless manner. Out of the corner of my eye I saw the stony-faced woman in the corner taking shorthand notes.

"I'm flattered," I said. "No one has ever thought anything I had to say important enough to record."

"The time has come," Devois said with a sharp irony.

Trying to match him, I said, "It is extremely pleasant to converse with you, monsieur, but not very illuminating. I still do not understand why ..."

"I will ask you some questions about the murder of Georges Fournier."

I didn't wait even a moment to react. I'd been expecting it. "I'll do anything I can to assist you, Monsieur Devois. I can't tell you how shocked I was when I read of it in the ship's paper."

His silence didn't help. I felt the necessity to fill the void. "Georges Fournier was very kind to me. If it had not been for him I would have had no success in Paris."

"So I understand."

He sat opposite me at the desk. He looked out somewhere over my head. "You understand that you are not compelled to answer my questions. As an American citizen you have the right to consult—"

"I'm only too delighted to tell you anything you might find of value. I was under the impression, however, that murder cases were handled by the civil authorities. Since when has such a crime become the concern of the Deuxième Bureau?"

"On that question," Devois said dryly, "I do not feel compelled to take you into my confidence."

"Sorry."

"Now then, since you see fit to be so co-operative, I shall take advantage of your affability by asking first some facts about yourself."

"My unimportant life has been pretty well recorded by the press."

"I have had some experience with members of your profession," he said. For the first time there was the suggestion of a bleak smile in his eyes. "My experience has taught me the sometimes astounding difference between public and private life in the theatre."

By his manner I didn't have to guess much about what experience he referred to, or with what sex.

"Allow me to congratulate you!"

Slightly taken aback for a moment, he recovered with a snap. "You will please tell me something of yourself."

"I'm an American citizen. Age, thirty-two. Born in—"

"The town of Madison. The province of Connecticut. This we know."

"Provincial, maybe, but not province! The *state* of Connecticut."

"No matter. Your father was keeper of a shop wherein was sold, as I understand, the hard goods?"

"Hardware store. Yes. If you know all this, why do you ask?"

"My information is meager. Please continue."

"I am the youngest of four children. My mother was a music teacher. My parents were killed in a motor accident when I was fourteen. I moved then to New Haven and lived for a time with an older brother. It didn't work out so well. His wife— well, anyway, I was on my own by the time I was seventeen."

"You found difficulty in your environment. You do not find stability. You have a feeling of being outside— unwanted?"

"What is this? An analysis?"

"Forgive me. I am always interested in background of this nature. Instability can account in later life for many—"

"Crimes?"

"I would not go so far."

"Well, don't look it, then."

"*Comment?*"

"Skip it. To continue with this fascinating case history, after I graduated from high school I worked at various jobs. Most of them were office or factory jobs and they bored me. You want all this?"

"If you please."

I didn't like his new politeness. It was more sinister than his old manner. I surmised that he had most of the facts I was giving him, but it was best, considering what might come, to give the impression of being completely, even naïvely, candid.

"It was the tail end of the depression in the States. There was a federal theatre— a government-sponsored plan to give work to actors and theatre technicians out of jobs. It looked like a good racket to me. I became an actor. I got to like it. I'd played the piano since I was a kid, and I had a natural ear for music and a voice that could at least keep on pitch. I found myself in a Federal Theatre revue in Chicago. A small part, but I thought I was on my way. Then the Federal Theatre folded. Congress wiped it off the slate and me along with it. I'd got the theatre in my blood by this time, and I tried to hit Broadway and the big time. Somehow the big street couldn't see me."

Devois acted as though he understood what I was talking about. Maybe he got half of it. Maybe more. I couldn't be sure.

"An artist sometimes finds difficulty in falling into the pattern of the *bourgeoisie*." He said it with a perfect dead pan, but somehow gave the impression of having actually said, "A bum can't fit into decent society."

I let it go and went on, "I finally landed a job as a pianist in a— a *boite* in Greenwich Village. It didn't pay much, but I kept hoping. Then along came Hitler. I enlisted in the Air Force. Some dimwit thought I should be an officer. I tried to dissuade them, but ended up in Pilot Training. I came out a second lieutenant. I was shipped overseas—"

"One minute."

"Yes?"

"You have forgotten one unimportant detail. You were married."

"Brother, when you say 'unimportant' you hit it right on the head. I knew the girl two weeks. She was blonde and beautiful and had the most innocent eyes in the world. She found certain things about me attractive. 'Certain things' being my allotment."

"Your war record we have found to be excellent." He said it as though whoever had made up my record must have been either a forger or a maniac. At any rate, he was not interested. "On your discharge you did not return to your wife. She divorced you."

"I found out a few unvarnished truths when I was home on unexpected leave. Part of said truths being a guy she was keeping on my allotment money."

"Perhaps." He shrugged distastefully. To the Frenchman my statement was obviously ungallant. "At any rate, she obtained the divorce."

"It was the simple way out."

"In the courts this lady stated that you were emotionally unstable, given to uncontrollable fits of temper, and refused to work to support her."

"You have to say something to get a divorce. It might not have been half so pleasant if I had done the saying."

"Yes. I see." It was quite plain that he did not care to see.

I was beginning to boil inside. I fought against it, knowing it must be part of Devois's technique to make me fly off the handle. It would fit beautifully into his case-history attack; "unstable," "given to unpredictable and fierce rages."

I contented myself with saying, "For a man who commandeers seaplanes to intercept liners in mid-Atlantic, your interest in the petty details of my life—"

"If I do not behave in the tradition of your cinema investigators you must forgive me. I would now like you to describe your reactions after your discharge from the Air Force. And your divorce."

"Reactions to what?"

"Let us say the world about you."

"They weren't much different from those of thousands of other guys. Most of us felt one thing was important above all else— no more war. We thought everyone else would be feeling the same way. Instead we found everyone having a good time, fattened up on war profits, yelling about taxes and 'foreigners.' Sometimes when I looked around I felt that I was in another country. I didn't feel easy any more. I wanted to get away from people who had everything and patted themselves on the back for it. So I went to Paris."

"Ah?"

For a moment I caught a gleam of sympathy in his eyes. But as he watched me I saw sympathy change to speculation and finally to skepticism. He had thought, incorrectly, that I was making a bid for understanding. Actually what I had told him was the truth.

"What's all this got to do with poor Fournier?"

"I am interested in your psychological state. You were bitter and disillusioned. In Paris you drank too much, talked too much, and did nothing."

I straightened up. "Just what does that mean?"

"You had lost all sense of what is normally considered social responsibility. You cared only about one thing. Yourself. You decided to concentrate on that fascinating subject. You were in a state of mind where other persons became only steps in your projected ladder."

"Now, wait a second!"

"You decided it was boring to be poor, but more boring to work for a living. You decided to wangle your way into the confidence of an honorable man who might, through his influence, help you to—"

"Just a minute, Dr. Freud! You're jumping the gun. Your facts are all wrong. If it's Fournier you're talking about, I didn't wangle any introduction or beg for assistance. It was an accident. I was playing the piano in a cheap joint back of Cannes. One of those all-night bars where sailors and their girls hang out after midnight. Fournier came in early one morning, about two o'clock. He was with a party in evening clothes. They had all been to some kind of party over in Monte. They were slumming. For some reason he took a fancy to the way I sang a couple of songs. He invited me to play at a party of his the following week. A lot of important people were there. They liked me. I was booked into the Casino at Cannes and I was a hit. I didn't wangle it. I didn't even ask for it. I am grateful as hell for what Fournier did, but—"

He snapped me off. "Yes!"

"Now, look here!" I said angrily. "You get me away from a perfectly good lunch with a charming lady. You tell me you want to ask some questions that might help you in your investigation of the Fournier case. I tell you I'm perfectly willing to co-operate, but I don't have to sit here and take your insults!"

He looked at me with cool insolence. "Calm down, Mr. McLean."

I gripped the arm of the chair to keep from taking a swing at Devois's smug face. I said one, two, three to myself, and then four, five, six.

"Would you be so good as to tell me the amount you have earned since your debut at the Casino in Cannes?"

Easy, I thought. Watch it.

"I'm no good at figures. I did pretty well, if that's what you mean."

"Come, monsieur! Surely you were not so naïve as not to know your own salary. Let me refresh your memory. You were paid forty-five thousand francs a week for your engagement at the Casino. About two hundred dollars in your money, I believe."

"Well?"

"Yet you moved into an expensive suite at the Miramar."

"I signed that contract with the Casino as a nobody. After I made a hit I knew my price would be triple that amount. I spent all my salary on that suite and entertaining for business reasons. In my profession—"

"Let us accept that much. You opened an engagement at Cabaret de Paris at a salary of one hundred and thirty thousand francs a week— about six hundred dollars. Is this correct?"

I began to feel cold inside. "That's right."

"Out of this money you paid the French government tax, a publicity manager, an agent, and other fees. It still left you with a respectable income. But persons with only a respectable income cannot afford a grand suite at the Georges Cinq Hotel, or enormous sums on parties, or a custom-built Jaguar automobile, or clothes from the most expensive tailor in London, or plane trips to England for week-end parties, or—"

"I've told you, an actor has to maintain a certain front. It attracts a better salary in the next engagement. I'm still in debt for a lot of the things you speak of."

"I beg to differ with you, monsieur," he said quietly. "We have investigated. All the items I speak of were paid for in cash. They amount to over twice the money you earned legitimately in Paris."

"What the hell are you implying?"

"I am implying nothing. I am stating facts, which in turn lead us to other facts. You have behaved with your customary impulsiveness. Your behavior must be considered, at best, unstable."

"What facts?"

I saw a flicker of irresolution behind the hardness of his eyes. He hadn't meant to use the word "facts." He proceeded to remedy the mistake.

"I am suggesting, monsieur, the motive for your presence in Georges Fournier's suite on the morning of his death."

"You're crazy! I wasn't anywhere near the Crillon!"

I said it almost without thought. Some instinct told me the truth was the least convincing of all arguments with this man, who obviously considered me his duck. My only chance was to brazen it out.

"There is no good denying it," he said with cold precision. "The night elevator boy recognized you from a picture that appeared in the magazine *Le Théâtre*."

"He's lying!"

"That may be up to the courts to decide."

"For God's sake, what motive would I—"

"Ah. We get back to what I was describing. We are quite certain, monsieur, that the man who murdered Fournier had been extorting blackmail from him for some time."

"What!"

I jumped to my feet. Devois didn't move. He looked up at me and went on calmly, "Fournier threatened to go to the police. He was murdered. The murderer, deprived through his own act of further large sums of money, saw fit to take with him a collection of jade valued at over twenty million francs."

I stood over him feeling as though the life were draining out of me to the gray carpet.

"It was impulsive," he said quietly. His small hands came up and outward in an expressive gesture. "It was impulsive, yes. And very stupid of you, Mr. McLean."

Chapter Twelve

SEPTEMBER 10, 3:00 P.M.

I was aware that behind me the girl had stopped scribbling on her pad and was sitting there in a frozen state of alarm. If Devois was disturbed by my threatening position above him, he gave no indication. He was the coolest bastard I'd ever seen.

"You are accusing me of the murder of Georges Fournier."

The little hands opened and shut expressively. He said nothing.

"You realize, of course, that my government takes a serious attitude about false accusations against its citizens. Accusations based on libelous speculation and the testimony of a doubtful witness."

The slight shift of the eyes encouraged me.

"Your entire case against me is based on the testimony of some dim-witted elevator boy at the Crillon. Instead of your phony psychological interpretation of my character, you might have spent a little more research into the symptoms of a pathological liar."

"You deny being at the Crillon?"

"Categorically!"

"In that case, you have proof of where you were from the time you left the party of a Mrs. Richards at the Ritz at one A.M. until you returned to your suite at the Georges Cinq at five in the morning."

I fought off the sinking sensation. So they had checked with the Georges Cinq. In a way I was grateful to him for the admission. It saved me from the pitfall of an obvious lie.

"This is a waste of time!" I tried to look outraged and important. "I intend to contact the American ambassador at Paris."

He shrugged. "This we cannot prevent. In the meantime, however, you will be confined to your cabin. If the weather holds, a plane will take us off in the morning. You will be returned to Paris for further questioning."

The bluff hadn't worked. I stood there by the desk wondering whether to make a clean breast of the whole story. But I dismissed the idea almost immediately. I hadn't an iota of proof against Pasquela. At best I would be detained in my cabin while they investigated my charges. In the meantime Elisabeth's life would be in jeopardy. Somehow I must be free to work it out in my own manner. I was certain now that the key to the whole filthy mess was in the jade owls. Elisabeth had some news about the jade. Somehow I must see her.

And then I remembered the Cole Porter song.

"Am I to consider myself under arrest?"

"I suggest that you do. Unless, of course, you could give me a satisfactory explanation of your movements from the time you left the Ritz until you arrived at the Georges Cinq. An explanation with proof."

"Very well."

He looked derisive. "Do not take too much time to dream up a fantasy, monsieur. Surely, if you had been able to account for your movements, you would have spoken up immediately."

I straightened up. I lit a cigarette and blew the smoke out in a long funnel over his head.

"My movements, as you so aptly put it, were movements not usually described by a gentleman. Or at least not in connection with specific names."

He laughed. "The rather shopworn alibi of a mysterious lady, monsieur? Come, you cannot be such a fool. Some charming and nameless lady of the Cabaret de Paris or the wife of a senator?"

"There is nothing vague about this lady. She is on the ship."

"A confederate, no doubt?"

"I doubt that even you would dare accuse the lady in question of complicity in a crime. Her position is unassailable."

One little hand reached for a pencil. My assurance was beginning to have its effect. Devois eyed me warily now.

"And, of course, as a gentleman you cannot name her? I will be forced to take your word? Come, now!"

"Because I am not a gentleman, I have a certain advantage. I'm just a guy on a spot."

His hand began to drum on the desk.

"Stop this performance! If there is, in reality, any such person— a lady who could vouch for your whereabouts during the critical hours of Friday morning, a lady whose word would carry weight— I advise you for your own good to speak out."

"The name is Lady Harcourt."

He looked at me without expression. Then he reached for the phone.

"She's in the dining salon." I said.

He never took his eyes off me, thinking perhaps that at the last minute I would refuse to go through with what he undoubtedly felt was sheer bluff. He got the dining salon on the phone and gave a sharp order. He hung on, still looking at me as though expecting me in this final moment to break down. Then he put down the phone.

"The lady will deny your story and you will of course claim that she is protecting herself."

"The lady is not a liar. When she corroborates my story, what then?"

He was getting rattled. "In that case, monsieur, you would be free."

The phone rang. Devois jerked it off the cradle. "*Oui... Oui... Merci.*" He hung up and turned away. "The lady has just left her table. She is on her way here."

My blood began to circulate in a more normal manner. I knew now that despite the embarrassment such an admission would involve, Irene would lie for me. This would give her the hold she had been wanting. It was the sort of moral intrigue she would find amusing. She felt herself too safe, too far above the crowd, to be aware of the criminal aspects of such a lie. It was she who had suggested just such an alibi should the need arise.

Devois was losing his self-confidence. He got up and began to pace back and forth. I knew that, aside from his disbelief in my story, he did not relish the delicate questions he must put to the wife of a British aristocrat. Lady Harcourt was, in his bourgeois mind, quite a different kettle of fish from an unstable member of a profession considered in France little better than that of prostitution. After a moment he stopped his pacing. He folded his arms. The little hands disappeared. He glared at me malevolently. "There has been a murder committed on this ship. We strongly suspect a connection with the Fournier case. After Lady Harcourt has denied your brazen fabrication, I will have some further questions to ask you."

There was a knock on the door and Irene sailed into the room with all the arrogance of a Bermuda Cup winner. For just a fraction of a second our eyes met. Again I was struck by an unaccustomed note of weariness beneath the smooth façade.

"Hello. What's up?" Her manner was casual and breezy, whatever she might have been feeling underneath.

"This is Monsieur Devois of the Deuxième Bureau."

"Charmed, I'm sure. But will someone please explain why I was called away from my luncheon guests?"

"I must apologize, madame." Devois was obsequious. "I am aboard this ship on an unpleasant mission. Time is of the essence. This gentleman claims your friendship. He is probably exaggerating."

"I know Mr. McLean quite well," she said calmly. "I've met him around and he has entertained at my own parties."

"I sang a Cole Porter song at the last one," I said carefully.

"May I ask why an acquaintance with Mr. McLean is so vitally important?"

"Madame, I am investigating the murder of Georges Fournier."

There was a moment's silence.

"Am I to understand that you wish to involve me in this investigation?" Irene's voice was like ice.

"Certainly not, madame!" Devois said quickly. "It is only that in questioning Mr. McLean about his whereabouts during the hours when—"

"You've been questioning Mr. McLean about Fournier's murder?" Her laughter rang out shrill and derisive. "But really! This man is a delightful night-club entertainer. Not at all the sort of person who goes about killing people. It's absurd."

Devois's hands tugged at the cuff of his coat. He looked toward the impassive girl in the corner as though for help, took a deep breath, and said, "Murder is often committed by the most unlikely persons."

"But what do you want of me?"

"This is most embarrassing, Lady Harcourt. Before I say more, I wish it understood that my only reason for asking you here is to disprove the slanderous statements of this gentleman."

"Slanderous statements?"

I began to feel easier. Irene was in complete control. Devois was due for a shock.

"Would you mind answering a question, Lady Harcourt?"

"Not if you make it quick. My guests are waiting."

"Please describe your actions after the ball given by Mrs. Richards at the Ritz last Friday night."

"My actions?" Irene's eyebrows went up into an incredulous arch. "What an extraordinary question!"

"I must ask your pardon if it sounds odd. I can only assure you it is of some importance."

"My actions? Well, really! What are one's actions after a party? I'm afraid mine were no more peculiar than those of most people. I went home to bed. Does that constitute a felony?"

"You went home alone?"

"No. Some friends dropped me in their car. My husband was in Lyon on business."

"You had no visitors at your apartment?"

"Visitors?"

Irene wasn't looking at me. I sensed that she was enjoying the little scene, leading up to an admission that would shock the smug detective.

"This gentleman claims to have spent the hours between one and five in the morning in your apartment."

Irene didn't even turn her head. "This gentleman, as you call him, is an unmitigated liar!"

I felt as though someone had slapped me over the head with a plank.

"Ah!" Devois's voice rose, triumphant and relieved.

"Irene! This is important!"

She didn't turn. She kept looking directly into Devois's eyes. She was as taut as a violin string.

"When I said that Mr. McLean was a friend, I was being kind," she went on in the same old mechanical voice. "After all, he is an entertainer. It is fashionable these days to be on intimate terms with such persons. If he claims anything more, he is what my husband would term— and correctly— a cad."

"I am in complete agreement with you, Lady Harcourt!"

My mind was beginning to work out of the shock of Irene's betrayal. There wasn't time to waste now on speculation as to her motive. I knew now that I was a sunk duck. I had to get out of this, and quick, no matter what the risks were. If Devois got me on that plane headed back to Paris, there would be little chance of clearing myself or saving Elisabeth Pasquela.

Irene, who had been standing beside me, moved slightly forward so that she was between me and the desk. Devois started around the desk toward me. His movements were no longer indolent. One small hand reached for his side pocket, the other made a signal to Irene to move aside. I acted now on pure reflex, without conscious thought. I lowered my head like a football tackle and charged into Irene's beautiful back. With a gasp of surprise she went sprawling headlong across the desk. In the moment that Devois leaned forward to catch her, I reached the door. I was dimly aware of the stenographer cowering in the corner. Behind me Irene screamed, "Don't let him get away!"

You and Cole Porter, I thought bitterly as I wrenched open the door, got out into the hall, and slammed it behind me. A ship's officer, who sat reading in a leather chair by the purser's desk, gave me a startled look, dropped his paper, and started to rise. But before he could get going I was past him, through the reception hall, vaulting the stairs. As I reached C deck I heard the sound of shouting below. I kept going— and fast. I scattered some startled passengers before I reached A deck. Here I turned away from the foyer and the public rooms into a long companionway. I had no plan, no point of destination. At the moment I wanted to put as much footage between me and Devois as possible. I figured there would not be a general alarm, at least not immediately; the peace of mind of the wealthy passengers came first. Besides, I couldn't get off the ship in mid-Atlantic.

Still, I was taking no chances. I had to get out of sight and stay there until I could figure the next move. I was working toward the bow of the ship with some idea of descending the rear stairwell to D deck and slipping through into second class when a name on one of the doors caught my eye: "La Suite Versailles." I drew up quickly and looked back over my shoulder. Luck was riding with me; the corridor was deserted. I fished the key Lili had given me from my pocket, opened the door of the suite, and stepped into the sitting room. I had been in this room on the previous afternoon at Lili Fenwick's cocktail party. I closed the door behind me and stood with my back against it, listening. The sitting room was empty, and there was no sound from the adjoining bedroom. I figured Lili was still in the dining salon. The poor girl had a shock in store for her. I crossed the sitting room and entered the bedroom. Everything there was soft and pink, a room for a woman as only a French decorator could design it. I slid open some blond wood paneling and stepped into the closet, closing the panel behind me, leaving just a crack for ventilation. I stood there pressed back among Lili's gowns. Inwardly I cursed Devois and myself, but most of all Irene. Whoever said a woman was unpredictable was being conservative. In her brittle airy way she had tried to stick my neck into the guillotine. Why?

I decided Irene deserved a little thought. For the first time I saw with new connotations her tête-à-tête with Pasquela in the bar of the Café Atlantique on the previous night. I felt a little ridiculous standing there in the perfume of Lili's closet. It would take them a little time to organize a room-to-room search. Everything would be done with discretion. No hint of "mad killer on the loose among the de luxe passengers." But I knew that when it came, despite all precautions not to alarm the paying guests, the search would be thorough. There was personnel trained for the purpose of digging out stowaways, and no reason why Devois couldn't put it to his use.

I went through the list of possible hiding places. A lifeboat, the luggage room, one of the great storerooms, a dressing room off the pool. I decided that for the time being I had been lucky enough to get to the best possible place. If there was anyone on this ship aside from Elisabeth on whom I could count for help, it was Lili Fenwick. I wished to hell she would get back from the dining salon. Somehow I must warn Elisabeth. There was no telling what steps Pasquela might take when he discovered what had happened in the purser's office, and I was fairly certain Irene would lose no time in warning him. I might be able to persuade Lili to act as errand boy.

I held my watch up to the crack of light. It was three-thirty. Lili might not be back for hours. I lowered myself to the floor and settled back as best I could in the cramped quarters, fighting off the overpowering desire for a cigarette. The minutes dragged on. I thought of the minutes as tiny pm pricks of time marching on the way to a gunshot or a knife in the back. After a while the sheer tension of waiting wore me down. There was nothing I could do until Lili returned, except to count the seconds and regret lost time. The thought of minutes became a sound in my ear, a rhythmical ticking impossible to obliterate. I caught myself dozing off and snapped my head up with a jerk. I felt guilty, as though I had committed a traitorous act.

Traitorous?

Fournier's words came back to me: "Like many Americans, you do not really understand the legend of Faust. You do not believe in the Devil." Fournier, the over-civilized European who had been my Mephistopheles, had decided at the last minute, when his highly cultivated mind could no longer bear its guilt, to be an avenging angel, to offer his Dr. Faust the chance at redemption never offered Goethe's original. He had clothed even this last act in a baroque fantasy. Directness must have seemed to this strange man almost ugly. On that last night when I had visited him in his suite, he must have decided, after having sent the jade to my stateroom on the *Dauphiné*, that his method was perhaps too devious for my crude American mind. In those last moments of his life he had struggled to break through the habits of a lifetime in order to state the facts in simple language. But even then some odd quirk, some barrier that was incomprehensible to me had limited the interview to implications and veiled warnings.

I had known for some time that despite his brilliant mind, his artistic sensibilities, his rapier irony, his weary cynicism, there were dark corridors of madness in his brain. I knew that he had loved that jade collection as other men love women. There was some dark symbolism in the fact that he had parted with it in an act of self-revelation. Perhaps he had acted as he had in some mystic belief in the Greek fates. The fates alone would ordain whether or not the jade would yield its secret.

Well, so far the fates were certainly acting as though they intended to keep his secret. Whatever proof lay hidden in the riddle of the jade owls was lost to me for the moment, and, unless a miracle happened, was lost to me forever.

Fournier and the jade and the ticking. The oppressive heat of the closet.

The ticking. Irene and her betrayal. My thoughts moved in slow motion through a maze of jade owls, and I fought a losing duel with sleep.

Chapter Thirteen

SEPTEMBER 10, 6:00 P.M.

I woke to the dreamlike sound of a voice faintly droning in the distance. I knew I must have slept for several hours, because through the crack I could see that the bedroom was plunged in darkness. With some difficulty I got to my feet, pounded circulation back into my legs, and slid open the panel. A shaft of violet light fell on the carpet near the sitting-room door. The voice was more distinct now, speaking out there in the other room. On tiptoe I crossed the bedroom and took a squint into the sitting room.

Lili was talking into the phone. She was alone in the room. I checked my first impulse to disclose my presence; something in her tone caught my attention. She was apparently excited about something. "... no reason at all. Of course I will. The sooner they get him the better. Oh, he's a cute one, all right, but not that cute! I understand the danger. Don't worry. I won't let you down."

She hung up and regarded the phone thoughtfully. Unconsciously she put her hand to her throat, then let it drop listlessly into her lap. She looked at her left shoe distastefully and kicked it off. It lay a few feet from her toe. She watched it with intense interest for a moment, as though it might come to life. Then she snapped one of her garters. The sound seemed to intrigue her, and she tried it once more. She sighed. She stood and did a sort of hopscotch toward the shoe. She looked down at it balefully, balanced on one foot. I was held in the doorway for a quiet moment, fascinated by the performance.

Then I said, "Who were you speaking to on the phone?"

She jumped as though she had been shot, twisted around still on one foot, and grinned.

"Have you come to do a little homemaking?"

"Who were you talking to, Lili?"

"Don't look so ferocious," she said calmly. "Mac, I've never been so glad to see anyone in my life! Have you been hiding in there all the time? Why didn't you show when I first came in?"

"Never mind that! I want to know who you were talking to."

She ducked down and retrieved the shoe. "If you must know, it was one of the ship's officers. They know I lunched with you. They called me in for some questioning— a horrible little goon called Devois or something. I told them I knew nothing about you except that you sang in night clubs. I talked fast and pretty damned well. I think I convinced them. Anyway, this guy just called to warn me you were still at large and dangerous."

"You sounded pretty damned chummy."

"I'm just democratic. I'm always chummy with the working classes. In the old family castle we used to—"

"You seem to think this is a picnic or something."

"Darling! Forgive me!" She danced across the room and put her hands on my shoulders. "It's just so good to see you alive and breathing. I've been so worried. And besides, I've got you in my power!"

"Listen, Lili, I haven't got time for games."

"You've got plenty of time, honey, and no place to go. They're turning this ship upside down for you right now. You should hear the gossip. Whee! You sure got yourself a million dollars' worth of publicity— if they ever let you loose to use it!"

"Publicity! You mean everyone knows?"

"They say it's in headlines in the Paris and New York papers. 'Murder suspect eludes police on luxury liner *Dauphiné!*'"

This surprised me. I wouldn't have thought Devois would advertise his incompetence.

"Well, as they say in Hollywood, don't just stand there. Sit down. Have a cigarette. Take it easy."

The idea appealed to me. I lit up and said, "What do you think of the news, Lili?"

"A lot of malarcky!" she said instantly. "I know my Mac. You could never have murdered anyone. I don't know what the hell you're mixed up in— what that guy with the gun was doing in your cabin— but I do know you never murdered anyone. I'm sold on you, honey. You should know that."

It struck me that her light tone was not quite genuine. She was talking awfully fast. Somewhere underneath there was suppressed excitement.

"Tell me about Devois."

"Boy! There's a real gone monsieur if I ever saw one. But I handled him. Although there was one bad moment."

"What was that?"

"Just in the middle of saying that I didn't know you very well, I suddenly remembered that the steward had seen me in your cabin last night and that they probably knew it. I made some quick revisions in my story. It meant making myself out the number one tramp of the ship, but what the hell. Devois had me down for one, anyway. I told them you propositioned me at my cocktail party and that I went to your cabin to— ah— well, I went to your cabin. I made out like I was in the habit of tearing one off with complete but attractive strangers."

"You told Devois that!"

"Well, honey, not in those exact bold words. But the same idea. The dope kept nodding as though he wasn't at all surprised. I told him my knowledge of you was confined to your activities in bed." She grinned maliciously. "Incidentally, I gave out like you promised more than you were able to deliver."

"For God's sake, Lili! Stop talking like a tart!"

"Then you do care!" she said mockingly.

"Go on. What happened then?"

"He seemed pleased at your reputed failure as a lover. He just don't seem to like you, kid. Anyway, I guess I'm not such a bad actress after all, because I put on the outraged act, saying that they should tie you to the mast or the funnel or whatever it is and burn you in oil. He agreed. Said you were a dangerous psychopath. Are you a dangerous psychopath, Mac darling? I must know for the sake of our children."

"You're sure they don't suspect I might have had your key? That I might be here?"

"Absolutely not. After I finished with Frenchie, he was convinced that this is just about the last place you would ever head for— and if you dared, I'd be on the phone in no time flat."

"Good work!"

"Do I get an A? The damnedest thing is that Mr. Greaseball actually tried to date me when he finished questioning me. Can you imagine those hands in the dark? Ugh!"

"What time did you leave Devois?"

"About four."

"Where have you been since?"

"Well, first I came back here hoping you might be here, but there was no sign of you."

"I guess I was asleep by that time. In the closet."

"Asleep! Of all the cool cucumbers! Half the ship hunting for him, and the guy curls up for a nap!"

"Where did you go then?"

"I got nervous waiting here. I decided to go out and hear what was being said— whether or not you had been picked up. Instead I got picked up myself. My Valentino type held me to my promise to see the movie with him.”

“Pasquela!” I sat up straight.

“It wasn’t exactly gay. Such a nervous type! Something’s eating that guy. When he held my hand in the movie I felt like he was doing it for reassurance. Halfway through he couldn’t take it any more, and we went up to the bar for a drink. A couple of drinks. His wife joined us and—”

“Elisabeth?”

“You know her?”

“Only casually,” I said.

“Very sweet. Too good for Mr. Jittery Pants. I got the impression they don’t get on any too well. Anyway, it ended up with their inviting me to sit at their table for the masquerade tonight.”

“You accepted?”

“No. I was too nervous about you. I don’t want to sit through a drunken party worrying.”

“It’s not too late,” I said in sudden excitement. “Call them and say you’ve changed your mind.”

She looked astonished. “Why?”

“Listen, Lili. You can help me. Accept their invitation. If Pasquela is really interested in you, you should be able to get him back to this room.”

“My God,” she said. “Don’t tell me Valentino is mixed up in this barrel of fun too.”

I stood up and took her hand. “Listen, Lili, this is no barrel of fun. I want you to get that into your head. I’ve been framed, and there’s only a hundred-to-one chance of getting out of it before Devois picks me up. We’ve got to use our heads. There are some tough characters laying for me.”

“Like the guy with the gun last night?”

“Not him. He’s out of the picture.”

She backed away from me. Her hands fell to her side. “Out of the picture? Mac, you don’t mean—”

“I told you, kid. This is for real!”

“That man— he’s dead?”

“Yes.”

The expression of horror was convincing. I tried to shake off the feeling that somewhere there was a false note. I couldn’t afford to think that now. Lili was in a position to help. I had to believe in her sincerity.

After a moment she said in a small voice, “What do you want me to do?”

“Have you any liquor in the room?”

With a gesture she indicated the bottles and glasses on a long table near the porthole. I mixed myself a stiff one. My mind was working fast now, caught up in a sudden wild plan. I turned back to find her waiting, white-faced and no longer smiling.

"Can I count on you?"

"Yes." And then rather desperately, "By God, if you turn out to be a phony, Mac, it will be the last mistake I'll ever make. But I'll take a chance on you."

"Good. I promise you won't regret it. Now listen. I want you to get hold of a mask, the kind they'll be wearing at that masquerade."

"You wouldn't dare! Besides, you haven't got a costume."

"Your closet is filled with clothes."

"Good God, Mac!"

"Don't argue, Lili," I said brusquely. "Can you get a mask?"

"Certainly. Everyone is buying them in the Bon Marché Shop on D deck. Come to think of it, I haven't got the costume yet that I ordered there yesterday. I'd better call them."

"No. Pick it up yourself. Get two masks and some make-up stuff. If the hairdresser is still open, get a couple of those switches women wear for extra hair. If not, I'll manage somehow."

She laughed in spite of her misgivings. "But darling, my gowns will never fit you."

"They will tonight. Now look. About a quarter of two I want you to steer Pasquela to the dance floor."

"But why?"

"Never mind. I'll tell you later. Then at two-thirty I want you to bring him back here."

"You flatter me. How can you be so sure I can inveigle him back here?"

"You've got to, that's all. I'm counting on you, Lili."

"All right," she said stoutly. "The guy is practically tied up and delivered already."

"Now, get on that phone and call the Pasquelas."

With a marked lack of enthusiasm Lili went to the phone. She hesitated with her hand on the mouthpiece. "I have a feeling this is a big mistake," she said.

"Call it a gamble," I said. "And if it works—"

"You're certain it isn't better for you to give yourself up to Devois? Surely you can clear yourself."

"Are you welshing on me?"

For answer she picked up the phone and said firmly, "Please get me Mr. Joseph Pasquela."

Chapter Fourteen

SEPTEMBER 11, 1:30 A.M.

The hour for unmasking was three A.M. Now, in that last hour and a half of anonymity, the first-class passengers were forgetting their inhibitions. Earlier there had been a gala performance in the theatre, at which I had been originally scheduled to appear, along with other theatrical celebrities aboard, but soon after eleven the scene had changed to the Café Atlantique, and now the usually chic atmosphere of the room was permeated with an unexpected frenzy. Dowagers and debutantes, whores and bankers, politicians and aristocrats, disguised now as harem girls, hula dancers, sailors, Greek goddesses, prize fighters, tramps, and nymphs, danced to a rude rumba among colored balloons and paper streamers while champagne flowed freely at the crowded tables. Violet light on white arms, the sheen of gold cloth and the sparkle of jewels, laughter and the shrill crescendo of excited voices, the heat of too many bodies in one room, and the insinuating beat of a jungle drum added to the impression of hectic unreality.

From my vantage point near the bar I imagined a note of desperation in the shrill gaiety. Only another hour and a half before the unmasking; only another hour and a half of illusion. Would withdrawn masks reveal a death's-head and a puppet's grinning face? Was there outside these walls some terrible plague about to enter the room in the form of Poe's masked death?

The brandy was inducing that strain of morbidity that always lay in wait just below the surface of my consciousness. The imminent unmasking became a kind of symbol in my mind, the hour and a half a predetermined time limit.

A jocular clown who stood next to me at the bar gave me a suspicious look. As well he might. I must have prerented a rather startling picture even for a shipboard masquerade, where costumes are usually improvised except by the more experienced and de luxe passengers who travel prepared. Lili had decked me out in odds and ends from her wardrobe. The effect was something between a disreputable nautch dancer from the toughest section of Port Said and a tattered gypsy down on her luck in some Kansas tank town. She had ripped a negligee up the back so I could get into it, tied it together again in the middle with a purple sash, torn the hem into untidy shreds, covered my arms with gold bracelets, smeared me with dark powder, draped my head in a shawl that was pinned under my chin, and— crowning indignity— painted my toenails, which were exposed in the red straw beach sandals she had procured in the men's shop. Any illusions I might have had about disguising my sex had been rudely shattered during the first minute at the bar when a waiter had said, "Pardon, sir, did you drop these cigarettes?" Aside from embarrassment, it didn't matter much. There were several other characters in the room cavorting joyously about as women. As long as my identity remained a secret, it was all right with me. Well, almost all right. The astonished and disdainful gaze of the jocular clown was becoming trying. I decided to get rid of him.

"Will you dance with me?" I minced.

The blood rose to his face. I saw his eyes dart about furtively through the holes of the mask. I expected a shot in the head or a torrent of abuse. To my amazement and consternation, he leaned close and said in a coy undertone, "I can't now. My wife is with me."

I controlled the shout of laughter that rose to my lips, downed the rest of my drink, and moved away from Pagliaccio. Live and learn, I thought. At the end of the bar I turned for another look into the main room. I caught a glimpse of Lili in her ballet costume sitting with a large party at the end of the dance floor. One of that party was Elisabeth. I was fairly certain she was the Renaissance princess in purple and gold. I looked at my watch. On the phone she had said she would meet me on the boat deck at one-forty-five. It was almost time to go.

Out on the boat deck the night was surprisingly mild for September on the Atlantic. The ship must have entered the Gulf Stream. A full moon hung over a satin-smooth sea. Long streaks of phosphorous streamed out in the *Dauphinés* wake. Far overhead, like a detached star, I saw the lights of a transatlantic plane moving to the east. A soft night, a lovely night, with no hint of death on the gentle breeze. As I walked back toward the appointed meeting place, I noticed the dim shadows here and there, merged as one. Harlequin and Columbine, Romeo and Juliet, Venus and Adonis, fighting against time. The sweet dream before the unmasking. Was there ever to be a time for Elisabeth and me when the night would mean not hidden terror but gentle moonlight?

Ironically enough, a couple stood in the shadow of the last lifeboat. Reluctantly I made myself obnoxious. I stood near them and brazenly lit a cigarette. They parted and the man said angrily, "What have we got here— a voyeur?" Then he whisked his slightly disheveled Dutch maiden off into the darkness.

From the distance came the sound of the orchestra playing a song that

Edith Piaf had made famous. It had a plaintive air and made me think of a sweet tune ground out on an ancient phonograph. For some odd reason it made me think of Lili.

And with Lili in my mind, the inexplicable sense of misgiving returned. It was nothing definite that she had said or done. It was an instinctive and, I felt, wholly unfounded sense of doubt. It was a coincidence that she had struck up an acquaintance with Pasquela; nothing more. And she had been perfectly frank about it. After all, she had agreed to help me in a manner that might be highly incriminating if it misfired. Surely if, for reasons beyond my understanding, she had intended to double-cross me, it would have been perfectly simple to inform Devois of my whereabouts. I was being unfair even to speculate about it.

Devois. The masquerade must have been a thorn in his side. I could almost see him ranting at the captain to cancel the affair. It was almost impossible to find a missing man among a thousand masked revelers. Despite the discreet but eagle-eyed attendants I had noticed stationed in the corridors and around the edges of the café, it was worse than a haystack surrounding the proverbial needle. I felt fairly secure until at least three o'clock.

I had been thinking a great deal about Irene, too, in the past few hours, and my thoughts had not been pleasant. I was fairly certain now that she must be involved in some manner with Pasquela and his gang. She had been playing with me like a mouse for weeks now, perhaps even under orders. It was shocking to think that a woman in her position could be involved with these international gangsters, but knowing Irene, I was not too surprised. Her morals were nonexistent and her ethics a dirty joke. She came of the Green Hat school, so fashionable a generation before, romantic only to an infantile mind and dangerous to an adult. Peter Pan gone delinquent, no longer able to fly in a world he couldn't understand; a Peter Pan who might have sold out to Captain Hook for want of recognition from any other world.

If Pasquela failed me, I intended to see Irene before the night was out.

Out of the darkness came the Renaissance princess. She looked like a breath-taking Goya portrait with the dark night sky as a background. She came into my arms without a word, removing the tiny gold mask as her mouth found mine. For an instant it was the night of distilled moonlight and no other. The secret, sinister life out in the darkness was obliterated for that one instant. But as she broke away it was there again, crouching, waiting, using up our precious time.

"I can only stay a minute."

"You've heard about what they're printing in the Paris and New

York papers?"

"Yes. It's monstrous. Darling, I'm terrified." When she saw my face, she hurried on, "Oh, not for myself. Joseph has been peculiarly indifferent to me, thank God. But for you."

"What were you able to find out about the jade?"

"It's heartbreaking to have to tell you this. When I talked to you on the phone this morning I had discovered that Joseph had those hideous owls hidden in our suite."

"What!"

"It was a lucky accident. Or at least it seemed lucky at the time. I was looking for accessories for this costume. I remembered a box of gold trinkets that had been put in Joseph's trunk. As I was going through the trunk, I noticed a soiled shirt tied into a knot behind the shoe rack. He was out of the stateroom at the time. I tore open the shirt. The owls tumbled out!"

"Good God!"

"I examined them carefully. There was nothing— absolutely nothing— that could be construed as the sort of proof that Gonzales hinted at. Just hard jade and solid mahogany."

The moment of elation passed. "I suspected that. As I told you, one of the owls was missing. It must be the one we want."

"At least it proves what we suspected, Mac. We know that Gonzales had those owls. Joseph must have murdered Gonzales to get them."

"It's only proof to us," I said dejectedly. "Devois will think the jade story is so much hooey. Besides, Pasquela has probably got rid of them by this time."

Someone passed close by in the darkness. Elisabeth drew near again. The scent of her perfume was maddening.

"There must be something we can do," she whispered. Her hands gripped my arm. "Mac, are you certain that missing piece of jade could not be in your stateroom?"

"Positive."

"Then the only other person who could have got hold of that missing piece, as far as we know, is the room steward."

I took a deep breath and said, "No. Two other people knew about the jade."

"What!" She drew away in surprise. "But Mac, you said yourself that—"

"I lied to you," I said miserably. "I didn't want you to think I was a rounder or something. Two women know."

"Who?" Her voice was sharp with anxiety.

"Lili Fenwick, for one. She was in my stateroom when Gonzales snatched the owls."

"In your stateroom. That movie actress? I didn't know. I—"

"It's not what you think. I swear I didn't ask her there."

"Then why did she come?"

"I don't know. She was drunk— or at least pretending to be drunk. Last night it seemed quite plausible. Now, I don't know."

For a moment she said nothing. Then she said, "She might be some sort of tool, but I can't believe it. She's a rather sweet and naïve little thing. Joseph has been flirting with her outrageously all evening. But—" She stopped. "It is strange, though. I mean that she and Joseph... But no. I can't believe it." Her voice took on an ironic edge. "And who else?"

"Irene."

"Lady Harcourt!"

Quickly I blurted out a clumsy explanation of Irene's presence in my stateroom. It sounded awfully phony even to me. But for the moment, at least, Elisabeth was not interested in the amorous implications.

"Mac! Why didn't you tell me this before? I know for a fact that Joseph met Lady Harcourt in the card room this morning. He used to see her before we were married. Malicious women used to take pleasure in telling me about it."

"But surely if she and Pasquela are hand in glove and she got hold of that owl, she would have turned it over to him by this time."

"Not necessarily." Her voice was low and excited. "Women are sometimes unpredictable. She might be holding out on Joseph."

"For what? Surely not—"

"Oh, not that," she said contemptuously. "She would know that about him by this time. I mean money."

"Money? Why would Irene need money? Everyone knows that Albert Harcourt is rich. Their place in Scotland is famous."

"The castle in Scotland is open to tourists— at a price. They haven't lived there since the war. An Englishman can get very little out of England. You know that. They've had to live somehow."

"Albert would never be a party to blackmail, I can assure you."

"My poor lamb! He probably knows nothing about it." She grabbed my arm. "The more I think of it ..."

"You may be right. She practically turned me over to Devois."

"There, you see!"

"I'll get to her somehow."

"No!" She pressed close to me. "Mac, please don't try anything foolish. I've been thinking. It's better for you— it would be better for you to give yourself up to Devois until—"

"Not until I get this settled!"

"You mustn't be rash, for my sake. I'll be all right. I'd feel so much better if I knew they couldn't get at you. You don't know them. They won't stop at anything!"

"I've made up my mind."

She sighed. "Where have you been hiding out?"

"I can't tell you now."

"Darling, please. I must leave you. I'll be worrying."

"Elisabeth, I think something will break in the next couple of hours. Get back to your stateroom and lock your door. Stay by the phone. If anyone tries to force his way in, call Devois immediately. I have a feeling Pasquela is desperate. If Irene has that jade owl, it's certain she's holding out on him. But if he gets hold of it he may decide to act fast. And acting fast might mean danger to anyone who might talk."

"What are you going to do?"

"There isn't time to tell you now. You've got to get back to that table before he becomes suspicious. When the party breaks up, do as I've just told you. I want you to swear you'll go to your room and lock the door. The minute anything breaks I'll telephone you."

"Darling, you frighten me. I can't let you... You must tell me what you have planned— where you are hiding."

"Not now. Promise me you will do as I say!"

After a moment she said quietly, "I promise."

I took her in my arms. "Everything will be all right," I said with more conviction than I felt.

She looked up at me. Her eyes were calm but infinitely sad. "Sometimes I feel that nothing will be right for me, Mac. But I'll do as you say. If you don't call me ..."

"You'll know that something has gone wrong. Then you must call Devois and tell him everything. He may not believe it, but you will have to take the chance."

"Dear God, don't let anything go wrong," she said.

Gently she touched my cheek. Then she was gone into the darkness. I stood there for a moment fighting off the premonition of disaster. Deep down was a sickening sensation, as though I were facing an irreparable loss.

Somewhere in the distance above the sound of the dream music I heard the ship's bells. Two A.M. An hour until the unmasking. I turned away from the lighted café toward a dimly lit companionway leading toward the stairs. A grinning satyr brushed against me and then was gone.

Chapter Fifteen

SEPTEMBER 11, 2:20 A.M.

Pasquela was drunk. In itself, that was not surprising, but there was something desperate, bitter, and resigned in his attitude that was completely at variance with the man as I had known him. Dressed as a conquistador, he looked like a decadent descendant of an ancestor who had come from Spain to find gold and glory in the New World. His body covered with black and gold, a white ruff at his neck, he sat on the yellow sofa in the sitting room of Lili's suite. On the commode beside the sofa lay his discarded mask. For the moment, as I watched his profile from my hiding place behind the bedroom door, I felt easier about Elisabeth. I prayed that by this time she was safe behind the locked door of her room.

Lili had reverted to her former role of glamorous Hollywood star. At the moment she was out of my sight on the far side of the room, fixing a drink for Pasquela. So far she had found no opportunity to lead the conversation in the direction in which I had rehearsed her.

She came into sight— a lovely sight in the white costume of the ballet dancer— carrying two highballs. She handed one to him.

"I don't usually drink so much," he said apologetically. "This is an excellent drink. I thank you."

"For a nondrinker you've done very well this evening," Lili said. I wished she wouldn't speak quite so loudly or so carefully, as though for the ears of an eavesdropper.

"I have never had much use for overindulgence of any kind. Tonight is a rare occasion."

"A celebration?"

"Hardly!" His voice was bitter.

"Well, I must say I've done pretty well myself," Lili said. "I needed some sustenance after the shock I had today."

"Shock?"

"The man I lunched with turned out to be a murderer. That night-club singer. Just think— if the police hadn't flown from Paris, I might have found myself with a nicely slit throat by this time."

"It is not easy to identify the murderers among us!"

"Oh, I don't know," Lili said lightly. "I wouldn't put much past that sort. Of course, I knew nothing about him. It only goes to prove that you must be careful about whom you pick up on a ship."

Lili sat with her back to me. Her neck looked tense, belying the careful measured voice. Pasquela gave her a long cowlike look. He got interested in his drink again. After a moment he said, "It was stupid of him to resist arrest. He would have been safer."

"Safer?"

Pasquela shrugged wearily, but did not explain.

"What do you suppose his motive was in eluding arrest?" Lili asked brightly. "Surely he knows how hopeless it is. He can't very well get off the boat in mid-Atlantic."

"Perhaps, my dear Miss Fenwick, he is foolish enough to attempt to settle some old score."

"Goodness!" Lili said with just the right note of alarm. "That sounds so sinister!"

"It is not you who have to worry, my dear child!"

Lili gave a gay laugh. "By the way you said it, I might almost think it was you who were worried!"

He gave her the look again; round-eyed and serious, almost speculative. "Yesterday I might have been." He shrugged. "Today ..."

"Yes?"

He shook himself like a tired bloodhound. "Today we will not talk of tomorrow. Eh? It was very good of you to allow me to come here with you. I was lonely."

"Lonely! Come, now! How could a man married to such a beautiful and charming woman be lonely?"

"We will not discuss my wife!" His voice was suddenly thick and harsh. Under ordinary circumstances Lili would probably have chucked him out at this point. Instead she went on playing the game.

"I didn't mean to offend you, Mr. Pasquela," she said with uncharacteristic coyness.

Pasquela descended from aristocratic arrogance to patronizing forgiveness. "I could not expect you to understand, my dear. I do not mean to be rude. How could I be rude to such a sweet child? A child who has been the only ray of light in this dark evening."

"I understand loneliness," Lili said. "Believe me."

"You, lonely?"

"Oh, not every minute of my life— no. But perhaps now."

Her hand moved expressively in a gesture that would have done credit to Duse.

Pasquela took notice of the trailing hand but made no move. His manner became more speculative. Remembering Elisabeth's statement about his difficulties with women, I thought I understood his inaction. But I felt that for the sake of his reputation he should put on a pretty good show anyway.

"You know, Miss Fenwick, this is quite extraordinary. At your party yesterday I looked upon you not as a human being, but as— well, something that had moved off the silver screen for an hour or so. Lovely to look upon, but somehow not flesh and blood."

"I've had that trouble before," Lili said with some conviction.

"When we got talking in the bar, I must say I was at first— how shall I say it— only politely interested. You came upon me, oddly enough, at one of the crises of my life. I should be worrying about other things. Instead I find myself here, and curiously grateful for it. Perhaps there will be one charming moment before ..."

"Before what? You sound so ominous."

"Life itself is ominous. It's only the moments. Moments like this." He drained his glass and set it on the small table by the sofa. His eyes seemed slightly out of focus. "I sit here with you and I am a person in fiction."

"I don't understand," Lili said truthfully.

"It is difficult to explain. I am for you a person who does not exist except in your mind. But I find in that a certain poignancy. Because the person you imagine is the person I might have been. If!" He smiled a sad smile of self-pity. I wondered how long the smile would have lasted if he had known what Lili really thought about him.

"I find you very sympathetic, Miss Fenwick. It would be unwise for me to dispel that sympathy. I should take advantage of it. Tonight, however, I feel at the end of wisdom." He leaned back on the sofa and looked at her through half-closed eyes. "You are probably congratulating yourself on what you consider a conquest."

The cold arrogance was infuriating. But Lili said mildly, "I hadn't thought of it just that way."

"Many women in Paris would think so at this moment, if they were in your position. But they would be wrong. You see, my dear Miss Fenwick, a conquest implies a prize. You could not call it a conquest to capture an empty shell."

"I don't know what you mean."

"It is simple. What you can see before you is an illusion. A conjurer's trick. A man can only be called a man when he possesses his soul and his pride. In my youth I had pride. Now you see before you a puppet, a mock conquistador, the product of a costumer who moves through his days in an empty dream."

Lili gave a nervous laugh. She wasn't used to dealing with Latin self-flagellation.

"I really don't know what you're talking about, Mr. Pasquela. All I see before me is a— a very handsome gentleman."

"Gentleman? Ah, yes."

"Let me pour you another drink."

"Why not? If I am to break the habits of a lifetime, I might as well do it well."

Lili took his glass and passed from view. Impatiently I looked at my watch. Lili was certainly doing her act in slow motion. Was she stalling?

Pasquela sighed. "I watched you this evening, Miss Fenwick, and I was charmed. I see in you a naïveté, a simplicity that has been very rare in my life. I do not understand what makes you like this. As a matter of fact, my childhood was spent in such a small circle of persons that I have had difficulty understanding people outside it." He hesitated a moment, then said, "You will not be offended, I hope, by what I will now tell you."

"I stopped being offended years ago," I heard Lili say from the other side of the room.

"Well, it is an odd thing, but the only understanding I have had in my life— the only real sympathy— was from women who... that is, from women of a different class."

I could imagine the expression on Lili's face, but apparently her back was to him because he went on, "I formed an odd habit when I was no more than fifteen. My mother was a very great lady, but she was remote and proud and our house was filled with stately ritual. We never spoke from our hearts. When I was fifteen I went one night with an older friend to a house of prostitution. It was my first such experience. I found warmth and a strange humanity there. I used to go back there, not entirely for the obvious compulsions of youth, but because there was a girl there to whom I could talk as I had never been allowed to talk in my life. This pattern became very strong in my life. Duty and family on one side, the place where I spoke of fears and doubts, yearnings and even my sins on the other."

Lili came back into sight with a fresh drink. She gave a quick, rather tortured look in my direction. He didn't notice. It was becoming obvious that Lili's presence was only a technicality to him. He was talking inward.

"About a year ago, because I could not face the confessional, I stopped attending mass. The odor of the church made me ill. Then in the nights the old pattern would reassert itself. There was one place where I could speak freely, undam the guilt and the fear; a place in which my identity was not known. These girls I paid to listen. I would find momentary relief. Do you understand?"

He had made it pretty obvious that Lili was merely a substitute for one of "these girls." Her back was to me once again. To my surprise there was no resentment in her voice when she spoke. Instead there was something I didn't like; a veiled warning.

"It's getting late, Mr. Pasquela. Perhaps ..."

But he interrupted, "You are a surprising young lady. I have been most fortunate to meet you at this moment in my life. I need to speak things. I know you will understand. There is a black night closing in about me."

"What do you mean, Mr. Pasquela?"

"You said I was a gentleman, and I suppose I am. I was born a gentleman and I was educated to be a gentleman, in the ancient sense of the word. Do you understand what that means? I should like to explain the tragedy of being a gentleman!" Pasquela said decisively. "In my country, the word has a rigid meaning. It means belonging to a class— the descendants of the conquistadors. The grandees. The blood of rulers is in our veins. In my youth there came to power in my country a government of the people. A vulgar revolution ruled by the mob and the facile slogans of democracy. My family, my relations, our friends never recognized the rights of this rabble. We went on living our lives as we had for centuries. Only now we were in seclusion, and spoke of politics only in the privacy of our haciendas. I was sent to school in Spain along with my young friends— a school for aristocrats. We despised the government of my country, and we planned, where our parents had only talked. Wild romantic plans that seemed utterly hopeless. We had not the power or the money or the military sense to carry them through."

He stopped and looked vaguely around the room.

"I believed with all my heart it was for the good of the people. Tradition and discipline, the old ways, the way of the cavalier. I was young and wild and foolhardy— but still, I was a man."

He rested his arm on the side of the sofa as though suddenly too tired to continue.

"Ah. I am telling stories again. Stories to lovely ladies who see perhaps a vestige of that young man in my eyes. I tell the stories and I go away and I never see them again. I tell them of this young knight who dreamed of riding at the head of a gleaming army, and the city square filled with the cheering people, and the old dreams revived. I tell them of a young lover, a hotheaded young lover whom women remembered with tenderness. I tell them of a young man who believed with all his romantic soul— believed ..."

He took another swallow of whisky. "And then, one day, they came."

"Who came?"

"The foreigners. The men who walked stiffly and looked at you with cold eyes. The men who flattered you. The men who hated the people and despised you for a fool!"

Shakily he lit a cigarette. He seemed to have forgotten Lili completely.

"The young man was not so young any more, but he had not stopped dreaming of glory. He thought he was clever. He thought he could use these Prussians and Spaniards for his own purpose. He took their money and watched the secret army grow under their direction. With their help there was a *coup d'état*. The government of the people was smashed. And for one blinding moment of illusion the young man thought the hour of his dreams had come."

He laughed bitterly. Lili did not move.

"One blinding moment! And then the night of dreaming was ended. Everything began slipping away. He and his friends were so many pawns caught up in a terrible machine. Soon they were at the mercy of the foreigners, who ruled from remote haciendas and hotel suites in the capital. All the purple trappings, all the moonlight vanished in an instant. Some of them saw the truth. Only a few. By this time the fear of the people had blinded them to what they had become. We learned to take orders and to die inside. One morning the young man who was no longer young awakened knowing that he had betrayed his country into the hands of a ruthless enemy. But it was too late for him. He was drowned in falsehood and corruption, and the day of dreaming was past. I will tell you to what depths he sank. He allowed—"

"No!" Lili said sharply. "You're drunk. You don't know what you're saying."

"Surely you do not object to stories. Stories out of unwritten books. Nothing to do with me, you understand …"

Lili jumped to her feet. She was white with anger.

"You sniveling coward! If things had gone right for you, you would have gone on smiling and listening to music and dining in luxurious restaurants, and shrugging while men were shot and murdered. You're a lousy skunk giving off a stink of fear. A knight! A romantic lover! That's a hot one!"

Pasquela looked stunned. Slowly he put down his glass. He didn't take his gaze from Lili's furious face.

"You wouldn't be here with this cheap sob story now if it weren't for one thing. You're out of your mind with worry. You're scared bloodless because you're terrified a missing piece of jade will turn up in the wrong hands!"

"The jade." His face sagged. "You. Surely not. You. You have the jade?"

I stepped out of the bedroom. He looked at the gun in my hand, but he didn't seem to see it. His eyes went back to Lili.

"You've tricked me," he said in a dazed voice. "You are one of them."

"It didn't help you to kill Gonzales, Pasquela," I said. "You didn't find what you wanted."

"I did not kill Gonzales."

"It didn't help you to murder Fournier. The jade is still missing."

"I did not kill Fournier," he said. The lack of tension in his body was disquieting. He sat there on the sofa like an empty hot-water bottle.

"All the killing didn't help you," I said. "There are too many of us to kill!"

"Perhaps." He sighed wearily. "You are a fool, McLean. Nothing you can do will help. You are surrounded by betrayal. There is an X beside your name. As long as they believed that you might still retain possession of the jade, you were safe until they got it from you. Now they know better. There is nothing, absolutely nothing you can do. You would be better off to give yourself up to Devois."

"Talk, Pasquela. And talk fast. Who are your confederates?"

His gaze slid to Lili, then away. He smiled a pale smile. "I am a little weary. You will forgive me."

He started to rise. I shoved him back. He shrugged again.

"What did you have on Fournier?"

"I? Not I. But there were those who had a very tight hold on Fournier. He was a victim of blackmail. For years the wife of one of the most prominent men in France was his mistress. They stumbled on the fact accidentally. The publicity would have destroyed the good lady. At first Fournier thought that what he was asked to do was comparatively harmless. He lived in a world of the arts and did not understand politics. It was only when he was in too deep to crawl out that they— how do you say— put on the screws. He was foolish enough to threaten to expose them."

"Them? Who? Who?"

He sighed. "There is only so far that a man can go."

"How long has Irene Harcourt been working for you?"

He averted his eyes. Behind me Lili gave a gasp of surprise. He looked beyond me to Lili. To my amazement, he smiled. "You see, even the moment was an illusion. A lady will destroy you, McLean."

Across his face flashed an expression I had never seen there. It was like a memory of life, of youth, of lost gallantry.

"Perhaps there is one last lady who will listen to my stories and have pity."

It happened so quickly, so unexpectedly, that I never had a chance to prevent it. With one hand he raised his glass in a mock toast. My eyes were on the raised glass so that I hardly noticed the quick movement of his other hand as it darted into the gold-braided pocket of his costume. I saw the tiny vial too late. I threw myself forward and forced open his mouth. He had already swallowed it. Convulsions gripped him almost immediately. He began to writhe around beneath me on the sofa. He seemed trying to say something, but no sound issued forth except a horrible dry gasping. I stumbled away from him and turned helplessly toward the phone. But halfway across the room the sound of his gasping sound ceased altogether. I had one hand on the instrument when I heard Lili's horrified "Mac!"

I turned, knowing what I would find.

Neither of us said a word. It was impossible to believe that a man could die so quickly.

Chapter Sixteen

SEPTEMBER 11, 2:40 A.M.

It was Lili's sob, which I recognized as a prelude to hysteria, that brought me to my senses. I took her by the shoulders and drew her close to me to shut out for the moment, at least, the Grand Guignol scene presented by Pasquela, face up on the rug, arm outstretched to an ironically clenched fist, still as wax. She trembled violently but made no further outcry. I knew she was making a heroic effort not to scream.

"It's not our fault," I said. "He would have done it anyway sooner or later. He's been heading for it for a long time."

"Are you sure he's ..." She gave him a desperate, unseeing look.

"Positive. I know the stuff he had in that vial. Some of the top Nazis used it when the going got hot."

"I can't believe it's real. What will we do?"

I put the revolver down on the table and wiped the perspiration from my forehead.

"We're not calling anyone, if that's what you mean."

"But Mac, his wife... There must be someone ..."

"Don't worry about mourners!"

Pasquela stared up at me with glassy sightless eyes. She turned and looked at him once more, this time forcing herself to hold her gaze.

"Oh, him!" she said after a moment, as though she had just comprehended the meaning of my remark. The contempt, the furious contempt was as surprising as it was shocking. I looked at her sharply. Something stirred in the back of my mind, some unresolved alertness.

"I'm thinking of you," she said. "Of you and me and what that French detective would make of it."

"Lili," I said quietly, "how did you know about the jade?"

"What do you mean?"

"Don't give me the innocent eyes, Lili. I heard you mention the missing jade piece to Pasquela."

"Oh, that! You know very well I was in your room when that character with the gun came for the jade. He made quite a fuss about the missing piece. I put two and two together."

"Pretty involved arithmetic!"

I started for the door.

"Mac! Where are you going?"

"I've got to get to Irene Harcourt, and quick. I'll be back. There are a couple of things I want to ask you. I haven't finished with you yet, Lili."

"No," she said. "You have not."

I turned to look into the barrel of my own gun. "You're not leaving this stateroom!"

"So!"

"You needn't look at me like that. There are things you don't know about. You're better off here."

"What makes you so sure?"

"Someone asked me to keep you here. What's happening out there is—"

"It couldn't be murder that's happening out there, could it?" I took a step toward her.

"You meddle too much!" she cried.

I took another step, slow and careful. She pressed her lips together, but the half step backward told me what I wanted to know.

"Listen, Mac! Now you listen!"

I threw myself on her and wrested the revolver from her hand. I moved in blind anger, hardly aware of my actions. I was aware of her face very close and the sharp crack of my fist on her jaw, the moan and the falling away. Then I was bending down over her.

In her white ballet costume she looked like a doll. I had hit her harder than I intended. She was out. And by the looks of things, it would be some time before she would be in again.

I didn't waste any time on either first aid or regrets. Quickly I left the suite. Out in the corridor a drunken Harlequin walked unsteadily toward the lounge, brushing past me just outside the door. Through the slits in his mask he gave me an indignant look and went on his way. He was like some monstrous tomcat heading for the back fence. I pulled the door closed behind me and hurried toward a corridor that ran from port to starboard amidship on A deck. I knew the Harcourts had a suite similar to Lili's on the opposite side of the deck.

I passed no one. The very fact that the corridors were empty was disquieting. It didn't speak very well for the safety of the passengers that, with an assumed murderer on the loose, this deck was not well patrolled. Devois had slipped up badly here.

When I reached the door of the Harcourt suite I hesitated a moment before knocking. There was only a chance in a million that Irene had left the masquerade before the hour of unmasking. Irene rarely left a party until the last tired tune had died out and the orchestra had left the stand. Elisabeth would be waiting nervously in her stateroom for my telephone call. On the other hand, there was no good frightening Elisabeth with the news about Pasquela until I could get Irene to talk.

There was a faint sound in the corridor. I wheeled about. Several doors away, a stout woman dressed as Marie Antoinette stopped in the act of unlocking her stateroom door and gave me a frightened look. I managed a sickly smile that was meant to be reassuring, but it didn't work. She stared back as though hypnotized with fear. The possibility of panic on her part ended all indecision on mine. I couldn't very well stand there in the corridor without purpose. I knocked on the door of the Harcourt suite.

The simple, normal act seemed to assuage Marie Antoinette's fear. She pushed open her door with a last doubtful glance and disappeared. I was about to knock again when the door was opened by a clown. It was a second before I recognized Albert.

"Is Irene here?" I brushed past him unceremoniously.

"I say, old chap, isn't this rather—"

"Where is she?"

Even as I spoke she appeared in the doorway separating her bedroom from the sitting room. She was got up to look like a French streetwalker in the traditional tight and brief black skirt, red blouse, and beret. She was obviously startled and dismayed.

Behind me Albert said, "Chap must be drunk. Where have you been hiding? Can't involve us in this sordid business, you know."

"Just a minute, Albert!" Irene hadn't taken her eyes off me. She was very pale.

"What's up, old girl?"

"Listen, Irene," I said. "I've come for—"

"Yes!" she interrupted sharply. She turned to Albert. "Albert, I know it sounds odd, but would you mind leaving me alone with him for a few minutes?"

"What's that? The man is wanted for murder!"

"Nonsense. He's not going to harm me. Please."

Albert looked dumbfounded. After a moment he pulled himself together. With a suggestion of humor in his eyes he said, "This tops everything, my dear. But I suppose, as usual, I will bow to your judgment. You've managed to crawl out of some nasty spots before. I'll take a turn around the deck."

"Thank you, Albert." Irene's voice was listless.

"Don't believe, myself, the chap is capable of murder. The Frenchman must be making the usual blunders of his type. However, keep a sharp eye, old girl."

"Yes, Albert."

"Don't cut my wife's throat, young man. I have use for it. Ha!"

Albert went out into the corridor and shut the door behind him. Irene reached over and switched off the sitting-room light, then turned and went back into her bedroom. Slowly I followed. She sat on a small gilt chair in front of a dressing table and turned to me. She looked exhausted.

"I told that girl—"

"Lili Fenwick?"

She shook her head impatiently. "I won't have it, Mac! I won't be bullied! You must stay out of this until—"

"Stay out of it! Jesus Christ, you'd think I was upsetting a cocktail party!"

"You've come for the jade owl?"

"So you *do* have it!"

"No."

I took a threatening step forward but she only shrugged wearily. "Will you please calm down? I only wanted you safely out of the way until—"

"Safely out of the way! Like turning me over to Devois for a murder rap!"

She sighed. "I thought at least it would keep you out of danger. I wanted a day to think."

Her manner was completely mystifying. If she was afraid of me, she was certainly concealing it with success. "To think?"

"It's all so hideous! Like waking up in hell. But I must know why and how and... I knew nothing much could happen between dinner and breakfast tomorrow, except possibly to me, and in that case ..."

"Nothing much has happened," I said ironically. "Pasquela is dead."

There was nothing phony about her reaction to that. She reached back to the dressing table for support. "I shouldn't have waited," she whispered.

The despair was genuine. I couldn't figure it out. My anger began to die down. There was something here I didn't understand. And suddenly, as I watched her sitting there devoid of all her former brittleness, cynicism, and chic, a faint stirring of the old camaraderie I had once felt for her returned.

"There isn't much time," she said dully. "Albert will be back. You must go before that."

"Irene, what in hell is wrong?"

"It started as a game, really. I was terribly curious about that jade in your stateroom. I knew you were lying when you said Fournier had given it to you to sell in the States. And then when the news came of his murder, I was certain you were mixed up in some fantastic intrigue. I never for an instant thought you had killed poor Georges, but I knew there was something awfully peculiar going on. I went to your cabin last night when the Fenwick girl was there. As you know, she was drunk. She went to the bathroom while I was there."

"She didn't tell me."

"Probably wasn't even aware of it. Anyway, I fished out the leather case from under your bed. I opened it and started to examine the owls. Immediately I saw that there was one different from the others— not the jade itself, but the base. The wood was of slightly different texture, and it was lighter when I held it in my hand. What I did then was sheer impulse. I stuffed the owl into my bag and put the case under the bed where I had found it before Miss Fenwick came back."

"Then you had it all the time you were talking to Pasquela and me in the bar?"

"Yes. And I was dying to get back to my stateroom to examine it. I was having fun then. God!"

"What did you expect to find?" I asked warily.

"God knows. Secret papers, a code message.... I thought maybe you were a government agent or an international crook. I didn't have any clear idea, except I thought it would be amusing to face you with it."

"Well?"

Her hand turned outward in a futile gesture. "Let me have a cigarette, Mac?"

It was like the plea of a tired child. I gave her one and lighted it.

"Thank you, darling."

"Go on!" I said impatiently.

She closed her eyes. "I suppose there's some kind of ironic justice that made me pry loose the owl from its base and find what was there. I had it coming to me!"

"Get to the point! What was in it?"

"A letter signed by Fournier. It was wrapped about something that I assume is microfilm."

"No wonder they're so anxious to get it! Where—"

She held up her hand. "No. Wait. I must explain something first. It's terribly important. I mean it's terribly important to me that you under-stand. It's as though I've suddenly grown up all in one dreadful day. I don't like it, Mac. It frightens me. I've been a child playing at life for so long."

I checked the impulse to interrupt.

"Everything was like a game, you know. Even the war was like some unreal dream in which I was the heroine of a chic canteen in London. Gay, chin up, and all that, but not knowing, not really knowing. You see, I knew people on the other side too."

"The other side?"

"Before the war we used to go hunting in Poland at house parties with Goering. I thought he was quite charming. And— oh, lots of others. We used to entertain them in London. Men like Ribbentrop. The German Legation was considered smart. We weren't the only ones. It was fash-ionable to have the Nazis to dinner in those days. At least, fashionable among a great many of the people we saw. So I couldn't understand— and I was very annoyed— when the government behaved as it did to-ward poor Albert."

"Albert?" I was puzzled. "The government?"

"I thought you might have heard the gossip. Albert was confined to our place in Scotland for the duration of the war."

"I never knew."

"Oh, it was all very hush-hush. You know how they do things in Eng-land. It didn't make sense to me. I was allowed to do war work in Lon-don, and at first most people didn't even suspect. Albert's family is a very ancient one, you know. I guess they felt it wasn't the sort of scandal to feed the public at the time. But actually he was under polite arrest."

Was Irene making up a fantastic lie? It seemed incredible that any gov-ernment would even bother to arrest Albert. You couldn't take him se-riously except as a sort of Colonel Blimp, affable, stupid, and merely a background for Irene's glitter.

"Naturally I was furious with the government. I thought they were discriminating against poor Albert. Politics was merely something to make amusing dinner conversation to me. And many times I had heard him make some good-natured remark about the stupidity of that Mosely man. It seemed to me simply absurd."

She took a puff at the cigarette and looked listlessly at her fingertips as the smoke drifted from her lips.

"But the gossip spread. After the war Albert was released, but we were not welcome at many British dinner tables. At the government's suggestion we left England. I thought the thing would blow over and that someday we would go back. We never went back. I've never seen England again."

"But in Paris you saw British people."

"Trash and climbers. You probably didn't notice that we were always out of town when any of the big embassy dinners were held. The set we knew in England— the people who matter, my dear— are very clannish and closemouthed. The gossip stayed within that set. After all, there was Albert's family to consider, and tradition, and that sort of thing. I went in for the South American and New York set. We were in Central and South America for two years after we left England."

The monstrous implications behind Irene's words began to take form.

"Oh, I knew Albert was involved in something, but I wasn't too interested. I thought it was probably some fast business deal. I was beginning to have a good time again. Amusing people were all that mattered, really."

She looked up at me with tortured eyes. "I don't expect you to understand this, Mac. I don't suppose anyone could. But you see, I have always been fond of Albert. He has been very patient and kind. I knew I should turn over the jade owl and all it implied to Devois. But I couldn't do it— not until I had given Albert a chance to explain. I think for a few hours I had some wild idea that I might be able to persuade him to give up this— this ghastly thing."

"You made a mistake."

"I know that now! I've known it all evening. I wanted to believe.... Besides I have some pride. It would have been stripping myself naked before the world. And I'm not big enough for that, Mac. At least I thought not. It was only when you didn't stay safely put in Devois's hands that I changed my mind. I couldn't have anything happen to you, darling. After all, you're the best playmate I ever had."

"If that's true, why didn't you tell Devois after I made my getaway?"

She averted her eyes. "I had to speak with Albert first."

"Have you told him?"

"No. I asked him to leave the party early. I was just about to go into it when you barged in."

"But my God, Irene! He must know what you're telling me now!"

"No. He hasn't the faintest idea that I had the owl. Why would he, unless someone told him, and who—"

"What a child you are!"

But I was somewhat reassured. Then a new and ugly thought came to my mind. Elisabeth was sitting alone in her cabin waiting for my call. Where was Albert? Had he really gone so docilely to the promenade deck? It wasn't likely. I had to get to Elisabeth quickly.

"Irene! Where the hell is the owl?"

"You see ..."

She stopped, her body suddenly tense. She sat very still, her hand upraised to silence me. I felt a chill creep up my back.

"Albert!" she called.

There was no answer. We both were absolutely motionless. After a moment she whispered, "Did you hear something?"

"No."

Not satisfied, she got to her feet, finger to lips, and silently crossed the room to the open door leading into the darkened sitting room. She stood there peering into the other room for a moment. Then she relaxed and turned.

"It must have been someone in the corridor."

"Irene ..."

"I can't bear this! I couldn't live a life like this. I don't understand how people can be such monsters. There must be—" She got hold of herself and suddenly smiled. "I wouldn't know what to do with myself now that the party is over!" Ruefully she indicated her costume. "I've been wearing this all my life, I guess."

"Irene!" I said urgently. "Surely you're not going to hold out now. There is someone whose life is in danger unless we get that owl to Devois."

"The owl? Oh, yes."

I was struck by a strange expression in her eyes. She stood there in the doorway facing me, looking at me, but speaking through and beyond me.

"Albert is a monster. I will tell you ..."

She lurched forward. There was no surprise in her eyes. She looked at me, kept looking at me, as though trying to say something she could not utter. In her brief black skirt she was like a child doing a senseless step to strange music. She half turned, her head still twisted around to me, her eyes filled in that last moment with the horror of final and complete realization. She kept on turning, slowly turning, her knees bending as she turned. The knife looked absurd buried between her shoulder blades, thrusting forth from the little red blouse. On her knees she reached for the doorframe, but her hand never touched it. She toppled forward on the pink carpet. Her hand crept away from her body, opened toward me, then moved convulsively and was still.

Too stunned for thought or motion, I stood there with my hand frozen on the revolver in my pocket. Albert stepped over Irene's body. He took the gun away from me as though I were a helpless child. He pushed me roughly toward the sitting room. I stumbled along ahead of him, still caught in a dream.

Only vaguely was I aware of his furious words. "You did it! If it hadn't been for you ..."

I managed somehow to get my feet over the white still hands, the black skirt, the silly little beret, still slanted rakishly to one side of her head. A monotone deep down within me said in cold despair, This is the way it will end. And I thought of the other woman who would wait by the telephone until it was too late.

Numb with shock and lost hope, I stepped over the threshold into the darkened room. She knew, I thought; she knew he was there. She knew it would happen. She couldn't have gone on living, knowing....

He prodded me with my own gun. I half expected a shattering explosion. Instead he pushed me forward.

Behind me he reached for the light switch. The sitting room was suffused in a soft pink glow. At the same moment a clock somewhere in the room began to chime three.

The woman in the costume of the Renaissance princess who stood facing me drew aside the tiny gold mask.

"It's three o'clock," she said. "The masquerade is over."

Chapter Seventeen

SEPTEMBER 11, 7:00 A.M.

Behind me Albert said, "She's dead."

"The fortunes of war," Elisabeth said. Her voice expressed a cool formality; the sort of regret one might profess at the news of the death of a hopelessly insane criminal.

Dead, I thought. Reason and decency and emotion. Dead. Everything.

"It took courage on my part," Albert said. "You know, I was rather fond of her."

"Thank God you were never weak, Albert."

She looked at me as she spoke to him, looked at me with cold contempt.

"I couldn't expect others to sacrifice if I were willing to compromise for my own pleasure," he said. "I have never tolerated self-indulgence in others. Still, I cannot help feeling that perhaps it was not necessary."

"Nonsense," she said. "It was an execution. The weak and the foolish can be fatally dangerous. And we must not waste our energies in academic regrets."

"What about him?"

"Mr. McLean will accomplish the act that he has been preparing for himself for some time now. Namely, suicide."

"Yes. Quite."

"That clever French detective will be able to put two and two together in practically no time at all. Titled British lady murdered by blackmailer. Blackmailer commits suicide when he realizes he cannot hope to escape. Monsieur Devois will be pleased to have closed the case with such ease."

They were discussing me as though I already didn't exist. At the moment I felt they were right.

"I can't imagine where Joseph is," she said. "But we must hurry. That jade owl must be somewhere in her room. You'd better get busy, Albert. Give me the revolver. I'll watch him."

Albert gave her the gun. She held it lightly. Albert went off to the bedroom. I could hear him in there pulling out bureau drawers.

I stood in the middle of the room feeling as though I were suspended in the middle of some vast and endless night. She regarded me thoughtfully for a moment, then said in a low voice, "Like Albert, I too have my regrets."

I opened my mouth to say something, but no sound came forth. There were literally no words in any language strong enough to express my feelings.

"I am a child of my times," she said with a sigh. "Ten years from now I will be able to afford the luxury of— how shall I say— enjoying a man like you."

"Ten years from now," I managed to say, "you'll either be rotting in prison or be merely an unpleasant memory in some persons' minds."

She smiled tolerantly. "No," she said. "This time there will be no mistakes. This time we will win."

"Never."

"Oh, come now. Do you imagine people like yourself will be able to stop us?"

"Not people like me. Better people than me. By the millions!"

She laughed. "You rather attracted me— in the way that something directly one's opposite is sometimes attractive. Your weakness, your stupidity... I almost blundered into your bed last night in your stateroom. I had sense enough not to give in to a passing fancy. You would have known, you see. Any man who has ever slept with me knows what sort of person I am."

"I bet! Like bedding down with a she-goat!"

She stopped smiling. "You don't seem to realize that I am admitting a certain feeling for you." She lowered her voice. "Even now ..."

"Even now you might save me! Is that it?"

"Don't speak so loud. This is between us."

"And the terms?"

She shrugged. "That you learn to take orders, submit to the sort of indoctrination that would rid you of your unspeakably muddled and weak sentimentality. I could save you, Mac, even now."

"For what?"

She looked up at me with a direct and brazen explanation in her eyes.

"Captain of the guards," I said. "Chief gentleman of the bedchamber!"

"Don't be a fool! If you knew me better you would understand what a concession I am making. And it isn't entirely selfish. I am convinced that in a few months I could make a valuable addition to our organization."

I controlled myself with an effort. In an almost conversational tone of voice I said, "Is that what you told Gonzales?"

"Gonzales! That scum! Nonsense. What I told you about him was true. He imagined I was working with him. He walked into the trap like the fool he was."

"You wrote that note that brought him to the gymnasium."

"Of course. We knew he had the jade. He told me he was going to your room to get it. But we didn't know there was a missing piece."

"And you murdered him!"

She drew herself up coldly. "The word 'murder' has no place in this connection. You don't understand the seriousness of my work. The life of one individual is of no significance. Gonzales was liquidated. We stepped on him as one might step on any worm."

"But you did it!"

"No. Albert did it. We hadn't expected that you would find that note in Gonzales' cabin. You came to the pool only a few moments after it happened. Albert was hiding in the dressing room next to the body. I had to think fast— but not too profoundly. You swallowed everything I told you like candy."

"You must be insane."

"Listen to me, Mac. I haven't time to argue. Do you agree ..."

I looked down into her eyes and said calmly and distinctly, "I hate to pass it up, sweetheart, but... no, thanks!"

Fury came into her eyes like fire across ice. Her hand tightened on the gun. For a moment I thought she was going to use it on me then and there. But the fire passed away, leaving only ice.

"You are even more of a fool than I thought."

"I'm worse than a fool! There was a time when I thought that holding you in my arms was the only thing that mattered in life. Now I'd as soon wallow in a sewer with a yellow sow!"

She disregarded me completely. "Albert!" she called. "What's keeping you? Do hurry. We have this business to settle."

"All those stories about how you hated the Nazis! All those touching tales about your hard life in the Fatherland!"

She laughed. "You're as gullible as the majority of your sentimental countrymen. My father was a general in the *Wehrmacht!* He was killed by order of that court of lies at Nurnberg! He was a soldier who fell in the line of duty in a war that never ceased. I carry on. I had false papers. The story I told you was the story of a girl who died in a Hannover hospital three days before the Allies came in. I carry her name and her papers. I worked at the Folies Bergère because they thought it would lead to the confidence of important men. They were right. Then they decided it would be advantageous to marry Joseph. He needs to be kept in line."

"But why did he come to me with that cock-and-bull story of your being a traitor?"

"We wanted to test you. At one time we thought you might be even more valuable to us than you had been." She laughed. "After my report of our conversation in the library, Joseph wanted to have you liquidated immediately. But by then we realized there was something important in the jade. I thought you might lead us to it after we discovered it was not on Gonzales. And I was right. You did!"

"I?" A cold snake of horror was coiling about my heart.

"Of course." She was enjoying my misery. "I couldn't imagine who had taken the missing jade owl. Especially when you said at first that no one had been in your stateroom but the steward. And, knowing that steward is one of Devois's men, we knew all hell would have broken loose long ago if he had got it." She leaned forward and smiled. "It had us worried. Terribly worried. Until you held me so tenderly in your arms on the boat deck and whispered in my ear that Irene Harcourt had been in your cabin. It was very sweet and helpful of you."

The terrible implication seeped into me, seemed to drown all my senses in despair. There was no doubt but that I had unwittingly laid a death trap for poor Irene. At this moment it no longer mattered much to me if and when Elisabeth decided to pull the trigger of the gun. Something died in me then that never will live again. I saw in this terrible irony, just as I now saw in my former emotion for Elisabeth, the symbol of my illusion and folly. In all the time I had been describing myself as a realist, I had never been able to see reality. My realism had been no more than a faded romantic cloak from some second-rate travesty of life. My world had been a puppet world where you talked hard out of the side of your mouth about "me first" and "fast deals" and the girls you made and the next drink. I had never really experienced genuine love or hate or known the potentialities for evil in men. Or women. My behavior had been that of a Lilliputian on a stage peopled by giants.

Elisabeth must have sensed what went on in my mind. At any rate she said, "The sort of guilty tortures you are now experiencing are for a dying world. Thank God I am free of such nonsense!"

"You are free of everything that makes a human being worth while. You are free of decency and conscience. You are free of heart and love."

"*Mein Gott!* Such beautiful phrases to come from a gigolo! The righteous gigolo! You are not even worthy to be my enemy. If Gonzales was a worm, you, my friend, are a bug!"

Her beauty was like marble, and, I saw at last, as devoid of life. Like the robots who used to goose-step beneath the Roman arches of Unter den Linden, she would move, untroubled, through a cold paranoiac dream until the living took their revenge.

"Pasquela is dead," I said quietly.

Her expression didn't change, but she slowly lowered the gun to her lap. "You're lying."

"It was one way to escape you," I said. "He had a vial of poison. I envy him."

For the first time uneasiness crept into her eyes. "Albert!" she called.

"Maybe he talked to Devois first," I said.

She laughed coldly. "That's the last thing Joseph would have done. He's too aware of the centuries behind him. He would never betray them, no matter what he may have thought of me. Recently he has seemed not too happy in his work, that is true, but you do not understand him at all if you think he would ever go to Devois."

I kept on looking at her.

"Albert!" she called again. This time there was a sharp note of anxiety in her voice.

"In a moment," Albert called from the next room. He sounded impatient and nervous.

The little gilt clock ticked on in the silence. Suddenly she leaned forward. "You think I am worried with this tale of Joseph's suicide! You don't know me. I despise you! You and your kind. Weak and stupid and bungling. You and your toy planes and the bombs you dropped on our cities— all child's play! Albert knows! He knew all along. Your people will have to fight the Russians now, and then we shall see! Both sides will come to us. They will beg us for help! We know. And we shall wait and choose! Choose not a leader, but the led! We will win. Oh, yes, my friend. Hitler knew! We will win in the end! It is almost an insult to have to kill you. You are something not to be shot, but to be swept into a sewer!"

Albert came back into the room and she straightened up. "Well?"

"I don't understand," he said in a worried voice. "It's not there!"

"Don't be a fool! We know she had it. It must be there!"

"No. We're wasting time. I've looked everywhere."

"But it's got to be there! You know as well as I—"

"She must have hidden it somewhere outside the suite."

"It's intolerable!" she cried. "If you had not been so certain that Fournier would be safe, none of this would have happened. I warned you. It wasn't until you heard with your own ears—"

"So!" I said. "It was Albert who was hidden in Fournier's suite while I was there. It was he who murdered Fournier. The business trip to Lyon!"

"He told Irene he was going to Lyon. He spent the night in our suite on the floor below Fournier!" She turned angrily back to Albert. "What now? Where—"

She stopped in the middle of the sentence, suddenly alert. I too had heard the faint sound.

"What's wrong?" Albert asked.

Slowly I began edging backward toward the bedroom door.

"Albert!" she whispered urgently. "I think—"

And then she saw me. I stopped.

She brought the gun up and fired.

It was a second before I realized it had not been fired at me, but beyond me toward the bedroom door. Something hurtled past me. She fired again. The man in the uniform of a ship's officer grabbed her wrist. Behind me Albert shouted, and then suddenly the room seemed filled with men. Elisabeth broke away and got to the far corner. She crouched there, her face distorted with hatred. Once more she fired. I felt the hot stab of pain in my right leg. Just before I blacked out, I saw, floating in the fading light, the face of Louis Devois.

Chapter Eighteen

SEPTEMBER 14, 8:00 A.M.

There was a heavy fog on the lower bay. The *Dauphiné* edged slowly through the Narrows. Far below the fat little tugs poked patiently at her sides. The air was damp and cold and permeated with the odor of salt and oil and smoke.

"What are you thinking about, Mac?"

"I'm too tired to say."

"With that bandage on your leg," Lili said, "you look like something out of *Gone with the Wind*."

We stood by the rail on a deserted section of the boat deck.

"Go on," I said.

"There's not much more to tell. Lady Harcourt got me in the powder room during the masquerade. For some reason she suspected you were hiding out in my stateroom, even though I denied it. She told me that under no circumstances was I to allow you to leave the stateroom. I guess she was afraid you'd get yourself quietly shot. She told me some other things that I can't tell you. Things that women talk about."

"I can imagine."

"No, you can't. Anyway, she gave me a small package. She seemed terribly upset. She said that if anything should happen to her, I should go immediately to Devois and give him the package. Otherwise she planned to take it back the next morning. It didn't seem any more crazy than some of the other things that had been happening. Besides, I liked her. I agreed."

I didn't want to dwell too much on the picture of Irene.

"You had that package all the time you were talking to Pasquela. You never told me about it."

"I think I suspected what it was. I was afraid you'd try something foolish. I wanted to keep you safe for the night, at least."

"But you changed your mind."

"Obviously. Or you wouldn't be here to ask questions! I changed my mind the minute I came to after that upper cut to the jaw. I opened the package— I had it in that innocent-looking evening bag— and when I found the owl, I called Devois."

For a moment I said nothing. I stared off into the fog, dimly making out a dark shape that must have been Fort Richmond.

Finally I said, "It's odd that Irene should have entrusted the jade owl to you."

"Women are funny. They have invisible antennas, like butterflies, about certain things. Things like knowing how I felt about you, and—"

"Yeah!"

"What did Devois say?"

"I'll have to go back to Paris for the trial. He seems to think I won't be thrown into a dungeon or anything lurid like that, but at least I'll have to testify."

"How long will you be there?"

"No idea. I imagine they'll push it through pretty quick. There's no doubt about the outcome."

"Both of them?"

"Yes."

"I wonder if they still use a guillotine. Her head would look good in a basket!"

"Shut up, Lili."

"Let's not stay at the Ritz," she said after a moment. "Let's find a quiet little hotel on the Left Bank."

"What do you mean, we?"

"You need someone to take care of you. A homemaker."

She was smiling up at me. I thought, Why not? Why not?

"Can you cook?"

"Darling! You're so romantic! No wonder all the women—"

"I'm just weak," I said. "Loss of blood. Too tired to argue."

"Aren't you going to kiss me?"

"Maybe later. Go down to my cabin and wait for it."

"You're so good to me."

She dropped the bantering tone and put her hand in mine. "Mac," she said, "you mustn't stay here and brood. There are years ahead to think of things, you know."

"Yes," I said wearily. "All the years of my life."

"You mustn't go on blaming yourself. I talked to her. It's funny, but I had the strangest idea that she had made up her mind then. I don't think she could have gone on living with the scandal and disgrace. I don't think she could have gone on living with herself."

"I can understand that," I said.

Her hand closed on mine. "Mac! You mustn't be morbid. There are so many things we can do— good things."

"Perhaps," I said. "That's what I want to think about. You realize, of course, that Albert and Elisabeth Pasquela will be tried on a civil murder charge. Politics won't enter into it except inadvertently. They can't prove a plot against the French government. And Albert and that woman aren't the big wheels. The big wheels are still safe, plotting, making their plans...."

"Darling, please. Not now."

"Go on down, Lili. I'll be down in a few minutes. I'll be all right."

Slowly she withdrew her hand. She looked up at me very seriously. "I read somewhere, Mac, that there are no heroes any more. They're all dead on the battlefields. You're no worse than the rest of us. We're all to blame. But we suffer and we learn. We may even learn how to be good again."

She left me, walking off into the fog. Still surprised by her unaccustomed solemnity, I was aware of a faint stirring of unease at her going. I wanted her back. And I knew I would be glad when in a few minutes I held her in my arms in the silence of my cabin.

For a moment the knowledge that she would be waiting dulled the sensation of loneliness and confusion. I looked out into the swirling mist as though for an answer. Someday I'll see the pattern, I thought. Someday I'll know what Fournier meant when he spoke of Faust. Someday, perhaps, out of the senseless violence and murder and betrayal, I will even find meaning for myself.

But at the moment, meaning was as veiled and obscured as the great statue somewhere up ahead hidden for an hour in the dense morning fog.

Excerpt from Variety, *October 1, 1950:*

Talk of the street is still the decision of Mac McLean, café performer who was involved in sensational murders on the French Line's swank *Dauphiné*, to quit show business on the eve of his scheduled opening at the Persian Room and devote himself to a minor job with the United Nations. What makes this move even more inexplicable is that, despite the fact that the international case has not yet come up for trial in Paris, the publicity, far from hurting McLean professionally, has made him just about the hottest draw in the business. Comment of columnists has ranged from outright approval to hints of a cheap grandstand play. The next few weeks should tell whether the singer is in earnest or not.

Excerpt from Variety, *October 9, 1950:*

Lili Fenwick, former Royale Films star, was married yesterday afternoon in the American Church in Paris to Mac McLean.

THE END

Faces Turned Against Him

John Flagg writing as John Gearon

The gilt clock on the mantel stood at ten twenty-five and through the French windows he could see a sliver of moon. The house was very still. He went to the phone and called Laura Williams.

"Bert Mason speaking. Is Myra there?"

"Myra? No. Should she be here?"

"Dunno. Just got in from a business dinner in town. We're supposed to go to the Wilsons' party. But—no wife."

"Wives get tired of waiting, darling. Especially in this damned town! She's probably gone on ahead to the Wilsons."

"Yes, I suppose. You and Roger going?"

"Virus has caught up with Roger again."

"Too bad; give him my best," he said and hung up.

He stood there a moment, his hand still on the phone, trying to shake off a vague uneasiness. Dead leaves rustled in the wood beyond the garden.

It was a mild night for October; a humid breeze stirred the silk draperies at the open windows. He heard a faint sound in the hall and stiffened. Perkins, the Maltese cat, appeared in the doorway, froze there tail erect, blue eyes transfixed. Bert laughed and said, "It's only me, Perkins. We've both got the jitters!"

He went upstairs to change into a dinner jacket and found the bedroom in a mess. Myra's day dress was thrown over the foot of the bed; underclothes and a large damp bath towel were draped over a chair; the dressing table was a litter of powder, used Kleenex and open bottles of lotions. People had picked up after Myra all her life.

Suddenly, irrationally, a sense of bereavement overcame him, a loneliness more complete, more final than anything he had experienced even during the lost and lonely days of his childhood. Their backs are turned, he thought; their faces are averted. He stood frozen in the act of knotting his tie, unable to account for the intensity of his emotion. A night-bird shrieked, far away and totally unreal, a dream bird uttering a dream sound.

If I don't watch out, he thought, I'll be as neurotic as the rest of them.

He shook off the mood, finished dressing, regarded the result in the mirror, then went down to the car and drove to the Wilsons'. They had been asked for ten-thirty, but so far there were only a few cars parked in the long sweep of the drive. Inside the big Tudor house an orchestra was playing one of those Nineteen-Twenty tunes. Irene Wilson, trailing tulle and ribbons and bows, bustled up to meet him at the door and immediately asked, "Where's Myra?"

"I thought I'd find her here."

He looked around. The furniture had been cleared out of the big hall. Over near the stairs was a five-piece orchestra. Two or three couples were dancing and they nodded and waved. Through an archway he could see Milt at the bar.

"Oh, you know Myra," Irene said. "She probably decided to go to dinner at the Bronsons' or somewhere."

He walked through the room smiling and waving and when he got to the bar said, "Started early, you son-of-a-gun."

"No earlier than usual," Milt said. "What are you having?"

"Where's Myra?" Lillian asked over Milt's shoulder. Bert noticed she didn't look as well as usual. Her well-scrubbed casual beauty was mitigated by a tightness around her eyes and her hair was plastered and set like iron.

"Run out on me, I guess," he said with a laugh.

Milt put down his glass on the bar. "Huh?"

"She wasn't home when I got back from town. Guess she decided to go to one of the dinners."

"Myra's, not the type who fills in at the last minute," Lillian said, voice curiously flat.

"Not home," Milt said blankly. Then he shot a quick look at his wife and said to the bartender, "Same again, Jake."

"Now, Milt ..." Lillian said.

"Don't begin nagging, Lil. I've had a helluva day."

"He's been over in Hartford on what we laughingly call 'business'," Lil said. "He didn't get home until nine."

Milt grinned. "But I always do get home, don't I, baby?"

"How is business, Milt?" Bert asked.

Milt stopped smiling. "Same old crap. What's it to you?"

The guests in the vicinity stopped talking. From the end of the bar Joe Mellon said, "Take it easy, Milt."

But Milt was already moving away from them. He waved to a tall blonde in white satin who had just entered the room. "It can't be real," Milt said gayly. "I've been waiting for it all my life!"

"He doesn't mean anything," Bert said to Lillian.

"Let's dance, Bert," she said.

They moved out into the hall and Lillian said: "He didn't mean to be rude, Bert. You know he thinks you're about tops. I don't know what's got into him tonight. You may not believe it but up until today he's been on the wagon for almost three weeks."

She moved stiffly in his arms. He thought she didn't follow very well and couldn't understand it. She seemed to dance all right with other men. It was the same, though, with all of them, he reminded himself.

"Sometimes I wish we could move away from here and get a fresh start," she said. "Somewhere where he could forget the responsibility of all those ancestors hanging on the walls. No one understands him here. No one but women. And you ..."

"What's wrong, Lil? Money again?"

"Oh, it's always money. But something more—"

"You're too attractive a woman to look so worried."

"Thanks, Bert," she said mechanically. She didn't look into his eyes. He held her tighter. She didn't resist nor did she respond.

"Later," she said, "when it won't be so noticeable, walk out to the pool with me. There's something I want to talk about."

"Sure, Lil," he whispered.

Still she didn't respond. She's being careful, he thought.

As they circled the room she chattered mechanically. Bert and Myra and the Wilsons were about the only ones who asked Lil and Milt to parties anymore. The room was filling up and Lil's last year's gown looked shabby against the shimmer of new silk and moire and satin.

"That's the Bronsons' dinner party coming in now," she said. "But I don't see Myra."

"That's funny," Bert said. "Where in the devil can she be?"

And then Bert was aware that she was trembling.

"What's wrong, Lil?"

"Wrong? Nothing." Then she added quickly, "Yes, there is too. You're a damned fool, Bert. A blind ..."

He steered her into a laughing group at the foot of the stairs. She stopped whatever she had started to say but she hung on to him. With a smile he disentangled himself.

"I'm going back to the house," he said.

He left her there, tight-lipped with annoyance, and found Irene Wilson.

"I think I'll run back to the house. I'm getting worried about Myra."

"Myra? My goodness! You mean to tell me she didn't come in with the Bronsons?" She smothered a derisive smile. "Maybe she found something more amusing?"

"What does that mean?"

Irene looked flustered. She put her hand on his arm. "Dear Bert. Any woman would be lucky to have you. But Myra is very beautiful and stubborn and used to her own way. The Commodore spoiled her. You never can tell what damned fool notion—"

"She's never done anything like this before."

"Yes. Well dear, I do hope she hasn't been taken suddenly ill or something. This awful virus. Albert says he thinks the Russians... Well, here he is! He can tell you about the Russians himself."

Albert Wilson, playful in his late forties, said, "Milt's behaving like a damned oaf in the bar."

"He has such charm!" Irene said with feeling. "I don't know any man with more ..."

"Charm!" Albert said. "The man can't even hold a job."

"Myra is missing," Irene broke in.

"Missing?"

"That does sound melodramatic, doesn't it? I mean we don't know where she is. Bert's going back to the house ..."

Albert grinned. "Myra can take care of herself," he said. "Always could."

Bert started for the door. Milt intercepted him. He put his hand on Bert's arm.

"Jus' wanna say... sorry... the way I acted in the bar. We've been pals so long, and what I've done to you ...!"

Bert managed a laugh. "Forget it!"

"I'm caught," Milt said. "I'm caught on a trolley. The one that's headed for the end of the line!"

"Nonsense!"

"Nuts, not nonsense, Bertie. Nonsense is an investment banker's word. Anyway... it's true. I try to make Lil jump. There's still time for her. She wants to stick. She paid her nickel and she wants to stick."

"Lil is a fine girl. Don't forget we have a date to go fishing on Friday. And skip a few drinks, Milt. Relax."

"What I know doesn't relax me. Bert... there's something...."

"Not now."

He left Milt quickly and went to the door. When he looked back he saw Lil crossing the room towards her husband, head high, oblivious to the amused glances.

Bert thought, I wonder if there's something wrong with my heart? His pulse was too fast. There was a sick empty feeling below his chest.

Peter Kelly refused the drink and said: "Don't let your imagination get you, boy. Calm down."

"But I've tried everyone I can think of. She would never have gone off without a word. I mean, of her own free will."

Kelly, though he wore a neat business suit, sat gingerly on the expensive flowered chintz as though afraid to soil it.

"I can tell you this, Bert," he said. "After fifteen years with the cops I've learned one thing. You can never tell what a woman will do next."

Kelly, chief of police, lived in a neat Georgian house—it had cost him fifteen thousand dollars—in a section where the more prosperous 'townies' lived. But Pete didn't belong to the country club and wouldn't have dreamed of trying to join it.

"How about the maid?" he asked.

"This is her day off. She usually spends the night with her folks."

Kelly looked at the coffee table in front of the sofa. On it stood a cocktail shaker, two glasses containing the dregs of martinis, and a twist of lemon peel gone brown.

"You have a drink when you got home?"

"No. I noticed that, too. It wasn't me who drank with her. No one at Irene's party said anything about having taken a drink here with her."

"In that case maybe it was someone you don't know. I understand that Mrs. Mason was... well, sort of democratic ...?"

Bert was startled. Democratic behavior was the last quality anyone ever had attributed to Myra. He wondered what Kelly was getting at. He waited.

"I mean she was always very friendly with... well, say the bartenders at the Golden Eagle or that other roadhouse on Route 21."

Bert suppressed a smile. But suddenly he found it was not easy to explain to Kelly that sort of 'democracy.' Myra called bartenders and caddies by their first names and assumed an easy air of comradeship with them. How could he explain that it was sort of a game, a snobbish one at that.

Kelly said, "Suppose some friend dropped in unexpectedly... she might have gone off with...."

"No. She most certainly would have called Irene Wilson and left a note for me."

Rather uncertain now, Kelly lit a cigarette and tried to look reassuring. He was worried. The Masons were important people. His wife called them a 'bunch of rich bums' but they were the group that had put him in office and kept him there.

"You and the missus have any difference of opinion lately?"

"None."

"When did you see her last?" Kelly made his voice casual.

"About three this afternoon. She took the station wagon and drove into New Haven to pick up an evening gown for the party."

Bert told Kelly he had taken the Lincoln and driven into town in the late afternoon to keep a business appointment with an associate from San Francisco. He had dined at the Metropolitan Club, and had left about eight-thirty to drive back to Elm Hill. When he arrived at the house he found the station wagon in the drive and the rooms lit up, but no sign of Myra. He explained how he had gone on to the Wilsons, assuming that Myra had joined someone for dinner. He told Kelly about the odd moment of uneasiness as he stood dressing in the bedroom.

"Uneasy? About what?"

"I don't know. Just one of those feelings. When I came back from the Wilsons and found she wasn't here the uneasiness increased. That's when I called you."

"Have you looked to see if anything is missing?"

"I thought of that. There's nothing missing. Only a diamond bracelet from Myra's jewel box but I imagine she would have worn that with her evening gown."

"If she changed."

"She must have. The box from the dress shop in New Haven was lying on the floor of the bedroom."

"Any relatives she might have gone to ...?"

"She has no immediate family."

Kelly stood. He tapped his cigarette in the direction of the ashtray but it missed and the ashes fell to the rug. He felt the color rising to his face. He took a deep breath and said; "Now I don't want to scare you, Bert... My hunch is she'll turn up with one of those simple explanations that only a woman could think of... but...." He stopped, stooped over, feeling clumsy, and stubbed out the cigarette... "It's always wise to take every precaution. I'm going to check on all the bars and roadhouses in the vicinity. After all, a woman in formal dress would be noticed. I'm going to set up a state wide alarm. And I'm going to ask for volunteers to search the woods."

"The woods!"

Kelly drew himself up. He felt more assured, noting the sudden panic in the other man.

"Now, take it easy. Don't touch anything in this room. I'll have Denby come up and take fingerprints... especially the cocktail shaker and glasses. I think when we find out who was here...."

He patted Bert's shoulder. "We're going to do everything in our power. Don't worry. She'll be home safe and sound in a few hours."

Bert wondered: would she?

Lil opened the door. She wore an old tweed skirt and a cashmere sweater and a single strand of pearls. She had lost her healthy outdoor look though. Her eyes dilated and she said rather breathily: "Oh, it's you, Bert. Come in."

Her living room was a litter of Early American, cigarette butts and yesterday's papers.

"Have you heard anything?" she asked tensely.

"Not a word."

"But my God, Bert, she's been gone almost twenty-four hours. She can't just have walked off the face of the earth. What's the matter with Kelly, anyway? Milt always did say he was a bootlicking lughead!"

"I don't know," he said wearily. "I've been out in the woods all night with the searching party. I managed to get a couple of hours sleep after breakfast. Is Milt in?"

"No. He lost the job with the wholesale food people, you know. Spent too much time chewing the rag with his customers. He's gone over to see some friend of Harry's in Middletown. It's to sell insurance again... if he gets it!"

"It's a shame," Bert said, "with his brains."

"Oh, we get along," she said defensively. "If only the cats—and I mean the male variety—would let up on him. He drinks a little and he likes people and women find him attractive. He's not the world's greatest business genius but to hear them talk you'd think ..."

"It's not fun for you," he said.

She looked directly at him for a moment then turned away. "I understand Milt," she said quietly.

"You're a remarkable woman, Lil," he said.

"I don't know why I'm talking about myself... with you worried half to death and...."

"I came to warn you," Bert said.

"Warn?" She clasped her hands tight then unclenched them and brushed a stray hair from her forehead. "I could use a drink," she said quickly, "How about you?"

It was bourbon-on-the-rocks in Elm Hill that year. She got rid of half her drink before she said, "O.K. Shoot. I can take it now."

"There's going to be a mess," Bert said. "Unpleasant gossip."

"Milt and Myra?"

"How did you know?"

Lil hesitated a moment, started to say something, stopped and said instead, "I've known for a long time. That's what I wanted to talk to you about at the party last night. It's a mess, all right, and someone's bound to be hurt."

"Kelly called me a half hour ago. He discovered that Milt met Myra at four yesterday afternoon at a roadhouse outside Southport. The Golden Eagle. They spent a couple of hours there drinking."

"God!" she said. "God, what a fool Milt can be!"

"'The business trip to Hartford!'"

"Bert," she said anxiously: "You don't think... Kelly doesn't think... I mean that there's any connection between...."

"*I* don't think so but Kelly may."

"That's ridiculous!"

"That's what I told him."

"I don't understand you!" she said in a shrill voice. "You seem to be taking it awfully calmly... I mean about Milt and Myra."

"Listen, Lil," he said quietly. "We all grew up in this town together... Milt and Myra and me... Milt is my best friend; always has been. Myra was sorry for the way things always seemed to break badly for him. She listened to his troubles. If he felt like drinking, it's just like Myra to keep him company. There is nothing else between them!"

"Saint Bertram!" she said with an incredulous laugh. "Myra certainly has the wool pulled over your eyes."

"You don't like her, do you, Lil?"

"That's neither here nor there. But to tell me she 'listens to his troubles!' Where the hell does that put me?"

"Sometimes a man can say things to another woman that he couldn't say to his wife."

"Oh, Bert! Really!" She finished her drink in one gulp. "Well, never mind what you believe or don't believe. Whatever else there is, I do know Milt had nothing to do with... with Myra's disappearance."

"I know that," he said. "I've already told Kelly he's wasting his time. And, I don't want a filthy scandal."

"Kelly should have more sense!"

"Please forgive me for saying this," Bert said quietly, "but we've got to face facts. In Kelly's set a married man meets another man's wife in a roadhouse for only one purpose ..."

"I know about that. It isn't his fault!"

"Lil!"

"I'm sorry, Bert. Myra was lucky to have found a guy like you."

"*Was* lucky?"

The color drained from her face. "Why did I say that...?" Then, "Let's face it, Bert. Most of the better citizens... the male most anyway... hate Milt. They hate him for enjoying life and odd ducks and misfits and fishermen and hunters and bums around the bars and truck-drivers in all-night lunchrooms. They hate him for not being a stuffed shirt like his father. And, most of all, they hate him because he confuses them."

Bert sighed. "If only Milt were a little more cooperative." He got up. "Kelly is coming over to get him this evening."

"Get him!" Lil put her glass down with a bang.

"Just routine," Bert said. "He wants to take his fingerprints. There were a couple of martini glasses and a shaker in the living room. Kelly thought maybe Milt came back with Myra from the roadhouse and ..."

"Fingerprints," she said. "My God, Bert... that sounds as though they think... They couldn't. Not Milt! Bert, they don't think... I mean with Myra... something bad."

He put his hands to his eyes, suddenly overcome with an overpowering sense of weariness. He didn't want to think.

"Oh, Bert," she said in a whisper.

At the door he turned. "I'll let you know... if ..." He went out.

The last sunlight, blood red, slanted through the French windows and across the rug that the Commodore's father had brought back from China. Hortense came in from the kitchen.

"There's something," the maid said in a frightened voice. "You'd better come, Mr. Mason."

Bert threw down his paper and followed her. Through the small window over the sink he saw the group of men coming out of the woods. One of them broke away from the others and came running through the garden. Bert met him on the terrace outside the kitchen.

"What's wrong?"

It was Red Smiler, the mechanic at Frost's garage. He stopped dead in his tracks. "I gotta call the Chief," he said.

"What's happened?"

There twas sweat on Smiler's forehead. He didn't look at Bert.

"I gotta call," he repeated evasively.

He went past Bert into the kitchen and through the pantry to the hall. He picked up the phone and got through to Kelly.

"Better get right over, Chief," he said. Then after a moment, "Yeah." He hung up, aware of Bert standing there behind him, and didn't turn.

"You've found her," Bert said.

Smiler didn't answer.

"She's dead," Bert said.

Smiler cleared his throat and said, "I'm sorry, Mr. Mason... Jesus, I'm sorry!"

Bert went across the hall into the living room and sat on the couch. Smiler followed him to the door, looking scared.

"Tell me," Bert said. "How ...?"

"Buried in that hollow back of Flat Rock."

"My God!"

"The side of her head," Smiler said and stopped.

"Tell me."

"I'd better not say anything more until the Chief comes."

He turned away and a moment later Bert saw him standing on the edge of the terrace by the drive. After a bit, Kelly arrived and the two talked in low voices. Kelly shook his head, ran his hand across his throat and looked apprehensively towards the French windows. Bert knew he dreaded coming in. He made it easier for Kelly by going out to him on the terrace.

"She was dressed for a party," Kelly said in a dazed voice. Then as though shocked by his own words, "You go inside, Bert. I don't want you to go out there. There's nothing you can do for the moment. We're going to get the son-of-a-bitch!"

"It must have been a lunatic."

"I'm working fast from now on in. I may want you to go with me when I get back."

"With you, yes," Bert said. "I think maybe ..." He leaned back against the wall. "It's all right, now. I'll go inside."

The light was fading fast. He went to the living room. On the coffee table lay a mystery book from the circulating library. Myra must have taken it out. I must return it before it mounts up, he thought.

After a while, Kelly came back from the woods. He looked pale and his mouth was set. He carried something bulky in his right hand, something wrapped in what looked like an old torn shirt.

"Maybe you'd better come with me," he said. "You have a right ..."

Bert stood, very careful and stiff, like a robot. "Certainly," he said. "Anything."

"Don't say anything, Bert," Kelly said as they went up the walk. "Let me handle it."

Lil answered the knock. She looked from Bert to Kelly, then to the bundle held ever so lightly in his hand.

"Sorry to bother you," Kelly said. "Is Mr. Richards in?"

"Yes," she said. "But he's in bed. I had the doctor right after you brought him home. He's running a temperature."

"Mind if I look around?"

"Look around?" Her voice rose an octave. "I certainly *do* mind. This isn't visiting day at the museum!"

Kelly walked right in past her. Startled, Lil said, "What does this mean, Bert? What's happened? What does he want?"

"Come on, Bert!" Kelly called with the warning in his voice.

She turned in the doorway to face Kelly, still not entering the room herself.

"It's Myra," she said.

"Where does your husband keep his tools?" Kelly asked.

"Tools?" She was very white now. "Where he's always kept them, of course," she said. "In the cellar."

Evasion would have been useless. Everyone knew about Milt's hobby. Kelly started for the cellar door.

"Look here, Pete Kelly," Lil said, "this is pretty damned high-handed!"

"What are you waiting for, Bert?" Kelly's voice was sharp.

Bert turned reluctantly and followed him. Kelly beckoned Bert to descend first. As they went down they heard Milt call, "What is it, Lil?" And Lil's toneless answer, "You'd better come down."

The workroom contained a long table with an electric saw and a lathe at one end. On the far wall, hanging on separate hooks, was an elaborate set of tools.

Kelly looked around the room, then seemed to lose interest. Milt came down the cellar stairs and into the workroom clutching a rather soiled bathrobe over his pajamas.

"What goes on?" he demanded.

Kelly spoke quietly, "You still deny going back for a cocktail with Mrs. Mason?"

Milt's shoulders sagged. He said, "I suppose you found my fingerprints on that damned glass. I was there."

"They were your fingerprints all right. How come you finally admitted being at the roadhouse with Mrs. Mason but went on denying having gone back to the house with her?"

Milt said nothing.

Lil said, "He didn't want to hurt Bert."

"Hurt him? In what way?"

"Oh, don't be a fool," Lil said. "Milt's going back to the house with her would have looked strange ..."

"Shut up, Lil!" Milt said. The color rose to his face. "I had a drink with Myra," Milt said doggedly. "Bert wouldn't mind that. I lied because I know the way the Elm Hill mind works. And, Bert ..."

"You made a mistake, Milt," Bert said. "You should have told Pete the truth. There was no reason not to."

"What did you and Mrs. Mason talk about at the Golden Eagle?" Kelly asked.

Milt hesitated and then said, "She was interested in insurance. We had a discussion."

"According to the bartender it was a pretty heated discussion!"

"What are you getting at!" Lil said. "What the hell are you getting at?"

Kelly pointed to the wall where the tools hung.

"One of your tools is missing, Milt," he said quietly.

Milt looked at the wall. After a moment he said, "That's funny. I hadn't noticed before. My wrench is gone."

"Be careful!" Lil said.

"I found your wrench for you, Milt," Kelly said.

He drew back the cloth from the bundle he held in his hand. There was the wrench with the blue steel handle.

"Found it? Where?"

"In a grave," Kelly said. "In a grave with Myra Mason's body. Get dressed; you're under arrest!"

After the maid had cleared the luncheon dishes, Kelly lit a cigarette. "What's happening now is more important than any silly bridge game," he said. "I can't play, that's all there is to it."

"Madge Roony will never forgive me if I have to call like this at the last minute. It just isn't done."

"I've got a red-hot murder case on my hands."

"Those bums!" Mrs. Kelly said vehemently. "It's no wonder one of them got murdered. Anyway, the way you've bungled the case!"

"Bungled?"

"Milt Richards never killed her!"

"Women!" Kelly said. But he looked troubled. "What makes you so sure? He lied about being with her. His fingerprints were found on the cocktail glass. His wrench was found ..."

"I don't care whether you caught him with a bomb in his pocket," Mrs. Kelly said with supreme irrelevance. "He didn't do it!"

"But what have you got to go on?"

"What you men never heard of," she said. "Common sense."

Kelly sighed and pushed back his chair.

"Maybe you think it was Bert Mason killed his own wife?"

"Maybe," she said. "More likely you'll find a jealous woman behind it. Just wait …"

"That's what I can't afford to do," he said. "I'm driving over to the county coop with Bert Mason this afternoon."

He pushed aside the velvet tassel on the archway separating the dining room from the hall.

"You just pick up that phone and call Madge Roony. It's getting so no one will ask us any more. Why did I ever marry a cop!"

Automatically, Kelly went and picked up the phone and stood there beneath the reproduction of the *Horse Fair* and tried to still the nagging headache. "It's too pat," he thought. "Even a moron couldn't be that stupid. I wonder …"

"I never thought I was a coward," Lil said. "But I can't go into the village to shop. I can't face them."

The midday sun filtered through a low hanging haze; the air was sultry. They sat in the little arbor near the kitchen door of the house on Magnolia Street. Lil's face was pinched from lack of sleep. Bert looked wan and his pallor was accentuated by the black tie and arm band.

"People are talking about your paying for Milt's lawyer. Imagine that!"

"Let them talk," he said.

"I saw him this morning," she said. "I behaved badly. I wasn't much of a help. Here he is in terrible danger and yet I let him annoy the hell out of me. There's some masochism in him, Bert.… I guess it's always been there. I think some part of him rather enjoys this whole thing. It's as though he regards it as the logical conclusion to some horrid comedy."

Above them a gull floated stiffly over the tree tops.

Presently Bert said, "Milt is a boy."

Lil said nothing. She seemed to be waiting.

Bert stiffened his arm, pulled down the white cuff, adjusted a cuff-link.

"He's never accepted responsibility," Bert went on. "We both are fond of him… we always will be. But …"

"Yes?"

"You need someone you can depend on," he said, casually, as though he did not expect his words to be taken seriously.

She threw her cigarette into the dead flowers on the edge of the garden and stood.

"There's a strange thing happening in town. Especially among the women. Despite all the evidence, there's a growing feeling that Milt didn't do it."

"I know," he said. "That may help."

"Who next?" she asked in a tight voice. "Someone did it."

Bert sighed and watched the gull floating like plywood and paper over the weed-choked garden.

"I want you to feel ..." he began, and stopped.

Without turning, still in that tight voice, Lil said, "It's getting colder."

"I guess you know," he said.

He followed her then into the kitchen and after a few minutes left to join Kelly.

The windows were up and the heater was on. An hour after noon, cold weather had descended suddenly on New England. The road to Bridgeville and the county jail was like a ribbon of toothpaste squeezed snakelike across the dull brown landscape.

Kelly had been smoking ever since they had left Elm Hill. There were crooked lines of worry across his broad forehead. For a long time the two men were quiet but after a while Kelly said, "I'd like you to tell me, Bert, just why you're so damned sure Milt didn't do it."

"The whole case against Milt is based on the supposition that he was having an affair with my wife. That I know to be completely untrue."

Kelly kept looking straight ahead. Rather painfully he said "Can you be so certain?"

"Yes," Bert said. "Myra would have laughed at the idea."

"This may sound funny," Kelly said after a minute. "But you know, damn it all, Bert, your attitude about Milt is almost *too* Christian."

"Nothing of the sort. Just common sense."

"Common sense!" Kelly repeated unhappily, remembering when last he had heard that word. "You're a great friend of Mrs. Richards?"

"A friend, yes. She's Milt's wife, after all." Bert gave Kelly a quick glance. "I've known Lil for eight years. Ever since Milt brought her home to Elm Hill as his wife."

"What's your opinion of her. I mean off the record?"

Bert's hesitation was barely noticeable. Then he said carefully: "I think she is an exceptionally fine woman. Although she was twenty-eight when she married Milt, I don't think she quite realized ..."

"What do you mean?"

"Let's face it, Kelly. Milt is not the marrying type. He met Lil when he was stationed at Wright Field during the war. They only knew each other a few weeks before they were married. She came here to Milt's town... a stranger... and Elm Hill is not an easy place for an outsider."

"It's not always easy for an insider," Kelly said with sharpness.

"Yes," Bert said. And then after a moment, "I think there were scenes in the beginning. I suppose there would have been with any high-spirited woman."

"Scenes about other women?"

Bert looked unhappy. He didn't answer.

"Then she was jealous of him!"

"I suppose you might say so. Not with Myra, of course. They were friends, Lil and Myra."

Kelly made no comment. Bert lowered his window and threw out a half-finished cigarette. His hand was shaking.

Just after midnight, Albert Williams came home from a meeting of the House Committee of the Elm Hill Country Club. His wife was propped among her pillows reading. Albert grinned at her and said, "Woman's intuition, indeed!"

Irene cocked one eye over the book.

"That shows some sort of secret resentment."

"Not at all. The rat confessed at ten o'clock tonight."

"What rat, dear?" she asked sweetly. "There are so many."

"I mean Milt Richards. He did it all right. He broke down and confessed to everything."

Irene let the book fall into her lap. "He must have been drugged."

"Don't be ridiculous. You can't very well crawl out of this one."

Irene thought a moment. "It's perfectly simple. He's protecting someone."

"Ye gods! Who?"

"Lil."

He laughed. "You women never give up, do you?"

"I can't say I blame her for hitting Myra over the head with a wrench," she said. "But I do think burying her was a bit too much!"

"Just a bit," he said. "You look like peaches and cream among all those pillows."

"Oh, Albert! Sometimes I think I'll send in an appendix about you to the Kinsey report."

"Sometimes I suspect you have a vulgar mind."

"Albert! Well... I'm glad I've convinced you about Lil, anyway."

Albert groaned.

Bert was late. Now, just a little before six, he drew up before the house on Magnolia Street. A large moving van stood parked outside.

He found Lil standing in the middle of the living room surrounded by half-packed trunks and packing cases. He stepped aside to let Hank Borden and his helper pass. They were carrying a table.

"I'm sorry...." Bert said, "I was in New Haven."

"It's all right. As long as you came." She wore a simple house dress and no makeup. Her hair hung in wisps from her forehead.

"What's this all about?"

"I'm going away," she said. She was close to tears.

"I'm sorry to hear that," he said. He took out a cigarette and lit it.

"It made me feel better," he said, "to find your message at the house."

"I suppose you think it's rotten of me. I'm deserting Milt."

Bert said nothing.

"It was like waking up from a bad dream. Everything I've lived has been a lie. Milt was never the man I thought him to be at all. He is warped and hideous. He's a liar and a cheat and a murderer."

He sat down on the couch. She went to the window and stood there with her back to him.

"Yesterday in the garden ..." he said.

"Oh, Bert."

"Don't go, Lil," he said.

He was waiting for her to turn. Now as she stood there, so still and tense, she was like the others, back turned, face averted.

"People think I'm cold and unfeeling," he said. "I think you know that isn't true."

"I believe you're capable of... capable of very great emotion," she said. Still she didn't turn.

"I'm like other people," he said. "I'm ..." He stopped and in a changed voice said, "How about some light?"

"I moved into the Inn today," she said. "I had the electric company turn off the power this afternoon."

He couldn't understand why she didn't turn.

"Did you hear what I said, Lil?"

"I think so," she said in a small voice. And now she turned. Her hands were clasped tight in front of her and her whole attitude expressed some sort of decision. "I believe you're just being kind. You'll never get Myra out of your mind."

"Myra was a bitch," he said.

And once having said it he continued compulsively, "I knew all about her and Milt."

"Yes," she said quietly as though what he had admitted was natural and completely acceptable. "But Bert, why did you pretend to Kelly... to everyone... that you thought there was nothing between them?"

"You must understand that, my dear. I think it's pretty obvious."

"You mean," she said carefully, "they might have suspected you, had there been a jealousy motive?"

He shrugged. "It was the better part of discretion."

"And you've always hated Milt!"

He hesitated a moment. "Yes," he finally said, "I think so. Always. Now that I know how you feel about him I can tell you this."

"It wasn't just because of Myra. It was all the others, too." Her voice was soft, almost kind.

"The others?"

"You never could understand how a worthless citizen like Milt was preferred by women to a distinguished character like yourself!"

Bert sat up straight.

"What's the matter with you?"

"You never could understand how Milt always won. Or why women sense the... the slug in you."

There were footsteps in the hall. Bert started to rise.

"Stay there," Lil said sharply. "There's more I have to say."

Hank Borden appeared in the doorway.

"That's all we can take tonight, Mrs. Richards," he said. "It's after six now. We'll get the rest of the stuff in the morning."

"Oh, Hank," she said, "... I didn't think you'd be through so early."

"The truck's full up."

She looked at Bert and then back to Hank and then said, "Well, then... yes. Yes, I suppose. Yes."

Her hesitant manner was so obvious that Borden said, "Anything wrong, Mrs. Richards?"

Before she could answer, Bert said in a light voice, "Mrs. Richards has been very upset, Hank. I'm sure she'll be all right now."

"I'm all right," Lil said. "You go ahead, Hank. Rita will give you hell if you're late to dinner."

"You ain't kidding," he said.

During the last part of the conversation Bert had walked to the window. He moved very carefully as though afraid to jostle a table or a chair in the darkness. He stood there where Lil had been, looking out to the lawn and the street. A street light had just been turned on, shining metallically through the bare limbs of the elm. He watched Hank stride down the sidewalk and hop into the truck beside his assistant. The truck drew off into the gathering gloom.

Bert touched the windowpane then looked at the finger as though he had been burned.

"So," he said wearily "You are the others."

She thought she'd misunderstood him. What he said made no sense.

"Even in the garden yesterday," he said, "you were laying a trap for me."

"Yes." Her voice shook with anger or fear or maybe both. "You couldn't really believe I would desert Milt. Even your warped ego couldn't really have accepted the fact that I thought Milt killed Myra. I knew... always... that he was innocent."

"Innocent!" he said harshly. "That filthy goat!"

"You thought you'd get rid of them both and you nearly succeeded!"

"Nearly?"

"And then in the end you thought you'd finally take away from him the one thing... the one person he loved... that's all you cared about. You had no emotion for me. It was simply to prove an insane point!"

"Insane?"

"For years your feeling for Milt has been psychopathic!"

"You forget," he said dryly, "Milt confessed."

"He confessed yesterday evening, a half hour after you had visited him. Somehow or other you convinced Milt that I had killed Myra. He confessed to protect me. You had to have that confession because you knew that despite the circumstantial evidence, Kelly was beginning to doubt that Milt had done it."

"You believe I killed Myra?"

"I know it," she said. "I think deep down I've known it all along. Ever since you came to warn me that Kelly had found out about Milt and Myra's meeting at the roadhouse... I knew you were lying when you said you believed there was nothing between them. It wasn't difficult to figure out why."

"No one will believe you."

"I don't know when you discovered about Milt and Myra. You must have known there was something before you married her. But you thought you had taken her away from Milt and that pleased you. Myra was quite a catch! But she married you for no other reason than that it was the sort of match she was expected to make... whatever her extra-curricular activities. She wouldn't let Milt alone when he tried to break it off after your marriage. And she held him by threatening to tell you everything. Milt considered you his best friend. He knew how it would hurt you. He tried to keep it from you and tried to break off with Myra. But she was a bitch if there ever was one. Even Milt's marriage to me made no difference. I imagine it took you some time to discover the truth and of course, I have no idea when you started to plan to kill her and implicate Milt as the murderer. But it was certainly planned in cold blood. You stole the wrench from Milt's toolroom... that must have been simple enough since you had the run of the house. You dug the grave in the woods. You arranged to have that business appointment in New York on the day you knew Milt was meeting her at the Golden Eagle.... How you discovered he was meeting her isn't important... probably you listened at one of the telephone extensions."

"You've figured it out fairly well," he said. "But who will believe you?"

"It's always puzzled me," she said, "what there was about you that revolted me even when I used to feel guilty about it. It's something inhuman about you."

To her surprise, he didn't respond in anger. Instead: "You see... My mother... Well, people here can tell you about her. She was beautiful and cold and she hated me because she had never wanted a child. As a child, I was always knocking on walls of ice. I had dreams in which the faces of people were always averted. Milt had all the faces turned towards him. Even as a kid he seemed to attract love. Why do I tell you this?"

"Don't," she said. "I don't want to hear! Did you think you could attract love through murder?"

He sighed. "Perhaps. I don't know. I bought an artist's smock and rubber gloves the day I drove to town for my business appointment. I left the club at eight, drove back fast. I had to be sure no one else was there with her so I walked in across the terrace and saw her on the sofa in that low-cut green thing they found her in. She looked like a Broadway tramp. She looked up from her book and with that fake smile of hers, said, 'Darling! What fun! You're home so early!'

"'I've got a surprise for you, Myra.'

"I went back to the car, put on the smock and the rubber gloves and took Milt's wrench from the rear. Then I returned to Myra ...'"

He shrugged. Easily he started to move towards Lil.

"Don't come near me!" she cried. "You don't seem aware of the consequences. I'm going to Kelly and ...'"

"So you've not confided in him?"

"No," she said. And then quickly, her voice rising, "Why?"

"I'm due at the Wilsons for dinner in a few minutes," he said. "I don't want to be late. I haven't much time."

"Time?" She looked over her shoulder into the black hall. "Bert! You're not that much of a fool. The furniture men saw you here."

"You fell down the steps after I left. You broke your neck."

With a sob of fear she stumbled out into the dark hall. She got to the front door, actually had the knob half turned before he caught her from behind. His arm closed around her neck and a hand covered her mouth. He drew her back powerfully. When she realized he was dragging her towards the kitchen she stopped fighting. It was all over now.

Bert kicked open the kitchen door and stepped across the threshold.

The room was suddenly ablaze with light. He let go of Lil and stood there. Lil staggered back against the wall. Through sobs, she cried, "I told you so, Pete! I told you I'd trap him if you gave me the chance."

Kelly, deathly pale, part of his world destroyed, said, "Milt will be free this evening."

Bert regarded the other men in the room with remote indifference. "Don't try to escape," Kelly said. He flushed as though ashamed of the melodramatic phrase.

Except for Lil's sobbing, there was no sound. Then Kelly cleared his throat. He looked like a man who had sustained a deep personal loss.

"Well, Bert...."

"Don't call me that," Bert said coldly. "You presume on a friendship that existed only in your mind."

Kelly's head went back as though he had been slapped.

"Come on!" he said harshly.

The men closed in on Bert. He turned a blank empty face to Lil and said, "It's as it's always been. In the end Milt wins!"

THE END

The Lady and the Cheetah

By John Flagg

Chapter One

When I opened my eyes I saw gilt-edged paneling and silk draperies at long windows. There was no doubt that someone had stuffed my head with oily rags. With some effort and only lethargic curiosity, I managed to twist around on the rumpled pillow. Sitting beside the bed was a young woman who obviously was not Florence Nightingale. She was a cool-looking blonde in a sheath-like gold gown with a neckline that plunged to China.

"Get up, you slob," she said sweetly. "We're going to the Casino."

There was a faint echo of Bow bells in her accent. I thought, All I need is a blonde cockney!

"Who are you?"

"Loretta," she said patiently.

"I don't know any Lorettas."

"Now then, Ducky, no need to be nasty, is there?"

"Where am I?"

"The Riviera. A suite in the Hotel Carlton at Cannes, to be exact."

"Oh, my God!"

I closed my eyes, hoping that when I opened them the blonde and the gilt-edged paneling would be gone. "What day is this?"

"Thursday."

"It can't be! My boat sails on Wednesday."

"The *Ile de France* went without you, sweetie. The captain was awfully dull about waiting around Le Havre for you a couple of days."

I groaned. "As James Durante, Esquire, would say, I've been sabotaged!"

"I've never met this Mr. Durante," she said quite seriously. "You said you didn't care if the ship sailed without you. You couldn't have been that spiffed."

"You don't know! I didn't marry you, did I? Sometimes I do when I'm spiffed."

"I wouldn't dream of taking advantage of a gentleman when he's in his cups," she said elegantly. "I'm not that sort."

"What else have I done?" I kept my eyes closed, prepared for the worst.

"Really, Ducky!"

"Don't call me Ducky. My name, as you probably know, is Rafferty Valois. And if you didn't know, don't make any cracks about having two last names. I'm sensitive about my name. Where did we meet?"

She fished out an unlikely-looking case from a sequined bag and lit a gold-tipped cigarette. She tilted her head like a movie queen and said, "You're a cad, but you're cute. We met two nights ago in the Ritz bar in Paris. I'd just had a row with my gentleman from Glasgow. He's very big in ships, you know, but a bloody boor the minute he gets a whiff of the Champs Elysées. You didn't like him. He didn't like you. You seemed to feel he was mistreating me. I went off with you and we did the rounds of the night spots and then you thought it would be fun to hop down here for a couple of days. So we took the Blue Train and—"

"Jesus! You must have money."

"Me?" She smiled. "Not a shilling."

"Why, that's wonderful," I said. "You couldn't have awakened me to better news. Very sweet of you. Be a nice girl even though you are poverty-stricken and order me a Bloody Mary from the bar."

Outside the windows a moon hung in the sky over the Côte d'Azur. I looked at my watch. It was ten-five. Then I closed my eyes again and tried to think. Nothing happened. The few innocent souls left from whom I might borrow money were conveniently out of my mind.

After she had ordered the Bloody Mary and hung up I asked her to bring my wallet from the dressing table. She moved as she talked, deadpan. She was one of those low-metabolism types that only England can produce. My mother's Irish ancestors and my father's French ancestors would have found her infuriating.

I counted the money in my wallet. "Exactly eighty bucks," I said.

"We shouldn't spend more than that tonight, even though it is a gala at the Casino."

"Tonight! My dear child. This is all the cash I have left in the world!"

"But someone at the Ritz bar told me you were a well-known newspaper correspondent. Can't you cable to the home office or whatever they do in the cinema?"

"There is no 'home office' for me. When I landed at Le Bourget from India there was a nasty cablegram waiting for me. I'm fired. This time for good."

She took that with a remote smile. "This is all very vulgar, I'm sure."

"Vulgar or not, you'd better take the eighty and scoot back to Paris and the daddy with the ships while the scooting is still good."

"You'd give me your last eighty dollars in the world?"

"For God's sake, don't look at me like that! It makes me think of treacle pudding."

She settled back on the gilt chair and sent a nauseating cloud of amber smoke out over the bed.

"You know," she said with all the emotion of a calculating machine, "you're not at all good-looking, really. You're rather too short and pixy-ish. Some people might like your red hair, but not I. You're extremely rude and obviously mad and you have no money."

"So?" I asked hopefully.

"So— I think I'll stick!"

"Loretta! I need you like I need another hole in the head."

"Yes," she said with stolid illogic, "I'll stick."

I looked at the night sky through the fluttering silk draperies. From somewhere came the sound of distant music floating out over the bay. I wasn't up to dealing with this remnant of the British Empire. I had other worries.

"Tell me," I said apprehensively. "What else have I done? I mean, aside from acquiring you."

"You treated half the tarts of Montmartre to champagne. You made several speeches— one very long one on the steps of the Louvre at three in the morning and another in the restaurant car of the train coming down from Paris."

"Speeches?" I muttered weakly.

"You told them all about some general out in Korea who had objected to the stories you filed and how you had been transferred to Malaya and how you got mad and sent back a ridiculous news story about a plague among the cats of Singapore and freedom of the press and you insisted on locking yourself in the gentlemen's room on the train singing 'Mad Dogs and Englishmen' until they had to force the door and—"

"Don't tell me any more!"

"And," she went on relentlessly, "you bought a dinner jacket from the maître d'hôtel at the Casino in Nice. See, sweetie, it's over there."

Glassy-eyed, I looked toward the offensive garment, neatly pressed and smugly waiting over the back of a chair.

"I wouldn't be caught dead in one of those things! It makes me think of my father standing in the center of the sawdust ring, bawling out the next act."

"Your people were in the circus?" she asked with a raised eyebrow.

"Damned right they were. My mother was known as 'The Irish Swallow.' The best trapeze single in the business. My old man was known as Count Valois, the most elegant barker under canvas."

"Well, I'm sure that's very nice," she said bleakly.

"You're not getting me into that soup and fish!"

"But, Rafferty! Those disgusting old tweeds you wear!"

I never allow anyone to make fun of either my name or my tweeds. In some ways the tweeds are even closer to me than my name. They've been with me a hell of along time and they're all the family I have left. But before I could think up a retort sufficient to crack the English ice, there was a knock on the door. Loretta called, "Come in," with an air of proprietorship that made me uneasy. Kissing Loretta good-by was going to be as much of a problem as finding my way out of the nasty financial spot I was in.

By the time the waiter left I had finished the Bloody Mary and managed to hoist myself into a sitting position. But the sight of the festive Loretta depressed me. The last thing I needed was a gala at a casino or another evening with this beautiful cockney. When a binge ends for me, all I want of it is in the past; none of the tawdry reminders of last night's foolishness. Besides, I had to figure a way of getting out of this de luxe hotel. The suite we were in looked like a good twenty a day or more, and I had no idea what kind of food and liquor bill had been run up.

As though she guessed my thoughts, Loretta said, "Don't worry, Ducky. There's always a silver lining. Every cloud, I always say, and let tomorrow take care of itself. Besides, I usually do rather well in casinos."

"A-pimping we will go! Not me!"

"You *are* so coarse! I didn't mean that. But gentlemen adore backing me at the roulette table, and—"

"Look, honey. I've done some pretty screwy things in my time, but I haven't yet sunk to—"

I was saved from finishing that one by the bell. The telephone, to be exact. Shakily I reached for it before Loretta could get her hand on it. "Yes?"

"Monsieur Valois?"

The voice was male and low and precise. The French accent was bad, even on the "monsieur." I said, "Yeah," and he switched over to the language that was obviously more familiar to him.

"Could I see you immediately? It's quite important."

"Who are you?"

"My name wouldn't mean anything to you, but it's Jeffery Hamden."

"How much do I owe you?"

He laughed rather uncertainly. "May I come up?"

Something said yes; something said no. I settled for the yes. I guess in the back of my mind I was hoping that the "home office" had had a change of heart.

"O.K. I'm dressing to go out, but I can give you a few minutes."

"That's very good of you indeed!" he said effusively.

And then in a lowered voice, "I should like— that is, if there's anyone with you— what I have to say is highly confidential."

"I'll be alone."

I hung up. Loretta was watching me without much interest.

"Some crank, probably," I said. "Maybe he thinks I'm still a working newspaperman and wants to give me a hot tip on De Gaulle." Then another thought struck me. "How the hell did anyone know I was here?"

"A great many people seem to know," Loretta said. "While we were lunching in the terrace café, people kept looking at you and whispering. Even Maurice Chevalier pointed you out to one of his guests."

"Was I behaving that badly?"

"No. Matter of fact, although you were bright to the gills, of course, you were acting with the dignity of a banker. I had no idea you were so well known."

"Are you kidding? I'm about as well known as the tenth starfish from the left at Brighton Beach."

"I'm simply reporting what—"

"Look, baby, I don't know what this upper-class voice wants, but how about going down to the bar and waiting for me there?"

She shrugged, took up a mink stole from the foot of the bed, draped it indifferently over one shoulder, and went to the door.

"Don't keep me waiting too long," she said. "It's possible I might end up working for the house on a percentage, basis. Cheerio."

After she had gone I managed to splash some cold water on my face and get into a dressing gown before the knock came at the door. I opened it to find a young man of about twenty-two. Right away I thought he was too good-looking for his own good; the sort of broad-shouldered Middle Western good looks that are at a premium in Europe. He wore an expensive-looking dark suit and he carried a dark Homburg and yellow gloves, which were two counts against him to begin with in my books.

"I must apologize for calling at this hour. I came directly from the Paris Express."

He didn't look or sound like a bill collector or detective. The Oxford accent was as phony as his studied nonchalance. Too suavely, he deposited the gloves and the hat on a commode and turned back to me. He seemed very intent on making an impression. He made one, all right, and it wasn't good. But then I noticed he was not quite so assured as he would have had me believe. When he lighted a cigarette his fingers trembled slightly.

When he seemed at a loss as to how to begin, I said, "Well?"

He looked at a thin gold watch on his wrist.

"It's ten-thirty," he said with a rueful smile. "At eleven-fifteen I must take the night train to Genoa. I hope to persuade you to accompany me."

"Is this to be an elopement?" I asked dryly.

He laughed. "I don't blame you for being somewhat puzzled. Although I should think that you, of all people, would be used to mystery by this time."

"I don't get it."

"Allow me to explain."

"For Christ's sake, do!"

He permitted himself to look somewhat pained. "I've had great difficulty in tracking you down, Mr. Valois. I missed you by ten minutes when your plane landed at Le Bourget from India, and I was always two cafés behind you around Paris. Then in this morning's *Paris Tribune* I saw that you were registered here at the Carlton and I hopped the first train I could get."

"Why the hell should the *Paris Tribune* be interested in where I'm registered? I've never made it before."

He smiled as though I had made a good joke. As he tried to move into a more dignified position, his feet got in his way and he looked at me furtively as though afraid I would jeer at his lack of poise. Despite the phony accent, I spotted him as an American, probably one of those types you see around the Paris night clubs and Riviera beaches with rich old women or rich old men. His next words added to this impression.

"Mr. Valois, I am secretary to the Countess Becellini."

He said it as though he were casting for God.

"So?"

"You know of her, of course?"

"Look, sonny," I said impatiently, "I know the name like I'd know the name Medici. From the history books. That's all."

"The present Countess Becellini," he said impressively, "was an American."

Suddenly it came back to me.

"I remember reading a lot about her in the tabloids fifteen years ago or so, it must be. They called her 'the Captivating Countess.' Didn't she used to go around with a tiger or something?"

"Not tigers. The Countess happens to be very fond of cheetahs," he said loftily.

"She was the toilet heiress, wasn't she?"

Jeffery Hamden looked pained. "I believe her fortune originated in plumbing fixtures. But of course she is not responsible for the manner in which her grandfather made his money."

"She may not be responsible, but she must be awfully grateful that the medicos haven't yet eliminated the actions of the alimentary canal."

"Quite!" Mr. Hamden said with all the dignity of his twenty-two years. "The Countess is one of the most fascinating women in Europe."

"Is that what you came to tell me?"

He cleared his throat and blinked and then said quickly, "Countess Becellini realizes you may be engaged in— in other activities. I don't wish to waste your time or hers, so I will come to the point. The Countess is very anxious that you come immediately to see her."

"Me? Are you sure you have the right guy?"

"I assure you," he said nervously, "that both the Countess and I are discreet. She wants me to make it clear to you that she fully appreciates the value of your time and— and your co-operation, shall we say?"

The synthetic poise was fast deserting him. I was amused to see a blush rising above the immaculate collar. When I said nothing, he stumbled on: "She understands that you might even have to postpone some other— other interests in order to— I mean to say that financially your advice and help— You see ..."

All I saw at the moment was a possible messenger from heaven in an overdressed and embarrassed young man. If the guy wasn't a mental case, he was talking about money. Just what "advice" the Countess wanted from a discredited newspaperman was hard to figure. But that was her worry, not mine.

"Where is she? Here in the hotel?"

"No. She's at her palace at Lago Maggiore."

"Lake Maggiore! In Italy? She wants me to go there?"

"I know it's presumptuous to expect— I mean on such short notice— If I'd been able to reach you in Paris— But as I say, I'm leaving in three quarters of an hour. I must be in Genoa early in the morning to meet the Countess' daughter, who is arriving back from the States on the *Vulcania*."

"What does she want to see me about?"

"The Countess doesn't confide in me," he said coldly. I bet! I thought.

"If you can't come with me tonight— and I guess it is ridiculous to think that you would— perhaps you could come in the next few days."

"Just a minute."

I walked to the window and looked down on the awning of the street café and the curving necklace of light that is the Croissant. A few gaily dressed couples were strolling on the water-front promenade beneath the palms and the lamps. Limousines and taxis moved slowly down the avenue in the direction of the Casino. The past months of anger and frustration ending with the binge and Loretta went swiftly through my mind. I didn't want to think about what I had left out there in Korea or my own hot temper and quixotic whims. This countess was probably looking for a ghost writer to help her with one of those idiotic memoirs that women like her write. At the very worst it might mean a few weeks of good lodging, food, and liquor, and at best it might mean a fat fee. Why she had picked on me was a question better left to a later date. Right now this might be one of those rare moments of good luck in my life; a way out of this expensive suite and Loretta's life.

Behind me the young man said, "The Countess is a remarkable woman. And *very* generous."

I turned. The knowing smile left his face. The blush took its place. He fumbled in an inner pocket and brought forth a small package. "As a matter of fact, the Countess instructed me to advance to you, shall we say, a retainer fee, if... if ..."

"How much?"

He held the package toward me. I managed not to snatch it from him and took my time opening it. Inside I found ten hundred-dollar bills.

To say that I was stunned is putting it mildly. I must have looked paralyzed. Hamden, misinterpreting the look, said quickly, "You understand that this is only a modest advance against your services."

"Jesus!" I said. "She must want someone bumped off!"

"Now, Mr. Valois, I hardly think ..."

"I was kidding," I said hoarsely.

"You mean you will go to see the Countess sometime this week?"

"I mean, sonny, that I'll go with you on the train tonight."

"But that's marvelous!" He seemed surprised at the speed with which I acquiesced. I thought maybe he didn't know what I might do for a thousand dollars.

"I've done a lot of crazy things in my life," I said, "but usually I'm not paid for them. I have some things to settle here. I'll meet you at the station in half an hour."

"Good! It's such a relief. The Countess would not have forgiven me if— I'll arrange the *wagon-lit* reservations."

He picked up his hat and gloves and then looked doubtfully at the money in my hand.

"I won't run out on you."

"Oh," he said quickly, "I wasn't thinking... You know, Mr. Valois"— he stopped and grinned and for the first time I got a glimpse of something resembling a human being beneath that façade of accent and phony sophistication—"I was scared of you when I walked in. After all, it's not every day that I'm supposed to deal with a guy who is a legend."

"A legend?"

He turned at the door and smiled. "It's like meeting— well, say Lawrence of Arabia!"

He went out on that one, leaving me alone with a thousand dollars in my hand and wondering if I were still in the midst of an alcoholic dream. I'd been called many things in my life, especially before I was booted out of some job, but never a legend. And as for that Lawrence of Arabia crack, either the guy had been reading some bad novels about newspapermen or he smoked. But no one had ever handed me a thousand dollars and I'd never visited a countess in a palace at Lake Maggiore. I felt the old sense of exhilaration that came only when I was setting out on something new and unknown.

Quickly now, I shaved and dressed and packed my bag. I was in the hotel lobby fifteen minutes after Hamden left the room. I instructed the clerk at the desk that Madame would be staying on for two days and paid the bill. I got very little change from a hundred dollars. Then I saw to it that an envelope with two hundred dollars in it was placed in Loretta's mailbox. The clerk seemed glad to see the last of me.

As I passed the entrance to the bar I saw Loretta sitting alone on the far side of the room, face turned in profile. For the first time I realized that she was very lovely-looking. For a moment I hesitated, experiencing a faint pang of regret. She looked so irrevocably placid and alone. But the mood was fleeting. Silently I wished her luck and went through the hotel entrance into the moonlit night.

Chapter Two

Genoans bound for work or revolution or merely pre-noon amorous reflexes eyed me with dark and wholly justified suspicion. Hamden and a liveried chauffeur had gone out onto the Italian Line pier leaving me in solitary grandeur, encased in about twenty-five thousand dollars' worth of Rolls Royce. Down here, in the grimy port area of Genoa, the enormous shining limousine bearing the Becellini coat of arms had all the arrogance of a diamond-laden dowager in a Bowery saloon. It was too early in the morning, too bright and noisy here, and too filled with the softness of spring. The passengers and porters streaming forth from the pier where the *Vulcania* had recently docked accepted the madhouse of shouting hackies, sputtering taxis, and complaining trams, and even the picture of me pretending that a Rolls was my natural habitat, with festive good humor.

I flicked ashes on the mauve upholstery with the disdain of a bored aristocrat and looked through the glass into the astonished eyes of a dock worker. To my chagrin the guy put his hands on his hips, leaned back, roared with laughter, and went his way out of my life. Then I remembered that, in the bleary-eyed confusion of dressing on the train as it crept through the suburbs of Genoa at seven A.M., I had forgotten to comb my hair.

I fished a comb from my pocket and was just going to work on the knots when I saw the chauffeur stalking through the crowd at the pier's entrance with a girl in his wake. The girl was tall and slim and dark and she walked like a dream. She was hatless, but wore a simple and very smart traveling suit. She looked as though she belonged to the Rolls Royce. It occurred to me that the dock worker would not have laughed at her; he might have spat.

When she was almost to the Rolls, a man who had been talking to a group that stood beside a flashy Ferrari sports car came hurrying toward her. He was dark and wiry, mustached and vasolined on top. She drew up politely enough, but I could see that she was annoyed. After a moment he shrugged, bowed with exaggerated gallantry, and stepped aside to let her pass. He looked after her as she came on toward the car, and when he saw me, the ironical smile died. There was a question mark in his expression that could have been seen in Pisa.

The girl got in beside me. She settled back and gave me a cool look of inquiry. She made no attempt to introduce herself. It was obvious that I could assume what I pleased, and it was just as obvious that she was Countess Becellini's daughter. She seemed amused by my hair.

"I'm Rafferty Valois," I said.

"You don't look like the usual run of Mother's guests."

"I've never met the Countess and I don't think you could call me a guest. I'm a newspaperman. She wants to see me about something."

"How odd," she said coolly. "After the way the poor dear has been misrepresented in the press, I should think she'd have sense enough to stay away from you people."

"Misrepresented?"

"Oh, you know— all that dreadful 'Captivating Countess' business. All so one-dimensional and unfair. However ..."

She wasn't too interested in pursuing the subject. She kept looking back toward the pier entrance. I thought she seemed tense about something. The guy with the mustache and the vasoline on top was leaning against the Ferrari, still watching us.

"Who is that man?" I asked.

"I haven't the faintest idea," she said quickly.

The frustrated Lothario finally stopped staring and got into the low-slung car with a stocky, amiable-looking guy in loud tweeds. The Ferrari leaped away through scattering porters and indignant passengers and disappeared toward the upper town. To my surprise, the girl still kept watching the entrance to the pier.

"What *is* that creature doing?" she asked impatiently.

"What creature?"

"That person who calls himself Jeffery Hamden." Her voice was edged with contempt. "My luggage is properly labeled. I've been through the customs. There's nothing for him to do out there on the pier except to act so terribly efficient. I do believe—"

She stopped talking very suddenly. One of her hands had been very tight on the little handbag she carried, and I noticed now that it relaxed. I followed the direction of her gaze. A tall young man in a shapeless tweed coat and gray flannels was standing outside the entrance to the pier looking towards the Rolls with a sort of rapture that would have been more suitable to one of the natives than to the clean-cut young American he obviously was. He grinned, winked, leaned down and picked up a rather battered valise, and walked away from us across the cobblestones toward the waiting tram.

It didn't take the released hand on the bag to tell me the girl had been waiting for that smile. It was reflected in her eyes as she followed the spasmodic progress of the ancient tram across the square and into the maze of narrow streets at the base of the hill. She tried without much success to make the rest of her features expressionless. When the streetcar had disappeared, she leaned back and gave me a furtive look. I pretended to be looking out across the harbor. She dug nervously into the bag and took out a cigarette. I lit it for her, still maintaining the silence. Through the little cloud of smoke she kept watching the entrance to the narrow street into which the tram had disappeared.

When I said nothing she gave me another worried glance. I was very much aware of the great brown eyes, eyes straight out of an Italian primitive, very expressive and sensitive eyes, eyes that contradicted the lovely but cold line of the aristocratic face.

"I didn't mean to stare at your hair," she finally said.

"That's all right."

"It's a nasty trick I have, left over from— I'm trying to cure myself of it. But there's so much I have to learn. So much...."

"Young men in old tweeds and baggy flannels don't like girls who stare,

I guess."

She sucked in her breath. "So! Mother has sent you to spy on me!"

"My dear child, I tell you I haven't met her yet, and I don't know what she wants me to do. If it's that I'll refuse."

"Then how did you— I mean—"

"Your eyes, honey, when you watched the tram disappear."

"So it shows that much! How inconvenient!" She put her hand impulsively on my arm. "Please don't say anything about— about young men in tweeds to Mother. It was just a casual shipboard flirtation, but Mother would think all sorts of silly things. It would worry her."

"She doesn't trust you?"

"Mother is the most wonderful woman in the world," she said stoutly, "but—"

"But you're afraid of her."

"Afraid? What an odd thing to say!"

The thought seemed to disturb her for a moment. Then she laughed. "What is this power you have, Mr. Valois? I've known you only a few minutes, and yet I've succumbed to the most personal sort of questioning. Do you always do this?"

"Usually," I said, "with people I like."

"Well! Thank you." I could see she wasn't certain whether or not I was kidding her.

"Have you been visiting in the States?"

"I'm going to college there. But not in the ordinary manner. You see, my past education didn't equip me to pass the entrance requirements. I was always with Mother, you know, except for a few years in a finishing school in Florence. I had tutors, but the things they taught me weren't very practical. So I've been living with an aunt in New York and taking extension courses at Columbia University."

"With your mother's blessings?"

"Lord, no!" She laughed. "But when she saw that I was so determined, we settled for sort of a bargain."

"A bargain?"

"You're not going to get that out of me, Mr. Valois. What a snooper you are, really!"

"I'm always curious. You'll get used to it."

"Anyway, aside from being away from Mother, I've adored the past year. I always hated the school in Florence so, and the unreal little ladies and the atmosphere of preparing for a perpetual party. This is the first time I've been with people my own age who said what they thought and— well, I've loved it. I'm afraid I'm going to break Mother's heart by being just another vulgar American!"

"But your mother's an American."

She laughed. "Don't remind her of it." She looked at me with a gay smile. "Really, Mr. Rafferty Valois, who are you, anyway? I feel as though I've known you for years. It can't be just your delightful red hair!"

"It's love," I said.

"You're going to make love to me? How charming!"

To my surprise I said, "You awaken the paternal in me, young lady." I'd used that line before, but rarely meant it. I must be aging fast, I thought.

She gave me a quick, searching look.

"Speaking of paternal," I said, "what about your father? Is he alive?"

"The Count Becellini is very much alive," she said in a cold voice, "and we won't discuss him."

The chauffeur had finished strapping her bags to the top of the car and now he stood waiting on the cobblestones for Hamden. I thought about the girl next to me with mixed reactions. She was hard to figure. I realized that she was younger than she appeared to be; probably not more than nineteen. Like many girls brought up in the European fashion, she had the social poise of a woman twice her age. But there was a child-like quality that kept creeping through that poise that might connote confusion or, on the other hand, might be intentionally deceptive. Certainly she could turn on the ice water when it suited her purpose.

My thoughts were interrupted by Hamden, who came hurrying from the pier. I moved over to make room for him between the girl and myself. The chauffeur shut the door behind him and climbed into the front seat behind the wheel. We crept through the port area and then began to climb swiftly up the narrow Via Garibaldi between the fading façades of ancient palaces. The city climbed with us, scrambling up the mountainside away from the sooty port.

"Forgive me," Hamden said breathlessly. "I should have been here to introduce you. Donna Bianca Becellini, allow me to present Mr. Valois."

"That's all right, Mr. Hamden," she said coolly. "Rafferty and I are old friends."

Hamden's mouth fell open. When he saw my grin, his lips pressed together in disapproval.

"How long have you been with Mother?" the girl asked.

"Six months."

"Six months. Let me see— six months ago was when Mother made that flying trip to New York."

"Yes. I met the Countess at the home of mutual friends in Connecticut."

Although he made it sound quite grand, I got the impression that he was lying. Apparently Bianca did too. But she merely said, "I hope, for your sake, that you last longer than your predecessor."

Which of course was enough to shut up even Hamden. "Let's play another game," I said easily. "This 'picking on Good Old Hamden' is getting boring."

After a moment she said contritely, "You're right, Rafferty. Forgive me, Mr. Hamden."

Hamden muttered something polite, but his feathers were pretty ruffled. He watched Bianca speculatively. I would have given a good deal to know what was going through what passed for his mind.

The limousine climbed out of the warmth of Liguria into the chill of the Apennines, and then, like a ship at sea topping a great wave, tilted downward for the descent into the bustle and matter-of-factness of Piemonte with its baroque and rococo strewn among rice fields and factories. As the Rolls fled across Piemonte toward the magic of Lombardia, I had the odd sensation of being in an archaic bark floating relentlessly into the center of a dream. Neither Donna Bianca nor Hamden nor the Countess had anything to do with my life or any reality. It was impossible to believe they existed in the same world in which the majority of mankind was either preparing for war or actually engaged in it. The symbols of other worlds and other times— ruins of Gothic and Renaissance on the landscape— added to the sense of fantasy.

We stopped for lunch at the Grand Hotel in Vercelli. As we walked across the courtyard I saw the Ferrari sports car parked around the corner. If Bianca recognized it she gave no sign. We went through the lobby and passed the bar and out to the rear of the hotel, where there is a charming open-air restaurant overlooking the valley and the monastery. I ordered a drink and let Hamden take care of the rest. He made a great fuss about the main course and the wine, but the results were just about what I would have expected: something impossible to identify concealed in rice and olive oil and raw, sour wine. He apologized as though he had prepared it with his own hands. Bianca looked impatient and bored.

Near the end of the meal, she excused herself on the pretext of buying some postcards in the lobby. I gave her a minute or so, then told Hamden I was going to find the men's room. As I suspected, she was in neither the lobby nor the adjoining bar. I walked to one of the open windows overlooking the courtyard. Bianca was just below the window, in a tiny enclosed garden, engaged in a heated discussion with the guy who had accosted her in front of the Italian Lines pier. On closer inspection,

I saw, beneath the leathery tan, the memory of youth and good looks in his face, like a badly constructed streamlined apartment house whose walls are beginning to crack, steel beginning to rust. Although they kept their voices low, I could hear every word quite distinctly in the still noon air.

"... despicable!" Bianca was saying. "I won't have you crawling to Mother with your horror tales!"

"Bianca! I beg you to listen! You must persuade her to call off the ball and all that it means! You have no idea of the danger!"

"Danger from what?"

"I cannot tell you."

"What rot! Are you working for Michel's mistress? Did she pay you to make a play for me in New York?"

"What I have to say I will say to your mother."

"You must not come to Stresa! If you do—"

She stopped. The air was absolutely still. I noticed a black butterfly floating, rigid as glass, above the dusty garden.

"Why don't you come to your senses?" the man said in sudden anger. "This Hank Dawson is the sort of man for you!"

"So!" she cried. "Hank is in it too! I might have known!"

"Bianca! Don't go. Listen. I must make you understand. We are in the hands of a monster!"

There was a sudden burst of laughter behind me from a group that had just come into the lobby from the garden restaurant. Quickly I left the window and found the men's room. I spent a little time there thinking. Bianca was not so candid as she would have had me believe. She had told me she did not know the man who accosted her in front of the pier. But the snatches of the conversation I had overheard certainly suggested intimacy, if not connivance.

When I emerged, Hamden and Bianca were waiting for me at the main entrance. As we went down the steps into the courtyard the flashy Ferrari was disappearing into the street.

"Quite a car!" I said.

"By Jove," Hamden said, "there's only one like it. It's a custom job. Don't tell me Tony Machero was lunching here and we didn't know it. How dull!"

"And who is Tony Machero?"

"Prince Machero. He's one of the most popular men in Florentine society. The Countess and I dined with him in Milan only last February. Before a performance at La Scala."

"Anyone can dine with him," Bianca said. "Anyone with the price of a meal."

"You know him, then," I said.

She looked me in the eye and said calmly, "I never laid eyes on him until he made a pest of himself on the boat. I told you I didn't know who he was because he's the sort of person Mother would think I should have been polite to. I didn't want to discuss it."

To my surprise and Bianca's, Hamden said, "Well, to be honest with you, I don't really see why he's so popular. He's amusing, but there's something slippery about him I don't like."

"But a moment ago you were bewailing the fact that we missed him at lunch."

"I thought it was the thing to say," Hamden said candidly.

After that honest confession I might have done some thinking about Hamden had it not been for my curiosity about Bianca. I tried to keep it just that, mild curiosity. I'd had my distressed maidens before and too goddamned many dragons. I didn't intend to do any jousting on this trip. I was going to stick to the job— whatever it might be— and let the maidens fend for themselves. Yet …

We set off once again, racing through the ancient towns toward the east. The drink at lunch hadn't helped much. As the conversation wasn't anything to keep me awake, I dozed off.

When I awakened it was dark and we were coming to a halt before the carriage entrance to a hotel in Stresa. Still half asleep, I followed Bianca and Hamden into the lobby. The chauffeur followed and handed my bag over to a bellhop, who immediately whisked it off to a destination unknown. I was too groggy to ask any questions, so I sat on a sofa with Bianca while Hamden, once more all bustle and importance, engaged in animated conversation with a guy in morning coat and striped trousers who was probably the hotel manager. The lobby was subdued and very elegant. A few people in evening clothes sat around chatting in low voices, and there was none of the hectic flashiness of the usual Italian hotel de luxe.

"I need a drink," I said to Bianca.

"I'll see that you get one as soon as we reach the island."

"The island?"

"Didn't you know? The palace— the Villa Dolorosa— is on an island in the lake. As soon as Mr. Hamden gets through his important conference with the hotel manager we will go."

"I don't swim well." I leaned close to her, my good resolutions forgotten. "If you're in trouble, honey, tell Pops about it. I might be able to help. Who knows?"

She had been sitting there pale and listless, but now she froze up. "Trouble? What in the world do you mean?"

"Forget it," I said.

"You *must* need a drink," she said. But a second later she put her hand on my arm and whispered, "Rafferty ..."

But Hamden killed the deal. He came back with the manager, who let forth a stream of effusions in Italian over Bianca's hand. While this was going on, Hamden said to me, "They have a very nice room for you, Valois. Overlooking the lake. I had your bags sent up, because you are expected at the villa for dinner. You'll go out with us."

"I thought I was to stay at the villa."

"I think you'll find this very comfortable. The launch will bring you back after dinner."

"O.K. by me. Let's go. I need a drink and I'm starved."

We went out through a charming garden where a few attractive people were sitting at tiny iron tables lighted by lanterns strung in the trees. A string orchestra played softly in the background and the May evening was filled with the scent of the lemon trees and roses. We left the hotel grounds, crossed the esplanade that runs along the lake front, and went down stone steps to the hotel pier. Across the lake the moon was rising behind the still snow-capped mountains of Switzerland. A few of the odd little canopied boats peculiar to Lake Maggiore drifted about in the soft night, lantern-lit and unreal.

A uniformed attendant helped us into a trim mahogany launch, where we settled among cushions under a blood-red awning. Bianca's hand touched mine. It felt icy cold.

The motor made a shocking sound in the unearthly peace of the evening as we swung in a wide arc away from the pier and headed out into the lake. In the pale moonlight I made out the ghostly shapes of the palaces rising from the water.

"This can't be real," I said.

"The lake is best at night," Bianca said. "In the daylight you are aware of the artificiality and the things that men can do. But at night it comes into its own. It's sheer magic."

The lights of the hotels and sugar-cake villas along the esplanade faded off to the rear. We were being carried away from the modern world into a star-struck May night. Bianca made no attempt to withdraw her hand. It lay against mine, cold and inert, expressing, more than all the words in the world could have, helplessness. It was not the hand of a traveler approaching the hearths of home.

And then ahead I saw for the first time the marble torch-lit steps of the

Villa Dolorosa, eighty feet wide, leading down from a great terrace and the palace above the waters of the lake. Beneath the flaming torches at the landing stage stood two footmen in purple breeches and cloth of gold.

"My God!" I said. "Is this produced by Sam Goldwyn?"

"It's the fifteenth century," Hamden said.

The motor died, and in the sudden stillness of the night I heard someone singing out on the lake, muted and far away.

Chapter Three

A major-domo who looked and acted like a general imparting necessary but dull information to the lower echelons answered some of my questions as he lead me through vast rooms and vaulted corridors hung with priceless treasures of Renaissance art. A monastery had once stood, grim and Gothic, on the tiny island. But in the eighteenth century it had passed into the hands of the Roman family Becellini, who had razed the monastery and built in its place a gleaming marble palace in the Venetian style. For a hundred years the Becellinis used this modest shack as a summer retreat, but by the advent of the twentieth century the family could no longer afford to keep up the palace and it had stood empty for thirty years until the infusion into the family of American plumbing-fixture profits. Later I discovered that the renovations, including repairs and additions, landscaping and bathrooms, electricity and heat, had cost over a million and a half dollars. The Villa Dolorosa was open one day a month to the public, and it was in a little guidebook printed for tourists that I was to discover, among other fascinating data, that it contained twenty-five bedrooms, an extravagant collection of Renaissance paintings, a ballroom of pink marble, a miniature and jewel-like eighteenth-century theatre, terraced gardens considered among the finest of their type in the world, and, down below in the rock of the island, the original subterranean tunnels and dungeons of the Gothic monastery.

The major-domo informed me that the Countess would join me directly and asked me to wait in a comparatively small room overlooking a tiny enclosed inner court where a fountain played. I realized with thanks that Bianca had not forgotten me when a footman arrived with a large silver tray containing a whisky decanter, soda, and ice in a bowl that might have been designed by Cellini.

Hamden and Bianca had disappeared into the far reaches of the palace, and I figured that, considering what Bianca might have to say to her mother, I might have a long wait ahead of me. It was after nine o'-

clock and I was hungry. My amazement at the size and luxury of the Villa Dolorosa was mixed with growing resentment. What kind of woman was this countess— American-born at that— to flaunt her wealth so theatrically in a country struggling out of the devastation of war and near economic ruin? Despite her great wealth, she could not have lived on this fantastic scale in her own country. Labor, taxes, and public opinion had put an end to living on such a plane (even a pale imitation of it) by the end of the thirties.

It seemed to me that if she had been working for the Soviet Union, the Countess could not have done more to strike a blow at our foreign policy. She must be either supremely callous or utterly stupid, I thought. And yet some troublesome part of my mind could not help admiring the sheer brass and imagination that had reconstructed the life of another century in a disapproving era. Whatever else she might be, I knew that the Countess Becellini would have strength of a kind and perhaps even that sort of individuality which has come to be maligned in our sheeplike times as "eccentric."

But what in God's name could the mistress of this palace want with me? As I finished the first drink I became more and more convinced that the next couple of hours were going to be damned embarrassing. I was beginning to be certain that Hamden had blundered into a ludicrous case of mistaken identity. That crack about Lawrence of Arabia seemed to prove it.

I poured another drink from the decanter on the silver tray. The small room was like a marble vault, still and suspended in time. Stone walls, stone floors, stone arches looking out into the stone-enclosed court. The Louis Quinze furniture scattered about the room looked doll-like and temporary. On the wall opposite me hung a painting that might have been a Botticelli. Against a pale green Lombardia landscape, a dark-robed figure wearing a scarlet cap watched me with the long-faced, crafty intelligence of the Medici. I didn't like what the eyes seemed to know.

What the hell, I thought. As Loretta says, let tomorrow take care of itself. Too many of my planned yesterdays had gone sour on me, anyway. Not only had I been the most scooped journalist in the profession, but every time I'd made a protective gesture to a lady in distress, the end had usually been laughter at my expense. No more, I thought. I'm really a hep guy at heart, a realist and a cynic, and from now on it's number one and no one else. Yet the vision of the enigmatic Loretta with a smile in her eyes was disturbing. I looked around the room again, trying to shake off the impression of being in a locked tomb.

The eyes of the Medici mocked me.

I reached again for the bottle and froze with my hand in mid-air. From behind me in the dead stillness of the stone room came a slight sound. I wheeled about expecting God knows what, but certainly not what confronted me.

Standing in the arch was a woman in a dull red robe-like gown tied in the middle with a wide green cord. She was one of the most strikingly beautiful women I have ever seen. Even though she must have been in her late thirties or early forties, her figure was magnificent, and part of it was quite apparent because of a casual neckline that swept from one shoulder down across almost completely exposed breasts. A pale but very alive face was dominated by dark and passionate eyes; eyes that would have made me think of Bianca except that they lacked any uncertainty or doubt. In a mass of midnight-black hair she wore a tiny gold net cap trimmed on the edge with green stones that glittered in the reflected light.

But all of this was registered only on my subconscious. For at the moment I had eyes only for the animal she held at leash on a thin gold chain. It was a full-grown cheetah, as large as a panther, sand-colored and spotted. At the moment its head was held high and it was sniffing in a manner I didn't like. Its small ears were flat against the great cat head.

Now it happens that I have a psychological allergy to even the most innocuous alley kitten. I have been known to leave a café or a party at the sudden appearance of a stray cat. How I managed to stay still, with a smile frozen on my face, is still a mystery to me.

The cheetah regarded me with some interest. Its mistress smiled.

"Iris likes you," she said. "That's a good sign."

"How can you be sure?"

"You'd know soon enough if she didn't. She always decides immediately. The first sniff is enough. She's really as gentle as a lamb, except in those very rare cases when she takes a dislike to someone. See?"

To my horror she lead the animal toward me. Standing my ground was the greatest act of will power in my life. Iris looked up at me with cold green eyes. Then she stretched out toward my hand. I was incapable of movement. My arms hung motionless, ready to be devoured. Instead I felt a rough warm tongue working over the back of my hand. I shuddered.

"Delightful!" the Countess said. "Now I'm certain I didn't make a mistake in asking you to come."

"If she had bitten off my hand you wouldn't have been so sure, eh?"

"Exactly. You can't fool an animal, you know."

With my free hand I finished off my drink. "Look, Iris," I said, "I promise I'll never lie to you."

The great cat looked up at me and made a frightening sound in her throat.

"See! She's purring. And it's such a relief to meet someone who doesn't get nervous at the first sight of Iris. Obviously you share my love for cats."

"I'm mad about them," I said with more truth than she could have suspected.

"Good. We've got off to an excellent start. Now then, Iris, darling, Mr. Valois will talk to you later. Lie down." Reluctantly the cheetah gave my hand back to me and, dragging her loose chain behind her, went to the far side of the room, where she proceeded to lie with her head in her paws, eyes fixed on me with a beady gaze.

"You let her run loose?"

"Certainly. At least, in the main part of the villa and gardens. I can't let her near the servants' quarters any more because she has taken a dislike to one of the chefs. If he weren't a *cordon bleu*, I would discharge him, but..."

To my relief the Countess sat on one of the gilt sofas. My legs would not have held out another minute. I managed to sink into a chair with some show of dignity.

The Countess leaned back, head to one side, and looked me over critically. For some reason the expression in her eyes made me think of Iris. "Has anyone told you that your face is definitely fifteenth century?"

"I'm aging."

"No. I'm quite serious. These things are important to me. A great many Italians have red hair, you know. Cesare Borgia was a redhead. Do you believe in reincarnation? Well, we won't discuss that now. I'm so glad we have this opportunity to have a little chat before dinner. We never dine until ten here, you know."

I didn't know, and I wasn't happy to hear it. Another half hour without food, sitting in the same room with an affectionate cheetah, and a woman who thought I was fifteenth century, wasn't going to help my state of mind. The Countess looked at my empty glass and gestured toward the decanter. I didn't waste time in being coy. I poured myself another stiff one.

"Forgive me," she said, "if I'm a bit distrait. My dear child has just returned from America and I can see the whole trip was a most unfortunate mistake. Not that it won't be of some value to her in the future, but her training has hardly fitted her for the sort of bourgeois atmosphere in which she has moved for the past months."

"She is a very sweet child," I said politely.

"Sweet!" The Countess' laugh was contralto and very pleasing. "My dear Mr. Valois, I adore my child. She's my treasure, my life. But you don't know the Becellinis. They could never be anything so tepid as sweet."

I took a gulp of the Scotch and tried not to look at Iris. The Countess opened a large jeweled case and took out a small brown cigar. I lighted it for her.

"Mr. Hamden has explained that you came to me with only a few minutes' notice. I'm deeply grateful. I think it best that we come to some sort of understanding immediately."

"Allow me to say," I said, "that I can hardly believe you are Bianca's mother."

"I was nineteen when Bianca was born," she said. But her eyes narrowed and I thought I detected a sort of speculation there that promised possible extracurricular activities. She remained silent just long enough to start a pleasant warmth in my circulation. Then she said in an impersonal voice, "The little service that you might perform for me will probably seem child's play after some of your fabulous adventures."

"Fabulous adventures?"

"Please don't be modest. I loathe modesty in men. It's the sort of thing one expects of shopkeepers or American businessmen. You've had the courage to seek romance and danger in an age when most people moan incessantly about safety and security. I've found that life is very much what you make of it. I admire you tremendously for daring to be— to be— a man!"

"I've always been aware of sex differentiation, if that's what you mean. I'm very much aware of it right now." Even if she is mad, I thought, she'd be terrific in bed.

"Ah?" She gave me another of those direct and challenging looks. Only fleeting, but enough to make the hair on the back of my neck stand on end.

"What I need," she said, "is a man with courage but also with utmost discretion. The matter in hand is, to say the least, extremely delicate. The slightest blunder could result only in disaster."

I didn't take the words too seriously. They were as melodramatic as the setting in which she lived and the cheetah on a gold chain. Here, I thought, but for the grace of God and about twenty million dollars, sits a potential Duse.

"What is it you want of me?"

She hesitated a moment, took a deep breath, and said, "I want you to recover some letters belonging to me."

"What sort of letters?"

"What sort of letters is a woman usually intent on recovering, Mr. Valois? It's not necessary to discuss their contents in detail. Needless to say, if they should fall into the wrong hands, they might prove somewhat embarrassing— and worse."

"The wrong hands?"

"My husband," she said. "The Count Lorenzo Becellini. The first legitimate bastard his family has produced. And I might add, quite literally, a son of a bitch."

"You're separated from your husband?"

"Not legally," she said. "We don't do things that way in Italy. But we haven't lived under the same roof for seventeen years. He lives in Rome and Torminia and we never meet."

"If it's been that way so long, why is it you are suddenly worried about these letters falling into his hands?"

"His mother— the bitch of Rome— has tried to make my life miserable for twenty years. For fifteen years Lorenzo has tried to arrange an annulment but failed. However, if he should get his hands on these letters ..."

"Why do you care?"

She leaned back, eyes half closed, and blew a cloud of the cigar smoke toward the ceiling. Then she snapped her head straight and looked at me with blazing eyes. "For twenty years Lorenzo's mother has made my life hell. When I married him, Father settled two million dollars on him and paid for the renovation of this palace. She liked that, of course, but once the money was in the bank, she tried everything in her power to get rid of me. She didn't know me very well! She thought I was a naïve little child who would be frightened out of Italy when she saw to it that Roman society closed its doors to me. I've fought her for twenty years, and by God, in the end I will win!"

"Win what?"

"Win the recognition for my daughter that she deserves as a Becellini!"

"Surely there are more important things than recognition by a few decadent Roman aristocrats who are on the way out anyway."

"*I* think it's important, Mr. Valois," she said with the first sign of hostility, "and as for the persons you speak of being on the way out, I should like to remind you that the Becellinis have survived seven centuries and God knows how many wars and revolutions!"

It was difficult to believe that this woman had been born an American. And it seemed incredible that, if she had received the rebuffs she had described, she could still feel the passionate necessity for achieving a position that had so little importance in the modern world.

"For years," she said, "I've held out. I've had to be satisfied with the fringes and the bobtails and the sort of international garbage they write about in the papers. But I've planned for my child, and right now, when the most fantastic sort of victory is in sight—"

She stopped. "I must have these letters back!"

"Do you know who has them?" I was far too curious now to tell her she had the wrong guy. I couldn't lose much by saying no a bit later.

"Yes. I've been paying blackmail for over six months."

"Blackmail!"

"Twenty thousand dollars," she said calmly, "and the last demand threatened to turn them over to my charming husband unless I increased the amount."

"Didn't you go to the authorities?"

"Really, Mr. Valois! You can't be that naïve. Surely you didn't ask such questions when you did that exciting job for the Maharaja of Punjabor."

"I beg your pardon?"

"You're carrying discretion too far. After all, I am taking a certain risk in confiding in you before I have had a definite promise of your assistance. I expect an equal amount of candor from you."

"Look, Countess," I said. "You've made some kind of mistake. This is not my line. I don't know what you mean about the Maharaja, but—"

"Ah!" she said. "Of course! Money! If you can return the letters to my hands, I will pay you twenty-five thousand dollars."

I managed to keep the glass from sliding to the floor. Shakily I got a cigarette lighted. I looked at Iris. If her instinct told her I was embarking on a deception, she concealed it beautifully. Her green eyes were fixed on me with hungry adoration.

"I thought it was a fair sum," she said into my silence.

"Yes," I said. "Quite fair. But first I'll have to ask a couple of questions."

"Naturally."

"You say you know who has the letters?"

She looked toward the arch and straightened up, listening for a moment. Then she lowered her voice and leaned closer.

"A very important personage is involved in this unpleasant business. He was a guest here in the Villa Dolorosa for three months. Then his mistress arrived in Stresa and I was stupid enough to invite her to stay in the palace for a few days. I thought then that the affair between them was over. It will be over soon! But at the moment the dreadful woman has him completely hypnotized. I was forced to suggest that they leave. He is a sweet boy, but rather weak. He left with— with this creature— for Rome."

"And it's this woman who has been blackmailing you. Have you been sending the money directly to her?"

"Certainly not. She doesn't realize that I know. I send the money to a post box in Florence."

"How can you be certain it is she who has the letters?"

"Because," she said, "the alternative is unthinkable! You see, on the evening before they left I came upon them both in my private sitting room. The woman seemed somewhat flustered and I thought it rather strange, but accepted the explanation that they had come in to examine a Cellini vase. It wasn't until the next day, after they had left, that I found the letters missing from the wall safe."

"Then the unthinkable alternative," I said, "is that the 'important personage' is involved."

"Impossible."

"Who is he?"

She darted another uneasy look toward the arch. "Michel of Movania," she said.

"Michel of what? Who?"

"King Michel of Movania," she said calmly.

I stared at her, dumfounded. I resisted the temptation to burst out laughing.

"The ex-king of Movania?" I finally managed to ask.

"Don't use that word 'ex,'" she said. "His present position is only temporary. I happen to know that he will be back on his throne by the first of July."

"But my God! He and this woman have been blackmailing you!"

"Nothing of the sort. I have told you that he is a charming young man. It's this dreadful woman. You see, he was financially embarrassed when he was forced to leave his country so suddenly. He was very grateful for my hospitality. However, I understand that since they have been in Rome, they have been living on a rather luxurious scale. I'm sure that she has told him some plausible tale about the source of her sudden wealth. The dear boy knows nothing of money, of course."

"This is incredible! Surely she would have returned them— if she is the one who has them— after receiving twenty thousand dollars."

"That's what I thought at first. I took it for granted that with that kind of creature, money was the only concern. It's only recently that I've realized the truth."

"And what is that?"

"Next Friday His Highness plans to announce his engagement. To a young woman of his own class, of course. This scheming creature hopes to prevent the marriage."

"But what have your letters got to do with that?"

"I believe she plans to turn them over to my husband. This would result in a filthy public scandal."

"I still don't see how that could affect his marriage."

She stood. At the same time the cheetah stretched and got to its feet. Countess Becellini held her head high, and there was that same unnatural blaze in her eyes.

"On June twenty-ninth I am giving a ball here at the Villa Dolorosa. For the first time in years this great palace will be filled with names worthy of its beauty. Even the bitch of Rome will not dare refuse. You see, on that night the world will hear the name of the next queen of Movania!"

I looked up at her, knowing, but unable to believe. "Now! Will you help me, Mr. Valois?"

"You'll have to give me until morning," I said. I felt suddenly ill and confused.

"As you choose. But I have no doubt you will help. Now then, let us join the others in a cocktail. And mind you, not a word!"

She marched toward the door as the cheetah moved to meet her. I put down my glass wearily and said aloud, "Poor Bianca!"

Chapter Four

Candlelight flickered on vine-covered arches and damask, and the faces about the dinner table in the loggia were like balloons suspended in space.

Aside from the Countess, Bianca, Hamden, and myself, there was a rather moth-eaten British couple, Sir Robert Haroll and his birdlike lady, who was distantly but determinedly related to the house of Windsor. Over cocktails Countess Becellini had informed me that Sir Robert had been a minor official in the British colonial service early in the century and was now retired on a pension that barely permitted his wife to hold her scrawny, tulle-draped neck at the rigid angle of her youth. Their position at the palace seemed to be that of permanent house guests, but they gave the impression of being unwilling hostages. They were both incredibly snobbish and exhausted and somewhat pathetic, and seemed to regard the Countess with the disapproving resignation of highly recommended servants in the household of a rich pawnbroker.

Bianca hardly touched her food or wine. She was giving a nauseating impression of a polite and vacuous schoolgirl home for the holidays. Once or twice I caught her watching me with a speculative expression that belied the act she was putting on. I found it possible to believe that the girl she was pretending to be would succumb docilely to her mother's ambition to marry her off to a broken-down ex-king. But then I remembered the stars in her eyes as she had watched the tall young man in the tweed coat and the baggy flannels walk across the cobblestones in front of the Italian Lines pier. And certainly the girl who had stood up to the Prince Machero in that odd and sinister conversation I had overheard in the courtyard of the restaurant where we had lunched was no simpering ingenue.

Just as dessert was being served, the major-domo handed the Countess a note. She read it, seemed to be thinking like a general deciding a strategic move, then looked up with what appeared to me to be synthetic pleasure.

"What fun! Bianca, my dear, Tony Machero has just arrived in Stresa!"

Carefully, primly, Bianca put down her fork. She gave me a quick, almost furtive look and then registered absolutely nothing. The Countess was smiling, but she watched her daughter with a bright— too bright— interest.

"My dear!" Lady Haroll croaked. "Not that dreadful young man! Henriette di Freier wrote from Florence and mentioned the most scandalous facts. It seems—"

"It's only eleven o'clock," the Countess interrupted, still watching Bianca. "Tony wouldn't think it at all odd if I had Renaldo call and ask him over for a few rubbers of bridge."

"It seems," the lady related to royalty continued as though no one had spoken, "that although everyone knows he and his family are absolutely penniless, he bought a vulgar villa at Porto Fino and appeared driving a fabulously expensive sports car. There is a very distasteful story about some impossible woman— the wife of a Greek importer, I believe."

"He plays an excellent game of bridge," the Countess said.

"And always wins!" Lady Haroll said, with an arched eyebrow for her husband.

"He'll cheer you up, Bianca. He's always full of the most amusing gossip, and one doesn't take him seriously, does one?"

"I haven't the faintest idea," Bianca said. "I've never met him."

The smile stayed fixed on the Countess' face. She crumpled the note into a small wad and flicked it from the table's edge.

"How odd," she said lightly. "He wrote me just before he sailed for New York and asked if he might call on you there."

"Did he? He apparently found other and more amusing things to do with his time."

"Well, no matter. I'll have Renaldo call and—"

Bianca pushed back her chair and stood. We all looked at her, struck by the obvious tension in her face.

"Not tonight, Mother. I have a splitting headache. There was a gala on the ship last night and I didn't get to my stateroom until almost dawn. I'm going to be very rude and ask if I may go to my room."

The Countess stopped smiling. Then she said quietly, "Darling, how thoughtless of me. Of course we *quite* understand. Tony can wait until tomorrow. Your health comes before a game of bridge."

"Thank you, Mother."

Bianca's footsteps receded across the stone terrace. Iris, from her position on the parapet, arched her neck and looked inquiringly at me. In the silence, Hamden seemed to be frantically reviewing his Emily Post for a precedent that would give him his cue.

Lady Haroll broke into the moment of tension.

"Well! I must say, Celia, young people *are* self-indulgent these days! In my time we bore up with our little aches and pains."

She looked as though she were still doing it.

The Countess disregarded Lady Haroll completely. She was looking toward the arch through which Bianca had disappeared.

Lady Haroll was not to be discouraged. "Don't you think it's odd that Prince Machero would not have called on Bianca in New York? You don't suppose, Celia, that—"

"I don't suppose anything!" the Countess said coldly. "I trust Bianca completely."

"Still, a man like that... A young girl might—"

"Oh, do shut up, Dorothy!" The Countess got hold of herself. "Do you play bridge, Mr. Valois?"

"Sorry. No."

"We still have four," Lady Haroll said anxiously. "Mr. Hamden, Robert, and you and I, Celia."

"That's fine," I said. "I must get back to the hotel."

After brandy and coffee in a red and gold drawing room, the bridge table was set up by an enormous fireplace. The Harolls gravitated to it like homing pigeons to the coop. Apparently they worked the graveyard shift at nonunion and highly speculative terms. The Countess walked with me across the vast room to the arched entrance into the hall.

"Tomorrow at luncheon you will give me your answer."

"Don't count on me too much," I said. "I don't think it's in my line."

She took my hand. I felt a tingle of pleasure as I looked into her eyes. "Oh, but I'm counting on you completely!"

Over her shoulders I saw Hamden and the Harolls at the bridge table. Hamden managed a farewell smile, but it cost him more effort than it was worth. He watched me with sultry impatience.

She wasn't in a hurry to withdraw her hand. When I didn't say anything she smiled. "Perhaps I'm incurably romantic," she said, "but I make decisions on such trivial attributes as red hair. You may not be completely honest, my dear Mr. Valois, but I am almost certain you have a highly inflammable sense of indignation. I'm counting on it."

"I'm sure it's not only my indignation that's inflamed, Countess."

She laughed as her fingers slid away from my hand. "Yes, I'm sure your perceptions are most acute. It is too bad you must leave now, but good night, Mr. Valois."

I left her then and walked through endless halls with Iris at my heels. At the top of the marble steps that led down to the landing stage, she rubbed against my legs and growled affectionately. I descended the steps in an aura of goose flesh. I got in among the scarlet cushions of the launch and looked back. The cheetah was where I had left her, gazing mournfully after me, flanked by the flaming torches.

The uniformed attendant leaped aboard and gave me an amused and insolent glance. I wondered what the hell it was he found so funny. We swung out and away from the island through the velvet softness of the lake toward Stresa. The reason for the boatman's amusement was disclosed almost immediately. The door to the tiny cabin in the center of the launch opened and out came Bianca. She had changed from the dinner gown to a simple dark suit and wore a scarf over her head.

"I thought you'd never come. I've been huddled down in that stuffy cabin for fifteen minutes. Can you give me a cigarette?"

She sat beside me on the cushions as I lit her cigarette. She leaned back and closed her eyes and blew a cloud of smoke back into the night. In the darkness her pallor was even more pronounced and the normally cool arch of her eyebrows was replaced by a sharp V of worry.

"Do you often play hooky like this?"

She said, "I'd rather save the tiresome explanations until after the deed."

"Deed?"

"Figuratively speaking. Besides, I'm a free agent. Mother has a fanatical belief in what she might call 'the dictates of my blood.' Whatever that may mean."

"It's a moonlight night. You're young. The kind of dictation your blood may be giving might be regretted in the morning."

"Good God!" she said. "How maudlin!"

Her voice had a bitter ring I didn't like. I waited. After a moment she said, "Twenty-four hours ago you might have been right. But a girl hears things. Things that open her eyes."

"Things that were said in the courtyard of that restaurant where we lunched?"

She straightened up. "So! You have been spying on me! How much does Mother pay you?"

"I didn't spy for your mother. It was to satisfy my own insatiable curiosity. I can't cure myself of it. Have it right now. Wonder who you are going to meet, for instance."

"You'll see. I'm out tonight to retrieve a little lost pride."

"And I'm curious about how a girl like you allowed herself to be bulldozed into a marriage with a broken-down king."

"Don't be absurd! Most girls would give their eyeteeth to walk down the aisle with a king. Besides, he's not broken down. He's really quite attractive."

"Cinderella will come down the marble stairs at the ball to be clutched in the arms of the anemic remnant of a worn-out family, and her children— if any— will live in syphilitic grandeur in resort hotels while the managers kiss my lady's— er— feet and Mother sends out engraved announcements of the sale."

"What rot! My mother is the most wonderful woman in the world. It's about time she had her inning."

"If that's the reason you're going through with this marriage, you'd better consult a good psychiatrist."

She clasped the little green bag. "Nothing will stop me now. Nothing."

"Not even Baggy Pants?"

"Who?"

"The Y.M.C.A. number who lit up your eyes in front of the Italian Lines pier."

"Hank? Not a chance! Not now! I've learned a good lesson. So will he!"

She threw the half-smoked cigarette back into the white wake.

"Rafferty Valois, will you help me?"

"How?"

"You're experienced in getting information. Digging things out."

"What makes you think so?"

"That Hamden creature told me." Before I could delve into just what Hamden had told her, she went on quickly, "Tony Machero admitted the last night on the boat that he had been employed by someone to prevent the announcement of my engagement to King Michel."

"Employed?"

"Apparently he was, as they say in America, supposed to 'make me.' The idea was that I was to fall desperately in love with him or some such nonsense and break off my engagement. When that failed ..." She stopped, biting her lip.

"Well?"

"From something Tony said in that courtyard today, it suddenly came over me that Hank had been employed by the same people and for the same reasons."

"Are you certain?"

"Practically. Once the idea registered with me, a lot of odd things about Hank suddenly fell into place. Well, he's going to fall into *his* place in just a few minutes!"

"He's here in Stresa?"

"Last night on the boat I made a date to meet him at the hotel pier at midnight. Just like a bad romantic novel, isn't it? What a fool I was!"

I touched her arm. "You're young yet, baby."

She drew away. "I have a little money. I can pay for the information. I want to find out who Tony and Hank are working for. That is, if I fail tonight."

"Fail at what?"

She clutched the little green bag: "Tony must not go to Mother with his melodramatic warnings. I won't have it. I intend to ..."

"What?"

"Never mind. Will you help me?"

"I'll try," I heard myself saying, as I had heard myself saying so many times before.

"It's an odd thing about you," she said, "but you invite confidence and trust."

I cleared my throat, hoping to clear the atmosphere of undue flattery. My own voice sounded like a travesty on the paternal.

"Now, honey, have you any idea who might be employing Machero and this American boy?"

"None."

The launch was approaching the lights of the hotel landing.

"Look," I said. "Why don't you go on back to the palace? I'll see what I can dig up. It's no time for a girl to be taking matters into her own hands.”

“I’m safe enough. I have two swains breathlessly awaiting my arrival!” The bitterness was back in her voice. “Besides, I’m expected to behave as a Becellini, you know.”

“That leaves you a pretty wide field.”

“How right you are! In the fifteenth century they made the Borgias look like bungling amateurs! Their poisons were more deadly and they were very adept with other weapons. For instance ...”

She opened the little green velvet handbag and drew forth what appeared to be a tiny figurine of a monk, carved in ivory, and no more than two and a half inches in length.

“For instance! This has been in the family for over four centuries. It’s said to have caused the death of a Medici— not to mention several minor Sforzas.”

“It looks innocent enough.”

“Doesn’t it!”

She held it high in the moonlight. There was a tiny click, and a blade, almost as long again as the figurine, shot from the feet of the monk. She sat there with the stiletto held high above our heads, smiling, but smiling in a way I didn’t like.

The launch’s engines were cut as we swept around the final arc toward the hotel landing stage. In the sudden silence she said, “So innocent! You merely touch the little Bible in the monk’s chaste hands, and out comes death!”

“What are you doing with that thing?”

The knife slid back into the body of the monk. She dropped it into her purse and snapped it shut.

“My father sent it to me on my ninth birthday. I’ve often suspected he was subtly suggesting I use it either on Mother or on myself. I carry it about with me. It gives me a feeling of ‘family’!”

“Why don’t you let me keep it tonight?”

“No,” she said. “Mother believes the Becellinis don’t rape easily, but you never can tell. Besides, I don’t like guns. Too damn much noise.”

“Have you been drinking, Bianca?”

She laughed, but without much humor. “Don’t tell me I’ve made the great Rafferty Valois nervous! I suppose you’ll rush to the phone as soon as you reach the hotel and report to Mother that her daughter is loose on the mainland with madness in her eyes and a stiletto in her bag!”

“I’m not hired to be a nursemaid for you, young lady. But if you run into any snags, I’ll be in my room.”

“I’ll remember that.”

The launch was nosing up to the pier. Standing at the foot of the steps leading up to the esplanade was the young American I had seen in front of the pier at Genoa. He still wore the old tweed coat and the baggy flannels. In the glare of the arc light he looked eagerly toward the launch. Bianca's hand closed on my arm. In a low voice she said, "Help me not to be weak, Rafferty!"

The attendant leaped to the pier and leaned down to help us out. Bianca jumped out first. The young man came hurrying across the cement. I looked up the steps to the esplanade. The low-slung Ferrari was just coming to a halt there.

"Bianca! I was afraid you had forgotten!"

"Henry," she said with polite surprise. "What in the world are you doing here?"

He stopped, uncertain, gave me a questioning look. "Doing here? We have a date."

Bianca laughed lightly. She spoke in a chiding, artificial voice that made me think of her mother.

"How delightful! Surely you didn't take that seriously. What a naïve creature you are!"

"What are you talking about, Bianca?" He gave me a suspicious glance. "Who's this?"

"An old friend," Bianca said. "Name of Rafferty Valois. Mr. Valois, unless I'm mistaken, this young man's name is Dawson. Henry Dawson. I believe he goes by the disarming nickname of Hank."

"What kind of act is this, Bianca?"

Bianca spoke with all the warmth of the Greenland icecap: "I never dreamed you would really believe I would see you here. I found you rather diverting for a few weeks, but really... And as for 'putting on an act,' as you so crudely put it, that is something you would know more about than I, Mr. Dawson."

Dawson looked startled, "What the hell does that mean?"

At the top of the steps I saw Prince Machero standing beside his shiny sports car, surveying the scene below. It struck me as odd that he would wait there instead of coming down the steps.

"Bianca, I've got to talk with you. It's desperately important!"

"I imagine it is— to your bank account!"

"Who has been talking to you?"

"I've developed the habit of talking to myself— fortunately!"

"Are you trying to give me a brush-off?"

"Please step aside. You're making a scene. Someone is waiting for me."

Dawson wheeled around and looked toward the esplanade. Machero leaned against his car smoking a cigarette, a weary smile on his too hand-some face.

"You're going out with that louse at midnight?"

Bianca laughed unpleasantly. "That's hardly the way to describe a colleague." Her voice was under control, but the anger thundered underneath her cool, cutting tone. "I don't want you to annoy me ever again."

With that she swept past the astounded young man, turned and waved a farewell to me, then marched up the steps to her waiting prince. There she said in a voice that carried down to us clearly, "Tony, darling! What a divine night! Let's drive up to the ruins of the castle."

Machero muttered something unintelligible. He hesitated a moment, looking down on us with a puzzled frown, then shrugged and went around to the driver's seat. A moment later the car roared off.

"Machero!" Dawson muttered. "I'll fix that noble gigolo so he won't be able to gig any more!"

"Tut-tut," I said. "Remember the old school tie."

Dawson didn't listen. Instead he bounded up the steps and disappeared from my view. The boat attendant caught my eye and grinned. I climbed the steps to the esplanade. Far down the boulevard, the Ferrari slid silently away under the street lights until it vanished into darkness. Dawson was nowhere in sight. I crossed the boulevard, trying to shake off the old Sir Galahad tendencies that had got me into so much trouble in the past. The sweet virgins I had assisted in their hours of need usually turned out to be the most hardened prostitutes in Port Said or dear little women who had murdered four husbands for insurance. This had all the signs of the same sort of trap. Bianca was young and beautiful and woefully alone, but there was something secretive and deceptive about her. It was difficult to tell whether she was naïve and acting sophisticated or sophisticated and acting naïve. Besides, I reasoned, the ordinary person wouldn't see anything particularly pathetic about a girl who would come into several million dollars and was going through with a marriage to a king in order to satisfy her mother's pathological lust for a position in a society that was already on the way out.

I had a strong hunch that my best bet would be to leave Stresa in the morning. The notion that I could retrieve the Countess' letters from a blackmailer or help Bianca was slightly ridiculous.

Still... there was something appealing about Bianca. And, of course, there was something definitely appealing about the twenty-five thousand dollars I would collect if I could get hold of the letters.

I entered the lounge to the sound of dance music from the adjoining garden. Manfully I kept my eyes off the bar and went to the desk. The clerk gave me a deadpan look arid said, "It is not necessary for the key, signor. Already the lady she has taken it."

"Already what lady?"

"Why, signor, your ..." His hesitation was so slight it could hardly be taken to be insolence. "Your niece."

"My what?"

"She is waiting this instant in your suite."

When he saw what my face was obviously registering, he began to look worried. "Ah, no, I have not made a mistake, surely not. The young lady is surely most convincing. She explains she is expected and wishes to wait in your suite. Signor, it did not occur to me ..."

"Keep your boutonniere in place, buddy. Maybe I could use a niece."

"I do not understand."

"I'll let you know when I do."

I left him gaping and crossed to the elevators. Might as well have a look, I thought. A local niece might be just what the doctor ordered tonight. Still, I was somewhat nonplused at what appeared to be an extra de luxe service in this highly respectable hotel.

I was lifted to the third floor in a softly lit, pink-paneled little elevator that was heavy with the scent of perfume. I stepped out and the elevator door slid silently shut behind me. Everything was muffled and still. The long hall was empty, and soundless as a tomb. For some reason I felt uneasy and alert. Irrelevantly, I thought of the green-eyed cat out in that fantastic palace on the lake, perhaps crouching now on a parapet staring toward the shore.

The door of the suite was slightly ajar. Carefully I pushed it inward and stepped across the threshold into a small but elegantly appointed sitting room. On a chaise longue was a girl wearing what appeared to be nothing but a rather worn and unflattering flannel bathrobe. Beside her on a small table was a glass of milk and a plate of crackers. For a moment she was unaware of my presence. She seemed deeply engrossed in a paper-backed novel. She reached for another cracker, looked up, and saw me.

"Hello, Uncle Rafferty," she said blandly. I must have groaned because she said, "That's not very polite after I've come all this way to help you."

Chapter Five

"Close the door, Ducky," Loretta said. "Open bedroom doors always make me nervous."

I banged the door shut behind me.

"How the hell did you get here?"

"Bertie brought me."

"And who in the name of jumping Jesus is Bertie?"

"A very vulgar little man with a bald head."

"Someone you're sleeping with?"

"You *are* a cad," she said without rancor. "I really don't know why I bother about you. I had a beastly few hours in the air in a plane that kept dipping and swirling like a bloody eagle. And that perfectly filthy little train from Milan to Stresa …"

"How in God's name did you find out where I was?"

"Bertie."

"Loretta! I've had enough riddles for one day. Make it quick and clean. Who is Bertie, what are you doing with him, how did he know where I was, and why would he want to know?"

"How I loathe literal minds! However, if you insist on a detailed explanation …"

She cupped the glass of milk in both hands like a child, sipped thoughtfully at it for a moment, yawned, curled her toes, put down the glass, and stretched her arms above her head. She was as unself-conscious as a ten-year-old. The flannel bathrobe would have looked more appropriate on an inmate of a home for the aged, but the long, slim, suntanned legs would have been definitely out of place there. I steeled myself into sightlessness in order to hear what she said.

"Well, Ducky, after you ran out on me in that perfectly childish manner in Cannes, I started to pack."

"At midnight?"

"Yes. I couldn't have stayed on in that suite. Not without you."

If she was kidding, she disguised the fact extremely well.

"I was planning to take a taxi to Nice and get an early-morning plane to Paris. I was weeping or cursing or something when there was a knock on the door, and when I said come in, in came Bertie."

"Someone you knew?"

"No, darling. He's someone no one could possibly know. Anyway, I demanded to know what the hell—I mean barging in on a lady like that unannounced and everything. He said he had to see you. That it was frightfully important. He seemed dreadfully steamed up about something and it was really rather difficult to understand what he was saying."

"A Frenchman?"

"Oh, no. An American. But he had one of those odd provincial accents. Chicago or Brooklyn or some unheard-of place like that."

"What did he want with me?"

"That's what I asked him, because naturally I assumed he was some dreary trades person with a bill in his pocket. He said it was something that might mean a great deal of money to you. I told him you had gone and I didn't have the faintest where. He thought I was lying to cover up for you, as they say in the films, and he became quite shrill and rude and finally stormed out. I guess he took it for granted that I was— well, that there was, shall I say, a warm friendship between you and me, Ducky."

"I feel warm about you, honey, but not in the way you think."

Unperturbed, she said, "Pet, you don't know *what* you feel. I'll have to tell you sometime. Anyway, as you may have learned, I don't de-mand—"

"Look, Loretta! Will you for God's sake get on with this unlikely story?"

"Well, I finished packing and drying my tears and finishing a champagne cocktail I had ordered from the bar, when up pops Bertie again. Only now he was all smiles and butter and milk. He made some kind of odd little speech about how you should be proud to have such a loyal girl and then he said he had discovered where you were heading for. That rather pleased me, and I must say I was awfully clever. I said, 'I believe you're trying to trap me. If you know, tell me.' And he said, 'Stresa.' I didn't have the foggiest notion where Stresa was, but I nodded and said as a matter of fact I was planning to join you there the next day. Bertie bowed and scraped and said he would arrange the plane reservations and I said wasn't that lovely of him and... well, here I am."

"So it seems. And this Bertie?"

"He's staying at the Regina Hotel. He muttered something about not wanting to be seen at this hotel. I can't imagine by whom, because it's quite impossible to believe that anyone could know him socially. He was very annoyed to discover you had gone over to that palace, and he wants you to call him the moment you come in."

"Why does he want to see me."

"I don't know, but I'm quite certain it's something shady. I'm glad I'm here to advise you. I wouldn't have much to do with him, Ducky."

"But I can't understand why he wants to see me."

"Probably wants to employ you professionally."

"Professionally?"

"Probably because of that absurd magazine article."

"Magazine article?"

She reached for the milk and looked at me with wide and too innocent eyes. "Pet! How delicious! You don't know about it? Bertie showed it to me on the plane. You're a celebrity!"

"Are you kidding me?"

"No. But somebody is. The person who wrote the article, I guess. It's all about 'The International Man of Mystery,' name of Rafferty Valois. I had no idea you had done such fantastic things, Ducky."

I began to feel weak. I sank into a chair.

"What fantastic things?" I asked with the glimmer of a horrid suspicion.

"Oh, confidential jobs for the Shah of Iran and two or three Indian maharajas and several minor Balkan countries and a British duke...."

"Don't say any more!"

I shuddered. A cold sweat was beginning to stand out on the back of my neck. I fumbled for a cigarette, trying to decide whether to laugh or to be sick. I settled for laugher. The shout that I produced made even the ordinarily lethargic Loretta sit up.

"You're not going to become hysterical, Ducky. I'm very bad with cases of hysteria."

"The article," I managed to gasp. "It was written by a woman? A woman who calls herself Geraldine Wiley?"

"Why, yes. That's the name."

"Oh, my God. This tops everything!"

"I knew it couldn't be true. Is she insane?"

"Not legally. She's a neurotic spinster who writes solemn gems of wisdom for the women's magazines."

"But where did she get these idiotic ideas about you?"

"From me. And a guy named Ed Haley who is a correspondent for the London *Morning Mail*."

"Will you please stop laughing like a hyena and explain?"

"I'll try to. I was coming out from Korea by way of Malaya and India. I ran into Ed Haley in Singapore. I needed a binge bad after some of the things I had seen in Korea and not been able to write about. Ed took me in hand and we did the bars together. About midnight we ended up at the bar of the Singapore Yacht Club, and there we had the misfortune to run into Miss Geraldine Wiley. Miss Wiley had been commissioned by some editor who must have been real sick to travel to the

Far East and write 'colorful' stuff about various characters who, as she put it, 'helped shape history.' She began to tell us in no uncertain terms what was wrong with the world and the Far East in general. She had put away quantities of pink gin and couldn't be stopped. She had a way of making the plight of millions of suffering Asiatics seem like a cozy film by Lubitsch, and the 'characters' she was writing about were old hat when Maugham first went to the South Seas."

"I suppose you lost your temper."

"Better than that. It was Ed who started it. Ed had one of those dead-pan senses of humor. He appears to be completely logical even when he's talking double talk. He informed the hatchet-faced Miss Wiley that she was standing right next to the greatest human-interest story in the East. Namely, me. He painted a picture that made me look like a cross between Philo Vance and Lawrence of Arabia.... Oh, my God!"

"What's wrong?"

"Lawrence of Arabia! That's what Hamden said. Now I'm beginning to understand why the Countess sent for me. She must have read that damned article."

"So! You're mixed up with a countess!"

"Never mind that now. Jesus! Can you imagine that fool editor passing that story? How the boys at Moriarity's must be laughing!"

"Bertie referred to Lawrance of Arabia, too. Of course, I knew the woman who wrote that stuff must be mad. 'Confidential agent' indeed! What rot!"

"You don't believe I could be one?"

"Certainly not. You forget, Ducky, I've heard you talk in your sleep."
Somewhat defeated, I said, "I'm going to take the job."

"I don't know what you're talking about, but I feel that you should discuss it with me. I'm certain you'll get into some kind of awful trouble."

"Go back to your room, Loretta. I've got to think."

"The man is beginning to believe his own publicity! Besides, you don't imagine that I'm the sort who traipses through hotel corridors in the bathrobe my poor papa left me when he died?"

"What! You mean to say ..."

"Yes, darling. My luggage is in the bedroom. And I actually do think it's about time that we—"

"Of all the goddamned cheek! I don't need you in or out of the bedroom."

"As usual, you're mistaken, Ducky," she said calmly. "And I must ask you to stop addressing me as though I were a— well, a tramp."

"How should I address you?"

"As a lady with principles."

"I'll investigate your principles in a few minutes. In the meantime, maybe I'd better call this Bertie guy."

"Let Bertie go until morning."

I looked at her and thought, Why not?

"You can stay tonight, Loretta, but I'm putting you on the Paris Express tomorrow."

She yawned. "I always say tomorrow can talk for itself."

She stood up, holding tightly the ridiculous bathrobe.

"It's so nice to be with you, Rafferty darling," she said quite simply. "Nicer than with anyone I ever knew."

She picked up her glass of milk and went off to the bedroom. I was surprised to find my annoyance with her vanishing. There was something different about Loretta, something childlike and very comforting. I decided I would forget Bertie in favor of some of that comfort.

I walked to the bedroom door.

"Among other ideas that are occurring to me," I said, "I just realized I don't even know your last name."

She swung her legs over the edge of the bed.

"It's Toastmaster."

"I beg your pardon?"

"Loretta Maximilian Toastmaster."

"I might have known."

"My uncle on my mother's side had a very successful pub in Birmingham and he was a bachelor and his name was Maximilian, but when he died he didn't leave me a shilling after all. Still, I do think the name is quite distinguished."

"Oh, quite. And now, Miss Loretta Maximilian Toastmaster, if you'll be good enough to get out of that ridiculous flannel bathrobe I will—"

But the phone started to ring.

"Ducky!" she said. "Don't answer. It's probably that impossible Bertie."

"Might as well get it over with."

I picked up the phone and said, "Hello?"

"Rafferty," the little pink earphone said, "I need help."

"Bianca!"

"Don't mention any names."

"Where are you?"

"A place called Alfredo's Café. Across the square from the railroad station. Can you come right away?" Vaguely I was aware of Loretta buttoning up the flannel bathrobe with an indescribable air of businesslike resignation.

Into the phone I said, "What's wrong?"

Bianca hesitated, then said in a low voice, "You remember the ivory monk?"

"Yes."

"It's been misplaced."

"Misplaced? Where?"

"In someone's back," she said.

Chapter Six

It was one-fifteen when I stepped out of the hotel lift into the lobby. The first person I saw was Jeffery Hamden, who checked his rapid pace toward the desk when he saw me and came hurrying in my direction.

"Mr. Valois," he said breathlessly. "Have you seen Bianca?"

"Not since dinner," I lied.

"The Countess is furious. We only played one hand of bridge when she got bored and said good night and went to Bianca's room hoping to find her still awake. Instead, Bianca was gone! She raised holy hell and had the boatman brought to her. He admitted taking Bianca across to Stresa and said she had dismissed him saying she would have the hotel boat bring her back. The Countess sent me across to get her. I've been to the Casino and the hotel gardens and everywhere and I can't find her."

"Don't get so excited," I said. "It's spring and the girl is young. Go back to the boat and wait until she shows up at the landing."

"You'd be excited too if you ever saw the Countess in a temper." Then he added angrily, "I knew she had a bad streak in her!"

"It's too late at night to be so morally indignant. I'll see you at lunch, I suppose."

I started toward the entrance but he put a detaining hand on my arm.

"Where are you going at this hour?"

I brushed his hand away. "Do you want a report, sir?"

"Listen, Valois. You're not trying to fool around with Bianca by any chance?"

"In books, young men who make cracks like that usually get their teeth knocked in."

I left him standing in the middle of the lobby, red-faced and worried, and made what is usually described as a dignified exit.

I found a carriage and directed the driver to Alfredo's Café. He gave me one of those "crazy American" looks, shrugged, and resorted to *sotto voce* conversation with his horse. The moon had disappeared behind some ominous-looking clouds and a cool wind was sweeping in from the lake. There is very little night life in Stresa; the esplanade was deserted except for another lone carriage far down the drive. The huge hotels, set back in gardens, were nearly dark save for an occasional lonely bedroom light shining forth from the stone façades. Out on the lake the Becellini palace was a dim, shapeless mass of dark shadow now that the torches had been extinguished.

After a bit the carriage turned away from the esplanade and the luxury hotels and headed through ill-lighted streets to the dreary square on which the railroad station is situated. The buildings around the square were dark and desolate in the reflection of the street lights, plaster peeling from their ancient façades, and here and there a torn and faded advertisement for vermouth or Olio Sasso. The carriage came to a halt before a small and uninviting-looking café opposite the darkened station. I got out and told the driver to wait.

The café was about what the exterior promised: a small room with six or seven marble-topped tables and a flyspecked zinc bar. The sole illumination came from a tired pink-shaded bulb hanging by a cord in the center of the room. Behind the bar was a thin, long-faced man in a dirty apron. He paused in the act of putting a bottle away to give me a hostile look. The only other person in the place was Bianca. I went directly to where she sat at a table in the shadow on the far side of the room.

"You've got courage to wait in this place alone with a villainous-looking pirate."

"Alfredo? I've known him since I was a child. He used to work at the palace. Mother set him up in this café. There isn't much he wouldn't do for Mother or me."

"Why didn't you call on him for help?"

"This is something special. Sit down and try to act casual. Order a drink or something."

She had something milky-green and evil-looking in a glass before her. I suspected it was Pernod. I ordered a brandy. Alfredo brought it reluctantly and retired once again to the bar. She looked down into her glass.

"Well?" I said.

She pointed to the dirty plate-glass window of the café. "Do you see that road that leads out across the railroad tracks?"

"Yes."

"You go down that road about five hundred yards until you come to a dirt road on the right. This road is used only in the daylight by tourists who want to visit the ruins of the old castle on the top of the hill.

The natives will not go there at night because of superstition. There's supposed to be some kind of curse on the place after dark— especially during a full moon."

"All right, Miss Baedeker," I said. "All very instructive, but ..."

"If you turn into the dirt road, you climb the hill for about half a mile. I want you to go up there for me."

"Ah," I said apprehensively. "You've been up there."

"Unfortunately, yes."

"Tell me."

"You remember at the hotel landing stage I asked Tony to drive me there? That was mostly for Hank's benefit. Actually it didn't matter much where we drove as long as I could talk to Tony. He parked the car up there and I started to ask him questions. He refused to answer. Said that what he had to say was for my mother. We got into an argument and suddenly in the midst of it his hot Italian blood or something got the better of him and he began to use cave-man tactics."

"You might have known that."

"I managed to elude his warm embrace and hopped out of the car."

"One of those 'walking home' routines?"

"I suppose so. I walked across the parking space and started down the dirt road. I was running, I guess. Anyway, I suddenly became aware that Tony had not started up the motor to follow me. I stopped there halfway down the hill and I remember the moon went behind a cloud and I felt a sudden chill. And then I thought to myself, This is absurd. I realized I had left my green velvet handbag in Tony's car. I decided I was behaving like a frightened schoolgirl. I started back toward the parking lot, intending to order Tony to drive me back to the boat landing. I ..."

She stopped, took a gulp of the green stuff, and closed her eyes.

"The moon came out again as I reached the edge of the parking space. Tony was slumped over the wheel of the car. I remember thinking, Of all the damned fool things, falling asleep like that. I crossed the gravel and then I saw his face was half turned on the wheel and his eyes were wide open. His mouth... Well. The monk was so innocent-looking— as though it were perched there in the middle of his back."

"Jesus."

"I couldn't believe it. There hadn't been a sound. At least, none that I remembered. No cry. No footsteps running across the gravel. And then suddenly it came over me that the murderer must still be there— probably crouched among the ruins. I turned and began stumbling down the road. I don't remember much more until I was on the phone calling you."

Blindly, unaware that her glass was empty, she lifted it to her lips and with great deliberation went through the motions of drinking. I saw now that her calm manner was a veil for controlled hysteria.

"Rafferty," she said, "there's only a chance in a million that they will discover— discover him until morning. I've got to get that stiletto and my bag back before the body is found."

"You mean to tell me you didn't take them?"

"I was mad with fear. I didn't think about that at all."

"And you want me to go up there to the castle and get them."

"Yes. I could never go back. I can't pay you what it's worth to me at the moment, but later— in a few months—"

"Forget the money!" I said sharply. "Let me think a moment."

I thought and didn't like my thoughts. An ugly little spider web of doubt got stuck on the corners. I tried to sweep it away, hoping to find innocence— or at least candidness— in her eyes. But she looked away.

My silence compelled her to speak.

"Surely you see. There must not be a scandal. Especially at this moment. It would break Mother's heart."

"People know you're in Stresa. How about the ones who saw you get into Machero's car at the pier?"

"There was only Mario, the boatman. He's safe. And Alfredo there. He won't open his mouth."

"And Baggy Pants."

"Yes," she said. "Hank."

"Hank heard you ask Machero to drive to the castle."

"No," she said. "No."

"How can you be so certain?"

"No."

Her hand was tight on the glass.

"You're in love with him, Bianca."

"No."

And suddenly she was weeping. She didn't try to conceal the tears as some women might have done; she sat there, her hands stretched before her on the soiled tablecloth, with the tears making a slow, unreal progress to the corners of her mouth.

"You can't bring yourself to believe he murdered Machero."

"I don't know," she said. "I don't know anything any more. Nor do I care."

"How long have you known him?"

She got hold of herself and spoke in a tired monotone. "Not long. He was in one of my classes at Columbia. I went out with him quite a lot. I knew I shouldn't be seeing him when I was about to be engaged to King

Michel, but I liked him so much, and I couldn't bring myself to tell him. And then when he heard I was sailing on the *Vulcania*... well, I got on the boat and there he was." She sighed and her tone changed abruptly. "He was clever and it almost worked."

"What almost worked?"

"I was intending to confide in Mother, and I thought when she understood how I felt about him, maybe ..."

"Maybe the engagement to King Michel would be called off."

"Yes, of course, I was an idiot. That's exactly what Hank wanted. It's what he had been hired to do."

"You're positive."

"It's so obvious. There were things that bothered me about him—things I hadn't let myself think about. A vagueness... a certain air of secrecy. They all came out into the light today in the courtyard of that restaurant. Only the night before, Tony Machero admitted he had been hired to try to break off my engagement, and today he began to tell me what a wonderful guy he thought Hank was. To my knowledge they had never even met! It was a stupid blunder on Tony's part and gave away their game completely. Hank had been employed to succeed where Tony had failed. And, as you see, it almost worked!"

"I see."

"So we'll forget the tears and the girlish crushes," she said bitterly, "and concentrate on getting me out of one hell of a mess!"

Her mother's caustic mask was back in place. She looked me in the eyes challengingly. "Well?"

"Your mother knows you came to Stresa. She sent Hamden to search for you."

"I think I can handle Mother," she said. "I'll tell her I came to Stresa to break off a silly flirtation with a ridiculous young American. It's the sort of thing that will amuse her— as long as she believes I didn't take it seriously."

"The boatman saw you get into Machero's car."

"I'll handle Mario in my own way!" She looked impatiently at her watch. "Are you on my side, Rafferty?"

"I'll play it that way," I said. I stood up. "You go back to the boat landing. You'll find Hamden chewing his fingernails down to the elbow. Go home and get a good night's sleep. I'll take care of it."

She got to her feet, tried to smile, then reached for the table for support. Her face was deathly white. After a second she said, "As a Becellini, I should be able to take murder in my stride."

I threw some lire on the table, took her arm, and guided her to the entrance. The waiting carriage looked painted on the empty square. Behind us Alfredo banged the door shut and threw a bolt into place. I helped her into the carriage. She leaned down and took my hand. It felt cold and lifeless.

"It's strange," she said in a tired voice, "but you're the only one in the world I can trust. I ..."

Her voice broke. Her hand tightened on mine, then slid away, trailing off my arm as the carriage lurched forward. I stood on the curb watching it as it creaked across the deserted square, out under the lamplights and off into the darkness toward the water front.

Chapter Seven

Behind me the light in Alfredo's was extinguished. I knew that in a few hours this place would be alive with peasants bringing their produce to market, but at the moment it looked cold and dead. Quickly I crossed the square and started to walk down the highway that led out across the railroad tracks. On the opposite side of the tracks the town gave way to open country. I walked several hundred yards to the dirt road on the right. I turned into the narrow, unlighted road and started up a sharp, twisting incline. Fortunately, for the moment, the moon was free of the dark clouds that had been gathering in the north and racing silently toward the south. On either side of the road, dark and sinister foliage grew dense over a ruined wall.

I had gone about half a mile when up ahead I saw the partly destroyed towers of the ancient castle looming against the night sky. A moment later the road opened into a wide graveled parking space.

I stood on the edge of the gravel, listening. Down in the town the church towers boomed twice. Distantly, from far out over the lake, came the screech of a night bird. In my immediate vicinity there was no sound save for the rising wind in the underbrush.

The Ferrari was parked on the far side of the clearing beside a stone wall that supported one of the castle's terraced gardens. Its low-slung bonnet was nosed up against a low parapet, beyond which was a sheer drop of several hundred feet. In the moonlight I could see clearly the body hunched over the wheel. Cautiously I started across the gravel. And then, when I was only a few yards from the car, the moon slid behind another cloud and I was submerged in blackness.

I started to grope my way forward, changed my mind, and fished in my pockets for matches. As my fingers touched the small box in my right-hand pocket I heard, from somewhere out in the darkness, a small sound. A bird or an animal moving through the underbrush? Or more sinister, a stone dislodged by a careless foot? I stood there, frozen, hand on matches, listening. The wind was rising. It began to sob through the gaping holes in the ruined towers of the castle. Below me the town seemed like a miniature toy village, far away and completely unreal. I thought of Bianca and the moment she had discovered Machero's body. No wonder she had turned and fled without thought of the incriminating knife or her handbag.

I tried to shake off the sense of sudden fear. I decided the sound I had heard was a sound anyone might hear in the country late at night. I wasn't an expert on country sounds. I managed to get the matches free of my pocket. With a certain amount of bravado I struck one and held it cupped in my hand. I'd never realized just how much light one tiny match can create. It flared up bravely in the shelter of my hand.

The sound of the shot was not more than a gentle ping.

The dive for the ground was one of the more undignified acts of a life peculiarly lacking in dignity. The gravel cut through the cloth of my trousers into my knees. I lay flat for a fraction of a second, then jackknifed up and, crouching, began to run a zigzag course across the clearing. I thanked the gods of this particular mountain for holding fast the clouds before the moon and for the fact that whoever had pulled the trigger was a lousy shot. I had been a target, match-lit in a shooting gallery for children. The gods were with me also when I found the road without much trouble and started down the incline, dragging my lady's colors with me. It's extraordinary how the sound of a shot can change a bold hero into a comic clown in a second flat. At least, if he has any sense.

I figured that a guy who coolly slipped a knife in Machero's back and then waited around on top of a darkened mountain for possible interesting visitors was no one with whom to fool around. When I had stumbled several hundred yards down the dirt road the moon sailed forth from behind the clouds, and by this time I was thankful for a little light. Perhaps as a reporter I was not upholding the standards of my profession in leaving a good story at the top of the mountain, but right now spot news was the last thing I wanted and a well-lit exit trail was more welcome than a possible by-line.

I must have been halfway down the twisting road when I heard the sound of a motor roaring to life above me. The only car up there, until a moment ago, had had a dead man at its wheel. I heard the gears growl and the engine roar into high. I looked back. Already the headlights were beginning to dance along the foliage at the curve in the road. There was no chance of my doing better time than a Ferrari to the foot of the hill. I plunged into the underbrush at the side of the road, vaulted a low stone wall, and ducked down.

The car was coming down fast but in a sudden sinister silence. The driver had cut the motor and it was descending swiftly under its own weight. The headlights cut across the stones above my head for an instant and then the car went sliding past. I lifted my head. The red tail-light vanished around a curve farther down.

I decided to wait where I was. A minute passed and then I heard once more the cry of the Ferrari's powerful motor, this time from the foot of the mountain. As I stepped out into the road I could see the headlights heading away from Stresa on the road to Milan.

By the time I reached the railroad square and the now darkened café, my mind was somewhat confused and suspicious. Had Bianca sent me up there for the benefit of someone's target practice? Did she want me out of the way for reasons beyond my comprehension, and if so, who was her collaborator?

It was difficult to believe.

On the other hand, the evil voice persisted, wasn't her call for help a bit too pat? Not to mention the casual manner in which she had announced that she was in the habit of traveling about with a businesslike stiletto in her handbag.

Was it possible that she was a party to the murder of Prince Machero in order to keep him from telling some unpleasant truths to her mother? And that she and her colleague thought my presence in and about Stresa might prove somewhat annoying?

If so, what were the unpleasant truths?

The shutters were up on Alfredo's Café. The deserted square was swept by a chill wind. There wasn't much chance of finding transportation here. I set off through the darkened streets toward the lake-front promenade. The more I walked, the more illogical became my suspicions of Bianca. I'd better begin on another and more plausible tack.

The only possible explanation for going to the trouble of trying to murder me seemed to be that somehow it was suspected I might make an attempt to recover the letters of the Countess from the blackmailer. And in that case, if the Countess' convictions were correct, Machero and Hank Dawson's employer must have been the mistress of King Michel. Or, fantastically enough, King Michel himself!

I reached the lighted esplanade and crossed to the lake side. The lights of a boat were just drawing away from the hotel landing. I stood by the parapet in the shadow of a poplar and saw the lighted boat move swiftly out in the direction of the palace. Suddenly everything seemed utterly unreal to me. The Countess and her cheetah, Hamden and the Harolls, Bianca and her American, the dead man at the wheel of the expensive sports car, the shot amid the lonely ruins of the castle. No one would believe it, I thought. And then quite suddenly I began to feel the old familiar sense of excitement. Here I had been in the midst of one of the most colorful stories of my career and I had done nothing about it. If I saw this thing through to the end, I might have a page-one story and a by-line. Not only would I be reinstated in the good graces of what Loretta called the "home office," but I could name my own figure. Maybe this would make up for all the stories I had been scooped on, for all the bad luck, for all the tough breaks, for all the ill-timed "temperament."

I walked briskly down the esplanade to the entrance of my hotel. The moon was free of clouds and the wind, sweeping down from the snow-covered Alps, was as cold as the lifeless appearance of everything I saw. The only moving object was the light of the launch, which was by this time a mere pin point far out in the lake.

The hotel lobby was dimly lit and deserted except for a night clerk who dozed behind the desk and an aged porter who opened the elevator door with obvious disapproval in his eyes.

The doors of the perfumed lift slid open and I stepped out into the third-floor hall. Tomorrow, I thought, I'll send Loretta packing and become a working newspaperman again. The porter banged the doors shut, and as I walked down the silent hall I heard the lift clattering down through the sleeping hotel.

Hoping that Loretta was asleep, I quietly unlocked my door and stepped into the sitting room. It was blazing with light and my cockney friend, wearing a smart suit and a hat with a gay red feather that might have been stolen from an organ grinder's monkey, sat primly on a sofa.

"What the hell are you doing?"

"Waiting for you," she said. "We're going on a little motor trip. We're going to see the Dolomites at night. I thought the Dolomites were monks or priests or something, but it turns out they're mountains."

"Have you gone nuts?"

"No, Ducky. I'm afraid you won't get much sleep tonight. Bertie wants to take us visiting."

"Bertie!"

She turned her head slightly and gestured toward the open bedroom door. A short, stout little man with a pug nose and a bald head and an expensive-looking camel's-hair coat stood there smiling politely. Politeness, however, ended with his face, because in his hand was a German Luger and it was pointed, not so politely, at me.

"It only goes to show," Loretta said, "what is apt to happen when a gentleman walks out on a lady at two in the morning."

Chapter Eight

Dawn was just touching the wild and barren peaks of the Dolomites when the black limousine climbed the last steep mile of a narrow mountain road that twisted about the rims of yawning chasms full of the remnants of night. For an hour now we had passed no sign of human habitation. The first grayish-pink light on the rocky crags cast up by God knows what sort of cataclysm added to the eerie impression of ascending high into the mountains of the moon. For almost three hours Loretta and I had carried on a tired and spasmodic conversation between uneasy cat naps, separated in the back seat by the uncommunicative Bertie. A chauffeur in a smart green uniform took to the precarious mountain roads as though he had been spawned by a goat. We rounded the last hairpin turn, slid between formidable-looking gateposts, and came to a halt in the courtyard of a low, sprawling, modern villa that seemed built into the highest peak of the mountain chain, hung now in cold and swirling mists.

When the motor died the silence was deafening.

The chauffeur climbed out of the front seat and opened the door beside me. Bertie nudged me with the Luger. I got out stiffly onto the cement pavement with Loretta close behind me.

The courtyard fitted snugly into the body of the house, which was formed into the shape of an E with the middle prong removed. In the center of the long stem of the E was a door guarded by two gigantic stone owls.

"Nice little hideaway you have," I said to Bertie.

"Don't belong to me. The Boss," Bertie said. That was the longest speech he had made since we had left Stresa.

A servant, half dressed and sleepy-eyed, opened the door. We went through a hall into a vast room with a great picture window overlooking miles of billowing fog and sinister mountain peaks. The lighting was indirect, the walls chartreuse and hung with some extremely bad modern pictures, the furniture low and overstuffed. It looked less like a room in a private house than the main lounge of a small ocean liner.

"Just wait here a minute," Bertie said.

"Is the execution to be at dawn?"

"Comic, huh? You and Miss Loretta make yourself to home. The Boss will be with you in a minute."

"From the looks of things, the Boss will probably turn out to be God Almighty Himself. This place must be the greatest engineering feat since the pyramids."

"If them Egyptians could do it, why couldn't the Boss?" Bertie asked. He didn't wait for an answer, if indeed there was one, but went out into the hall and into the silence of the thick carpets.

"I must say!" Loretta said.

"If you must, I suppose you will."

"Well, I mean, Ducky, you must admit it is just a bit of too much. It's like the Dark Ages or something equally absurd. People— even impossible bald-headed ones like Bertie— just don't do such things."

"I'm afraid quite a few of them, bald-headed and otherwise, have been doing such things recently."

"Perhaps I'm simply naïve in saying that I find the whole business quite novel."

"From the looks of this fortress, I'd guess the Boss, whoever he is, must be afraid of something."

"Oh, dear. Terrified people always make me nervous. There's no telling what they might—"

She stopped very suddenly and looked beyond me. I turned fast. A woman was standing in the hall doorway, eying us with cool speculation. She was certainly an object for some speculation herself. Flaming red hair, pale skin, a scarlet slash for a mouth, full-blown and startling breasts, and curves that seemed to be in constant motion even as she stood still. All of this was carelessly and barely contained in a diaphanous black lace negligee, which she used in the manner of a striptease artist as it kept slipping away from various interesting parts of her anatomy. She appeared to be in her late twenties, but whatever her years, they obviously had not been wasted in a nunnery.

"Hi," she said. "A hell of a time of day to have to be a hostess, isn't it, but C. C. always wants things done just right. I'm Annie Harrison. You're Rafferty Valois, and your girl friend there is Loretta, so we don't have to go through that. It's too goddamned early to be polite. Get your asses down and I'll fix you a drink."

Loretta, who looked somewhat pained, said, "I couldn't possibly touch a drink."

The two women were eying each other like old hands in Macy's basement. Annie Harrison shrugged and said, "Far be it from me to start an innocent young thing toward a drunkard's grave. Someone will be bringing coffee in a minute. What will it be, Rafferty?"

She opened a cabinet containing many bottles, the fixings, and an ice bucket. I settled for a brandy and a splash of soda. I noticed that she poured herself a mild vermouth and soda.

"Who is C. C.?" I asked as I took the drink.

"You mean to tell me you don't know where you are? Bertie is sure carrying discretion to the limit." She sank onto the sofa beside me, and in doing so disarranged the black lace so that it slipped to one side, exposing completely for a moment one magnificent breast. "Whoops! Sorry." Calmly she adjusted her neckline. Loretta sat very primly on a chair opposite and didn't smile.

"C. C.'s old lady is getting coffee and buns or something. You want to know who C. C. is?"

"It might help."

"Well, C. C. is Carlo Cattoriere."

I stared at her, hoping she was making some kind of joke. When I saw she wasn't, I began to feel weak. "'Cat' Cattoriere!" I managed to murmur.

"Don't pull a faint on me, honey. He's in a friendly mood. That is, if you play ball. He's quite a guy. Really quite a guy."

"Did you say 'Cat'?" Loretta asked.

"A nickname," I said. "Because he's crawled out of so many tough spots. A cat has nine lives, you know."

"And C. C. has used up eight of them!" Miss Harrison said.

"I don't understand," Loretta said.

At the moment I couldn't enlighten her further. It was hardly the time to explain that Cat Cattoriere was considered by many back in the States to be public enemy number one. Convicted as the brains of a drug-smuggling ring, not to mention his control over organized prostitution, the numbers racket, and gambling, he had been pardoned and deported back to his native Italy. Rumor had it that for the past eight years he had controlled organized crime in America, as a sort of international czar, by remote control from Italy. What he wanted with Loretta and me couldn't even be imagined.

"You're English, dear," Miss Harrison said to Loretta.

"Yes."

"I adore the British. They're very fond of Americans like me. Middle Western accents and no side. I did fine in London. Gave parties at the Savoy Grill and the Embassy Club and had the lords and earls purring in my lap. Some of them tried more than purring, if you know what I mean."

"Quite!" Loretta said with the frigidity of a duchess.

"Aw, now, darling! Come off it, as they say in your country. I'll bet you've had plenty of purring around that cute little lap of yours. But then, maybe you never rated the aristocracy."

Loretta seemed about to break her record for placidity. I could almost hear the hair stand up on the back of her neck. I gave her a warning look. Miss Harrison leaned over and patted her stiff wrists.

"I'm joking, honey. Take it easy. I'm on your side."

It was quite plain that this was one ally that Loretta could do without. But before any international incidents could occur, the ladies were diverted from warfare by the entrance into the room of a stout, swarthy-skinned, elderly woman with flashing black eyes. She was dressed in peasant style but she didn't look like a native of northern Italy. I figured her for a Sicilian. She carried an enormous tray laden with pitchers and cups and a plate of bread. As she put the tray down on a low table in front of the sofa she gave us a warm smile.

"C. C.'s mother," Annie Harrison explained. "No speaka da English. She thinks her son was a big-shot businessman back in the States, and I guess he was, at that. C. C. is a family man. Likes lots of relatives around. You can't go to the can without tripping over a second cousin or a half-wit nephew."

"Won't she think it odd that her son receives visitors at this hour?"

"Her? Everything is odd to her. She lived most of her life in some kind of a fishing hut in Sicily. She probably just thinks it's the crazy American way of doing things— if she thinks at all. Anyway, C. C. can do no wrong as far as she's concerned. Have you ever seen such a dumb-looking slob?"

"She looks sweet," Loretta said coldly.

"I suppose she is, if you like that kind of thing. No sweets for me. Can't touch the stuff. How about you, Rafferty?"

"Now I know who you are," I said. "I didn't connect you at first with *that* Miss Harrison. You certainly twisted the noses of that Senate investigating committee. This young lady, Loretta, spent twenty thousand dollars in two weeks, entertaining in a resort hotel, and then told the committee she just couldn't account for where the money came from."

Annie Harrison laughed. "Am I supposed to be an accountant? Can I help it if gentlemen want to give me little gifts like negotiable bonds?" She looked maliciously at Loretta. "Ask *her* if she'd turn it down!"

In command of herself once again, Loretta said with lofty remoteness, "I've always made it a point that the gentlemen give only for value received. I've never given twenty thousand dollars' worth in my life!"

"I can believe that!" Annie said with sweet venom. She smiled at C. C.'s mother with mock politeness and said, "Scram, you old bag!"

The woman looked at us uncertainly. Loretta tasted the coffee and made a pantomime of pleasure. I put my brandy aside long enough to do likewise. The Sicilian was delighted. She nodded her head back and forth and chuckled, then edged out of the room, showing us a great expanse of very white teeth.

"This dump is as dead as the Copa at eight o'clock on a Monday morning," Miss Harrison said. "I'll be glad when we clear out for the summer. C. C. has a little marble pile of a summer shack up at San Remo. I'm going down to Rome tomorrow to buy myself a slew of summer rags."

I had been watching her closely since my first realization of her identity. She was common and hard and supremely shrewd, and yet there was something else about her that was difficult to pin down. Something underneath the streamlined façade that was like a continuous ripple of tense nerves.

On a sudden impulse I decided to try the shock treatment on her. "Poor Vince," I said.

She froze in the act of lighting a cigarette and looked at me through narrowed eyes, the match still flaming between her fingers.

"Poor Vince," I repeated lightly. "He thought you were coming to Italy to plead for his life. He got a bullet through the head anyway. I guess he would have been surprised to see his girl friend being chummy with the man who is reputed to have ordered the— shall we say— liquidation?"

She said nothing, nor did she move. The match burned down to her fingers. She snapped it away to the rug and crushed it. She flipped the unlighted cigarette into my face.

"We got a son of a bitch in the room, huh?"

"I only know what I read in the papers," I said.

"I warned C. C. not to get mixed up with you!"

"Take it easy, Annie. Don't try so hard."

Very quietly she said, "How would you like that pitcher of coffee up your—"

We were saved from anatomical exactness by a low voice, male and rather tired. "That's not nice, Annie. Not nice at all."

In the hall doorway stood a thin man of middle height with a narrow, sallow face, and brooding black eyes. He was immaculately garbed in silk pajamas, gold slippers, a brocade dressing gown, and a yellow scarf tied at his throat. His hair was plastered back on his thin head, and even from a distance I thought I detected the odor of bay rum and perfume. He smiled politely and gestured what I assumed was a greeting with an amber cigarette holder. Mr. Cat Cattoriere looked as though he had seen one too many George Raft movies.

"The bum was talking about Vince!"

"Mr. Valois was probably kidding you, Annie. We don't talk about Vince in this house, Mr. Valois. The paper's done— I mean did— enough talking for us all. Huh?"

He advanced on us languidly.

"But I told you, Annie, I won't have that sort of language on the premises."

"What sort of language?"

"About where you was going to put Mamma's pitcher of coffee. And things. I don't like that. It isn't ladylike."

Annie shrugged. "Sorry, C. C. I'm not used to getting up at this stinking hour."

"Nor are our guests, I assume," C. C. said elegantly. On closer inspection his manners were nearer to the leading man of a third-rate stock company just hitting Saskatchewan than Mr. Raft's. He bowed to Loretta and then to me. "Allow me to apologize for the abruptness of your departure from Stresa. Bertie is sometimes a bit too impetuous. However, in this case, time was of the essence, and I found it most necessary to employ methods— methods— that ..." He stopped, apparently unable to find the finishing words, and added instead, "You know what I mean."

"Not exactly."

"It was necessary to bring your lady friend so that there might not be any unpleasant publicity."

"Oh, Loretta is used to moving about. Wherever I go I'm apt to find Loretta."

"I've always admired loyalty," C. C. said. "Even in a woman."

"How about dogs?" Loretta asked innocently.

"Dogs, too," he said quite seriously. "I love dogs."

Outside the picture windows the sunrise was becoming spectacular against the jagged mountain peaks. C. C. pushed a wall button and the electric lights were extinguished. He gestured with silent reverence to the scene, as though he had created it especially for our benefit. In the gloom of the room, reflected in the pinkish light filtering through the windows, his face looked more sallow than ever.

"The fact of the matter is," C. C. explained, "I didn't mean for Bertie to take my instructions so literal. I wanted you here, but no rough stuff.

But talking of dogs, as the lady just was, you can't teach the old ones new tricks."

Having coined this phrase, he sat a little distance from us. His movements, as he adjusted his robe neatly over his knees, made me think of a china doll. I noticed his hands were abnormally tiny.

"You tried Mamma's coffee?"

"Delicious," I said sincerely.

"Mamma does everything wonderful. Wonderfully. She does everything wonderfully."

In the moment of respectful silence that followed this pronouncement, Annie's gaze slid away from mine. I found Loretta looking at the ceiling.

"It's very pleasant to be drinking your mother's excellent coffee and watching that highly exaggerated sunrise, Mr. Cattoriere, but kindly, please, just what the hell is it all about?"

"In a moment," he said, somewhat pained at my vulgarity. "But first allow me to say how very pleased I am to meet you. My line of work has been somewhat different from yours, but I've always had a kid's hero worship for a guy like you. A real honest-to-God international adventurer."

"You read that damned magazine article!"

"Yes. That Geraldine Wiley! There's a writer. That last book of hers was wonderful. I'll never forget that scene where Amelia managed to get the message to General Lee just as her blood ran out."

"I beg your pardon?"

"Don't you remember? She bled to death from a musket bullet fired by the Mississippi gambler who had raped her in Chapter Two and then turned up later as a Yankee spy, and she ran through half of Richmond with the top of her dress torn off and stuffed into the wound. Some writing!"

"Did you bring us all the way from Stresa to tell us about Amelia of the bloody bosom?"

He sighed, obviously among Philistines. He turned to his hostess. "Annie, why don't you take the lady on a tour of the premises?"

Loretta, with the courageous expression of Marie Antoinette bound for the guillotine, followed Miss Harrison's swaying hips into the hall.

In a man-to-man voice, C. C. said, "Annie gets out of hand sometimes in her talk. But she's a smart girl."

"I can see that."

"Maybe too smart," he said softly. "I don't know yet."

I felt a little chill for Annie Harrison.

"Well?" I said.

He leaned back and blew a cloud of smoke toward the ceiling. "I got a job for you, Valois."

"Thanks," I said. "I don't need a job. I'm just playing around for a couple of months."

"A guy like you couldn't waste too much time playing around. I know, it's in your blood."

I opened my mouth and shut it. Might as well hear what the perfumed bastard was up to.

"What's the job?"

"Well, I'll tell you, Valois— you do pronounce it Valwah, don't you? I took French lessons same time I took diction. Yes? Good." He leaned back and regarded me through a cigarette-smoke screen with dead black eyes. "I've had to do a little rough stuff in my time, just like any other businessman, but I don't use it unless there's no other way, see? This particular job might end up rough, but when I read about you, it came over me you were just my baby. You could handle the operation smooth."

"Thanks for the compliment."

"I had you on my mind even before I heard you were going to Stresa. I sent Bertie to contact you in Cannes when I read in the *Paris Herald* you were there. Then Bertie calls me to say you had left for Stresa and that cinched it. It was the goddamnedest coincidence I ever heard of."

"Coincidence?"

"Yeah, yeah. But first, the thing I gotta know is this: Why did the Countess Becellini send for you?"

So! I thought. And my heart skipped a beat. I looked him straight in the eyes and said, "She had a job for me. Small change. Not interested."

"What job?"

I thought fast. Better make it plausible, I thought. This baby doesn't stand fooling around with.

"She has some crazy notion that someone is trying to prevent the coming announcement of her daughter's marriage to a big shot. She wanted me to find out who they were. I told her to get a Pinkerton man or Emily Post."

"You're sure you turned it down, sweetheart?" His voice was natural now, and I didn't like the sound of it.

"I've got more to do than to play nurse to a spoiled little rich girl. It isn't in my line. Anyway, I told her she was probably imagining things."

Cattoriere flicked ashes on the carpet. His eyes were as beady and as cold as a cobra's. He waited a moment, then said, "She's not imagining things, Valois. Not at all."

"I don't get it."

"Someone's going to stop that announcement, all right."

"Who?"

"I am," he said softly.

I managed not to register anything but mild curiosity.

"Why?"

I thought at first he had not heard me. He was looking toward the ceiling. He seemed to be in a trance. Then slowly, as though operated by wires, his head came back into position.

He stood and looked down at me. In the lurid sunrise his face was almost purple.

"I'm reasonable, Valois. I got longer patience than in the early days. I can afford to carry a little steam now. But I think you understand how I operate. You work for me. Nobody else. You do the job I want and you won't complain at what you get for it. You double-cross me and you won't complain anyway. You won't be able to complain. That's the way I do business."

I settled for a discreet silence. I could understand why they called him Cat. There was something taut beneath the perfumed softness, something deadly and feline. As he walked to the window and stood there with his back to me, he made me think of Iris.

Over his shoulder he said, "You saw my mamma?"

"Yes."

"You have traveled a lot. Met a lot of people. Did you notice anything about Mamma's face?"

"It's a very lovely face," I said.

"You don't see faces like that often," he said. "Behind it is hundreds of years of breeding. My family was in Sicily when them two brats were suckling off a wolf up around Rome. They were great landowners in Sicily in the days of the first Greek settlers. I paid a guy who knows about those things to look it up. He wrote it all down for me. My family's descended from aristocrats. And yet my mamma knew nothing but poverty and hard work and no education for us kids. See? I went to America when I was fifteen. The Mafia got me started. I rose quick. Being a leader is in my blood. I always wanted to get high— high like this house— on top. I haven't gone high enough yet. But I'm going!"

Behind his back, his hands met and clenched tight.

"I got a niece, Valois. My sister's child. She's a good girl, brought up right with money I sent back from the States. She got mixed up with a guy. When I first heard it, I was going to finish off the bastard with my own bare hands. Then I got a better idea. I decided the guy was going to marry her."

"Shotgun style, eh?"

"Machine gun, in this case. You see, the guy happens to be a king. My niece— sweet, gentle little Maria— will be the queen of Movania!"

I managed to think, Now nothing can surprise me.

"It was as though it had been planned that way, Valois. Like a pattern. It was the opening I've been waiting for. I have a certain amount of political power back in the States. Got three or four senators and a couple of governors jumping through hoops for me. But it isn't enough. Now I've got ten million bucks sewed up in Movania. I got a general there— General Metachas— working for me. We've been secretly arming his followers. In a few weeks there's going to be a military *coup d'état* in Movania. King Michel will be back on the throne and Maria is going with him!"

"And you?"

Very quietly he said, "Spain has its Franco, hasn't it? I'm going to do what I've always done. Run the show. Only this time out in the open and with respect!"

In his emotion he had completely discarded the stock-company elegance. There was more of Sicily in his voice now than the elocution teacher. If almost anyone else in the world had spoken these words, I would have dismissed them as emanating from a mad paranoiac. There was no doubt that paranoia was present, but I knew it was barely possible that Cattoriere could carry out his fantastic plan.

"I didn't know that the King and his mother had arranged a marriage with the daughter of Countess Becellini," he said.

"What did your niece think of that?"

"She's too shy to make a fuss about anything. It never seemed to occur to her that he'd marry her. And it didn't occur to him, either, until I put the idea into his head. But strong!"

"How did he react?"

"Jesus! Such double talk you never heard. He informed me that he regretted he could not go back on his word as a gentleman. That the marriage plans were already advanced and nothing could prevent it except a change of mind on the part of the Countess or her daughter. I thought he was joking at first, but after three weeks trying to make headway, I realized I was wasting time. The best thing was to get the Countess or the girl to call it off. I decided to play it soft. No rough stuff. It didn't seem necessary. I knew the girl was young and vulnerable. I had a guy who had done a couple of jobs for me— good-looking, young, the type women go for. I put him on her trail in New York, but the bum failed me."

"Prince Machero!" I said almost without thinking.

He whipped around. "How did you know that?"

"The girl told me Prince Machero had made passes at her in New York and that she had given him the brush."

Eyes narrowed to slits, he gave the impression of being about to spring. But after a moment he relaxed.

"He wasted a lot of my time and money. He was a lousy amateur."

"Was?"

"'Was in my books. He's off my payroll."

He sure is! I thought, but didn't say it.

"What about Hank Dawson?" I asked. "The young American."

"Never heard of him. Should I have heard of him?"

His answer was so immediate I was almost convinced.

"Just some guy the girl met on the boat," I said.

"Not interested. I've given up that type of operation. If Machero couldn't do it, no one could."

A sudden thought struck me.

"The girl could always be framed for a murder," I said as casually as though I were suggesting a game of golf.

"Who, for instance?"

"Oh, I dunno. Dawson... Machero ..."

"You been reading too many books. I said I wanted this to be smooth. No rough stuff unless everything else fails. If you can pull off the job I have in mind, the Countess and her daughter will be able to go on enjoying their millions in good health. Otherwise ..."

The shrug said it. A chill ran up my spine. It made me think of bodies encased in cement and dumped into the East River and bloody corpses found at night along deserted highways.

"What do you want me to do?"

"It's an inside job. Only someone who can get into the palace and into the good graces of the Countess could succeed. None of my boys are right for that operation except Machero— and he's no good to me any more."

"Getting into the good graces of the Countess" might be pleasant work. I had a hunch what would happen after would not be so pleasant. I asked for it.

"What then?"

"Well, you see, the Countess is a stubborn bitch. She's not going to let King Michel off the hook unless it's for a damned good reason. I think

I know the good reason and I'd like you to get hold of it for me."

"What is it?"

"I'll give you a week. If you haven't succeeded by then, I'm going to get rough. Real rough. I happen to know that there's something you could take from the Countess that's so hot she'd give in to any demand in order to get it back."

"Her virtue?"

"This is no joke, Valois."

"Sorry. What is it you want me to get?"

"A package of letters."

Carefully I put down the cup of cold coffee. Was he offering me the job of getting hold of the same letters that the Countess had commissioned me to get from his niece? I began to be more and more curious about those letters.

"What's in these letters?"

"I don't know exactly, except they're dynamite. They were written over twenty years ago, and my informant tells me they're hot enough to melt Little America."

"Who is your informant?"

"None of your goddamned business, Valois."

I thought, I'll make it mine. I crossed my fingers under the table and said, "If I get them for you, how much is there in it for me?"

"Fifty thousand."

My worth was going up. Twenty-four hours before I had been worth exactly zero. With the Countess' twenty-five thousand and Cattoriere's fifty, I was potentially richer than ever I had dreamed I would be.

"Fair enough," I said without too much enthusiasm.

Cattoriere said nothing. For the first time, looking at him, I felt a twinge of real fear. His face was impassive. I would have given a great deal to know what was running through his mind.

Behind him the mountain peaks were radiating barbaric flame.

"Just one thing," he said softly. "In my business there are no cancellation clauses in the contract. Understand?"

I understood, all right.

Chapter Nine

It was four-thirty in the afternoon when the launch with the red awning dropped me at the palace landing stage. In the great reception hall with its curved staircase of red marble, the major-domo met me and said, "Madame asks that you will please wait. She is resting for the next half hour. In the meantime, Donna Bianca wishes to see you. If you will come with me ..."

Considering that Loretta and I had not reached the hotel from C. C.'s mountain retreat until almost ten A.M. and I had not been able to doze off, I felt remarkably alert. For the first time in a long while I had managed to begin a day— in this case an afternoon— without a drink. With a new resolve I had told Loretta to pack and be ready to take the night train for Paris. To my surprise, she didn't put up any resistance. I supposed that involvement with a notorious American gangster was too much even for her customary placid indifference. I'd left her among the debris of luncheon, served in our suite, and gone down to the concierge's desk and sent off a fifty-word cable to McLaughlan of the I.P. In it I informed him that I was on the inside track of one of the biggest stories in Europe: a planned military *coup d'état* in Movania, involving the ex-king and a well-known American mobster. I was certain McLaughlan would forgive past transgressions and put me back on the payroll with a front-page by-line. Once again I felt the buoyancy I used to feel when I was on the track of a good story.

The major-domo conducted me to a small sitting room done in Chinese Chippendale, where I found Bianca waiting impatiently. When we were alone she drew me to the sofa. She looked as though she hadn't had much sleep. "Rafferty, I've been mad with worry. Why didn't you come earlier? Did you get my— my things?"

"Someone beat me to it, Bianca."

She fell back as though I had slapped her.

"Someone? The police?"

"No. Your bag and the stiletto were gone when I reached the top of the hill."

She pressed her lips together, touched my arm with trembling fingers, and said, "I'm terrified. Mother called the hotel to ask Tony Machero to luncheon. They said quite calmly there was no answer in his room. Surely they must have found him by this time."

"They have," I said. "Everyone was talking about it at the hotel when

I left. He was found stabbed to death by the side of the Milan road early this morning."

"The Milan road!"

"About fifteen miles back from Stresa. The theory seems to be that he got out of his car to change a flat tire. The front of the car was jacked up and the wheel half off. It is being said that whoever killed him must have sneaked up on him in the darkness. His wallet and personal papers were missing, so it's assumed that the motive was robbery."

"But the ivory monk— and my handbag?"

"The weapon that killed him wasn't found. Nor anything else incriminating."

Her fingers tightened on my arm. "Rafferty! You moved that car with Tony in it from the castle to the Milan road!"

"Don't thank me. I didn't do it. But it could be," I said, "that Baggy Pants is covering up for you."

"Hank?" The look of surprise and even hope in her eyes was quite convincing.

"He heard you ask Machero to take you to the castle."

"You think he might have followed and ..." She stopped. "But Rafferty... in that case... you're not trying to say that it was Hank who killed Tony!"

"It seems to me the most logical deduction."

"No! Hank may be many things I didn't suspect, but I know he couldn't commit a murder. I know it!"

I lighted a cigarette.

"I tried every hotel and pension in Stresa. There's no Hank Dawson registered at any of them. I also discovered that the night train from Geneva to Rome stops at Stresa at three-fifteen A.M. He could have been on it."

"But it doesn't make sense! Why would Hank have killed Tony? There's absolutely no motive."

"There is one motive that occurred to me. Not a very pretty one, either."

"What?"

"If Baggy Pants has the stiletto and your bag, he may use them."

"Use them?"

"Blackmail."

She thought about that for a moment. I could see she didn't like her thoughts. Despite last night's bitter denunciation of Hank Dawson, it was apparent that she was resisting the idea of his being a murderer and blackmailer. She started to say something, checked herself, and settled for the camouflage gesture of fumbling in an ivory box for a cigarette.

"Bianca. Have you any idea for whom Tony was working?"

"Not the faintest."

"Suppose you discovered that the persons he worked for were powerful and ruthless. That they will stop at nothing to prevent the announcement of your marriage to King Michel."

"That's absurd! In this day and age ..."

"Remember— if you changed your mind, it might break your mother's heart for a while but she would get over it. She might not get over a bullet through the head."

She drew away and looked at me with sudden bright suspicion. "You too, Rafferty? You sound suspiciously like Tony and Hank." She smashed out her cigarette. "I don't scare easily. Nor does Mother. I'm going through with this marriage if it's the last thing I ever do!"

"Is it worth it?"

"I won't have you or anyone else—"

She stopped abruptly. I looked up. Jeffery Hamden, dressed for an afternoon on a country-club veranda, was standing in the arch that opened out onto a terrace. "Sorry," he said. "I didn't mean to interrupt anything."

Bianca stood.

"You're not interrupting anything. I'm just leaving. I'm going into Stresa with the Harolls for tea." And then in a tone that carried with it the sting of a whip, "Has Mother's siesta been satisfactory?"

The color rose on Hamden's face.

"I'm sure I wouldn't know. I haven't seen her since lunch."

"In that case, you're not as efficient as I thought you were!" Before Hamden could catch his breath she went out into the hall.

The young man made an explosive sound. "What a hell of a thing for a young girl to say! Implying that I usually spend the afternoon in the countess' bedroom!"

"A little crude. Is she right?"

"What the hell do you take me for?"

"It's what the Countess takes you for that counts."

Hamden sank into a chair. His handsome, suntanned face was screwed up unhappily.

"I'm sick and tired of being treated like some kind of lower animal by that snippy kid. She's got too much money— that's her trouble. If she's got that kind of disposition now, you can imagine what's she'll be like with a crown on her dome!"

"So. You know about that."

"The Countess just told me."

I grinned. "At the luncheon table, no doubt?"

"Eh? Oh— oh, yes. I mean just before... just after... lunch." He looked up at me with the eyes of a sick spaniel and said, "O.K., you think what the kid thinks— that I'm just a lousy gigolo."

"It doesn't necessarily follow that a gigolo must be lousy."

His arms flopped dejectedly to the sofa cushions. "Well, let's face it. I suppose I am."

"Lousy?"

He refused to be light about it. I sensed an atmosphere of confession and self-flagellation. Uneasily I tried to put off the day of soul-baring. "Listen, Hamden," I said, "I haven't even thought about it. I—"

But he was off to the races and nothing would stop him.

"It hurts that a guy like you would think that about me, Valois. I've got to make you understand."

"Why me?"

"Because, goddamn it, no one else will!"

Here comes the life story, I thought grimly. I looked at my watch and hoped he'd make it short. I settled back with a fixed looked of interest on my face and tried to make my mind a blank.

"You were born... ?" I said resignedly.

"Iowa. A farm. I hated it. I used to go into town whenever I could and spend hours in the library, reading about all the places in the world that I wanted to visit. The librarian had a bug on genealogy and heraldry, and she got me interested in it."

"Heraldry? I've always wondered what they did on Saturday nights in Iowa."

"It fascinated me. I read all the books about it the library had. I discovered that the Hamden family had once had a title in England— back in the fifteenth century. I copied the coat of arms. My old man and brother thought it was the biggest joke they'd ever heard. I was sixteen then. I ran away the next day. I jumped a freight to Chicago. And I never went back."

"What happened?"

"It wasn't like Horatio Alger— at least, for some time. I did all kinds of odd jobs in all kinds of odd places. Finally I got to New York and landed a job in a department store. I took a secretarial course at night. I read a lot and listened to the rich people who came to my counter in the store... and I met a few people. One night the store manager's wife asked me to fill in at a party in a night club. Very swank. Countess Becellini was there. She was intrigued with my interest in heraldry and in

Europe. Three weeks later I sailed on the *Liberté* as her private secretary."

"The Countess makes up her mind quickly!"

"I'd never met anyone like her. I didn't think there could be anyone more wonderful than she."

"She was interested in your heraldry, no doubt."

"I was pretty gauche at first. The Countess was extremely patient. She taught me how to navigate socially. I worked hard at being a good secretary, and God knows she really needs one, but I never thought of myself as... well, I found her damned attractive and it seemed only natural that ..."

"What could have been more natural?"

"I'm sick of everything I've become!"

"I wouldn't take it so hard."

He went right on, compulsive to the end:

"She used to tell me that I was as good socially as the people I met through her. That my family could be traced back to the Plantagenets. That I had the natural manners of an aristocrat. I wanted to believe it. But of course, in the end I couldn't help but notice what other people were thinking. It was more or less accepted that I would be asked to parties and things with her. But even then it didn't matter too much. Because— because by that time I was in love with Celia."

"Ah, love. A relationship that had nothing to do with the vulgar bond of employer and employed."

"You're laughing at me."

"Only sympathetically. But now, I gather from your attitude, you have lost some of the earlier fervor."

"Not at all. On the contrary. It may seem comic to you, Mr. Valois, but my feelings for Celia are stronger than ever. It's she who has changed her mind."

"How?"

He looked wildly about the room as though for help, then blurted out, "She's given me the sack!"

For the first time since his mention of his peculiar interest in heraldry, Mr. Hamden succeeded in surprising me. "I'll be damned!"

"I'm finished the night after the ball. Oh, she was very generous. Three months' pay and my passage back. Back to what?"

"Sorry to hear it."

"God, what a fool I've been! I must be the laughingstock of Italy."

I felt the young man was exaggerating his own importance somewhat, but it seemed hardly the kindest of observations to make at the moment. I kept silent.

"Just an hour ago she told me. In her bedroom. So damned cool, so damned logical, and so goddamned cruel. She said, 'Jeff, darling, I find myself bored with you. We both need a change. Why don't you go back to the States and pick out some full-blown, healthy young widow with money?' Isn't that a hell of a thing to say to a man who feels about her as I do?"

I kept my face straight. His torment was as genuine and extreme as his sense of outrage.

"I've been nothing more than a paid stud!"

I leaned over and gave his arm a paternal pat. "Sonny," I said, "the Countess is a wiser woman than I would have suspected. Someday you'll thank her for it. This isn't the kind of pond for a kid like you. It's stale and polluted. Go back where there's sunlight and forget about heraldry and the Countess. She's old enough to be your mother."

"If mothers were like that, incest would be a common practice! What can I do? I've lost my pride!"

Watching him closely, I wondered whether it was the woman or the lush surroundings he found so difficult to part with. I decided that, strangely enough, this slightly stupid young man whose accomplishments in life seemed to be confined to heraldry and the bedroom was in a state of utter infatuation.

"If only Bianca hadn't come back right now!" he said bitterly. "If only this damned engagement ball weren't in the offing. If only we were alone together the way we used to be. And if it's someone else Celia is interested in, Bianca certainly wouldn't help my cause."

The idea of a daughter pleading the cause of her mother's ex-lover didn't strike him as being ludicrous. "Someone else? Who, for instance?"

"I don't know. But I have my suspicions. Tony Machero."

I checked myself in time. Hamden obviously had not heard the news that was circulating like wildfire on the mainland.

I wondered if there might not be a germ of truth in Hamden's suspicion. Perhaps the Countess had been thinking of Machero as Hamden's successor. A woman like that always carries some sort of insurance in these cases.

"What makes you think she's interested in Machero?"

"Well, you know how furious she was last night when she heard Bianca had gone to the mainland. I thought then that she was worried only about possible scandal, but it occurred to me that maybe she suspected who Bianca was really meeting and thought Tony was making a pass at the wrong member of the family."

"What makes you think Bianca went ashore to meet Machero?"

"Who else?"

I decided to nip that dangerous idea in the bud. "Me, for instance."

He gave me the look of a startled goldfish. "You!"

"She wanted my advice on something."

"And you were going out to meet her when I ran into you in the hotel lobby?"

"Exactly."

"But Bianca had been in Stresa over an hour at that time."

"That's right," I said glibly. "We met in a café in the town and then I thought of some papers I wanted to show her so I ran back to my room for them. I was just on my way out again when I met you."

"Papers?" To say that he looked skeptical is putting it mildly. "I think you're covering up for her."

I straightened up. "Covering up? For what?"

"I don't know. I wish I did. There are a lot of things going on around here I wish I understood."

I didn't like this turn of events at all. Hamden didn't like Bianca. In case of trouble he most certainly would not be one of her more reliable character witnesses.

Nervously he lighted a cigarette. The air of candid confession was past. I sensed he regretted having told me anything. Before I could set his mind at rest, something rubbed against my leg. I looked down, without pleasure, into the glowing eyes of Iris.

"That goddamned cat!" Hamden said shrilly. "Celia must be crazy to let it run loose like that."

"Look, Iris," I said. "To another cheetah you might look like Helen of Troy, but I'd prefer you as a rug."

The sound of my voice sent a tremor of some unknown emotion through the cat's body. Fervently I hoped the emotion was sympathetic to me. I tried to move my legs but I seemed to have been afflicted with a sudden case of paralysis.

The major-domo saved the day by appearing in the doorway and announcing that the Countess was ready to see me. Iris moved politely aside to allow me to pass. Hamden gave me a sudden, and too bright, look.

"My God," he said. "Why didn't I think of it?"

"Of what?"

"Here I've been telling you everything, all the time thinking it was Tony Machero who was on the way in. Jesus, how you must have been laughing!"

I didn't get it for a moment.

"She always did like red hair!" he said.

I got it then. I was flattered but somewhat nonplused. "Look here, sonny ..."

"Don't you 'sonny' me, you goat! If you try anything funny, Valois, I'll fix you so you'll never be funny again in your life!"

With that he strode out onto the terrace like the hero on his second-act exit line. Iris looked up at me inquiringly. "It's all right," I said. "No drastic measures required yet, my pet."

The major-domo— stony-faced during Hamden's angry outburst— and Iris and I made a regal procession through the halls and up the marble staircase.

Chapter Ten

Iris and I, treated with equal deference, were ushered into a dimly lit sitting room with satin-covered walls and silver draperies drawn against the afternoon sun. The major-domo backed out, shutting the door behind him. Iris settled down in a corner and proceeded once again to stare me down.

On a table by a chaise longue were tea things. And a whisky decanter! My good resolutions of the early afternoon vanished in an instant. I wanted, and wanted very badly, a drink. I poured myself a stiff one. When it was halfway down I wondered why the sudden and urgent need of that drink. I decided that it must be the unseen presence of the Countess. Was it possible that this ridiculously snobbish, spoiled woman could make me uncertain? I was forced to the conclusion that intellectual rationalization was comparatively weak against the onslaught of the Countess Becellini's extraordinary personality.

Rather awkwardly, drink in hand, I stood in the center of a pink rug and surveyed the room. It was a highly feminine little bandbox in which my tweeds seemed as out of place as a bonfire. It occurred to me that the very daintiness of this chamber might have been planned to flatter the maleness of certain visitors. Hamden's suspicions were still in my mind and I was disconcerted to find myself pleasantly speculating along the same lines. It was absurd to think of myself as a successor to Hamden. And yet ...

Near the glass fireplace I noticed a small wall safe. I thought of the missing letters. What the hell was in them? Surely ancient love letters could not cause a scandal at this late date. Hamden's ungentlemanly references to the Countess' behavior certainly added to the possibility that C. C.'s description of the letters as "hot" was probably justified. But it wasn't likely that even very lurid letters from or to some former lover could prevent the engagement announcement. What were they about?

I looked toward the bedroom door. I remembered the way the Countess had held my hand when we parted the night before. Breathing began to be somewhat difficult. My imagination, fed perhaps on certain pictures suggested by Hamden's few unsaid words, worked up to the point where I half expected her to appear in the doorway either in transparent lace or stark naked with a whip in one hand.

It was something of an anticlimax when she walked briskly in wearing a heavy Chinese robe that covered her from chin to foot.

"It was naughty of you not to appear at lunch," she said.

"Something came up last night."

"Blonde and cockney, no doubt."

I sank into a chair. "Who told you that?"

"I know everything that goes on in Stresa."

Fervently I hoped, Not quite everything!

"Tea or whisky?"

"I've begun on whisky."

"Good. Let me fix you another."

She poured me a stiff one and fixed herself some tea and leaned back on the sofa. She looked as though she expected something, but not what I would have preferred. I filled the waiting silence: "About what we discussed yesterday ..."

"Before we go into that, I should like to thank you for taking care of my child last night."

"She told you?"

"No. She told me some idiotic tale about a mythical American she met on the boat."

"Idiotic?"

"I knew she was lying. You see, when she said at dinner last night that she had never met Tony Machero I knew she was up to something. Her aunt had written me from New York and mentioned that Tony had taken Bianca to dinner several times. When I discovered that she had gone ashore, I put a rather nasty two and two together. I must say I was deeply disturbed. It isn't like Bianca to be deceptive, or to get herself involved in a sordid intrigue. I didn't tell Jeff Hamden what I suspected. He's so unbelievably moral, you know. I simply sent him ashore with instructions to find her and bring her back."

"Bianca doesn't know what you suspect?"

"Certainly not. There is no reason to create any more unpleasantness about the episode. Especially now that there is no more danger from that particular source."

"No danger?"

"Fortunately," she said in a cool voice, "Tony Machero was stabbed to death on the Milan road last night. He had charm, certainly, but not *that* much! My Bianca is extraordinarily innocent. If someone else had not done it, I might have arranged it myself."

"Perhaps you did arrange it."

She smiled at me over her teacup. "I'm afraid that even I could not have arranged things that quickly."

"Alfredo, for instance?"

"Alfredo might have done it for me had I asked him. I didn't. However, he told me you had met Bianca in his place and that my poor child seemed terribly upset. Now, then, what happened?"

I took a good swig of the whisky. Behind her cool manner the Countess Becellini was more upset than she cared to admit by Bianca's supposed intrigue with Machero.

"It's not as bad as it appears," I said. "Bianca had been carrying on a little flirtation with Machero. Innocuous enough."

"'Innocuous' I cannot accept! 'Amusing,' perhaps, or even 'dangerous.' The Becellinis are incapable of behavior you would describe as merely 'innocuous.'"

"Well, then, she thought it would be 'amusing' to meet Tony for a drink. Apparently he got out of hand, and..."

"Come, come, Mr. Valois, you can't believe that I'm that stupid! Mario, my boatman, is more observant. Bianca went off in Tony's car. But before that, she met another man on the hotel landing stage. Now, who was this other man?"

I took a minute to light a cigarette. "A young American she met in New York. He came over on the same boat."

"Ah. Then that part of her story was true. She told me she had gone to meet this creature to break off a flirtation that had got out of hand—at least on his part."

"That's correct."

"Who is he?"

"Some poor student she met at the university."

"Even poor students have names, I assume."

"Henry Dawson. At least, that's what he claims."

"But I really don't understand for the life of me why she met Tony after that. It *was* Tony she intended to meet all the time, wasn't it?"

"In a way. Yes. I suppose." I took a deep breath and looked her in the eye. "He behaved like a boor. Tried to attack her in his car. She got out and walked to Alfredo's."

She busied herself with fitting a cigarette into a jade holder. "It doesn't sound at all like Tony's strategy. However, even if it were true, why would she call you?"

"Maybe I seem like a fatherly type."

"Fatherly!" The expected smile didn't appear. She put down the holder beside her cup and looked thoughtful. "It's possible Bianca might think of you in that way. And very odd."

"Odd?"

"Yes," she said. "Odd." She drew the robe about her as though she had felt a sudden chill. Then she tilted her head up and said, "She's always confided in me. We are much closer than most mothers and their daughters. Bianca is my life. I can't understand why she didn't tell me."

"Perhaps she thought it would upset you, knowing that Machero was a friend of yours."

"Friend! My dear man! One didn't think of Tony in such serious terms. He was merely someone you invited to parties."

She lifted the holder to her mouth. I reached over and lighted the cigarette. In the moment that we were close her eyes looked deeply into mine. It was a searching, provocative look, intense and green and very disturbing. I drew back as though I had been burned. It made me think of the expression in other eyes, and then suddenly I thought of Cattoriere as he had talked of becoming the power behind the throne of Movania.

"Tony was found fifteen miles from Stresa. Bianca couldn't have walked back from that spot in fifteen minutes. She must have left him before he headed out the Milan road. I suppose I am safe in assuming that my daughter didn't kill Machero?"

"Quite safe," I said with more conviction than I felt.

"Good. It might have created trouble if she had done it. The ball is only three days away."

"It *would* have been dull to have your ball spoiled by a messy murder trial!"

"Yes," she said in a businesslike voice. "Even discussing it troubles me. Let's have an end to such discussions. At the moment I'm interested in my own extremely annoying problem."

"The letters."

"Yes. I assume you have decided to accept the assignment. Otherwise, you wouldn't be here."

"I'll do my best to help you."

"Excellent! I have some good news for you."

"News?"

"I spoke to King Michel on the phone this morning. I mentioned casually that I had met an amusing and delightful person, name of Rafferty Valois. My dear! I've never heard the dear boy so interested in any subject. It seems he is an avid reader of American magazines and detective fiction. He had read that article about you in that American magazine. He suggested himself that you come to his suite at the Excelsior Hotel in Rome tomorrow for tea."

"He wasn't suspicious?"

"Why should he be? I thought I made it quite clear, Mr. Valois, that there must be no question of Michel's being involved in this annoying business. He knows nothing about it. It's that creature. She's the one you will have to approach."

"Approach. How?"

"That's what I will be paying you for. That's what other people have paid you for. If I knew how to get those letters back, I wouldn't be confiding in you."

"*Touché!*" I stood and approached the table. "May I?"

"Please do."

I poured another drink. Newsmen work better drunk, I reassured myself. At least in the movies.

She looked up at me with an expression that might be expectant. But that damned cheetah sat looking at me. Baffled, I returned to my chair.

"There is one question I will ask," I said. "And that's a pretty important one. Without being specific, are the contents of these letters merely what I or any other literal-minded person might suspect, or is the subject matter even more embarrassing to you?"

Right away I knew the shot in the dark had hit home. She stiffened and said, "They are rather silly love letters written by a wildly romantic young man."

"Surely that can't be so dangerous. Surely that isn't worth the amount you have already paid the blackmailer."

"Allow me to be the judge of that!"

I shrugged. "Sorry." I stood.

"Must you go?" Her voice which a moment before had been sharp and decisive, was now soft and inviting.

I must, I thought, unless you want trouble, lady. But I didn't answer. The sound of her voice was like an aphrodisiac. It dissipated completely the somewhat chaste effect of the Chinese gown. As I hesitated, Iris made an alternate decision difficult. She bounded across the room and stood barring the door to the hall. For the first time I saw something in her eyes that was not altogether sympathetic.

"Tell her to move," I said without much conviction.

Softly the countess said, "I don't believe I will."

The room was very still. The air was heavy with the scent of perfume. My pulse began to do funny things.

"Surely you're not afraid," she said.

"Afraid?"

She laughed, got up from the sofa, and moved toward the bedroom door. The cat's eyes seemed to reflect the mockery of her mistress' voice.

I didn't need the cat to keep me in the room now. But for a moment the comic aspect of the situation were smothered in resentment against the arrogant assumption of this beautiful woman, who had turned to face me once more in the entrance to her bedroom.

I said, "Surely you don't have to go through a wild-animal-training act every time you... I mean ..."

"It's insurance," she said. "A beauty specialist in Paris once prescribed certain activities to keep my complexion toned up. It's a form of pleasant exercise— more or less daily."

On that calm announcement she turned and disappeared into the bedroom. Iris made a sound that might have been her version of laughter. The perspiration was damp on my forehead. My feet refused to move. For once in my life I felt like a callow farm hand. From the bedroom I heard a sound like the faint rustle of heavy silk.

My feet, behaving now with more logic, started me toward the door of the bedroom. I crossed the threshold and stopped, catching my breath. The woman on the bed bore a striking resemblance to Goya's famous painting of the Duchess of Alba. Divested of the Chinese gown and any other encumbering garment she may have worn, the perfection of her body was nothing less than incredible.

She drew one arm back languidly and said, "It's unseasonably warm."

"You're damned right it is!" I said as I moved forward to participate in skin-toning exercises with Celia Becellini, Contessa di Friemonte e Maggiore.

Chapter Eleven

Loretta looked up at the station clock.

"Ten minutes," she said.

Through the windows of the café in the Milan station we could see the Paris-Rome Express resting in a cloud of steam in the great glass-covered shed. The clock stood at ten minutes before midnight. I gulped some more of the diluted chickory misnamed coffee and tried to drown the faint gnawing feeling of guilt that overcame me every time I looked into Loretta's passive face.

"The train from the south comes in a half hour after my train leaves. You'll be in Paris at eight in the morning. Here are your tickets and *wagon-lit* reservation. Be sure you don't lose them."

She took them indifferently and stuffed them into her handbag.

"Maybe you'll run into your Glasgow gentleman again," I said brightly.

"Maybe."

"Who knows... I might even be in Paris myself in another few weeks."

"How delightful," she said politely.

"Paris is lovely at this time of year. Much more fun than being mixed up with gangsters and things."

"Quite," she said. And then, "Is she really so attractive?"

"Who?"

"The Countess."

"For the tenth time, Loretta, I swear that there's nothing between us!"

Well, there hadn't been. "I'm sure it's none of my business."

She looked like a well-behaved schoolgirl in the neat traveling suit with the starched collar and the absurd little monkey hat.

"Stop looking at me like that!"

"Like what, Rafferty?"

"As though I were turning you out into a blizzard in a forest filled with wolves."

"Well, I must say no such idea ever entered my mind. After all, a lady doesn't stay where she isn't wanted, does she?"

Feeling like Simon Legree, I fumbled with a package of cigarettes and avoided her eyes.

"I'm really quite fond of you, Loretta. You have a way of growing on a guy."

"You needn't be polite and there's no necessity for making me sound like something you graft onto a tree."

"I mean it. But you see, honey, I'm mixed up in something that might be very important to me and it's no place for a nice girl like you. I wouldn't want to see that lovely little head blown off."

She sighed. "How thoughtful of you, Rafferty darling. But I'm very much afraid it's you who will get his head blown off. It's not very solidly attached to your shoulders anyway."

"Don't worry about me!"

"Oh, dear," she said. "If only that silly article hadn't been published. I do believe you're beginning to be convinced that you actually did do all those unlikely things."

"I can handle myself. I'm on the track of the biggest story of my life."

"I might have helped you," she said. "But it's too late to discuss that now. Isn't it?"

"Yes," I said.

Outside in the great station shed the Rome Express let out a warning shriek on its toylike whistle. Somewhere an electric bell began to ring. I stood up and threw some lire on the table for the check.

"Well ..." I said.

She looked up at me with wide, placid eyes. "Good-by, Rafferty."

"Don't forget to write."

"I'll never forget, Rafferty. Now, go quickly without any more words."

I leaned down and kissed her and then hurried away through the café to where my porter waited by the entrance to the platform. As I walked down the long line of darkened sleeping cars, I looked back through the steam-covered plate-glass window of the café. Loretta still sat at the table where I had left her, very still, looking down into the empty coffee cup. My heart did a little skip. And then I thought, Don't be a dope. I averted my eyes and followed my porter to my car.

The narrow corridor was dimly lighted and most of the sleeping compartments were already dark. The porter left me in my compartment, which I was relieved to find I would have to myself. I unpacked my pajamas and shaving kit, trying not to speculate on the future of the odd little cockney girl named Loretta Maximilian Toastmaster. But as the train began to slide out of the shed into the rain-drenched night, I couldn't resist pressing my face to the window for a last look back at the station café. Instead of the lonely, pathetic picture I had envisaged, I was astonished and rather deflated to see Loretta smiling up into the face of a distinguished-looking man with a spade beard.

That's that! I thought, and then the train was speeding out through the industrial suburbs of Milan to the accompaniment of great gashes of lightning across the night sky and tremendous claps of thunder. The city flew swiftly past and soon we were in the midst of a dark and wild countryside where the lights of my window played an obbligato to the forks of lightning on massive rock beside the road bed. I sat on the berth and stared dejectedly at my pajamas and shaving kit. I had planned to get to bed immediately, but the little blow to my ego brought about by that last sight of Loretta got me to thinking of a drink. I knew that on some of the international expresses the restaurant car was open all night for late brandy and coffee drinkers. I decided to take a chance.

The narrow, swaying corridor had that lonely, unsubstantial look of all sleeping cars late at night. I made my way forward, and after traversing three cars found the lighted restaurant car. I entered the narrow corridor skirting the kitchen and suddenly checked my pace and drew back into the hallway. There were only two persons in the midst of the somewhat shabby elegance of the ancient restaurant car, a man and a woman. The woman's back was to me but there was no mistaking who the man facing me was.

It was Baggy Pants, known also as Henry Dawson, Bianca's former swain. He hadn't noticed me in the corridor and seemed completely engrossed in his companion. One glance was enough to prove that the Baggy Pants nickname was no longer applicable. Mr. Dawson was expensively attired in a well-cut pin-stripe suit, and the tie looked like Charvet's best. This was no poor student doing the Continent the hard way; he was sleek and sophisticated and much better-looking than I had remembered.

Dawson was obviously explaining something to the girl. I thought his face looked rather grim. The girl wore one of those large-brimmed straw picture hats, but as she leaned forward to answer him I caught a glimpse of red hair.

A waiter came out of the alcove at the other end of the car and saw me. I stepped forward into the aisle. Dawson's eyes met mine over the straw hat.

The waiter came forward. "Signor?"

"I'm alone. Coffee and Cointreau, please."

The straw hat jerked up. The head was rigid for a moment, then the girl turned. I looked into the face of Annie Harrison.

"Well, for God's sake," she said.

I moved down the aisle and took her hand. I thought it was cold and tense. I thought that beneath the poker face was uneasiness.

"I didn't recognize you with your clothes on," I said.

"That's a hell of a thing to say. What do you think Mr.— Mr. Brent will think? Up to this point he probably thought he'd picked up a *lady* to have a drink with."

"Mr. Brent?" I said.

"That's right," Dawson said blandly. "Bill Brent. Shaker Heights, Ohio."

"This is Mr. Rafferty Valois," Annie said, spacing the words too precisely, I thought, giving them a certain warning significance. And then quickly, "Here I was dying of boredom over a lone brandy when along came Mr. Brent. I always meet such nice people on trains."

"Rafferty Valois," Dawson said. "I've heard that name somewhere. Or maybe I read it."

"Sit down, Rafferty," Annie said. "I heard you order a Cointreau and coffee. How ladylike!"

"It's too late at night to prove my virility by drinking dark stuff neat."

"It's never too late," Annie said, indicating her pony of brandy. She rattled on, her eyes restless as the hands that moved back and forth across the white tablecloth. "I thought you were doing a job for C. C."

"I am. That's why I'm on my way to Rome."

"Why Rome?"

"You ask too many questions."

Dawson leaned back in his chair and lighted a cigarette. He seemed remarkably cool.

"Where is your lady friend Loretta?" Annie asked.

"Left the country," I said. "For her health."

"Wise girl!" Her vehemence was genuine enough.

"Funny I didn't see you in the Milan station."

"I got on at Como. C. C.'s car dropped me there."

The waiter brought my coffee and Cointreau. Nervously Annie Harrison sipped at her brandy. I caught her giving Dawson a worried, questioning look when she thought I was not looking. An idea began to formulate in my mind.

Casually I said, "I had to walk about a mile for this drink. I'm way back in Car Twenty-one."

Annie rushed to the bait. "I hope you were lucky enough to get an end compartment like me. They're larger. The end ones are usually numbered one and nineteen."

"Nope," I said. "Mine's twelve."

Annie gave a little start, as though something had bitten her under the table. It didn't take a Sherlock Holmes to figure that what had bitten her was the end of Dawson's shoe. Annie gulped down the rest of her drink.

"I'll leave the coast clear for man talk," she said, getting to her feet. "A lady like me needs her beauty sleep. That is, if she's to go on traveling first class. Look me up at the Grand Hotel di Suisse in Rome, Rafferty. And you too, Mr. Brent. Thanks for the drink."

"I'll be seeing you," Brent said.

Swaying beneath the enormous picture hat, she went down the aisle and out of the car.

"Quite a gal," Brent said.

I looked at him. "I dunno. C. C. is easily pleased."

"C. C.? What's that? City College?"

"It's an education, usually with a degree at the end. Slipped to you in your back."

"I don't get it."

"Maybe you've been luckier than Machero, Dawson." There was the merest flicker of surprise in his eyes. He took time to sip his drink. He put down the glass, puffed at his cigarette, and said easily, "I like the name Brent. Thought it might appeal to the lady who just left."

"I saw you yesterday morning disguised as an honest young student. In front of the Italian Lines pier in Genoa. I was in the Becellini limousine."

"With Bianca. Bad luck."

"Bianca?"

"Hell, no! Bianca is the sweetest kid ..." He stopped.

"But not as stupid as you thought, eh? You didn't succeed as you thought you would when Machero failed."

"Is that what she told you?"

"Never mind what she told me. I have a little message for you to relay."

"Relay?"

"To your boss, C. C. Tell him for me I don't like being tailed while I'm on a job. If he wants it done, it's got to be done my way."

"You think this C. C. put me on your tail?"

"What else are you doing on this train?"

Instead of answering he said softly, "Who *are* you working for, Valois?"

I stood up. "You can tell him I take that no-cancellation clause seriously."

"I wonder," he said. "I wonder."

"You can put my drink on the expense account," I said, and started down the aisle.

Behind me he called, "Stay and have another."

"I'm choosy," I said over my shoulder.

"O.K., but you can relay a message for me."

I turned at the entrance. "To whom?"

"To Bianca."

"Bianca wouldn't be interested."

"Perhaps not. But tell her this. Tell her the monk is in safe hands."

I felt my blood beginning to boil. "For how much?"

He grinned insolently. "Ask her to call me at the Hotel Flora in

Rome."

"Anything else?"

"Yes. Tell her I think she's a damned little fool."

"Is that all?"

"You might add that I love her very much."

The gall of the guy was spectacular.

"Bianca wouldn't touch you with rubber gloves!"

"Bad as that, eh?"

He crushed out his cigarette, looked over his shoulder to make certain the waiter had retired to his alcove, lowered his voice, and said, "Stay out of this, Valois. You'll only get burned."

"Is that a threat?"

"A friendly warning."

"You're an awfully clean-cut type to be such a stinking rat," I said. I turned on my heel and left the restaurant car, and hurried through swaying corridors to my compartment. The door was slightly open but the lights inside were doused. I threw open the doors and stepped inside. Quickly I shut them behind me and grappled in the dark. Someone tried to get past me. I heard heavy breathing and felt silk tear in my hands and then I got my fingers around a mass of hair and yanked back. The girl— and it obviously was a woman— fell over the berth. I reached back and switched on the lights.

Annie Harrison sat up on the edge of the bed, holding her hands to her head.

"You bastard! You almost tore my hair out."

"Next time remind me to do it. What are you doing here, as though I didn't know?"

"You're my type," she said with brazen indifference.

"So is my luggage." I indicated the contents of my suitcase strewn over the compartment. "You should have told your colleague to hold me in the restaurant car by force. What did you expect to find?"

She disregarded the last question and looked up at me with something like fear in her eyes.

"What colleague?"

"Mr. Brent of Shaker Heights, otherwise known as Hank Dawson."

"No," she said quickly. "Honest to God, I never saw the guy before. I don't know what you're talking about. Don't go to C. C. with any lies like that!"

I couldn't figure it. The girl was terrified.

"What were you after?"

"I was just checking up. C. C. wanted to be sure of you.

"That's a damned lie. You thought maybe I had the letters already, didn't you?"

"Letters?" She gave a hopeless shrug. "Oh, for Christ's sake. Give me a cigarette, will you? Cool off. You had nothing to worry about in that bag except some dirty socks. They should be a worry to anyone."

She shook out her hair, leaned back on her elbows at an angle that accentuated her breasts. Her dress was in disarray and she didn't bother to rearrange it.

"Look," I said, "if C. C. doesn't trust me any more than to send Dawson and you snooping after me, I may not go on working for him."

She snorted. "That's a noble speech. You only stop working for C. C. when you're too stiff to do work of any kind."

"Like Machero?"

"I heard about that," she said. "Too bad. He was a bum, but he was kind of cute."

"C. C.'s work?"

She looked me in the eyes, hesitated, and said, "I don't know. Could be. I just don't know."

"C. C.'s work through your friend Hank Dawson." Her chin came up. "Listen. I told you I never laid eyes on the guy before tonight. This is serious. Keep that straight in your mind for future reference."

She was obviously upset every time I mentioned her friendship with Dawson. It occurred to me that she had been two-timing C. C. with the good-looking American. It was possible C. C. didn't know what his left hand was doing to his right hand for once.

"If I keep quiet," I said, "what's it worth?"

"Jesus! How crude can you get? If you want to sleep with me, say so. I'm not doing anything tonight and it's raining outside."

"I want to sleep, all right," I said. I certainly did, too. The Countess— or her cheetah— hadn't been exactly soporific. "But I want to sleep alone. Go on back and report my dirty socks to Dawson."

She shrugged. She got to her feet, mouth set, eyes hard.

"You might at least have offered me a cigarette, you bum."

I stepped aside to let her pass. She started past me, turned suddenly, violently, threw her arms about my neck, and pressed her lips to mine.

"Honey," she said, "I'm so lonely!"

The intensity of her feeling was astounding.

"There isn't anything else but this... now," she said.

I disentangled myself with some difficulty. She clung like a drowning sailor to a rock.

"We're both alone in the middle of nowhere," she said. "I'm scared."

"Find Dawson," I said harshly, "and be scared with him."

Her hands dropped to her side. She was suddenly limp and tired with the first signs of the middle age that would be her destruction showing like a dim prophecy about her eyes.

"It was an idea," she said.

"An idea that C. C. would have loved," I said.

"That bastard!" she said. She shrugged and left the compartment. Outside the window of the swiftly moving train was a blinding flash like the flash of doom and then the metallic, anguished cry of thunder.

I awakened from a nightmare with a cold sweat on my forehead. A sickly dawn was trickling in at the window of my sleeping compartment. The train was standing still. I looked at my watch. It was six-forty-three. We were less than three quarters of an hour from Rome. Everything was very still.

I got out of the berth, planning to get some cigarettes from my trouser pocket. I saw that the train had stopped in the midst of a small village. The sign on the dingy station read: Palini. It struck me as odd that the Paris-Rome Express would stop at this tiny hamlet. I went to the window and looked out at the rain-streaked platform. Almost directly below my window a smart limousine stood waiting. I caught a glimpse of a green-uniformed chauffeur and in the rear a woman who sat back in the far corner, furs drawn up about her face. It looked as though the train had stopped to discharge some big shot; probably a government official. I was about to turn back when a man came hurrying down the platform, obviously having left a car farther up ahead. His hat was pulled low and his coat collar was up against the rain and in one hand he clutched a brief case. The woman leaned forward to greet him as he reached the car. Even in the half-light I was struck by her youth and beauty and the expression of anxiety on her lovely face.

The train began to move. The man got into the car, settled back, and looked back toward the train. For one instant as the train slid past I looked into his eyes. It was Hank Dawson.

From far up ahead the whistle gave a lonely shriek.

I thought, Good God! Cattoriere has got so big they'll stop the Rome-Paris Express at his command. And then I thought, Maybe I'm still dreaming. The train gathered speed, racing now to make up for lost time, bearing down on Rome. I stood there a moment staring out at the rain-streaked plains of Italy. Then mechanically I turned back toward my trousers and the cigarettes.

It was then I noticed the white slip of paper by my compartment door.

Quickly I stooped and picked it up. It was a note written in scrawling pencil: "Long live the Republic of Movania! He whose masters are more than one rarely lives to see the fun!"

Chapter Twelve

The aide-de-camp was built like a wrestler, wore a drooping mustache, and looked at me with ferocious black eyes. He barred the door of the suite like a eunuch at the gates of a harem.

"I am not in knowledge of such an appointment," he announced in an operatic baritone.

"I am here at the invitation of His Highness."

"So! And what is the reason of the business?"

I remembered that the Countess had told me the King was an avid reader of detective fiction.

"His Highness was kind enough to like one of my books."

"Books!" he said with passionate distaste. "What is this book you are writing?"

"Murder stories."

"Murder?" he said with a faint glimmering of respect. "This is not to be connected with the goddamned newspapers?"

"Certainly not. I hardly read the goddamned newspapers, must less write for them."

"Men of the newspapers we do not want. You will wait here."

The door was shut in my face. I looked down the third-floor corridor of the Excelsior Hotel. It was cream-paneled and softly lit and utterly still. I had been told that the King's aide was a Colonel Wersisoviski, and he certainly looked it. After a moment the door was opened and the Colonel, formally polite but completely disinterested, said, "You will go on the inside now and wait."

He stepped aside and I went "on the inside" through a small foyer that had been transformed into a sort of office and through another door into a sitting room.

"But ten minutes will be yours!" the Colonel said. "His majesty must be permitted his divertissements. But ten minutes. No more!"

He made it sound as if the eleventh minute was the minute of be-heading. He left me alone in the bright little sitting room, wondering whether he had gone to saddle his horse for the return trip to Graustark. I lit a cigarette and cased the joint. It was as impersonal as any suite in a de luxe hotel. But on a long table by the windows were several American magazines devoted to detective fiction.

A minute or so passed, and then the door opened and a slim, rather pale young man advanced toward me. He wore an ill-fitting double-breasted suit and he didn't seem to know what to do with his long, very white hands. He stood there regarding me somewhat uncertainly. I could see he was painfully shy and embarrassed.

"Mr. Valois," he said. "I am very pleased that you have come to see me."

I knew then I was looking into the face of the former king of Movania. Awkwardly I tried to bow, but he stopped me with a gesture. With a youthful bound he crossed the room, grabbed hold of a small gilt chair, straddled it, and faced me over its back.

"We must not waste time!" he said in a dramatic undertone. "We have but a few moments. I must make the most of them. They watch me like hawks!"

"They?"

"Metachas' men. Wersisoviski and the others." He darted a look toward the door of the office and said with all of the melodrama of a boy just home from his first Grade B thriller, "I am their prisoner!"

"A nice prison you've got," I said, indicating the room. I was finding it difficult to think of this kid as a "royal personage." Even my typically American romanticism about royalty couldn't surround this boy with any purple glamour. He was more like a gawky member of the graduating class of Centerville High.

"It is true!" he said like one of the characters in the magazines he read. "I am an unwilling pawn in a web of intrigue. I have no one to whom I can turn for help."

"This Wersisoviski— he is holding you by force?"

"Not exactly. It is more subtle than that. But in the end it is the same."

"Why don't you go to the authorities?"

He turned his pale hands outward in a sign of hopelessness. "It is a matter over which the Italian authorities have no jurisdiction. I get only polite shrugs and words of sympathy, and besides, they do not allow me out of their sight long enough. I could hardly believe it when the Countess Becellini told me by phone that you would be in Rome. I had just finished reading that exciting article about your breath-taking exploits and ..."

"Oh," I said. "I see."

"Mr. Valois, if anyone can help me it is you. At the very least, you could give me advice."

This is where I came in, I thought. I waited for the next move in what was becoming, apparently, a pattern in my life— thanks to Miss Geraldine Wiley. The move came on cue.

"I should like to engage your services, Mr. Valois."

"So would a great many people," I said.

He wrung his hands together and looked away. "I imagine you demand a rather high fee."

"Rather."

"It may seem odd to you, Mr. Valois, but at the moment I am suffering from some financial embarrassment. However, in a certain vault in a certain bank in the city of New York" (His Majesty's dialogue seemed to have been written at a cent a word) "there are certain jewels. I will see to it that ..."

Slipping! I thought. No retainer fee this time.

"Sir, I am sure that you could find others more qualified to advise you."

"You do not understand! There is no one I can trust. Not even my own mother."

"That is a sad state of affairs for anyone."

He looked nervously toward the door. "After the revolution, my mother and I fled to Italy. The Countess Becellini was good enough to offer us the hospitality of her villa at Lake Maggiore. My mother went to London hoping to enlist the help of the British royal family in restoring the throne to Movania. She was, as they say in the American magazines, given the heave-ho. Politely, of course; Uncle George has charming manners. It seems the British and American governments were very happy with the new Movanian republic. They felt it was a healthy bulwark against Stalin or some such idea. I know nothing about politics."

"Nothing?"

"My father, the former king, thought politics were in bad taste. He refused to have them discussed in the palace. He had some sort of persons who collected the taxes from the peasants, and in Movania the peasants are about everyone except the court."

"And how did the peasants feel about that?"

"Well, I'm not exactly clear on that. You see, I never saw many Movanians. I was sent to school in America when I was nine. I was there all through the Second World War. Father thought the Movanians would be a bad influence on me. Then when I returned to Movania after the war there had been a great change. General Metachas had become all-powerful. My father was... well, shall we say... senile, and he and my mother were separated. My mother, as you probably know, is British. She dreamed and planned for the day when I would become king. But she hadn't counted on my eight years in the United States and what they would do to me. I didn't want to be king. I wanted to settle down in the United States and write detective stories."

"An ambition of doubtful merit."

He disregarded my flippancy. "Apparently the Movanian people had the same idea."

"About writing detective stories?"

"About my leaving Movania. Two days after my coronation, they chucked me out. Metachas' toy army was no match for the anger of the peasants. We all did a quick powder. I was the only one happy about it."

In the outer room there was a sound as though a door had closed. King Michel lowered his voice.

"We stayed with the Countess Becellini, as I told you. Then Mother went to England and I went to Rome for a few weeks. It was during that visit that the most wonderful thing happened to me."

"Maria Cattoriere."

"Yes! A charming young lady who has made me very happy." He tried without much success to sound like a man of the world. "Somehow Mother got wind of it in England. She had failed in her mission there, and without my knowledge arranged a marriage with the daughter of the Countess Becellini."

"She never consulted you?"

He looked surprised. "That wouldn't have been necessary. I have no objections to the marriage. The girl is rich and quite nice, I am told: But it placed me in an embarrassing position, because, you see, not knowing about the marriage plans, I brought Maria back to visit at the palace of the Countess Becellini. Naturally, the Countess was somewhat annoyed, and so I decided it was more discreet to come to Rome until after the engagement announcement at the ball on Friday night."

"How did Maria Cattoriere feel about all this?"

"She has been marvelous. She understands perfectly and feels that the marriage will be a good thing for me."

"She must be extraordinarily tolerant."

"She is. And, as for herself, she has always understood that marriage is quite out of the question between us."

"Why?"

He looked down at his long white hands. "It would break Mamma's heart. I must consider her."

"And what will happen to Maria?"

"There are ways of arranging things. She makes absolutely no demands. She will do whatever is for my own good."

A likely story, I thought. This young man was apparently even more naïve than he seemed.

"You seem to have everything fairly well settled. Why do you fear Metachas now? And what advice could I give you?"

Once again he looked nervously toward the door. "Maria has an uncle...."

"Ah. The Cat."

"Yes," he said unhappily. "I believe he is referred to as Cat. He is a sinister man and very powerful. Somehow he contacted Metachas. He has been supplying Metachas with arms. They plan to seize the government by a *coup d'état* within a week. They have been bringing pressure to bear on me to break my engagement with the American girl because they have some mad idea about putting me back on the throne with Maria as queen."

"But wouldn't that make you happy?"

"Happy! Life would be miserable."

"Even with the woman you love as your legal wife?"

"But you don't understand. It is Maria most of all who fears this. She does not want it any more than I. Maria says that if I do not go through with my engagement to the American girl, we are lost!"

He really surprised me with that one. It was the Countess' assumption that Maria had taken the letters not only for purposes of financial blackmail but also to force a cancellation of the engagement between the King and Bianca. Yet the guy sincerely believed the girl wanted him to marry Bianca. It was beginning to look as though Cattoriere's niece was not in sympathy with her uncle's plans, or she was an extremely subtle young lady. Subtle or not, she certainly had him tied up and delivered.

He sighed. "You see, life is very complicated. Without Maria's uncle, Metachas would not have the power to hold me as a pawn. My poor deluded mother thinks Metachas is a great man. And without the fortune of the Countess Becellini, Maria and I would not be able to get to America and settle in peace."

I wondered what Bianca would have thought had she heard the King's postnuptial plans.

"What do you want from me?" I asked.

"The Countess Becellini is, I believe, innocent of these facts. The engagement is to be announced at the ball, day after tomorrow. I have a high regard for the Countess and her daughter. I do not wish any harm to come to them."

"From Cattoriere?"

"Yes."

I hesitated a moment, then said quietly, "Then you have not thought of turning the Countess' letters over to Cattoriere?"

"Letters?" he said blankly. "What letters?"

"Sir, if you wish me to help you, you must be absolutely on the level with me. I'm going to ask you a very rude question."

"That's fair enough."

"Where does the money come from to pay for this layout at the Excelsior?"

He pushed the little gilt chair back and stood. I saw the color rising on his neck above his collar.

"Well?"

"I wish you hadn't asked that question."

"It's important that I know."

He sighed. "Very well. As you know, my mother disapproves of my... of my friendship with Maria Cattoriere. She cut off what small allowance I had. It's controlled by my uncle in England."

"Then how ..."

He said miserably, "Maria loaned me the money."

"And where did she get it?"

He turned quickly. "Where? Why, it never occurred to me to ask. Perhaps from her uncle. I don't know about money, you know. It never occurred to me... What are you driving at?"

"Sir," I said quietly, "it is not easy for me to tell you this. On the night you and Maria Cattoriere left the palace of the Countess Becellini, certain very personal letters belonging to the Countess disappeared. Since that time, the Countess has been paying large sums to an unknown blackmailer."

The boy looked at me in horror. "My God! Surely the Countess doesn't think... But this is outrageous! The very thought of Maria ..." He stopped.

"Well?"

He looked suddenly haggard. "No," he said. "Impossible!"

"Then what are you worried about?"

He turned abruptly on his heel and walked to the window. Indignation had been replaced by some other emotion. After a moment he said over his shoulder, "Poison darts are being placed in my heart. Maria is the only one I have trusted. If ... I must speak with her."

And then, almost in answer to his wish, the door to the office opened and a young woman with clear olive skin and brooding dark eyes— an extremely beautiful young woman— came into the room. She wore a simple linen afternoon dress and in her arms she carried a great bunch of wild lilies.

"Look, Michel!" she cried. "The countryside is alive with them."

The young man who had been king turned. "I have been calling you all morning, Maria."

"But, Michel! I thought I told you. I spent the night at my aunt's at… in the country."

"At Palini?" I asked quietly.

Aware of me for the first time, she stiffened.

"Michel! Who is this man?"

"Forgive me," Michel said in a tired voice. "This is Signor Rafferty Valois."

Mechanically she thrust the flowers to a table and moved toward the King.

"Michel! How long has he been here? What have you been saying to him?"

"My dear Maria," he said with a show at dignity, "I don't think that is a matter which …"

"Tell him to go away," she said tensely. "He is not a friend. Of this I am certain!"

"Have you gone mad, Maria?"

The girl looked behind her toward the open door to the office. She lowered her voice. "He is a fraud. He has taken money from people under false pretenses. He works for anyone."

"'For everyone' would be more like it," I said as lightly as possible. However, I got to my feet.

"What do you mean, fraud?" the King asked, his voice suddenly sharp with nerves.

"I know, Michel! Believe me …"

"Ask her where her friend Hank Dawson is," I said. There was a dead silence. The King looked at her questioningly. She was very pale.

"I don't know what he means," she whispered.

"Ask her how her uncle arranged to have the Paris-Rome Express stopped at Palini at six o'clock this morning. And ask her how she happened to be there to meet a guy who calls himself Dawson."

I walked toward the door and turned and bowed with mock politeness.

"When you get the answers, let me know, Your Highness."

Chapter Thirteen

Bianca came into the sitting room of her mother's suite at the Excelsior and threw her hat in the general direction of a chair.

"What are you doing here?" she asked.

"Waiting for your mother. I got the message at the desk."

"I'm hot and tired and generally fed up."

She sank into a chair. "Mother stopped to talk with some old hag in the lobby. She'll be right up. Don't expect me to entertain you. I don't feel entertaining."

"Been shopping?"

"For a king. For the past hour I've been on exhibition at Fireolo's. Very smart for tea. All Rome was there to see me talk to a king while Mother simpered between us."

"I saw him earlier today," I said. "If that's what you were shopping for, its price should be cut down."

"Don't be rude. Or funny. I'm in a mood to bite."

I walked across the room and looked out of the window across the rooftops of Rome. The dome of St. Peter's glistened in the late-afternoon sun.

After a moment she said, "Did you really see Michel?"

"In person."

"Why?"

"Ask your mamma."

"What exactly is Mother up to, Rafferty?"

"Getting you safely married. Beyond that, I'm not free to say. I have a message for you."

"Message?"

I turned so that I could see the reaction on her face. "The first part of it you can disregard. It's purely sentimental. The young man told me to tell you that he loved you very much."

"Michel?" Her hand went trailing along the sofa to the arm.

"Hank Dawson."

The hand closed tight over the arm. For a moment she said nothing. I expected her to scoff or even fly into a blinding rage. I wasn't prepared for the softness in her voice when she said, "He really said that, Rafferty?"

"Does it matter much what he says?"

She got hold of herself and said in a matter-of-fact voice, "Of course not. Where did you see him?"

"Last night on the Rome-Paris Express. He said to tell you he would be at the Hotel Flora."

"Why, that's just up the street. How can he have the gall to think I would see him?"

"It might be worth it. I think he knows where to put his hands on the ivory monk."

"Rafferty! He didn't say that!"

"I'm afraid he did."

She stared at me for a moment, then walked decisively toward the phone.

Before she got her hands on the instrument I said, "It might interest you to know that he got off the Paris-Rome Express at about six-thirty this morning in a place called Palini. He was met there by a very attractive young lady."

She drew back her hand. She turned. She waited.

"Perhaps this isn't in the best possible taste, but I think I'd better tell you that the young lady is the same beauty who has been so interesting to King Michel."

"What! What would Hank be doing with her?"

"I'd give a lot to know. I'm afraid I'm not living up to my reputation as a great international sleuth."

"I don't understand at all."

I took a drag on my cigarette and said, "I don't mind telling you I'm nervous. I wish to hell your mother would give up the idea of a crown on your head."

"Nonsense." She looked at the phone, reached for it, changed her mind, and went back to the sofa. The sparkle was gone from her eyes.

The Countess came bustling into the room. She sat down, threw her furs back, and laughed.

"What's the joke?" I asked.

"Jeffery Hamden!"

"I'm glad you finally see it that way, Mother."

"No. I didn't mean that. He's really quite sweet, if somewhat boring. The joke is really on me. On my colossal ego."

"How come?" I asked.

"Well, I must say I thought the boy was insanely in love with me. It should teach me a lesson. I just saw him having tea in the lounge with a perfectly lovely-looking young girl. My dear, his eyes were practically falling from his head, he was so engrossed in her. Ah, well... it makes things all the easier."

"Hamden in Rome?"

"He flew down with Bianca and me. He seemed so depressed that I thought the change would do him good."

Bianca excused herself in order to change for dinner. Celia Becellini leaned back with her head on the sofa and closed her eyes.

"It's coming true, Rafferty. Everything! Just as I dreamed it would. Michel was perfectly charming at tea. People who haven't spoken to me in years broke their necks to say hello."

"I hope everyone involved will be as happy as you."

"Now, don't be depressing. I won't have it! Only two more nights till the ball. I shan't sleep at all. And what a ball! It will open all their jaded eyes. Italy hasn't seen anything like it in years."

"Let's hope we all live to see it."

She jerked her head back into position and her smile died. "Did you get the letters?"

"No."

She frowned. "But it can't be that difficult. We must get them before Friday. If the girl is going to be stubborn, I suppose I will simply have to pay her more money."

"I'm not at all certain she has the letters."

"But who else?"

I walked to the bedroom door through which Bianca had disappeared and closed it. When I came back toward the sofa the Countess was waiting for me, tensely now.

"I won't have all this absurd intrigue!" she said angrily. "Of course the girl has them! It's perfectly obvious. She has most to gain."

"There are others."

"For instance?"

"Well, I might say Cattoriere if he were not under the impression that he has hired me to get the letters for him."

She sucked in her breath. "So! He knows about their existence. Why didn't you tell me this before?"

"I was fool enough to think I could do something about it without involving you or Bianca."

"Rafferty, we must get those letters! It's vitally important. Who else could have them?"

"Any number of persons. Any one of your servants. Hamden. The Harolls. A man called Dawson."

"Bianca's American friend?"

"Yes."

"But how? And why?"

"They may have been in the possession of Prince Machero. He may have been murdered for them."

"You believe this Dawson person murdered Tony?"

"I don't know. I'm stumped. There are so many queer things about this business. I'm damned if I know what to think."

"But I'm not paying you to tell me that you are stumped! I rely on you absolutely! You must get those letters. It's of no interest to me what methods you use."

"Look, Celia," I said. "About that magazine article ..."

But before I could continue there was a knock on the hall door and a moment later Jeffery Hamden entered. He looked indecently cheerful for a young man who only yesterday had been inconsolable.

"Hope I'm not interrupting anything."

"Don't be vulgar," the Countess said coldly.

"I'm sorry, Celia. I didn't mean ..."

The Countess took a deep breath and changed the mood. "I refuse to be serious about anything!" she cried. "Now, Jeff darling, out with it! Who was that charming creature you were having tea with?"

Without the slightest embarrassment, the Countess' former lover said, "Isn't she something, Celia? One of the most fascinating women I've ever... I mean aside from you..."

"Oh, quite. Who is she?"

"The daughter of a British earl," Hamden said reverently.

"What earl?"

"She won't say. She's in Rome sort of incognito. It seems she has some sort of uncle who is a regular ogre." He looked at me cheerfully. "Matter of fact, Rafferty, she described the uncle as having red hair."

"We're all ogres," I said.

The Countess gave me a wicked smile. "Incognito, eh? How romantic!"

"I just left her in the lobby. By an odd coincidence, she's going to Maggiore. I knew you wouldn't mind, so I asked her to the ball."

Obviously the Countess did mind.

"I won't have a lot of tourists appearing at the ball, Jeff. I do think it was presumptuous of you to ..."

"But, Celia... the daughter of an earl!"

"Daughter of an earl— perhaps. What name is she using?"

"Toastmaster," Hamden said.

"I beg your pardon?"

"Miss Loretta Maximilian Toastmaster."

The Countess leaned back and shouted with laughter. Jeff gave me a puzzled look, and then when he saw the expression on my face he said, "Are you sick, Mr. Valois?"

"Yes," I said. "It seems I have something I'll never get rid of."

"I don't understand. Celia, what is it?"

"Oh, Jeff! You are priceless. You know very well that no one ever had such a name. I'm afraid the young lady was joking. I guess I don't have to fear her turning up at the ball."

Hamden looked stricken.

"She's not that sort," he said. "Very serious and candid."

I sat down. What Loretta was doing with Jeff Hamden could wait until I got back to Maggiore. I began to feel as though I were in a dream that made utterly no sense at all.

There was another knock at the door. Hamden answered it and took a note from a bellhop. "It's for you, Celia."

The Countess took the envelope and glanced at it. Then she sat up very straight.

"At last!" she cried triumphantly.

"What is it?"

"The bitch of Rome! She's finally come around. I knew she couldn't hold out."

"The bitch of Rome?"

"Bianca's grandmother. The Marchesa Becellini. She hasn't written me a note in twenty years. I sent her an invitation to the ball. She can't refuse this time."

Feverishly she tore open the envelope. As she read it the light died in her eyes. She frowned in a puzzled manner. Finally she looked up at me.

"This is fantastic!" she said.

"Anything wrong?"

"She doesn't mention the ball. She wants Bianca to come to tea. And she wants her to bring you."

"Me! Why in God's name me?"

"I can't imagine." She crumpled up the note and stood. She turned and spoke crisply to Hamden. "Tell Bianca to get ready to go to tea at her grandmother's immediately!"

"But she's already had tea," I said.

"She must go. I don't know what that monster has in her mind, but we'll soon find out. And you must go with her."

I looked at my watch. It was five-twenty.

Chapter Fourteen

"I'm afraid," Bianca said.

"Of what?"

"I don't know. My childhood, I guess. I came here only once when I was ten. I dreamed about it for years after."

The streaked façade of the Marchesa's villa was not inviting. A great blank wall pierced only by an enormous heavy door and several barred windows hung over the narrow cobblestoned street. We alighted from the taxi that had brought us from the Excelsior Hotel. On the rooftops the sun glistened, but on the Via Florina one had the sensation of an eternal twilit world.

"Or perhaps I'm afraid of myself," she said. "Of what I might say."

"I still can't understand why they want to see me."

"Neither can I," she said.

I yanked on a chain beside the oak door and a bell tolled dismally from somewhere in the depths of the house. After a moment an ancient servant opened the door and we were led through dank, halls into a large, musty sitting room. Though the day was hot and sunny, the windows, hung with dusty velvet, were sealed tight, and the air was unpleasantly reminiscent of a tomb.

Out of the midst of a hideous collection of furniture appeared a stout but unhealthy-looking individual wearing a tight-fitting black suit and long, pointed shoes. His face, which seemed to be composed mostly of jowls and puffy bags and an enormous drooping underlip, was unexpectedly punctuated by an eagle-like nose. He looked petulantly at his watch and said in excellent English but in a high whine, "You're late."

"I'm sorry, Father," Bianca said. "Allow me to present Mr. Valois."

He bowed formally without offering his hand. I was stunned. It seemed impossible that this monster— who obviously was the Count Becellini— could have been party to the creation of a beauty such as Bianca.

"I will take you directly to Mamma," he said. "She expected you at least ten minutes ago."

He might have been talking to a complete stranger. I looked at Bianca. She was managing to look coolly detached. In silence we followed him through some more dark halls, up a stone staircase, and finally into a sitting room that was more or less a replica of the one we had left, only more so. Here there was a sickening odor of heavy perfume and stale air. On a chaise longue reclined— or rather balanced— an enormous woman, encased in purple silk. She looked not unlike a walrus, even to a slight mustache on her upper lip. Beside her was a table with the tea things. There was no welcome in either her eyes or her voice.

"You have come at last. Good. Come here where I can see you. Not you, Mr. Valois. The girl."

Bianca held her chin high and walked forward into the meager light that trickled through faded lace curtains. She stood before her grandmother, the Marchesa Becellini, and said nothing. The Count cleared his throat nervously.

A minute ticked by. I felt my blood begin to boil. The old walrus grunted and reached for the teapot.

"I will give you tea."

"It's not necessary," Bianca said clearly.

"If it pleases me, I give tea to my housekeeper!"

"Mamma ..." the Count said timidly.

"Lorenzo, you will be quiet! The best for you is silence. When you attempt words, one can only pray to the god of fools!"

Lorenzo whined something unintelligible and subsided into a corner. Bianca said, "You have asked me here to insult me."

"That is not necessarily true. I cannot blame you. Who could blame beauty but another woman far younger than I? No. I wished to see."

"Well! You have seen!" Bianca said angrily.

"You have spirit, which is more than I can say for the surviving Becellinis."

Something in the phrasing of her words caught my attention. I have met some exceedingly unpleasant people in my life, but I think that the Marchesa Becellini topped them all for the immediate impact of sheer unpleasantness. I knew now why Celia Becellini had referred to her as the bitch of Rome.

"I didn't want to come," Bianca said. "I came because Mother wished it and because... well, considering the circumstances ..."

"Ah, yes. The circumstances. Surely you are not fool enough to go through with this silly masquerade. This vulgar ball at Maggiore— this idiotic engagement announcement."

"I do not think it idiotic," Bianca said tensely.

"Nonsense. We ..." The Marchesa stopped thoughtfully and then continued on another vein: "That gown. Where did you get it?"

"Fontana."

"Ah. I might have guessed. It must have cost you many lire."

"I don't see what ..."

"How much?"

Bianca gave me a helpless look, shrugged, and said, "I believe it was about a hundred and fifty dollars."

"Scandalous! Only a whore would be seen in a gown of that price!"

"Mamma ..." came the pleading voice from the darkest corner.

The Marchesa paid no heed. "Here, girl. Drink your tea."

"No, thank you," Bianca said.

"You might as well. I suppose that even the tea was bought with your mother's money."

Very distinctly Bianca said, "Mamma is very generous. She has bought many things out of the kindness of her heart that were not worth it." She turned and looked toward the dark corner where the Count lurked. "Not worth a lira on any market."

"Well said," the Marchesa surprised me by saying. "Now sit down. I must tell you something. Sit down!" Bianca hesitated. I saw her look toward the door as if for flight. But she changed her mind and sat on a horsehair sofa near her formidable grandmother. I felt my nerves tensing with a sense of disaster.

"Mr. Valois, your tea!"

Against my will I found myself crossing the room to take a cup of lukewarm tea. There was no question of sugar or lemon or milk. One took what was offered, grateful or no. I took it and moved back again out of the little circle of faded light.

"I am going to tell you something, girl, for your own good."

Bianca looked as skeptical as I felt, but remained silent. The Marchesa sucked noisily at her teacup, belched, and slid the cup back into the saucer, spilling a good deal of the liquid in the process.

"Your mother is a fool. No. Just a moment, please. No more of a fool than many others of her compatriots. She tried to buy her way into something that can't be bought. Oh, I know... you will tell me of other American women who have married men of my class. They receive everyone and they go everywhere, but before they die they know that it has been no use. I have not received one of these women in my house. Ever! No matter how much wealth they represent or how illustrious the name they acquired. I despise snobs. I despise those who cannot take pride in who they really are, whether it be the lowest peasant on my country estate or a ruler of great nations. It would be as absurd for me to try to be part of a present I loathe— to be healthy, with my heart in the future. All that I know in my blood is dead— as dead as the soul of my son." She hesitated a moment and then said quietly, "All that I am— all that is my son, God help him— is sick with the past. Sick. Corrupt. And yet... this you will not understand... we are who we are because we were once great.

Not sniveling exhibitionists— great! With something in our souls!"

The angry hostility was dying on Bianca's face. She was listening now, intently.

"You see," the Marchesa said quietly, "the greatness was once there. The generosity of heart; the passion; the sense of responsibility; the daring! But it was for other times. Your mother comes of a nation where every man in the street can feel this, and sometimes does. And she rejected it in order to buy a stage on which to play a foolish game. Now she wishes to barter the Becellini name for a kingdom. The maddest fantasy of all. You must make her realize I will not permit it!"

"Permit it! What can you do?"

"What can I do?" The Marchesa settled back and closed her eyes. "Child, you are lovely and young and terribly naïve. Follow your heart. Do not make the mistake she has made."

"How can you lie there and speak so coolly about what you don't understand!" Bianca cried out. "My mother was generous to a fault. She restored your houses and gave you the money to live as you feel you should, and in return you made her the laughingstock of Italy. You saw to it that she was not received by certain people. You..."

"Child! You love her and that is good. I have tried to explain. You do not wish to understand."

"You've hated her!"

"Perhaps. But not for reasons you think."

She propped herself up on one fat elbow.

"I will tell you something. Your mother believes that if you marry a king, all the doors of Europe will be opened to her. And they will be opened. But when they are, her dream will be shattered. She is an incurable romantic and a fool. The kindest thing you could do is to let her retain her illusions. But because you will not heed me, I am forced ..." She sighed. "Child, go back to your country. Europe is a graveyard. At least, for my class. You are far too lovely to waste away among the tombstones. Now, then, I have told you this without sentiment. I feel none for you. You are not one of those I love. But I have pity. You will see."

She turned to the corner and signaled. Her son came waddling forward. "Take her down to the taxi. Send her back to her hotel. Now I will speak with Mr. Valois."

Bianca stood, her hands clasped tight before her. She looked down into the face of the fat old woman.

"I hate you!" she said. "I hate you with all my heart!"

She rushed blindly from the room, with the Count Lorenzo Becellini puffing at her heels. A servant appeared from the darkness and shut the door to the hall.

The Marchesa put her hands to her face for a moment. I thought she had forgotten my presence, but finally she spoke softly: "I'm so very tired."

I waited. After a moment she sighed again, reached into a silver box at her elbow, and drew forth a cigarette. Automatically I went forward and lit it for her.

"Perhaps I am sentimental," she said. "I could not tell her."

She looked up at me, and when I said nothing, she smiled. "You are different. I will not speak to you in riddles."

"Why did you wish to see me?"

"I will not waste words. I wish to employ your unique services."

"Good God! You too?"

"So. There are others. Celia?"

I shrugged.

"No matter. You would like to help this girl. See that she is happy. I saw it in your eyes."

"Yes," I said. "At least, it would be something decent out of this mess."

"Good. Then when I explain to you certain unpleasant facts, I believe you will agree to do what I ask."

"What is it you want?"

"I want a package of letters belonging to Celia."

I looked down at her and grinned. "So do several other people, including the Countess Becellini herself."

Her shoe-button eyes snapped in alarm. "They are missing!"

"Someone stole them from the Countess' safe."

Her hands came together in a pudgy fist. "Have you any idea who has them?"

"Only a suspicion."

"You must get them back. You must get them back and deliver them into my hands."

"I have prior commitments," I said with some relish.

"No. Listen to me. No." She pushed herself into a sitting position. "I will pay you a great sum!"

"Why are they so important? What's in them?"

She leaned forward with some effort and looked me in the eyes. "The proof of a fact that would prove highly embarrassing and even tragic for the woman and her daughter."

"Proof of what?"

She turned and looked away from the soiled light of the window. "You see, signor, it is and was a biological impossibility for my son to have fathered a child.”

“What!”

“The letters in question were written by the true father of the girl who just left this room.”

Somewhere, far away in the silent house, a door was slammed.

Chapter Fifteen

A light cold rain was falling over Rome; over the churches and tenements, the monuments and palaces, the ruins of the Caesars’ great capital. The bronze sound of a clock striking one A.M. echoed through the dim, deserted street. Countess Becellini, wrapped in a dark coat, a wide-brimmed felt hat pulled low over her eyes, strode beside me in silence. We came to a deserted plaza where an equestrian statue gazed stonily at dark and silent windows.

“Haven’t you had enough?” I asked.

“Nervous?”

“Not for myself.”

She laughed shortly. “All my life I’ve loved to walk in the rain at night. I think I’ve covered most of the capitals of Europe after midnight. Nothing melodramatic has ever happened to me.”

We crossed the plaza, went down another narrow street, and came to a low parapet that looked out over the rooftops of grim-looking tenements strewn down the hill at our feet. She stopped there and looked out into the hissing rain.

“All these years she has known,” she said at last.

“Apparently.”

“Lorenzo has utterly no pride.”

“From what I could see, Lorenzo has utterly nothing.”

“He must have known years ago about the letters. He must somehow have discovered I had them before he left me for good.”

“Why did he leave you?”

She shrugged. “He does whatever his mother wishes. Besides, he has a weakness for the young fishermen of Torminia.”

Somewhere behind us came the slow clop-clop of horses’ hoofs on the wet cobblestones. An empty carriage crossed the deserted plaza.

“Why did you keep the letters?” I asked.

For a moment she didn’t reply. She stared out into the darkness over the glistening rooftops.

“I suppose they represented something... something I might have been. That is," she added quickly, "had I been foolish."

"Foolish?"

"He was a young attaché at the United States Embassy in Rome. He was exceedingly handsome and romantic. He said he wanted to marry me. I was in love with him. Two weeks before my marriage to Lorenzo we spent a night at an inn near Florence. After that I would have been willing to throw Lorenzo over. But then I heard ..."

"Yes?"

She cleared her throat and said without emotion, "He was married already. His wife was in Boston. He swore that he had meant to tell me. That he and his wife were estranged. That he intended to get a divorce. But I said good-by and I never saw him again."

"And the letters?"

"They were written just before and just after Bianca was born. I wrote him the truth— that Bianca was his child. I wanted to hurt him. He wrote several letters. He had managed his divorce. He begged me to get rid of Lorenzo and marry him. Finally I wrote him a letter without heart. I put all of my hurt into that letter. I never heard from him again. He remarried and became an ambassador years later. He died three years ago."

"And you still kept his letters?"

"I don't know why. I don't know why!"

A wind blew in from over the rooftops, sending gusts of rain into our faces.

"It was the only real thing in your life," I said.

"Oh, rot!" she cried.

"Celia," I said, "if Bianca had the same choice to make, surely you'd have her follow her heart."

"No," she said coldly. "That sort of happiness is only a delusion. And its duration is short. After that there are all the years of regret."

"The years of regret," I repeated.

She turned her back on the rooftops.

"Come!" she said almost angrily. "Let us go back to the hotel."

We went back across the empty plaza, into the maze of narrow streets that lead toward the Corso.

"There is nothing the Marchesa can do without proof," she said. "All the rumor and gossip in the world will not help unless she can get her hands on those letters. And she will never get them, because you will find them for me."

We came out on the great square on which stands the palace of the Colonnas. Here there were more lights. A few taxis and motor cars slid silently past in the rain.

"Celia," I said, "perhaps I'm merely a sentimental fool, but there's one thing I should like to see above all else in this mess, and that is Bianca's happiness."

She stopped and turned and looked up into my face. She reached out, and our hands, wet with rain, touched.

"Good," she said. "Then you will do as I ask."

"I must tell you," I said quickly, holding tight to her hand, "I am not the guy you think. That magazine article is a bad joke— a hoax. I have never been anything more than a second-rate newspaperman."

She snatched her hand away and fell back. "Rafferty! You're trying to scare me!"

"No," I said miserably. "I thought I'd see how far it went, but I realize now ..."

"You couldn't have done this to me!" she cried. "The ball is tomorrow night! I've staked everything on your getting hold of those letters. I ..."

"I've tried. At this point I'm at a complete loss. I have some ideas, but they seem so ..."

She cried angrily, "You've tricked me. It's too late to employ a good detective, or... You've attempted to destroy me!"

"Celia ..."

"Go away! I never want to see you again!"

I took a step forward but it was too late. She turned and fled across the great square and in a moment she was gone out into the darkness.

I stood there feeling suddenly ashamed and futile. Then disconsolately I started back toward my hotel. But for once a drink held no promise. I veered off the Corso through the back streets toward the Capitoline hill.

Ahead was the great flight of stone steps leading down into the Forum. Everything was very still except for the murmur of the rain. I walked to the head of the steps. For some reason I thought of Iris, the cheetah, with her green eyes staring out over the lake. And then with my foot on the top step, an idea entered my head. I stood there, with the ancient city, sunk in the silence of the past, crouching darkly at my feet, and a sudden ray of hope seemed to lighten up the night.

It was at that moment that something hit me from behind. I threw my arms up, tried to wheel about, felt my feet slip on the wet stone, heard my own cry muffled by the relentless rain, saw myself as in a film, falling forward frantically and vainly attempting to regain my balance, saw the endless flight of gleaming steps rushing up to meet my face, pitched down and outward into darkness.

Chapter Sixteen

There were whispering voices in a black funnel and the next minute there was blinding whiteness. Everything was white and gleaming, and someone laughed softly.

I turned my head on the pillow. There was a dull, throbbing ache like the accumulation of all my hangovers come back to haunt me. A tall, gaunt woman hung above me; a leathery horse face attached to a white uniform.

"Good," she said.

I looked beyond her. The room was sparse and neat and very white. A blue sky seemed pinned between cheap chintz draperies. I began to remember.

"What is this?" I asked. My own voice sounded thick and hoarse.

"You are surrounded by the Villa Rosa," she said. She spoke English with a slight German accent. "A private sanatorium."

"What happened?"

She shrugged. "One too much cocktail. One slip of the foot. One too many stone steps."

"I was pushed," I said.

"Perhaps," she said in a bored voice. "It is not wise to walk through Rome in the dark and the rain. Take this." She thrust a pill and a glass of water at me.

I pushed them aside and looked fearfully down at my arms and then the length of my body. No casts; no severed limbs.

"What's my trouble?"

"Who knows? Slight concussion, maybe. Perhaps you need only a long rest. Take what I offer you."

Automatically I reached for my wrist watch on the bedside table. I was relieved to see my wallet there also. It was two o'clock. Obviously two in the afternoon. And suddenly I was right back where I was in that moment before I had hurtled down into darkness.

"How do I happen to be in a private sanatorium?"

She shrugged. "How do I know? We have few patients. Most of them are here for— for a rest."

I didn't like the way she said that. I pushed myself up on one elbow. "I've been asleep a long time?"

She made a sound faintly resembling laughter. "Thirty-seven hours!"

"What? Jesus Christ! It's Friday!"

"No blasphemy, please."

"I've got to get out of here. Stop waving that damned pill in my face."
She began to look angry and worried. "You are to do as you are told!"

"The hell I will! I've got to get to a phone!"

"Dr. Heinrich left orders that you are not to use the telephone under any circumstances."

"I'm not taking orders from Dr. Heinrich or anyone else." I looked up into her grim face. "I've been drugged. That's why I've slept so long!"

She slammed the glass of water down on the little table. "I have not time to waste with you. I've been warned you might be a difficult patient. If you do not do as you are told, you will be placed in restraint."

"Restraint!" I felt a little chill creep up my spine. I looked toward the window. For the first time I noticed the discreet aluminum bars. I swung my legs over the side of the bed. "By you and who else?"

"So!"

She turned on her heel and marched to the door. She went out and slammed it. I saw that there was no handle on the smooth inner surface of the door. I fought the rising panic and looked around me. In a half-opened wardrobe drawer I saw my clothes folded neatly. I leaped from the bed and stumbled across the room. Dizzily I leaned against the wardrobe for a moment, then frantically began to dress. Even during the last war I never got into my clothes so quickly. With shoelaces still untied, shirt stuffed unbuttoned into my trousers, tie in pocket, I picked up my wallet and watch and took up a position just inside the door. The minutes ticked on. I would have given a lot to know who had had me brought to this place. I was beginning to have my suspicions. My head felt as though it contained little revolving knives. Just when I thought I was to be left alone forever I heard the faint sound of voices through the door. I braced myself.

The door swung inward. I was flat against the wall beside it. The horse-faced nurse stepped in, followed by a stocky, flat-nosed guy in a dirty white coat.

Before they had a chance to do a double take at the empty bed, I flung my full weight between them. The nurse flapped back against the wall with a cry. The stocky guy recoiled, stooped low, and made a grab for me. I felt his hands making a wild, fruitless effort to catch my leg. Then I was out in a narrow white hall.

I dashed down the hall to a stair well at the end and took the steps downward like a gazelle in flight. Behind me I heard a hoarse shout and then heavy footsteps. Two flights down I came out into a small reception room. A woman was just rising from the desk with a look of alarm on her face. She screamed. I went past her through a small foyer and out into the sunlight.

The sanatorium was a small place, apparently a former private residence, set back in an unkempt garden. I ran blindly down a graveled drive to some iron gates. Just before I reached them they started to close. There was no one there; the action was purely mechanical, controlled apparently from the main building. I slipped through when there was but three feet left between me and freedom. Behind me I heard a shrill whistle and more shouting. I didn't look back.

Outside the high wall I found myself in a narrow alley, empty and silent. My footsteps made a shocking clatter in the still afternoon as I ran across the cobblestones toward a tiny square at the end of the alley. Just as I reached the square I was overcome with dizziness. I fell against a wall and looked back. Far down the alley the guy in the white coat was standing outside the gate to the sanatorium. He simply stood there staring after me, not making an effort at further pursuit. I ducked around the corner.

A small motor lorry came rattling across the square. I signaled frantically to the driver. He gave me a startled look and stepped on the gas and disappeared like a frightened duck into the mouth of the alley. I took a deep breath, pushed myself away from the wall, and made for a street on the other side of the square. There was no one in sight. The place seemed devoid of human life.

I reached the entrance to the street, which was no more than another alley, slightly wider and sunk in silence. I had the sensation of running through a city laid low by a plague. And then I saw the man in the white coat.

I stopped dead. He had come out of a side street. He just stood there waiting. I thought, This is a nightmare. I looked toward the doors and windows on either side. And then I realized the reason for the sinister silence. These were war ruins, the mere shells of houses. I turned and fled back toward the square.

And then, as in a dream, an ancient taxi came rolling out into the sunlit stillness of the square. I waved my arms and ran toward it. The driver stopped. He was a very old man wearing a green fedora. He looked at me without interest. I jumped into the back and slammed the door.

"Rome Airport," I said. "And quick."

We didn't move. He looked at me over his shoulder, still waiting. I couldn't think of a word of Italian. The man in the white coat came running out of the alley. I tapped the driver on the shoulder.

"Albergo Excelsior," I shouted in desperation.

The man in the white coat started toward the taxi. The driver looked at him without the slightest sign of interest. We began to move forward. The man in the white coat jumped onto the running board. His face was very close and very ugly. I smashed my fist into it and he fell out and backward without a sound. The driver looked back over his shoulder and smiled. He looked like an angel to me in that moment. The ancient taxi jerked forward and we left the square behind.

We came out on a wide boulevard. Far in the distance I saw the dome of St. Peter's gleaming in the afternoon sun. The sky was cloudless. It was a perfect day for the Countess' ball. It was a perfect day for death.

Words came back to me. I tapped the driver on the shoulder again and directed him to drive as fast as possible to the Rome Airport. Then I busied myself with buttoning my shirt, tying my shoes and my necktie.

My wallet contained about six thousand lire and a traveler's check for fifty dollars. When we arrived at the airport I handed the six thousand lire to the driver, patted him on the cheek, and wished him and his children and his children's children eternal prosperity. He shrugged, smiled, and rattled off into the bright afternoon and out of my life.

I found that I had an hour to wait until the next plane to Milan. I cashed my check and booked a seat, then headed for the public phone.

I put in a call to the Villa Dolorosa at Lake Maggiore. I waited a long time while dreamlike voices conferred in unintelligible double talk. Then my operator came back and muttered something in Italian. I asked her if she spoke English, and when she said, "But yes, signor," asked for a translation.

"Ah... yes. The operator in Stresa has informed me that the telephone lines to the Villa Dolorosa have been out of order since one P.M."

I felt a chill of fear. I asked her to connect me with the hotel where I had stayed in Stresa.

I waited while the dream voices took over, trying to fight off the sense of approaching disaster. I thought of the bustle of preparation at the great palace in the lake, cut off now from telephone communication with the mainland. Why? Was it merely an accident?

I was put through to the hotel.

"Is there a Miss Loretta Toastmaster registered there?"

"One minute, signor."

Time was annihilating itself again. The pain in my head was subsiding into a dull thickness. After a while the voice on the other end spoke again. "We have a reservation for Miss Toastmaster. As yet she has not arrived."

"My name is Rafferty Valois. I was in Stresa recently, visiting the

Countess Becellini."

"Ah, yes, signor."

"I am flying up from Rome. Will you have a room for me?"

"Ah... I am most sorry, signor. We are booked full. Many guests have taken reservations because of the ball at the palace tonight."

"Well, listen," I said. "The telephone is out of order at the Becellini palace. Can you get a message across to the Countess?"

He hesitated. "I believe it can be arranged, signor. What is the message?"

"Tell the Countess that Mr. Rafferty Valois is arriving as soon as possible with a message of utmost importance. It concerns the health of Donna Bianca."

After that I hung up and found a barber and rested for a bit under a hot towel. Then I bought a copy of that morning's *London Mail* and walked out onto the raised curve of the promenade that overlooks the airport to wait for my plane. I found a chair in the shade of a columned portico. I looked at my watch. Still a half hour. I opened the paper casually and then sat up very straight.

"Trouble in Movania. Capital cut off from communication with outside world. Military *Putsch* feared. Reliable sources state General Metachas has been secretly in Movania for past weeks. London and Washington take serious view."

The details were meager but alarming. All efforts of foreign governments to contact their embassies had been in vain. Rumor told of stores of arms secretly cached by insurgent army officers in a suburb several miles north of the capital, where General Metachas was said to have been in hiding. The story went on to explain that a successful *coup d'état* would be considered a distinct setback to the arming of the West. It was felt that a restoration of the throne and a military dictatorship would lead only to dissension and revolt among the people and even an invitation to extremist parties favoring the Soviet Union.

Nowhere was the name of Cattoriere mentioned. But at the end of the story came these significant words: "Efforts to obtain a statement from former King Michel have been fruitless. It is known that this evening he is to attend a ball at the palace of the American-born Countess Becellini at Lake Maggiore. Well-informed sources have linked the name of the youthful King Michel with that of the Countess' beautiful daughter, Donna Bianca Becellini."

I folded the paper. If the *coup d'état* was successful, Cattoriere would stop at nothing to prevent the announcement of the King's engagement to Bianca. Again I felt the maddening fingers of time tearing away at the edges of the margin of safety.

Impatiently I looked out across the great airport. An Air France liner was just taking off from the end of one of the large ramps while a K.L.M. stratoliner was slowly wheeling into position in midfield. Idly I watched an American military transport plane creep slowly down the length of the long promenade like a great bug. The steps were wheeled out up against its belly and several men hurried toward it from one of the waiting rooms beneath the promenade. They were swallowed into the body of the plane. A man in a pin-stripe suit came running out to the steps, climbed them quickly, then turned in the open doorway and shouted something back to someone who was below me and out of my sight. In the bright afternoon light his features were clearly distinguishable. It was Hank Dawson, alias Mr. Brent of Shaker Heights.

He ducked inside. The door was slammed. The plane nosed out onto one of the runways for the take-off. I sat there staring at it as it crept far out in the sunlight, wondering whether I was dreaming. What in God's name was Hank Dawson, whom I had suspected of being one of Cattoriere's henchmen, doing in a United States military plane? My head was throbbing with the faint beat of its engines. Mechanically I stood up as it suddenly turned into the wind, gathered speed, became airborne, and circled over the field heading north.

At that moment the loud-speakers began to announce the Milan plane. I hurried down to the proper gate and out under a striped awning to the waiting plane. It was a two-motored job that looked obsolete to me. I realized this was hardly the star flight of the day. I climbed the steps. There were only two or three other persons in the plane, and none of them looked particularly happy.

Now I was more impatient than ever to reach Maggiore. I felt that there were certain new aspects on Hank Dawson that would prove of great interest to Bianca. In my mind I visualized the bustle of preparation for the ball, which was scheduled for ten o'clock that night. The hour of departure came and went. The pilot had not boarded the plane. I was the only one that seemed concerned. Perhaps the others had learned the comparative unimportance of Mussolini's fanatical desire to have trains and planes leave on time. Finally two uniformed men sauntered to the pilot's cabin. Their faces expressed a certain disquieting contempt for the plane. One of them pointed toward the idling propeller and made an observation concerning some detail of the plane's apparatus that was obviously not conducive to the security of the passengers. The other pilot shrugged fatalistically and swung up into the navigation compartment. And then, just as the attendants were about to drag away the stair ramp, a woman came hurrying down under the awning and a moment later entered the cabin in a breathless state. The stewardess slammed the door, the steps were dragged away, and the plane groaned slowly toward mid-field. The new arrival started down the aisle, hesitated when she saw me, decided to smile, and took the seat beside me.

"What next?" I said. "Why the hell are you heading for Milan?"

Miss Annie Harrison shrugged and said, "To see the Last Supper."

"And you don't mean the painting of the same name!"

"Maybe."

"Seriously."

"I'm going to a ball," she said coolly.

"At whose invitation?"

"People are always glad to see me," she said, somewhat grimly, I thought. "I never disappoint."

"Anyone in particular?"

"Have you got anyone in mind?"

"Hank Dawson."

She looked startled. "I don't know about that," she said. "What he does from now on is his own damned business. Me, I got business of my own."

"With whom?"

"A creep," she said.

The plane roared down the runway, engines screaming in protest, and then suddenly we were lifted high into the warm Italian afternoon.

Chapter Seventeen

This was an enchanted palace drifting toward me out of the soft spring night. The barges, emptied now of the guests brought over from the mainland, were huddled up against the marble steps, trailing gold cloth into water that reflected the pagan light of torches. Bargemen, dressed for this occasion as fifteenth-century Venetian sailors, were grouped around an accordionist in the farthest barge, doing very well with a large cask of wine. Because of the presence of royalty, guests had been requested to be in the ballroom by ten, yet the footmen stood, still rigid, lined up the steps, while behind them the torches flamed up into the night.

My boatman, supplied by Alfredo, in whose café across from the station I had changed into makeshift dress clothes borrowed from God knows what source, navigated the tiny sailing craft in between the barges to the foot of the stairs. I got out with all the dignity my low-comedy appearance would permit, and marched up between the stony-eyed footmen. Renaldo, the major-domo, was waiting for me at the entrance to the reception hall.

"Madame received your message, signor. She asks that you wait in her sitting room until she is free to leave the ballroom."

I looked at my watch. It was just after eleven. I knew the Countess had planned to make the engagement announcement at midnight.

"Renaldo, is everything all right?"

"All right, signor?" For a moment he looked startled. Then his mask slid back into place. "Such a magnificent ball has not been seen in years. It is a great success."

"You've noticed nothing disturbing?"

He hesitated. "As yet the telephone cable has not been repaired. It has caused some inconvenience. However …"

"Nothing else?"

Again that slight hesitation. He cleared his throat and looked away. "Nothing, signor."

The great hall was empty except for liveried servants who rushed back and forth from the entrance to the kitchen quarters to the hall that led toward the ballroom. Faintly I heard the strains of violins playing a Viennese waltz. It was difficult to believe that a ball was in progress. When I remarked on this to Renaldo, he explained that the guests were all in the ballroom and its adjoining suites and terraces.

"How is Donna Bianca?"

"Radiant!" he said.

I followed him up to the Countess' sitting room. Renaldo closed the door and smiled for the first time. "Perhaps you would like a glimpse of the ball while you are waiting, signor?"

I didn't get it. Renaldo, as pleased as a child, walked across the pink rug to a painting that hung on the silk-draped wall. He touched a corner of the frame and the picture slid slowly upward. Behind it was a latticed window, Curious, I went to his side. To my amazement I found myself looking down into the great ballroom. The sight that met my eyes was breath-taking. Far below on the polished floor women in brilliant gowns and jewels were whirling about in the arms of men in evening dress or uniforms covered with decorations. Across the arched ceiling, directly on the level with my eyes, were four enormous crystal chandeliers literally blazing with the light of what must have been a thousand candles, reflected a hundred times in the mirrored walls. Around the edges of the floor were tables covered with scarlet cloth and silver candelabra. Champagne buckets glistened beside every table. Orchids were hung on the delicate Moorish pillars and the balustrade of the grand staircase, at the far side of the room.

At first the scene was merely a kaleidoscope of moving color peopled by animated wax dolls. But after a bit I made out a few familiar faces. Celia Becellini, in a daring gown of gold cloth, with rubies gleaming at her throat and in her hair, was leaning over a table laughing down into the face of a distinguished middle-aged man with a ribbon across his white shirt front. At a table near the stairs the old Marchesa Becellini, dowdy in faded black silk, carrying a large lace fan, sat with a group of ancient white-haired relics and her son, who looked like a great mass of dough squeezed into his evening clothes. King Michel was dancing with Bianca, who was a dream in white sprinkled with silver stars. The Harolls, looking somewhat stunned, sat in solitary grandeur at a table near the Marchesa. On the floor, Hamden, who looked very suave in well-cut evening clothes, guided a pretty girl through the measures of the waltz. The girl looked up toward the crystal chandeliers. I was not too surprised to recognize my extraordinary little cockney friend, Miss Loretta Maximilian Toastmaster.

Here were a great many of the actors in the melodramatic puppet show that I was fairly certain would take place. But it was the missing actors that worried me.

Fascinated, I watched the extravagant scene. Celia Becellini was certainly having her night of nights. The noble, the celebrated, and the rich had not only come to her ball, but were obviously having themselves a time.

As I watched, a footman approached Celia. She nodded, excused herself to the group to whom she had been talking, and started toward the grand staircase.

Beside me Renaldo said, "It is a historic night."

"I hope not a bloody one," I said.

Renaldo took a deep breath and said, "Very well. I will admit I am worried. Perhaps foolishly. But the signor's words make me uneasy. Yet what worries me may be only a sign of the times."

"What?"

"The extra servants."

"Extra servants. Do you mean to tell me you had to hire more servants with your large staff?"

"Oh, yes, signor. There were the extra footmen, the bargemen, and the waiters to serve the supper. We have employed such men before. Always they have come through an agency in Milan. They have always been at least competent... until tonight."

His own uneasiness spread to me. "And tonight?"

"They are hopeless. They arrived late, to begin with. They are completely untrained and very rude. I fear for the supper. And I do not recognize one face!"

"What do you think?"

"I do not dare to think. I thought perhaps the signor might have some ideas. I thought ..."

He stopped as the door opened and the Countess Becellini swept into the room.

"Renaldo! What in the world are you doing here? You must go down. Some of the servants must be drunk. One of the louts just spilled a bottle of champagne on the Duchesse de Révélon. It's outrageous!"

"Madame! This is a tragedy! I will see what I can do."

When he left the room Celia said, "You were picked up on the streets of Rome. They called me at the Excelsior. I had you sent to the sanatorium. It was understood that you would be kept there until after the ball."

"Why did you want me out of the way?"

"I have a sense that you are meddling!"

"You look lovely."

"Flattery will do you no good. What is this urgent message?"

"I'm afraid that you and Bianca are in danger."

"Surrounded by three hundred friends? Really!"

"Some of those 'charming friends' wouldn't bat an eye if your throat were slashed. They might even celebrate!"

"Is that what you've come to tell me? Is that the urgent message?"

"Celia, for God's sake! Cattoriere will stop at nothing now. His general is on the move in Movania. He's not going to let that slip out of his hands because you wish Bianca married to Michel."

"You're mad!" she said. "You don't imagine he could force his way into the palace and ..."

"He may be in it now! Why do you think the telephone cables were cut this afternoon?"

"What rot!" She drew herself up and her face was bright with excitement. "Have you seen it? The ball? I've waited for this for twenty years. They all came! Even the bitch of Rome!"

"And poor Bianca will be served up on a platter at midnight."

"You have only one excuse for being here, Mr. Valois. My letters. Do you have them?"

"No."

"Who has?"

"I wish to hell I knew." I took a step toward her. "Look. This isn't play-acting. You can't fool around with a weasel like Cattoriere."

She made a gesture of annoyance. "I refuse to allow you to spoil things. I won't even consider anything so ugly." She smiled gaily. "Please do stop being so dreary. We can talk about the letters later. I forgive you for not being the person I thought you were. Come down and have some champagne."

There was no use trying to impress her with the danger. She almost made me believe that perhaps I was a little hysterical about it myself.

"Would you mind if I stayed here and watched the ball from your window for a few minutes?"

"Certainly not. But do come down in time for the announcement. I want you to have a close-up of the Marchesa's face!"

She went out, closing the door softly behind her.

I stood watching the dream scene below me, and once again the absurdity of my own position overcame me. The only answer I had received to the cable to McLaughlan had been one sentence: "Have another drink on me!" Apparently he believed that this was another gag like that business back in Malaya. Here I stood in borrowed dress clothes, a newspaperman without a newspaper to write for, with about fifty dollars left in the world, and fabulous promises of great sums if I could produce the missing letters for any one of four people. As usual, I had allowed sentiment to interfere with my own economic well-being. If it had not been for Bianca, things might be different. But at the moment I was no closer to the identity of the blackmailer than I had been on the night of my first interview with the Countess.

Beneath the thousand candles the jewels glittered and silver slippers glided over polished wood. Once again the dancers looked like wax puppets, utterly unreal, with something of death about them. I thought of Bianca, so full of youth and life, taking her place in this useless waxworks.

And then I was aware of a sudden cool draft around my legs.

I turned. The sight that met my eyes was so ludicrous I almost forgot to be afraid. Standing in the doorway were two beefy men dressed in ill-fitting purple and gold livery. And in front of them, like a badly constructed doll, his purple breeches sagging like a burlesque comedian's, was Bertie, Cattoriere's right hand.

There was no use attempting any escape antics. There was nothing to swing from or over, and anyway, my acrobatics have never been of that variety. Besides, Bertie held a Luger in a manner that told me he was all too familiar with its mechanism.

"Get that rat!" he said elegantly.

The hatchet men out of Minsky's obeyed. They got me firmly by each arm and propelled me toward Bertie and the door.

"You made a mistake coming back here," Bertie said. "A bad mistake."

That was obvious enough. I was dragged out into the hall, through a long corridor and a deserted loggia, and down many steps into a square stone tower that stood in one of the darkened gardens in the rear. I took a last glimpse of the moon as I was shoved through a low archway into a moldy interior. I thought, Why the hell couldn't I have stuck to my profession? My career as an international adventurer appeared to be ending as melodramatically as it had begun. And I thought of all the wax dolls whirling mechanically to the music of the waltz.

One of my apelike escorts produced a flashlight. Here the ancient stones were covered with green slime and the place was as inviting as an Egyptian tomb at midnight. The guy with the flashlight led the way over the lip of a giant well and onto unrailed stone steps that circled the walls of the well, down into endless darkness. With Bertie and the other footman behind me, I began to descend. Our footsteps echoed up from the depths of the evil-smelling hole. Just when I thought we were probably bound for China the short way, we reached bottom. On three sides were arches leading into black tunnels. Our guide ducked down and, beckoning me to follow, entered the tunnel at the left. The air became cold and heavy and I could see water seeping from the rough stones of the walls. The tunnel curved around, and suddenly up ahead I saw the light of flames dancing on the walls.

The next moment I was shoved through a low opening and into a large chamber lit by flaming torches. At one end of the chamber was a raised stone platform, and hanging from the ceiling above it I saw rusted iron rings on which had been tied new rope. In the center of the platform was the man I had known I would probably be seeing: Mr. Carlo Cattoriere.

"You took too long," he said.

"We missed him on the steps, Boss. And then he went into the huddle with the Becellini bag. You said to do things smooth."

"Yeah, yeah. Bring him over here. We got to work fast."

I realized without happiness that I was in the inquisition chamber of the old monastery that had stood on the site of the palace. When they got me close to Cattoriere, he raised his hand indolently and slapped me very gently on the face. I clenched my fists in the attitude of heroism but thought better of following through.

"Where are the letters?" he asked.

"I wish to hell I knew."

He sighed. "I got news for you. You got three minutes to tell me where they are. If you don't ..." He flicked a bit of dust off the sleeve of his evening clothes. "If you don't, the Becellini girl is going to have a bad accident. She's going to slip on the top of some steps and break her neck. You wouldn't like that."

"For Christ's sake, leave the girl out of it. It's not her fault!"

"You're a lousy amateur, Valois. A phony. But you're just dumb enough to have luck. Only it's running out."

"Listen, Cattoriere," I said quickly. "I don't know where the letters are. I don't want this engagement to be announced any more than you do."

"Are you going to talk, sweetheart?"

"You're wasting your time."

"Maybe you got something there."

He signaled to the two dressed-up apes and they jumped me. Before I realized what was happening, they had me strung up on the iron rings, dangling there like a sack, with my feet a good foot off the stone floor. The ropes began to cut into my wrists almost immediately. Cattoriere gave me a kick and I swung back and forth like a boxer's dummy. Even in the midst of my pain and desperation I was aware of the fantastic scene before me. Gold and purple, flaming torches on ancient masonry, giant shadows playing across the vaulted ceiling, and Cattoriere, pale and immaculate, staring up at me with his shoe-button eyes.

"Talk!" he said.

"You bastard!"

"You don't think I'm playing hopscotch, Valois? This is for the biggest stakes of my life! At this very moment Metachas is probably sitting in the capitol building of Movania. Tomorrow my little toy king is going home, and by God, he's going to do what I tell him!"

My arms felt as though they were being yanked from their sockets. The slight head pain that had been with me since I left the sanatorium in Rome was now a hot knife in my brain. I wondered how many victims had hung from these very rungs with nothing to say that would have saved their lives.

Give him a little encouragement," Cattoriere said.

The encouragement consisted of grabbing my legs and pulling downward. The pain in my armpits was excruciating. I gasped and wished for the blackout that wouldn't come. Bertie moved away and grinned. He was enjoying himself.

No one said anything now. They all looked at me, waiting, as I swung slowly back and forth. After a moment Bent Cattoriere lifted his hand. Bertie stooped down and picked up a rusted iron bar. I thought, This is it. I thought, No marines for me!

Bertie moved forward, crouched, and drew back the arm with the bar. I closed my eyes.

The second seemed an eternity. Instead of the blow I heard a woman say quite calmly, "I wouldn't do that, Bertie."

I opened my eyes. Bertie had turned in amazement. I saw Annie Harrison just inside the entrance from the tunnel. She looked as though she were dressed for a gala evening.

"Annie?" Cattoriere said. "What the hell are you doing here?"

"Maybe I like parties," she said.

"Who let you in and why?"

"I told the boys you wanted to see me right away. They told me where you were. Then I told my friends."

"Friends!" Cattoriere's voice rose.

"I'll introduce you," she said. "Come in, boys."

And they came in. Three members of the Italian police. The one with the carbine interested me most. The other two worked quickly. The footmen didn't have a chance to reach for their guns. The whole stunned mob was corralled into one corner with Cattoriere in their midst.

"Hello, Red," Annie called to me. "You don't look too comfortable."

"I like it here. The view is fine."

Hank Dawson, looking extremely handsome in evening clothes, stepped through the archway like an actor making his first entrance.

Cattoriere found his voice. "Call these monkeys off. They don't know who I am!"

"They know who you are, all right," Dawson said. "They've been waiting for some time to get the goods on you. You certainly gave it to them tonight." He looked at me and grinned. "You look positively silly, Valois." He shouted an order to another officer who came into the room. They cut me down. I fell in a heap on the stone platform.

"You double-crossing bitch!" Cattoriere screamed at Annie Harrison.

She smiled contemptuously. "I've been waiting a long while, you rat. This is for Vince."

"You dumb whore, this will finish you! You and your boy friend there."

"He's not my boy friend. He's with the State Department. They've been trying for a long time to get the dope on whoever was behind Metachas. Even when he knew he had to get a rap on you that would hold in Italy. I've been working with him for quite a time."

"State Department!" Cattoriere yelled. "You think that scares me? I got friends everywhere. My man Metachas is ...”

“Your man Metachas is dead,” Dawson said quietly.

“You’re lying!”

“I’ve got some more news for you, Cattoriere. Metachas was killed at seven o’clock this evening in front of the parliament building in Movania. His little *coup d’état* was a miserable failure. All the officers who worked with him are under arrest. The news came through a half hour ago. My job is done.”

Cattoriere looked as though he had been turned to stone. His henchmen turned away as though he were a fallen idol. Bertie’s face was a picture of astonished reproach.

“I got friends!” Cattoriere screamed.

“It will be hard to find them this time.”

I struggled to my feet, rubbing my raw wrists.

“Dawson of the State Department, I presume,” I said. “Damned grateful for everything and all that sort of rot, old chap, old chap.”

Dawson laughed. “You look like a beat-up turnip.”

“What about his niece?” I asked, indicating Cattoriere. “What was all that chummy business at six in the morning when you left the Rome Express?”

“She’s a good kid,” Dawson said. “She’s been working for us for several months. She hates her uncle. She’s really in love with the King, but she had no intention of becoming a queen with a machine gun in her back.”

“This is a hell of a time and place to discuss plot,” Annie Harrison said. “I’m cold.”

The police were prodding their captives toward the tunnel. The would-be footmen moved like characters in some macabre comedy. I found myself near the arch facing them as they came toward me with Cattoriere, unexpectedly docile now, in their midst. And then, when they were almost at the threshold, it happened. Catlike, Cattoriere sprang out of the welter of fading gold and purple silk and disappeared into the mouth of the tunnel.

In the instant that he sprang I knew that he could have only one purpose for the break. He was not so stupid as to think he could get off the island. With all the cards stacked against him, he was probably going to try to kill the woman who had won.

But even as the thought flashed through my mind, I ducked through the arch into the tunnel. Up ahead I saw his shadow growing larger against the flickering light that came from the stair well. I raced down between the black stone walls in pursuit of a man whom I knew to be very near to madness.

As I reached the railless circular staircase I could see him above me, his shadow thrown grotesquely on the stone walls over the intervening and ever deepening space of the stair well.

I had not climbed many of the stairs before I saw I was gaining on him. It was obvious that his habits had not equipped him for such physical activity.

I had almost reached him when I stumbled and my chest smashed into the stone steps. I thought, God! What if I go over the edge?

I didn't. My fingers caught the cuff of Cattoriere's pants and I hung on. I felt my nails rip and tear as his weight swung on them.

Around me the light suddenly grew brighter. Clinging to Cattoriere's cuff, inching my way upward in an attempt to get a grasp on his ankle, I turned my head slightly and gasped. A few feet below us on the other side of the stair well, holding a flaming torch in both hands, stood Annie Harrison.

Cattoriere gave one desperate jerk of his leg and the cuff of his trousers ripped. I was holding him now by only a frayed tatter of cloth, and in order to get to my feet I would have to let go of that.

Suddenly Annie Harrison's voice filled the vast, echoing stair well.

"This is for Vince," she said, and the flaming torch came hurtling across the empty space, directly at Cattoriere's face.

He stumbled back against the wall, and I let go of the torn cuff. The torch went hurtling down to the stone floor and was extinguished. For a moment there was pitch darkness, and then, still looking up, I saw a sputter of light. It receded from me, and then, farther up now, flame sputtered and grew. To my horror I saw Cattoriere outlined in flame. The lighted torch had ignited his clothing.

"Jesus!" he screamed. His voice wailed downward. "Mother! Help! *Mama mia!*"

And then the ball of fire leaped outward and seemed to float gently to the stone floor far below.

Chapter Eighteen

The guests danced on in the ballroom, unaware of the unusual events that had culminated in Cattoriere's unpleasant death. Countess Celia Becellini was not to be dissuaded because of sudden death, the invasion of a trainful of mobsters, the Italian police, or the U.S. State Department. On the contrary, she looked politely across her pink and gold sitting room to Dawson and said, "I'm very grateful to you for handling matters so discreetly. But it doesn't in the least change my plans."

"But, Countess, you don't understand. I was under orders. I couldn't tell Bianca the truth. Perhaps it's egotistical of me, but I believe she really loves me as much as I love her."

"My dear young man, this is charming but irrelevant."

"Suppose Bianca thinks otherwise?"

"I am quite certain that she will not."

"You don't dare send for her!"

The Countess puffed at her cigarette. She hesitated a moment and then said, "I must get back to my guests. But just to clear things up in your own mind, I see no reason why Bianca should not tell you herself."

She pulled a bell cord and when a servant appeared gave orders in rapid Italian. Dawson looked at me uncomfortably. The Countess seemed supremely certain.

"I have put off the announcement until twelve-thirty because of... shall we say... the disturbance below stairs."

Bianca came into the room. She looked extraordinarily beautiful in the white gown sprinkled with tiny silver stars. When she saw Hank Dawson she clasped her hands tight and looked from one to the other of us with something like panic in her eyes.

"Bianca, my dear. This very nice young man has just prevented a most unpleasant scene. We must thank him."

"Scene?"

"Some idiotic gangster thought it was Halloween."

"Gangster! Mother! What has this man been telling you?"

"It's all right, darling. He is not anything more sinister than a spy."

"Spy! For whom?"

"The United States State Department. It seems that the present administration has been awfully dull about Michel's taking his rightful place— at least for the present. However, there will be other administrations and other ideas."

"State Department!" She turned and said in deadly earnest, "So! You made love to me for the State Department!"

"In the beginning. But I like you better now than the State Department. Much better, Bianca dear."

"Rather sweet, isn't it, darling?" the Countess said with a yawn. "One young lady burned a man to death tonight. That was for 'love' also. Now, darling, put this earnest young man in his— I mean, tell him that he is being absurd. He has some mad thought that you might give up marriage to Michel for his callow charms."

"Does he?" Bianca spoke in a dull monotone. She never averted her eyes from her mother.

"We are touched and rather flattered, aren't we, darling?" the Countess said, with only the slightest touch of irony.

"Yes," said Bianca mechanically. "We are."

And then she burst into tears. She flinched away from Hank as he came toward her and sank onto the sofa and turned her face against its back.

Her mother regarded her calmly for a moment, then stamped out her cigarette. Perhaps it was only I who imagined the little shadow of pain in her eyes.

"She's been under a strain," she said. "And, unfortunately, she is young. So terribly young."

"Bianca!" Hank said. "You've got to tell her the truth! You're throwing your life away for her pathological ambition! You've ..."

Bianca turned. Her face was very pale but she had stopped weeping. "You don't understand," she said in a tired voice. "I don't expect you to."

"You're behaving like a little fool," I said. "Those wax dolls down in the ballroom belong in a museum!"

Bianca stood.

"I'm sorry, Hank," she said in a firm voice. "Life is not quite so simple as it may have seemed to us for a few months. That's all part of a dream."

"It's the only reality you've ever known!" I said. And then I remembered. "It's odd, but reality seems somehow mixed up with the State Department in your family."

"That's enough!" the Countess said icily. "Now, gentlemen, we shall be delighted if you will join us in the ballroom. In the meantime, I hope there will be no misunderstanding as to Bianca's intention. Enough of this talk of 'reality.' At best, it is a rather sordid illusion."

Bianca followed her mother to the door. There she turned back to us and said with surprising gentleness, "I won't forget, Hank... ever." And then she was gone.

"Let's go down and get drunk!" Hank said bitterly.

"An excellent idea."

We went down to the ballroom and supplied ourselves with champagne. Hank found himself a gorgeous brunette who spoke no English but understood the proper verbs, and he moved with her out onto the floor. Despite the gaiety of the music, a certain tension was spreading throughout the room. It was after midnight and the expected announcement had not been made. I stood on the edge of the crowd, feeling unaccountably unhappy. The sight of Bianca in the doorway was something I would not soon forget.

I saw Annie Harrison dancing in the arms of a bearded diplomat. She was laughing hysterically at something. I wondered whether the sight of that ball of fire floating out into the dark stair well could be as easily forgotten as she was pretending.

At my side someone said, "How much do you charge for a dance?"

I looked down into the too innocent eyes of Miss Loretta Maximilian Toastmaster.

"More than you can afford, baby."

"Ducky," she said, "about that man with the beard in the Milan station ..."

"I'm not interested."

"He was merely a delightful gentleman who offered to arrange a refund on my ticket to Paris."

"Why did you want the refund?"

"To help you, Ducky."

"Very thoughtful, I'm sure."

"And now I'm going to help you."

Something in her voice caught my attention.

"What are you up to, Loretta?"

"A gentleman has made me a very nice offer."

"What do you want? Advice?"

"In a way. The gentleman has just bought a lovely villa outside of Monte Carlo. He's asked me to stay with him for the rest of the summer."

"Why do you tell me this?"

"I thought you might like to know his name."

"Well?"

"It's a Mr. Jefferey Hamden."

The orchestra was giving a very peculiar and Italian rendition of a tune from, of all things, "Guys and Dolls." The tune jumped in and out of my mind.

"Are you kidding? Where would Hamden get the cash for a villa at Monte?"

"Maybe you'd better find out," she said quietly.

I didn't wait for more. I left the ballroom quickly. Renaldo, a good third of his staff hauled off to the jail in Stresa, was giving frantic last-minute instructions to a group of worried waiters. I asked for directions and he gave them to me without question. I hurried up the marble steps to the second floor and down the long hall that led out into the south wing, past the sitting room of the Countess, to the last door. It was unlocked.

It was a pleasant room overlooking a balcony and the lake. Near the windows was a suitcase with the lid up. I don't know what instinct made me go for the suitcase instead of the trunk, but whatever it was, it was right. I found the packet of letters under some shirts at the bottom of the suitcase. There must have been ten of them, tucked into an elastic band. One glance at the top letter was enough. I shoved them into my pocket and turned back to the door.

Hamden was standing there with, of course, a gun in his hand.

Chapter Nineteen

"I saw Loretta talking to you," he said. "I had a hunch. It was right."

I tried to act nonchalant. "I was looking for a book on heraldry," I said.

"I don't believe in lending things. Books or letters."

He shut the door behind him.

"I've never met a blackmailer from Iowa," I said.

"I never saw Iowa in my life. I was born in Perth Amboy, New Jersey, and I didn't like it. I've done pretty damned well."

"You fooled me."

"That wasn't difficult. I knew that story in the magazine was a phony the minute I read it. I didn't mind at all when Celia called you in on the case. I knew you'd never get onto the truth in a million years."

"Let's talk things over," I said.

"Not me. I'm not splitting with anyone. I don't have to."

"What else?"

He fingered the gun significantly. "What do you think?"

"You wouldn't be stupid enough to kill me, Hamden."

"I wouldn't be stupid enough not to!"

He meant it. I fought for time.

"How do you expect to account for the presence of a body in your room?"

"It won't be found in my room. That balcony overlooks the lake. They'll have one hell of a time accounting for a corpse found floating in the water with four or five hundred suspects dancing in the ballroom."

"I hadn't thought of that." I managed to keep calm, although my legs felt as though they were freezing. "Tell me, Hamden, how did you manage to pick up your payments in Florence?"

"That was simple. Machero's valet picked them up."

"So Machero was in it with you?"

"It was he who gave me the idea. Cattoriere had hired him to try to get the letters. He came to me with a cash offer if I could get them. It was money from heaven to me. I was sick to death of Celia. I got the letters from the safe the last night the King and that Cattoriere girl were in the palace. It was simple. I'd seen Celia open the safe many times. But when I got my hands on them and read them, I had a better idea. Why split with Cattoriere? Machero fell in with it at first. He wrote the letters demanding cash. But then he began to develop an inconvenient conscience. He implied that he was coming back here to spill the beans to Celia. And when I saw him at that restaurant where we lunched on the day Bianca landed, I knew he was going to rat."

"I see. So when the Countess sent you ashore to find Bianca, you saw your golden opportunity. You found out from the boatman where she had gone with Machero and followed them to the castle. When Bianca left the car you jumped Machero, probably knocked him cold, and then finished the job with the little ivory monk in Bianca's handbag."

"That's about right. I thought I might get rid of the little bitch that way. I hadn't counted on Sir Galahad in the guise of Dawson moving the car to the Milan road and taking away the evidence."

Out of the corner of my eye I thought I saw something move out on the balcony. I tried to keep him talking.

"Why not be sensible and talk business?" I said.

"The hell I will. I don't need you. Even if Celia eventually suspects who has the letters, she won't dare do a thing about them. A nice little scandal if I made it public that the wife of the ex-king of Movania is a bastard!"

"They make them smart in Perth Amboy!"

"No," he said. "I was the exception. And I'm smart enough not to waste any more time gabbing with you."

He raised the gun and I threw myself headlong on the carpet. For one terrible moment I saw him over me with the automatic pointed at my head. I would like to be able to say that what happened next was expected. But I hadn't counted too much on that shadow on the balcony. I was aware of a growl and then something large and furry flying through the air. Hamden went over backward with the great cat on top of him. The gun went thudding across the pink carpet. I scrambled to my feet. Iris had him pinned to the floor. She looked surprisingly gentle. She turned her head and gave me a questioning look.

"Get her off!" Hamden screamed. "She'll kill me!"

He tried to move out from under. Iris slapped him gently with one paw and he flattened out on the carpet.

"Good work, Iris," I said. "For this you'll get a plate of nice warm milk."

Daintily, as though not to soil her paws, she stepped off Hamden and came loping to my side. I retrieved his gun and said, "Get up!"

Still shaking with fright, he managed to get to his feet. "Watch out for her! She hates my guts!"

"She doesn't think you're worth the trouble," I said.

"Listen, Valois, I'll split with you. You're a smart operator. We could go places, you and me."

"The place you're going is into that closet!"

And, despite his protests, he did. I slammed the door and turned the key.

"Come on, Iris. We may still have time to do our good deed for the day."

She followed me out into the hall and down the red marble stairs. Renaldo was just moving toward the ballroom.

"Renaldo! Has the announcement been made?"

"No, signor. It is just about to happen. I am ..."

"Listen. This is a matter of life and death. Go immediately to the Countess. Tell her I have important news of the letters and that under no circumstance is she to make the announcement until she sees me. I will wait in her sitting room."

He looked pained, but he turned and went off to the ballroom. I went back to the Countess' sitting room. I peeled off the top letter from under the elastic and stuffed the rest back into my pocket. Again I looked through the window down into the ballroom.

I thought of the letters and the motives of the people who wanted them. Greed, ambition, lust for power, the desire to preserve a dead and moldering past. The burning reality that their words described had been perverted in an attempt to kill their very meaning. The wax dolls twisted and turned, whirled and faded from my sight. I turned as the Countess came into the room.

"The letters," she said eagerly.

"I have bad news for you."

She caught her breath. "Bad news?"

"I know who has the letters. They have asked me to act as their representative. I know what they want for them."

"Who? What is it? You're trying to frighten me!"

"Celia," I said, "the masquerade is over. It's midnight. You've got a pumpkin waiting for you. Your letters are in the hands of the Marchesa Becellini."

She laughed a wild and tinkling laugh. "You're joking! For a moment I thought you were serious. You're joking." And then, "Oh, God, you're joking!"

"I've never been more serious in my life."

I held the lone letter I had taken from the packet toward her. "The Marchesa asked me to show you this as proof that she has the rest of them."

She had gone deathly pale. She refused to take the letter. She backed away and leaned on the arm of a chair. "What does she want? How much?"

"This time your money will do you no good."

"What, then?"

I took a deep breath. "She demands that you do not announce Bianca's engagement to King Michel. Tonight or ever. She demands also that you will leave Italy forever within two months."

Slowly she sank into the chair. She looked at me as though I were pronouncing her death sentence.

"And if I refuse?"

"She will make the letters public."

The dance music came to us faintly, like the tinkling of a distant calliope. She said nothing. I opened the letter and began to read: "Dearest Celia: At the risk of being dramatic, I should like to plead with you for the last time. I want you to be alive as you were during those precious few nights near Florence. I beg you to choose life and not ..."

"No," she said. "Stop!"

I looked up to find her face absolutely expressionless. Even in this moment of defeat she was the most beautiful woman I had ever seen. But at the moment it was difficult for me to believe that I had actually held her in my arms. She seemed as remote as a lovely statue.

"He lied to me," she said in a dead voice. "And I felt that all men lie. I didn't want Bianca to be hurt as I was. I dreamed of something else for her. For twenty years I've planned this night ..."

"What will you do?"

"Leave me," she managed to say. "Leave me."

Iris looked at me with great sad eyes and whimpered. She moved slowly toward the proud and unbending woman on the absurd gilt chair. I left the room and shut the door.

I felt guilty and uneasy. I had never believed in trying to arrange other people's lives. I'd always despised the sort of person who did. Besides, there was no telling what a woman like Celia might do. It was quite conceivable that she would still play the long shot.

Loretta was waiting for me by the entrance to the ballroom.

"I was worried about you," she said.

"Thanks."

"Wasn't it clever of me to trap Hamden?"

"Very."

"I knew you'd never be able to figure out things by yourself. The first minute I talked to that dreadful young man, I knew his sort. It takes a woman, you know."

I took her hand. "Let's get a last drink."

We found the champagne. As I lifted the glass to my lips I realized the dance music had stopped and an expectant murmur was spreading over the room. It was twelve-forty-five. I saw Bianca, tense and pale, making brave conversation with King Michel. Dawson, drink in hand, stood near the orchestra. His face was drawn.

And then suddenly there was a melodramatic roll of drums. A complete silence fell over the ballroom. I felt the muscles in the back of my neck tighten up. Loretta's fingers closed over mine.

Celia came slowly out of the shadows at the top of the grand staircase. At her side moved Iris. She stopped at the edge of the top step. She was very calm and there was something in her manner that held the room absolutely silent. In that moment— the moment before the end— she looked absolutely magnificent. She looked over the crowd with a cool sort of detachment. It occurred to me that she was seeing them— really seeing them— for the first time.

She raised her hand and spoke in a quiet voice:

"I ask you to share in my happiness. I have the very great honor to announce ..." The break in her voice was hardly noticeable. "To announce the engagement of my daughter, Bianca, to my... my fellow countryman... Mr. Henry Dawson."

No one spoke. From somewhere in the distance, as in a dream, came the sound of a slamming door. Then the old Marchesa, her face beaming with victory, rose from her table and started across the empty ballroom floor, arms outstretched toward Celia.

Celia regarded the approaching old woman without any expression. She allowed her to reach the foot of the steps and then, with great deliberation, turned her back and left the room. I realized that in that one gesture Celia Becellini had turned her back forever on the world she had once dreamed of attaining. The old Marchesa turned back to the room, her face scarlet.

It was only then that the silence was broken. A gasp swept over the room and then bedlam broke loose. In the confusion I saw Dawson and

Bianca moving blindly toward each other through the crowd. The expression on Bianca's face eradicated any lingering feeling of guilt in my mind. I looked for King Michel. To my surprise, he was smiling.

The orchestra struck up an inane dance tune. But already many of the guests were heading toward the doors. I was thinking that in the end Celia Becellini had come through with the spirit of the aristocrat she had so pathetically hoped to be. I didn't like to think of her now, alone behind the locked doors of her sitting room.

"Let's get out," I said to Loretta.

She came with me without question. I got her wrap and we hurried through the reception hall to the marble steps that led down to the lake. There were many small craft waiting there, aside from the theatrical barges. I hurried Loretta into one of them and directed the boatman to take us to the landing stage of the hotel. We drifted out into the lake.

I took the letters from my pocket and held them for a moment in my hand.

"What is that, Ducky?"

"A fortune, if I play my cards right."

"You'll never do that, Ducky."

"You know, I think you're right."

One by one I took the letters, tore them into small pieces, and scattered them on the still, black waters.

A mist was settling over the lake. It was falling down around the palace like a mysterious curtain. It gave the place its true quality of utter unreality. I thought of Iris sitting with the lonely woman in the little pink and gold sitting room. The mist thickened and soon the island was part of a dream, part of an impossible past.

"Let's get away from the rich," I said.

"It takes money to do that, darling Rafferty."

"No. It's really simple. We'll just walk back from the water front to a little café called Alfredo's."

"And then?"

"I always say," I said, "let tomorrow take care of itself!"

THE END